"Let's see how they like the Christmas lights."

Erica carried the twins into the front room.

She sat on the couch and put Mikey on the floor, then Teddy. She waved her hand toward the tree. "Pretty!" she said.

The twins' brown eyes grew round as they surveyed the sparkling lights and ornaments.

"Priiiiy," Mikey said, cocking his head to one side.

Teddy started to scoot toward the tree.

"Whoa, little man," Jason said, intercepting him before he could reach the shining ornaments.

"Better put the ornaments higher up and anchor that tree to the wall." Papa laughed.

Teddy then turned and crawled toward Mistletoe, who gave his face a few licks. Teddy chortled and waved his arms.

"Not very sanitary," Papa commented.

"Oh, well," Erica and Jason said at the same time. Jason grinned at her.

It was like watching a Christmas movie. The perfect setting. A happy home. She'd always longed to be in such a family.

And it was all a lie.

Lee Tobin McClain read *Gone with the Wind* in the third grade and has been a hopeless romantic ever since. When she's not writing angst-filled love stories with happy endings, she's getting inspiration from her church singles group, her gymnastics-obsessed teenage daughter and her rescue dog and cat. In her day job, Lee gets to encourage aspiring romance writers in Seton Hill University's low-residency MFA program. Visit her at leetobinmcclain.com.

Books by Lee Tobin McClain

Love Inspired

Christmas Twins
Secret Christmas Twins

Rescue River
Engaged to the Single Mom
His Secret Child
Small-Town Nanny
The Soldier and the Single Mom
The Soldier's Secret Child

Lone Star Cowboy League: Boys Ranch
The Nanny's Texas Christmas

Secret Christmas Twins

Lee Tobin McClain

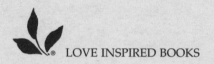

Recycling programs for this product may not exist in your area.

LOVE INSPIRED BOOKS

ISBN-13: 978-0-373-62308-2

Secret Christmas Twins

Copyright © 2017 by Lee Tobin McClain

www.Harlequin.com

Printed in U.S.A.

Two are better than one, because they have a good return for their labor: if either of them falls down, one can help the other up. But pity anyone who falls and has no one to help them up.
—*Ecclesiastes* 4:9–10

To Shana Asaro and Melissa Endlich,
who offered me the opportunity to work on
this special Christmas project, and to Mark S.,
with appreciation for the informal legal counsel
and the delicious cider.

Chapter One

Detective Jason Stephanidis steered his truck down the narrow, icy road, feeling better than anytime since being placed on administrative leave. He'd checked on several elderly neighbors near Holly Creek Farm and promised to plow them out after the storm ended. Now he was headed back to the farm to spend some much-needed time with his grandfather.

It wasn't that he was feeling the Christmas spirit, not exactly. Being useful was how he tamed the wolves inside him.

Slowly, cautiously, he guided the truck around a bend. Amid the rapidly falling snow, something flashed. Headlights? In the middle of the road?

What was a little passenger car doing out on a night like this? This part of Pennsylvania definitely required all-wheel drive and heavy snow tires in winter.

He swerved right to avoid hitting the small vehicle. Perilously close to the edge of the gulch, he stopped his truck, positioning it to provide a barrier against the other car going over the edge.

There. The car should be able to pass him now, safely on the side away from the ledge.

Rather than slowing down gradually, though, the other driver hit the brakes hard. The little car spun and careened into an icy snowdrift, stopping with a resounding thump.

Jason put on his flashers, leaped from his truck and ran toward the vehicle. He couldn't see through the fogged-up window on the driver's side, so he carefully tried the door. The moment he opened it, he heard a baby's cry.

Oh no.

"The babies. My babies! Are they okay?" The driver clicked open her seat belt and twisted toward the back seat. "Mikey! Teddy!"

There were two of them? "Sit still, ma'am. I'll check on your children." He eased open the back door and saw two car seats. A baby in each. One laughing, one crying, but they both looked uninjured, at least to his inexperienced eye.

Between the front seats, the driver's face appeared. "Oh, my sweet boys, are you okay?" There was an edge of hysteria in her voice.

"They seem fine, ma'am. You need to turn off your vehicle."

She looked at him as if he were speaking Greek, then reached a shaky hand toward the baby who was wailing. "It's okay, Mikey. You're okay." She patted and clucked in that way women seemed to naturally know how to do.

The baby's crying slowed down a little.

"Turn off your vehicle," he repeated.

"What?" She was still rubbing the crying baby's leg, making soothing sounds. It seemed to work; the baby took one more gasping breath, let it out in a hiccupy sigh and subsided into silence.

She fumbled around, found a pacifier and stuck it in the baby's mouth. Then she cooed at the nearer baby, found his pacifier pinned to his clothes and did the same.

Unhurt, quiet babies. Jason felt his shoulders relax a little. "Turn the car off. For safety. We don't want any engine fires."

"Engine fires?" She gasped, then spun and did as he'd instructed.

He straightened and closed the rear car door to keep the heat inside.

She got out, looked back in at the babies and closed the door. And then she collapsed against it, hands going to her face, breathing rapid.

"Are you all right?" He stepped closer and noticed a flowery scent. It seemed to come from her masses of long red hair.

"Just a little shaky. Delayed reaction." Her voice was surprisingly husky.

"How old are your babies?"

She hesitated just a little bit. "They're twins. Fifteen months."

He focused on her lightweight leather jacket, the nonwaterproof sneakers she wore. *Not* on her long legs nicely showcased by slim-fitting jeans. "Ma'am, you shouldn't be out on a night like this. If I hadn't come along—"

"If you hadn't come along, I wouldn't have gone off the road!"

"Yes, you would've. You can't slam on your brakes in the snow."

"How was I supposed to know that?"

"Ma'am, any teenager would know not to…" He trailed off. No point rubbing in how foolish she'd been.

She bit her lip and held up a hand. "Actually, you're right that I shouldn't be out. I was slipping and sliding all over the place." Walking up to the front end of the car, she studied it, frowning. "Wonder if I can just back out?"

Jason knelt and checked for damage, but fortunately, the car looked okay. Good and stuck, though. "You probably can't, but I can tow you." As he walked around the car to study the rear bumper in preparation for towing, he noticed the Arizona plates.

So that was why she didn't know how to drive in the snow.

He set up some flares, just in case another vehicle came their way, and then made short order of connecting the tow rope and pulling her out of the drift.

He turned off his truck, jumped out and walked over to her. Snow still fell around them, blanketing the forest with quiet.

"Thank you so much." She held out a hand to shake his.

He felt the strangest urge to wrap her cold fingers in his palm, to warm them. To comfort her, which would shock the daylights out of his ex-fiancée, who'd rightly assessed him as cold and heartless. He was bad at relationships and family life, but at least now he knew it. "You should wear gloves," he said sternly instead of holding on to that small, delicate hand.

For just the briefest second he thought she rolled her eyes. "Cold hands are the least of my problems."

Really? "It didn't look like your children are dressed warmly enough, either."

She turned her back to him, opened her car door and grabbed a woven, Southwestern-looking purse. "Can I pay you for your help?"

"*Pay* me? Ma'am, that's not how we do things around here."

She arched an eyebrow. "Look, I'd love to hang out and discuss local customs, but I need to get my boys to shelter. Since, as you've pointed out so helpfully, they're inadequately dressed."

"I'll lead you back to a road that's straighter, cleared off better," he said. "Where were you headed?"

"Holly Creek Farm."

Jason stared at her.

"It's supposed to be just a few miles down this road, I think. I should be fine."

"Are you sure that's the name of the place? There's a lot of Holly-this and Holly-that around here, especially since the closest town is Holly Springs."

"I know where I'm going!" She crossed her arms, tucking her hands close to her sides. "It's a farm owned by the Stephanidis family. The grandparents…er, an older couple lives there." A frown creased her forehead, and she fingered her necklace, a distinctive silver cross embedded with rose quartz and turquoise.

A chill ran down Jason's spine. The necklace was familiar. He leaned closer. "That looks like a cross my sister used to wear." Sadness flooded him as he remembered the older sister who'd once been like a mother to him, warm and loving, protecting him from their parents' whims.

Before she'd gone underground, out of sight.

"A friend gave it to me."

Surely Kimmie hadn't ended up back in Arizona, where they'd spent their early childhood. An odd thrumming started in his head. "Why did you say you were going to the Holly Creek Farm?"

"I didn't say." She cocked her head, looking at him strangely. "The twins…um, my boys and I are going there to live for a while. Our friend Kimmie Stephanidis gave us permission, since it's her family home. What did you say your name is?"

"I didn't say." He echoed her words through a dry throat. "But I'm Jason. Jason Stephanidis."

She gasped and her hand flew to her mouth. She went pale and leaned back against her car.

Jason didn't feel so steady himself. What had this redheaded stranger been to Kimmie? And was she seriously thinking of staying at the farm—with babies— when she obviously knew nothing about managing a country winter? "Look, do you want to bring your kids and come sit in my truck? I have bottled water in there, and it's warm. You're not looking so good."

She ignored the suggestion. "You're Jason Stephanidis? Oh, wow." She didn't sound happy as she glanced at the babies in the back seat of her car.

"And your name is…"

"Erica. Erica Lindholm."

"Well, Erica, we need to talk." He needed to pump her for information and then send her on her way. The farm was no place for her and her boys, not at this time of year. And Jason's grandfather didn't need the stress.

On the other hand, given the rusty appearance of her small car, a model popular at least ten years ago, she probably didn't have a lot of money for a hotel. If she could even get to one at this time of night, in this storm.

She straightened her back and gave him a steady look that suggested she had courage, at least. "If you're Kimmie's brother, we do need to talk. She needs help, if you're willing. But for now, I need to get the boys to shelter. If you could just point me toward the farm—"

He made a snap decision to take her there, at least for tonight. "I'll clear the road and you can follow me there." She'd obviously been close to Kimmie. Maybe a fellow addict who needed a place to stay, dry out.

If he caught one whiff of drug use around those babies, though, he'd have her arrested so fast she wouldn't know what had hit her.

"I don't want to put you out." Her voice sounded tight, shaky. "I'm sure you have somewhere to go."

"It's no trouble to lead you there," he said, "since I live at Holly Creek Farm."

The detective in him couldn't help but notice that his announcement made the pretty redhead very, very uncomfortable.

Erica Lindholm clutched the steering wheel and squinted through the heavily falling snow, her eyes on the red taillights in front of her.

Jason Stephanidis *lived* there. In the place Kimmie had said belonged to her grandparents. What nightmare was this?

How could she take care of the babies here? Kimmie's brother, being a detective, was sure to find out she'd taken them and run with no official guardianship papers. That had to be a crime.

And he might—probably would—attempt to take them away from her.

She couldn't let him—that was all. Which meant she couldn't let him know that the boys were actually Kimmie's sons.

Somewhere on the long road trip, caring for the twins and worrying about them, comforting them and feeding them, she'd come to love them with pure maternal fierceness. She'd protect them with her life.

Including protecting them from Kimmie's rigid, controlling brother, if need be. She'd promised Kimmie that.

In just ten minutes, which somehow felt all too soon, they turned off the main road. The truck ahead slowed down, and a moment later she realized Jason had lowered the plow on the front of his truck and was clearing the small road that curved up a little hill and over a quaint-looking bridge.

A moment later they pulled up to a white farmhouse, its front door light revealing a wraparound front porch, the stuff of a million farm movies.

Behind her, Teddy started to fuss. From the smell of things, one or both of the boys needed a diaper change.

Jason had emerged from the truck and was coming back toward her, and she got out of her car to meet him. He looked as big as a mountain: giant, stubbly and dangerous.

Erica's heart beat faster. "Thank you for all you've done for us tonight," she said. "I understand there's a cabin on the property. We can go directly there, if you'll point the way."

"No, you can't."

"Why not?"

"That cabin hasn't been opened up in a couple of years. The heat's off, water's off, who knows what critters have been living there…" He shook his head. "I don't know what you were thinking, bringing those babies out in this storm."

Guilt surged up in her. He was right.

"For now, you'll have to stay at the farmhouse with me."

Whoa. No *way.* "That's not safe or appropriate. I don't know you from—"

The front door burst open. "There you are! I was ready to call the rescue squad. Who'd you bring with you?"

All she could see of the man in the doorway was a tall blur, backlit by a golden, homey light that looked mercifully warm.

"Open up the guest room, would you, Papa? We've got Kimmie's friend here, and she has babies."

"Babies! Get them inside. I'll put on the soup pot and pull out the crib." The front door closed.

Jason looked at Erica, and for the first time, she saw a trace of humor in his eyes. "My grandfather's house. He'll keep you and the twins safe from me and anything else."

Behind her, through the car's closed windows, she could hear both twins crying. She didn't have another solution, at least not tonight. "All right. Thank you."

Moments later they were inside a large, well-heated farmhouse kitchen. Erica spread a blanket and changed the twins' diapers while Jason's grandfather took a dishrag to an ancient-looking high chair. "There you go," he said, giving the chair's wooden tray a final polish. "One of 'em can sit there. You'll have to hold the other for now." He extended a weathered hand. "Andrew Stephanidis. You can call me Papa Andy."

"Thank you." She shook his hand and then lifted Teddy into the high chair. "This is Teddy, and—" she bent down and picked up Mikey "—this is Mikey, and I'm Erica. Erica Lindholm." *Who might be wanted by the police right about now.* "I'm very grateful to you for taking us in."

"Always room for the little ones. That's what Mama used to say." The old man looked away for a moment, then turned back to face Erica. "Sorry we're not decorated for Christmas. Used to have holly and evergreens and tinsel to the roof, but…seems like I just don't have the heart for it this year."

Jason carried in the last of her boxes and set it on the table. "I put your suitcases up in the guest room, but this box looks like food." He was removing his enormous boots as he spoke. "Sorry about the mess, Papa. I'll clean it up."

The old man waved a hand. "Later. Sit down and have some soup."

Erica's head was spinning. How had Kimmie gotten it so wrong, telling her the mean brother never came to the farm? And it sure seemed like Kimmie's grandmother, the "Mama" Papa Andy had spoken of, had passed on. Obviously, Kimmie had completely lost touch with her own family.

In front of Erica, a steaming bowl of vegetable soup sent up amazing smells, pushing aside her questions. She'd been so focused on feeding and caring for the twins during four long days of travel that she'd barely managed to eat. The occasional drive-through burger and the packets of cheese and crackers in the cheap motels where they'd crashed each night couldn't compare to the deliciousness in front of her.

"Go ahead. Dig in. I'll hold the little one." Papa Andy lifted Mikey from her lap and sat down, bouncing him on his knee with a practiced movement.

Erica held her breath. With the twins' developmental delays came some fussiness, and she wanted to avoid questions she wouldn't know how to answer. Wanted to avoid a tantrum, too.

But Mikey seemed content with Papa Andy's bouncing, while Teddy plucked cereal from the wooden high chair tray and looked around, wide-eyed. The babies cared for, Erica scooped up soup and ate two big pieces of buttered corn bread, matching Jason bite for bite even though he was twice her size.

When her hunger was sated, she studied him from under her eyelashes and tried to quell her own fear. Kimmie had been afraid of her brother's wrath if he discovered that she'd gone back to drugs and gotten pregnant out of wedlock. And she'd feared disappointing her grandparents. That was why she'd become estranged from the family. She hadn't said it outright, but Erica had gotten the feeling that Kimmie might have stolen money from some of them, as well.

None of that was the twins' fault, and if Kimmie's family history were the only barrier, Erica wouldn't hesitate to let Jason and Papa Andy know that the twins were their own relatives. She wasn't foolish enough to think she could raise them herself with no help, and having a caring uncle and great-grandfather and more resources on their side would be only to their benefit.

But Kimmie had said Jason would try to get custody

of the twins, and seeing how authoritative he seemed to be, Erica didn't doubt it.

Kimmie hadn't wanted her brother to have them. She'd insisted there were good reasons for it.

Erica wished she could call and ask, but Kimmie wasn't answering her phone. In fact, she'd left a teary message two days ago, saying she was moving into a rehab center. She'd assured Erica that she was getting good care, but might not be reachable by phone.

Now that Erica was sitting still, for the moment not worried about her and the twins' survival, sadness washed over her. For Kimmie, for the twins and for herself. With all her flaws, Kimmie had been a loving friend, and they'd spent almost every moment of the past month together. Like a vivid movie, she remembered when Kimmie—addicted, terminally ill and in trouble with the law—had begged her to take the twins.

"I know it's a lot to ask. You're so young. You'll find a husband and have babies of your own..."

"No, I won't," Erica had responded. "But that's not what's important now."

"You have time. You can get over your past." Kimmie had pulled a lock of hair out of Erica's ponytail. "You could be beautiful if you'd stop hiding it. And you need to realize that there are a few men out there worth trusting."

Remembering Kimmie's attempt at mothering, even at such a horrible moment, brought tears to Erica's eyes even now, in the bright farmhouse kitchen. Erica *wouldn't* get over her past, wouldn't have kids of her own, as Kimmie would have realized if she hadn't been so ill.

But Erica had these babies, and she'd protect them with her life. They were her family now.

The old black wall phone rang, and Papa answered it.

"Yes, he's here." She listened. "No, Heather Marie, he's not coming out again in the storm just because you forgot to buy nail polish or some such crazy thing!" He held the phone away from his ear and indistinguishable, agitated words buzzed out from it. "You saw a *what*? A *dog*?"

Jason took one more bite of corn bread, wiped his mouth and stood. He might have even looked relieved. "It's okay, Papa. I'll talk to her."

Papa narrowed his eyes at him. "You're an enabler."

Jason took the phone and moved into the hall, the long cord stretching to accommodate. Minutes later he came back in. "She thinks she saw a dog out wandering on Bear Creek Road, but she was afraid if she stopped she couldn't get going again. I'm going to run out there and see if I can find it."

"And visit her? Maybe get snowed in? Because that's what she wants."

Jason waved a dismissive hand. "I don't mind helping." Then he turned to Erica. "We have to talk, but I'm sure you're exhausted. We can figure all of this out tomorrow." He left the room, a giant in sock feet. Moments later, a chilly breeze blew through the kitchen, and then the front door slammed shut.

A chill remained in Erica's heart, though. She had the feeling that Kimmie's big brother would have plenty of questions for her when he returned. Questions she didn't dare to answer.

It was almost midnight by the time Jason arrived back at the house. Exhausted, cold and wet, he went around to the passenger side to get leverage enough to lift the large dog he'd finally found limping through the woods near Bear Creek.

He carried the dog to the house and fumbled with the door, trying to open it without putting down the dog.

Suddenly, it swung open, and there was Erica, her hair glowing like fire in the hallway's golden light. "Oh, wow, what can I do?" She hurried out to hold open the storm door for him, regardless of the cold. "Want me to grab towels? A blanket?"

"Both. Closet at the top of the stairs."

She ran up and came back down and into the front room quickly, her green eyes full of concern. Her soft jeans had holes at the knees, and not the on-purpose kind teenagers wore.

After she'd spread the blankets on the floor in front of the gas fireplace, he carefully set the dog down and studied him. Dirty, yellow fur, a heavy build: probably a Lab-shepherd mix. The dog didn't try to move much but sighed and dropped his head to the floor as if relieved to have found a safe haven.

"Go take off your wet things," Erica ordered Jason. "I'll watch the dog."

"The twins are asleep?"

"Like logs."

Jason shed his jacket, boots and hat, got two bowls of water and a couple of thin dishrags, and came back into the warm room. It hadn't changed much since he was a kid. He half expected his grandmother to come around the corner, bringing cookies and hot chocolate.

But that wasn't happening, ever again.

"Was he in a fight?" Erica asked. She was gently

plucking sticks and berries out of the dog's fur. "His leg seems awful tender."

"I'll try to clean it and wrap it. He's friendly, like he's had a good home, though maybe not for a while." He put the cold water down, and the dog lifted his big golden head and drank loud and long, spilling water all over the floor.

"He's skinny under his fur," Erica said. "And a mess. What are all these sticky berries on him?" She plucked a sprig from the dog's back, green with a few white berries.

"It's mistletoe." Made him think of Christmas parties full of music and laughter. Of happy, care-free times.

Erica didn't look at Jason as she pulled more debris from the dog's fur. "Then that's what we'll call him. Mistletoe."

"You're *naming* the dog?"

"We have to call him something," she said reasonably. "You work on him. I'll be right back."

He puzzled over Erica as he carefully examined the dog's leg. She seemed kind and helpful and well-spoken. So how had Kimmie connected with her? Had Kimmie gotten her life together, started running with a better crowd? Was Erica some kind of emissary from his sister?

He breathed in and out and tried to focus on the present moment. This homey room, the quiet, the dog's warm brown eyes. Letting his thoughts run away with him was dangerous, was what had made him okay with administrative leave. The only crime he'd committed was trusting his partner, who'd turned out to be corrupt, taking bribes. With time, Jason knew he'd be exonerated of wrongdoing.

But still, he was all too aware that he'd lost perspective. He'd been working too hard and getting angrier and angrier, partly because of worrying about his sister's situation and wondering where she was. He'd had no life. Coming here, taking a break, was the right thing to do, especially given his grandmother's death earlier this year.

He should have come home more. He'd made so many mistakes as a brother, a son, a grandson. And a fiancé, according to what Renea had screamed as she'd stormed out for the last time. Funny how that was the weakness that bothered him the least.

Erica came back into the room and set a tray down on the end table beside the couch.

A familiar, delicious smell wafted toward him. *Déjà vu.* "You made hot chocolate?"

She looked worried. "Papa Andy showed me where to find everything before he went to bed. I hope it's okay. You just looked so cold."

He took one of the two mugs and sipped, then drank. "Almost as good as Gran's."

Her face broke into a relieved smile, and if she'd been pretty before, her smile made her absolutely gorgeous. Wow.

"How's Mistletoe?" She set down the other mug and knelt by the dog.

He snorted out a laugh at the name. "He let me look at his leg. Whether he'll let me wash it remains to be seen." He put down the hot chocolate and dipped a rag into the warm water.

"Want me to hold his head?"

"No." Was she crazy? "If he bites anybody, it's going to be me, not you."

"I'm not afraid." She scooted over, gently lifted the dog's large head and crossed her legs beneath. "It's okay, boy," she said, stroking his face and ears. "Jason's going to fix it."

Jason parted the dog's fur. "Don't look—it's not pretty."

She ignored his instruction, leaning over to see. "Aw, ouch. Wonder what happened?"

"A fight, or clipped by a car. He's limping pretty bad, so I'm worried the bone is involved." As gently as possible, he squeezed water onto the wound and then wiped away as much dirt as he could. Once, the dog yelped, but Erica soothed him immediately and he relaxed back into her lap.

Smart dog.

Jason ripped strips of towel and wrapped the leg, aiming for gentle compression. "There you go, fella. We'll call the vet in the morning."

"That wasn't so bad, was it?" Erica eased out from under the dog's head, gave him a few more ear scratches and then moved to the couch, picking up her mug on the way. "I love hot chocolate, but in Phoenix, we didn't have much occasion to drink it."

Jason picked up his half-full cup and sat in the adjacent armchair. "How did you know Kimmie?"

The question was abrupt, and he meant it to be. People answered more honestly when they hadn't had a chance to relax and figure out what their interrogator wanted to hear.

She drew in a deep breath and blew it out. "Fair question. I met her at Canyon Lodge." She looked at him, but when he didn't react, she clarified. "It's a drug rehab center."

"You're an addict, too?"

"Noooo." She lifted an eyebrow at his assumption. "My mom was. I met Kimmie, wow, ten years ago, on visits to Mom. When they both got out, we stayed in touch."

And yet she hadn't turned to her mom when she'd needed a place to stay. "How's your mom doing?" he asked.

She looked away. "She didn't make it."

"I'm sorry."

"Thanks." She slid down off the couch to sit beside the dog again, petting him in long, gentle strokes.

"Where's Kimmie now? Is she in Phoenix?"

Erica hesitated.

"Look, we've been out of touch for years. But if she's sober now…" He saw Erica's expression change. "*Is* she sober now?"

Erica looked down at the dog, into the fire, anywhere but at him.

Hope leaked out of him like air from a deflating tire. "She's not."

Finally, she blew out a breath and met his eyes. "I don't know how to answer that."

"What do you mean? She's straight or she's not."

Erica's face went tense, and he realized he'd spoken harshly. Not the way to gain trust and information. "Sorry. Let's start over. Why did she send you to Holly Creek Farm?"

Simple enough question, he'd thought. Apparently not.

"It's complicated," she said.

He ground his teeth to maintain patience. His superiors had been right; he was too much on the edge to be working the streets right now. For a fleeting, fearful moment, he wondered if he could ever do it again.

But interviewing someone about your own kin was different, obviously, than asking questions about a stranger.

"Kimmie isn't…well," she said finally.

Jason jerked to attention at her tone. "What's wrong?"

She opened her mouth to speak, but his cell phone buzzed. Wretched thing. And as a cop, even one on leave, he had to take it.

"It's late for a phone call." Then she waved a hand, looking embarrassed. "Not my business. Sorry."

A feeling of foreboding came over Jason as he looked at the unfamiliar number. "Area code 602. Phoenix, isn't it?"

She gasped, her hand going to her mouth. "Yes."

He clicked to answer. "Jason Stephanidis."

"Mr. Stephanidis." The voice on the other end was male, and there was background noise Jason couldn't identify. "Are you the brother of Kimberly Stephanidis?"

Jason closed his eyes. "Yes."

"Okay. This is Officer John Jiminez. Phoenix PD. You're a cop, too?"

"That's right."

"Good. My information's accurate. Do you know… Have you seen your sister recently?"

"No."

Silence. Then: "Look, I'm sorry to inform you that she's passed away. I've been assigned to locate her next of kin."

A chasm opened in his chest. "Drugs?"

"The coroner listed the cause of death as an overdose. But it also looks like she had advanced lung cancer."

Jason squeezed his eyes closed, tighter, as if that could block out the words he was hearing. What he wanted to do was to shout back: *No. No. No.*

Erica sat on the couch, her arms wrapped around herself. Trying to hold herself together.

Kimmie was gone.

The twins were motherless.

Grief warred with worry and fear, and she jumped up and paced the room.

After Jason had barked out the news, said that a lawyer would call back tomorrow with more information, he'd banged out of the house.

What had happened? Had Kimmie gone peacefully, with good care, or died alone and in pain? Or, given the mention of overdose, had she taken the low road one last time?

Erica sank her head into her hands and offered up wordless prayers. Finally, a little peace came to her as the truth she believed with all her heart sank in: Kimmie had gone home to a forgiving God, happy, all pain gone.

She paced over to the window and looked out. The snow had stopped, and as she watched, the moon came out from under a cloud, sending a cold, silvery light over the rolling farmland.

Off to the side, Jason shoveled a walkway, fast, furious, robotic.

Wanting air herself, wanting to see that moon better and remind herself that God had a plan, Erica found a heavy jacket in the hall closet and slipped outside.

Sharp cold took her breath away. A wide creek ran

alongside the house, a little stone bridge arching over it. Snow blanketed hills and trees and barns.

And the moonlight! It reflected off snow and water, rendering the scene almost as bright as daytime, bright enough that a wooden fence and a line of tall pines cast shadows on the snow.

The only sound was the steady *chink-chink-chink* of Jason's shovel.

The newness, the majesty, the fearfulness of the scene made her tremble. God's creation, beautiful and dangerous. A Sunday school verse flashed through her mind: *"In His hand is the life of every creature and the breath of all mankind."*

The shovel stopped. Heavy boot steps came toward her.

"You should have contacted me!" Jason's voice was loud, angry. "How long were you with her? Didn't you think her family might want to know?"

His accusatory tone stung. "She didn't want me to contact you!"

"You listened to an addict?"

"She said you told her you were through helping her."

"I didn't know she had cancer!" He sank down on the front step and let his head fall into his hands. "I would have helped." The last word came out choked.

Erica's desire to fight left her. He was Kimmie's brother, and he was hurting.

She sat down beside him. "She wasn't alone, until just a short while ago. I was with her."

He turned his head to face her. "I don't get it. On top of everything else she had to deal with, she took in you and your kids?"

She saw how it looked to him. But what was she

supposed to say? Kimmie hadn't wanted her to tell Jason about the twins. She'd spoken of him bitterly. "I was a support to her, not a burden," she said. "You can believe that or not."

He leaned back on his elbows, staring out across the moon-bright countryside. "Tough love," he muttered. "Everyone says to use tough love."

Behind them, there was a scratching sound and then a mournful howl.

Jason stood and opened the door, and Mistletoe limped outside. He lifted his golden head and sniffed the air.

"Guess he got lonely." Jason sat back down.

Mistletoe shoved in between them and rested his head on Jason's lap.

They were silent for a few minutes. Erica was cold, especially where her thin jeans met the stone porch steps. But she felt lonely, too. She didn't want to leave the dog. And strangely enough, she didn't want to leave Jason. Although he was obviously angry, and even blaming her, he was the only person in the world right now, besides her, who was grieving Kimmie's terribly early death.

"I just don't get your story," he burst out. "How'd you help her when you were trying to care for your babies, too? And why'd she send you and your kids here?"

Mistletoe nudged his head under Jason's hand, demanding attention.

"I want some answers, Erica."

Praying for the words to come to her, Erica spoke. "She said this was a good place, a safe place. She knew I…didn't have much."

He lifted a brow like he didn't believe her.

"She'd loved my mom." Which was true. "She was kind of like a big sister to me."

"She was a *real* big sister to me." Suddenly, Jason pounded a fist into his open hand. "I can't believe this. Can't believe she OD'd alone." He paused and drew in a ragged breath, then looked at Erica. "I'm going to find out more about you and what went on out there. I'm going to get some answers."

Erica looked away from his intensity. She didn't want him to see the fear in her eyes.

And she especially didn't want him to find one particular answer: that Kimmie was the biological mother of the twins sleeping upstairs.

Chapter Two

Sunday morning, just after sunrise, Jason followed the smell of coffee into the farmhouse kitchen. He poured himself a cup and strolled around, looking for his grandfather and listening to the morning sounds of Erica and the twins upstairs.

Yesterday had been rough. He'd called their mother overseas—the easier telling, strangely—and then he'd let Papa know about Kimmie. Papa hadn't cried; he'd just said, "I'm glad Mama wasn't alive to hear of this." Then he'd gone out to the barn all day, coming in only to eat a sandwich and go to bed.

Erica and the twins had stayed mostly in the guest room. Jason had made a trip to the vet to get Mistletoe looked over, and then rattled around the downstairs, alone and miserable, battling his own feelings of guilt and failure.

Tough love hadn't worked. His sister had died alone.

It was sadness times two, especially for his grandfather. And though the old man was healthy, an active farmer at age seventy-eight, Jason still worried about him.

Where was his grandfather now, anyway? Jason looked out the windows and saw a trail broken through newly drifted snow. Papa had gone out to do morning chores without him.

A door opened upstairs, and he heard Erica talking to the twins. Maybe bringing them down for breakfast.

She was too pretty and he didn't trust her. Coward that he was, he poured his coffee into a travel cup and headed out, only stopping to lace his boots and zip his jacket when he'd closed the door behind him.

Jason approached the big red barn and saw Papa moving around inside. After taking a moment to admire the rosy morning sky crisscrossed by tree limbs, he went inside.

Somehow, Papa had pulled the old red sleigh out into the center of the barn and was cleaning off the cobwebs. In the stalls, the two horses they still kept stomped and snorted.

Papa gave him a half smile and nodded toward the horses. "They know what day it is.

"What day?

"You've really been gone that long? It's Sleigh Bell Sunday."

"You don't plan on…" He trailed off, because Papa obviously did intend to hitch up the horses and drive the sleigh to church. It was tradition. The first Sunday in December, all the farm families that still kept horses came in by sleigh, if there was anything resembling enough snow to do it. There was a makeshift stable at the church and volunteers to tend the horses, and after church, all the town kids got sleigh rides. The church ladies served hot cider and cocoa and homemade doughnuts, and the choir sang carols.

It was a great event, but Papa already looked tired. "We don't have to do it this year. Everyone would understand."

"It's important to the people in this community." Papa knelt to polish the sleigh's runner, adding in a muffled voice, "It was important to your grandmother."

Jason blew out a sigh, picked up a rag and started cleaning the inside of the old sleigh.

They fed and watered the horses. As they started to pull out the harnesses, Jason noticed the old sleigh bells he and Kimmie had always fought over, each of them wanting to be the one to pin them to the front of the sleigh.

Carefully, eyes watering a little, he hooked the bells in place.

"You know," Papa said, "this place belongs to you and Kimmie. We set it up so I'm a life tenant, but it's already yours."

Jason nodded. He knew about the provisions allowed to family farmers, made to ensure later generations like Jason and Kimmie wouldn't have to pay heavy inheritance taxes.

"I'm working the farm okay now. But you'll need to think about the future. There's gonna come a time when I'm not able."

"I'm thinking on it." They'd had this conversation soon after Gran had died, so Jason wondered where his grandfather was going with it.

"I imagine Kimmie left her half to you."

Oh. That was why. He coughed away the sudden roughness in his throat. "Lawyer's going to call back tomorrow and go through her will."

"That's fine, then." Papa went to the barn door.

"Need a break and some coffee. You finish hitching and pull it up." He paused, then added, "If you remember how."

The dig wasn't lost on Jason. It had been years since he'd driven horses or, for that matter, helped with the farm.

It wasn't like he'd been eating bonbons or walking on the beach. But he'd definitely let his family down. He had to do better.

By the time he'd figured out the hitches and pulled the sleigh up to the front door of the old white house, Papa was on the porch with a huge armload of blankets. "They'll be right out," he said.

"Who?"

"Erica and the babies."

"Those babies can't come! They're little!"

Papa waved a dismissive hand. "We've always taken the little ones. Safer than a car."

"But it's cold!" Even though it wasn't frostbite weather, the twins weren't used to Pennsylvania winters. "They're from Arizona!"

"So were you, up until you started elementary school." Papa chuckled. "Why, your parents brought you to visit at Christmas when you were only three months old, and Kimmie was, what, five? You both loved the ride, and no harm done."

And they'd continued to visit the farm and ride in the sleigh every Christmas after they'd moved back to the Pittsburgh area. Even when their parents had declined to go to church, Gran and Papa had insisted on taking them. Christmases on the farm had been one of the best parts of his childhood.

Maybe Kimmie had held on to some of those memories, too.

He fought down his emotions. "I don't trust Erica. There's something going on with her."

Papa didn't answer, and when Jason looked up, he saw that Erica had come out onto the porch. Papa just lifted an eyebrow and went to help her get the twins into the sleigh.

Had she heard what he'd said? But what did it matter if she had; she already knew he thought she was hiding something.

"This is amazing!" She stared at the sleigh and horses, round-eyed. "It's like a movie! Only better. Look, Mikey, horses!" She pointed toward the big furry-footed draft horses, their breath steaming in the cold, crisp air.

"Uuusss," Mikey said.

Erica's gloved hand—at least Papa had found her gloves—flew to her mouth. "That's his second word! Wow!"

"What did he say?" It had sounded like nonsense to Jason.

"He said *horse*. Didn't you, you smart boy?" Erica danced the twins around until they both giggled and yelled.

Papa lifted one of the babies from her arms and held him out to Jason. "Hold this one, will you?"

"But I…" He didn't have a choice, so he took the baby, even though he knew less than nothing about them. In his police work, whenever there'd been a baby to handle, he'd foisted it off on other officers who already had kids.

He put the baby on his knee, and the baby—was

this Mikey?—gestured toward the horses and chortled. "Uuusss! Uuusss!"

Oh. Uuusss meant horse.

"I'll hold this one, and you climb in," Papa said to Erica. "Then I'll hand 'em to you one at a time, and you wrap 'em up in those blankets." Papa sounded like a pro at all of this, and given that he'd done it already for two generations, Jason guessed he was.

Once both twins were bundled, snug between Papa and Erica, Jason set the horses to trotting forward. The sun was up now, making millions of diamonds on the snow that stretched across the hills, far into the distance. He smelled pine, a sharp, resin-laden sweetness.

When he picked up the pace, the sleigh bells jingled.

"Real sleigh bells!" Erica said, and then, as they approached the white covered bridge, decorated with a simple wreath for Christmas, she gasped. "This is the most beautiful place I've ever seen."

Jason glanced back, unable to resist watching her fall in love with his home.

Papa was smiling for the first time since he'd learned of Kimmie's death. And as they crossed the bridge and trotted toward the church, converging with other horse-drawn sleighs, Jason felt a sense of rightness.

"Over here, Mr. S!" cried a couple of chest-high boys, and Jason pulled the sleigh over to their side of the temporary hitching post.

"I'll tie 'em up," Papa said, climbing out of the sleigh.

Mikey started babbling to Teddy, accompanied by gestures and much repetition of his new word, *uuusss*. Teddy tilted his head to one side and burst forth with his own stream of nonsense syllables, seeming to ask a question, batting Mikey on the arm. Mikey waved toward the horses and jabbered some more, as if he were explaining something important.

They were such personalities, even as little as they were. Jason couldn't help smiling as he watched them interact.

Once Papa had the reins set and the horses tied up, Jason jumped out of the sleigh and then turned to help Erica down. She handed him a twin. "Can you hold Mikey?"

He caught a whiff of baby powder and pulled the little one tight against his shoulder. Then he reached out to help Erica, and she took his hand to climb down, Teddy on her hip.

When he held her hand, something electric seemed to travel right to his heart. Involuntarily he squeezed and held on.

She drew in a sharp breath as she looked at him, some mixture of puzzlement and awareness in her eyes.

And then Teddy grabbed her hair and yanked, and Mikey struggled to get to her, and the connection was lost.

The next few minutes were a blur of greetings and "been too long" came from seemingly everyone in the congregation.

"Jason Stephanidis," said Mrs. Habler, a good-hearted pillar of the church whom he'd known since childhood. She'd held back until the other congregants had drifted toward the church, probably so she could probe for the latest news. "I didn't know you were in town."

He put an arm around her. "Good to see you, Mrs. Habler."

"And this must be your wife and boys. Isn't that

sweet. Twins have always run in your family. You know, I don't think your mother ever got over losing her twin so young."

Mother had been a twin?

Erica cleared her throat. "We're actually just family friends, passing through. No relation to Jason."

The words sounded like she'd rehearsed them, not quite natural. And from Mrs. Habler's pursed lips and wrinkled brow, it looked like she felt the same.

What was Erica's secret?

And why hadn't he ever known his mother was a twin?

And wasn't it curious that, after all these years, there were twins in the farmhouse again?

When they returned to the farm, Erica's heart was both aching and full.

After dropping Jason, Erica and the twins in front of the farmhouse—along with the real Christmas tree they'd brought home—Papa insisted on taking the horses and sleigh to the barn himself, even though Erica saw the worried look on Jason's face.

"Is he going to be okay?" she asked as they hauled the twins' gear into the house in the midst of Mistletoe's excited barking.

Jason turned to watch his grandfather drive the sleigh into the barn. "He enjoyed the sleigh ride, but I think picking out a tree brought up too many memories. He'll spend a few hours in the barn, is my guess. That's his therapy."

"He's upset about Kimmie?"

"Yes. And on top of that, this is his first Christmas without my grandma."

Her face crinkled with sympathy. "How long were they married?"

"We had a fiftieth-anniversary party for them a couple of years ago," he said, thinking back. "So I think it was fifty-two years by the time she passed."

"Did Kimmie come?"

He barked out a disgusted-sounding laugh. "No."

Not wanting to get into any Kimmie-bashing, Erica changed the subject. "Could we do something to cheer him up?"

He looked thoughtful. "Gran always did a ton of decorating. I'd guess the stuff is up in the attic." He quirked his mouth. "I'm not very good at it. Neither is Papa. It's not a guy thing."

"Sexist," she scolded. "You don't need two X chromosomes to decorate."

"In this family you do. Will you... Would you mind helping me put up at least some of the decorations?" He sounded tentative, unsure of himself, and Erica could understand why. She wasn't sure if they had a truce or if he was still upset with her about the way she'd handled things with Kimmie.

But it was Christmastime, and an old man needed comfort. "Sure. I just need to put these guys down for a nap. Look at Mikey. He's about half-asleep already."

"I'll start bringing stuff down from the attic."

Erica carried the babies up the stairs, their large diaper bag slung across her shoulders. Man, she'd never realized how hard it was to single-parent twins.

Not that she'd give up a bit of it. They'd been so adorable wrapped up in their blankets in the sleigh, and everyone at church had made a fuss over them. One of the other mothers in the church, a woman named

Sheila, had insisted on going to her truck and getting out a hand-me-down, Mikey-sized snowsuit right then and there. She'd promised to see if she could locate another spare one among her mom friends.

Erica saw, now, why Kimmie had sent her here. It was a beautiful community, aesthetically and heartwise, perfect for raising kids.

She'd love to stay. If only she wasn't terrified of having them taken from her by the man downstairs.

Kimmie had seemed to feel a mix of love and regret and anger toward her brother. Now that she'd met him, Erica could understand it better.

A free spirit, Kimmie had often been irresponsible, unwilling to do things by the book or follow rules. It was part of why she'd smoked cigarettes and done drugs and gotten in trouble with the police.

Jason seemed to be the exact opposite: responsible, concerned about his grandfather, an officer of the law.

Erica wished with all her heart that she could just reveal the truth to Jason and Papa. She hated this secrecy.

But she would hate even more for Jason to take the twins away from her. This last thing she could do for Kimmie, she'd do.

And it wasn't one-sided. Kimmie had actually done Erica a favor, offered her a huge blessing.

Erica rarely dated, didn't really understand the give-and-take of relationships. Certainly, her mother hadn't modeled anything healthy in that regard. So it was no big surprise that Erica wasn't attractive to men. She didn't want to be. She dressed purposefully in utilitarian clothes and didn't wear makeup. She just didn't trust men, not with her childhood. And men didn't like her, at least not romantically.

So the incredible gift that Kimmie had given her that she could never have gotten for herself was a family.

She put the twins down in their portable playpen, settling them on opposite sides, knowing they'd end up tangled together by the end of the nap. Mikey was out immediately, but Teddy needed some back rubbing and quiet talk before he relaxed into sleep.

Pretty soon, they'd need toddler beds. They'd need a lot of things. Including insurance and winter clothing and early intervention services for their developmental delays.

And just how was she going to manage that, when she didn't have a job, a savings account or a real right to parent the twins?

Teddy kicked and fussed a little, seeming to sense her tension. So she pushed aside her anxiety and prayed for peace and for the twins to be okay and for Papa to receive comfort.

And for Kimmie's soul.

When she got toward the bottom of the stairs, she paused. Jason was lying on the floor, pouring water into a green-and-red tree stand. Somehow, he'd gotten the tree they'd quickly chosen into the house by himself and set it upright, and it emitted a pungent, earthy scent that was worlds better than the pine room freshener her mother had sometimes sprayed around at Christmastime.

Jason had changed out of church clothes. He wore faded jeans and a sage-green T-shirt that clung to his impressive chest and arms.

Weight lifting was a part of being a cop, she supposed. And obviously, he'd excelled at it.

Her face heating at the direction of her own thoughts,

she came the rest of the way down the stairs. "It smells so good! I never had a live tree before."

"Never?" He looked at her as if she must have been raised in a third world country. "What were your Christmases like?" He eased back from the tree and started opening boxes of decorations.

"Nothing like a TV Christmas movie, but who has that, really? Sometimes Mom would get me a present, and sometimes a Secret Santa or church program would leave something on our doorstep."

Jason looked at her with curiosity and something that might have been compassion, and she didn't want that kind of attention. "What about you? Did you and Kimmie and your parents come here for the holidays?"

"My parents loved to travel." He dug through a box and pulled out a set of green, heart-shaped ornaments. "See? From Ireland. They usually went on an overseas trip or a cruise at Christmas, and every year they brought back ornaments. We have 'em from every continent."

"Wow. Pretty." But it didn't sound very warm and family oriented. "Didn't they ever take you and Kimmie with them?"

"Nope. Dumped us here. But that was fine with us." He waved an arm around the high-ceilinged, sunlit room. "Imagine it all decorated, with a whole heap of presents under the tree. Snowball fights and gingerbread cookies and sleigh rides. For a kid, it couldn't get much better."

"For a grown-up, too," she murmured without thinking.

He nodded. "I'm glad to be here. For Papa and for me, too."

"Where are your parents now?"

"Dad passed about five years ago, and Mom's living on the French Riviera with her new husband. We exchange Christmas cards." He sounded blasé about it. But Erica knew how much emotion and hurt a blasé tone could cover.

They spent a couple of hours decorating the tree, spreading garland along the mantel and stringing lights. By the time Erica heard a cry from upstairs, indicating that the twins were waking up, they'd created a practically perfect farm-style Christmas environment.

"Do you need help with the babies?" Jason asked.

She would love to have help, but she knew she shouldn't start getting used to it. "It's fine. I'll get them."

"I'm going to check on Papa, then."

Erica's back was aching by the time she'd changed the twins' diapers and brought them downstairs, one on each hip. But the couple of hours they'd spent decorating were worth it. When Jason opened the door and Papa came in, his face lit up, even as his hands went to his hips. He shook his head. "You didn't have to do this. I wasn't..." He looked away and Erica realized he was choking up. "I wasn't going to put anything up this year. But seeing as how we have children in the house again..." He broke off.

Erica carried the twins into the front room. "Let's see how they like all the lights," she said, and both men seemed glad to have another focus than the losses they were facing.

She sat on the couch and put Mikey on the floor, then Teddy. She waved her hand toward the tree. "Pretty!" she said, and then her own throat tightened, remembering the silver foil tree she'd put up in Kimmie's apartment. They'd taken a lot of photographs in front of it,

Kimmie in her wheelchair holding the twins. Erica had promised to show the twins when they were older, so they'd know how much their mother had loved them.

The boys' brown eyes grew round as they surveyed the sparkling lights and ornaments.

"Priiiiiy," Mikey said, cocking his head to one side.

Erica had no time to get excited about Mikey learning another new word because Teddy started to scoot toward the tree, then rocked forward into an awkward crawl.

"Whoa, little man," Jason said, intercepting him before he could reach the shining ornaments.

"Better put the ornaments higher up and anchor the tree to the wall," Papa said. "It's what we used to do for you and your sister. You were a terrible one for pulling things off the tree. One year, you even managed to climb it!"

Jason picked up Teddy and plunked him back down on the floor beside Mikey, but not before Erica had seen the red spots on the baby's knees. "I need to get them some long pants," she fretted. "Sturdy ones, if he's going to be mobile."

"Can you afford it?" Jason asked.

Erica thought of the stash of money Kimmie had given her. She'd spent more than half of it on the cross-country drive; even being as frugal as possible in terms of motels and meals, diapers didn't come cheap. "I can afford some."

Questions lurked in his eyes, but he didn't give them voice.

Teddy rocked back and forth and got himself on hands and knees again, then crawled—backward—

toward Mistletoe, who lay by the gas fire. Quickly, Jason positioned himself to block the baby if needed.

Mistletoe nuzzled Teddy, then gave his face a couple of licks.

Teddy laughed and waved his arms.

"Not very sanitary," Papa commented.

"Oh, well," Erica and Jason said at the same time.

From the kitchen came a buzzing sound and Erica realized it was her phone. She went in and grabbed it. An Arizona number. She walked back into the front room's doorway and clicked to accept the call.

"Hello," came an unfamiliar voice. "Erica Lindholm?"

"That's me."

"This is Ryan Finnigan. An old friend of Kimmie Stephanidis. Do you have a moment to talk?"

She looked at the twins. "Can you watch the boys?" she asked the two men.

Jason looked a little daunted, but Papa nodded and waved a hand. "Go ahead. We'll be fine."

She headed through the kitchen to the dining room. "I'm here."

"I'm not only an old friend, but I'm Miss Stephanidis's attorney," the man said.

"Kimmie had an attorney?" Kimmie had barely been organized enough to buy groceries.

"Not exactly. The medical personnel who brought her to the hospital, after her overdose, happened to find one of my business cards and gave me a call. I went to see her, and we made a will right there in the hospital. None too soon, I'm afraid."

She was glad to know that Kimmie had had a friend near and that she'd been under medical care, and said so.

"I did what I could. I was…rather fond of her, at one time." He cleared his throat. "She let me know her wishes, and I was able to carry those out. But as for her estate…she's left you her half of the Holly Creek Farm."

"What?" Erica's voice rose up into a squeak and she felt for the nearest chair and sat down.

"She's left you half the farm her family owns. It's a small, working farm in Western Pennsylvania. The other half belongs to her brother."

"Half of Holly Creek Farm? And it's, like, legal?"

"It certainly is."

She sat a moment, trying to digest this news.

"I'm sure it's a lot to take in," the lawyer said after a moment. "Do you have any questions for me, off the top of your head?"

"Did Kimmie…" She trailed off, peeked through the kitchen into the front room to make sure no one could hear. "Look, is this confidential?"

"Absolutely."

"Did she leave any instructions about her children?"

"Her *children*?"

"I take it that's a no." *Oh, Kimmie, why would you provide for them with the farm, but not grant me guardianship?*

"If Kimmie did have children…the most important thing would be that they're safe, in an acceptable home."

"Right. That's right." She didn't want to admit to anything, but if he'd been fond of Kimmie at one time, as he'd mentioned, he would obviously be concerned.

He cleared his throat. "Just speaking hypothetically, if Kimmie had children and died without leaving any written instructions, they would become wards of the state."

Erica's heart sank.

"Unless…is there a father in the picture?"

"No," she said through an impossibly dry mouth. Kimmie had told her that after abandoning her and the twins, the babies' father had gone to prison with a life sentence, some drug-related theft gone bad.

"If there's no evidence that someone like you— hypothetically—had permission to take her children, no birth certificates, nothing, then any concerned party could make a phone call to Children and Youth Services."

"And they'd take the children?" She could hear the breathy fear in her voice.

"They might."

"But…this is hypothetical. You wouldn't—"

"Purely hypothetical. I'm not calling anyone. Now, even if the state has legal custody, if you have physical custody—and the children in question are doing well in your care—then the courts might decide it's in the best interest of the children for you to retain physical custody."

"I see." *It's not enough.*

"None of this might come up for a while, not until medical attention is needed or the children start school."

Or early intervention. Erica's heart sank even as she berated herself for not thinking it all through. "If it did come up…would there be some kind of hearing?"

"Yes, and at that time, any relative who had questions or concerns could raise them." He paused. "It seems Kimmie had very few personal effects, but whatever there is will be sent to her family as soon as possible."

Her hands were so sweaty she could barely keep

a grip on the cell phone. "Thank you. This has been very helpful."

"Oh, one more thing," the lawyer said. "You'll be wanting to know the executor of Kimmie's will."

"It's not you?"

"No. I'm happy to help, of course, but if there's a capable family member, I usually recommend that individual."

Erica had a sinking feeling she knew where this was going. "Who is it?"

"It's her brother. Jason Stephanidis."

Chapter Three

The next morning, Jason padded down the stairs toward the warmth of coffee and the kitchen. Noticing a movement in the front room, he stopped to look in.

There was his grandfather, in his everyday flannel shirt and jeans, staring out the window while holding a ceramic angel they'd set on the mantel yesterday. As Jason watched, Papa set it down and moved over to a framed Christmas photo of Jason and Kimmie as young kids, visiting Santa. Papa looked at it, ran a finger over it, shook his head.

Jason's chest felt heavy, knowing there was precious little he could do to relieve his grandfather's suffering.

But whatever he could do, he would. He'd been a negligent grandson, but no more.

Mistletoe leaned against his leg and panted up at him.

He gave the dog a quick head rub and then walked into the room just as Papa set down the photograph he'd been studying and turned. His face lit up. "Just the man I want to see. Come get some coffee. Got an idea to run by you."

"Yeah?" Jason slung an arm around his grandfather's shoulders as they walked into the kitchen. He poured them both a fresh cup of coffee, black. "What've you got in mind?"

Papa pulled a chair up to the old wooden table and sat down. "Got someone coming over to do a little investigating about our guests."

"You, too?" Jason was relieved that he wasn't the only one who felt suspicious. In a corner of his mind, he'd worried that it was as Renea had said: he couldn't trust, couldn't be a family person. "I can't figure out why Kimmie left the farm to her. What were they to each other?" As executor of the estate, he needed to know.

The mere thought of there being an estate—of Kimmie being gone—racked his chest with a sudden ache so strong he had to sit down at the table to keep from falling apart.

"I'm thinking about those babies, for one thing," Papa said unexpectedly.

"What about them?"

"Something's not right about them, but I don't know what it is. So I've got Ruthie Delacroix coming over this morning. There's nobody knows as much about babies as Ruthie."

Jason remembered the woman, vaguely, from visits home; she'd always had a child on her hip at church, and he seemed to recall she ran a child care operation on the edge of town.

"And that's not all I'm wondering," Papa said darkly, "but first things first."

Jason grinned. Papa conniving and plotting was better than Papa grieving.

"I figure I have to take the lead on this, since you haven't shown a whole lot of sense about women. When you brought home that skinny thing—what was her name? Renea?—and said you were going to marry her, your grandmother had a fit."

Jason wasn't going to rise to that bait. And he wasn't going to think about Renea. He got up and started wiping down the already-clean counters.

No sooner had his grandfather headed upstairs to his bedroom than Jason heard the sound of babies babbling and laughing, matched by Erica's melodic, soothing voice. A moment later, she appeared, a baby in each arm.

Even without a trace of makeup, her fair skin seemed to glow. Her hair wasn't styled, but clipped back, with strands already escaping.

His heart rate picked up just looking at her.

As she nuzzled one of the baby's heads—was that Mikey or Teddy?—he was drawn into her force field. "Want me to hold one of them?"

And where did *that* come from? He never, but never, offered to hold a baby.

"Um…sure!" She nodded toward the wigglier baby. "Take Teddy. But keep a grip on him. He's a handful. I just need to get them some breakfast." As she spoke, she strapped Mikey into the old wooden high chair.

Jason sat down and held the baby on his knee, studying him, wondering what Papa saw that made him worry. But the kid looked healthy and lively to him as he waved his arms and banged the table, trying to get Erica's attention.

Which seemed perfectly sensible to Jason. Even in

old jeans and a loose blue sweater, Erica was a knock-out. Any male would want her attention.

Nostalgia pierced him. Erica moved around the room easily, already comfortable, starting to know where things were. It made him think of his grandfather sitting at this very table after a long day of farmwork, his grandmother bustling around fixing food, declining all offers of help in the kingdom that was her kitchen.

Papa was grieving the loss of his wife now, but his life had been immeasurably enriched by his family. In fact, it was impossible to think of Papa without thinking of all those who loved him. And when Jason and Kimmie had needed some extra parenting, Papa and Gran had opened their arms without a second thought. They'd been the making of Jason's childhood.

Unfortunately, Kimmie had seen more neglect before Papa and Gran had stepped in. She'd never quite recovered from their parents' lack of real love.

"Would you like some oatmeal?" Erica asked a few minutes later, already dishing up four bowls, two big and two small. "I'm sorry, I should've asked rather than assuming. The twins love oatmeal, and so do I, and it's about the most economical breakfast you can find."

"That would be great." He shifted Teddy on his knee. "Put his down here and I'll try to feed him. No guarantees, though."

"You don't have to do that."

"It's no problem. You had the care of them all night. At least you ought to get a minute to eat a bowl of oatmeal yourself."

"That would be a treat." She placed a small bowl beside his larger one and handed him a bib and a spoon. "Go to it."

Trying to get spoonfuls of oatmeal into a curious baby proved a challenge, and as Erica expertly scooped the cereal into Mikey's mouth, she laughed at Jason's attempts. How she managed two, as a single mom, he couldn't fathom.

"Hey now," he said when Teddy blew a raspberry that spattered oatmeal all over himself, the high chair and Jason. "Give me a break. I don't know what I'm doing here."

"Teddy! Behave yourself!" A smile tugged at Erica's face as she passed Jason a cloth. "When he spits like that, he's probably done. Just wipe his face and we'll let them crawl around a little."

Mistletoe had been weaving between their legs, licking up the bits of oatmeal and banana that hit the floor. Jason reached down to pat the dog at the same moment Erica did.

Their hands brushed—and Jason felt it to his core. "Nothing like a canine vacuum cleaner," he tried to joke. And kept his hand on the dog, hoping for another moment of contact with Erica.

"I know, right? We totally should have gotten them a dog back in Arizona."

And then her hand went still. When he looked up at her face, it had gone still, too.

"Who?" Jason asked. "You and their dad?"

"*I* should have gotten them a dog," she said, not looking at him. "I meant, *I* should have."

The detective in him stored away that remark as relevant. And it was a good reminder, he reflected as they both scarfed down the rest of their breakfast without more talk. He couldn't trust Erica, didn't know what she had been to Kimmie. Getting domestic with her would only cloud his judgment. More than likely, she'd been a bad influence, dragging Kimmie down.

Beyond that likelihood, he needed to remember that he was no good at family relationships. He was here, in part, to see if he could reset his values, and he'd vowed to himself that he wouldn't even try to start anything with a woman until he'd improved significantly in that regard. It wasn't fair to either him or the woman.

Just moments later, as Jason finished up the breakfast dishes, there was a pounding on the door. Mistletoe ran toward it, barking, as Papa came out of his room and trotted down the stairs to the entryway. Jason heard the door open and then his grandfather's hearty greeting.

Immediately, the noise level jumped up a notch. "Hey there, Andy! What's this I hear about babies in the place?"

An accompanying wail revealed that she'd brought at least one baby with her. Probably her grandson, whom she seemed to bring everywhere.

Jason walked into the front room, where Erica was sitting on the floor with the twins. "Ruth Delacroix," he said in answer to Erica's questioning expression. "She's a force of nature. Prepare yourself."

"Good morning, everyone!" Ruth cried as she came in, giving Jason a big hug and kiss around the baby she held on one hip. Then she spun toward Erica. "And you must be Erica. Andy was telling me about you, that you're here for a visit with some... Oh my, aren't they adorable!"

"Let's sit down," Papa suggested, "and Jason will bring us all out some coffee. Isn't that right?"

"Sure." Jason didn't mind playing host. He was glad to see his grandfather seeming a little peppier.

When he carried a tray with coffee cups, sugar and milk into the front room, the three babies were all on the floor, and Ruth and Erica were there with them. The pine scent from the Christmas tree was strong, and the sun sparkled bright through the windows, making the ornaments glisten. Papa had turned on the radio and Christmas music poured out.

"Mason! Stop that!" Ruth scrambled after her toddling grandbaby with more agility than Jason could muster up, most days, even though Ruth had to have thirty years on him. "He's a handful, ever since he started to walk."

Teddy, not to be outdone, started scooting toward the shiny tree, and Mikey observed with round eyes, legs straight out in front of him.

"Like I said," Ruth continued, "I'm down a kid, so I'd be glad to watch these little sweethearts anytime you need. A couple of my regular clients are off this week and kept their little ones at home."

"Thanks." Erica was dangling a toy in front of Mikey, who reached for it. "I'm not sure quite what I'll be doing, but knowing there's someone who could look after the twins for a few hours is wonderful. I really appreciate you thinking of it," she added to Papa Andy.

"No problem, sweetheart." Papa took a small ornament off the tree and held it out to Jason. "Remember this?"

"The lump!" Jason laughed at the misshapen clay blob. "Haven't seen that in years. That's my masterpiece, right?"

"You were pretty proud of it. Insisted on hanging it

in a place of honor every Christmas, at least until you turned into an embarrassed teenager. And so here it is right now."

Jason smiled as Papa reminisced, egged on by Ruth and Erica. This was important, and Jason was starting to realize it was what he wanted for himself. Traditions and family, carried on from generation to generation. Just because his own parents hadn't done a good job of making a true home for him and Kimmie, that didn't mean he had to follow their patterns. He wanted to be more like Papa.

He had some work to do on himself first.

While he reflected, he'd been absently watching Erica—she was easy on the eyes, for sure—so he noticed when her expression got guarded and he tuned back into the conversation.

"What are they, seven, eight months?" Ruth was saying. "They're big boys."

"They're fifteen months," Erica said.

"Oh." Ruth frowned, and then her face cleared. "Well, Mason, here, he's real advanced. Started walking at ten months."

"They have some delays." Erica picked up Mikey and held him high, then down, high, then down, jumping him until he chortled.

Teddy did his strange little scoot crawl in their direction. Jason noticed then that Ruth's grandson was indeed a lot more mobile than the twins, a real pro at pushing himself to his feet and toddling around.

"Why are they delayed?" Ruth asked. "Problems at birth?"

"You might say that." Erica swooped Mikey down in front of his brother, and the two laughed.

Teddy pointed at the tree. "Da-da-da-DA-da-da," he said, leaning forward to look at Mikey.

"Da-da-da-da-da!" Mikey waved a hand as if to agree with what his twin brother had said.

Teddy burst out with a short laugh, and that made Mikey laugh, too.

"Now, isn't that cute. Twin talk." Ruth went off into a story about some twins she'd known who had communicated together in a mysterious language all through elementary school.

As the women got deeper into conversation about babies, Papa gestured Jason into the kitchen. He pulled a baggie from a box and started spooning baking soda into it.

"What are you doing?"

"You'll see." He tossed the baggie onto the counter and then pulled out a couple of syringes. He grabbed a spoon from the silverware drawer.

Jason stared. "Where'd you get that stuff and what are you doing with it?"

"From your narco kit, and it's just a little test. You'll see."

"But you can't… That's not—"

"Come on, hide in the pantry!" Papa shoved Jason toward the small room just off the kitchen. "Hey, Erica, where did you put those baby snack puffs?" he called into the front room.

There was a little murmuring between the two women as Papa hastily stepped into the pantry and edged around Jason. "Watch for anything suspicious," he ordered.

Helpless to stop the plan Papa had set into motion, Jason watched as Erica came into the kitchen, opened a cupboard and pulled out some kind of baby treats. Behind her, Mistletoe sat, held up a paw and cocked his head.

Erica laughed down at him. "It's not treats for you, silly. It's for the babies." She squatted, petted the dog and then stood and reached toward the jar of dog treats on the counter. "All right, beggar, I'll get you just one…"

She froze. Stared at the pseudo drug supplies. Looked around the kitchen.

Then she leaned back against the counter, hand pressed against her mouth, eyes closed.

She drew in a breath, let it out in a big sigh and picked up the baggie between two fingers as if it were going to jump up and bite her. "Papa Andy," she called. "Could you come in here a minute?"

Papa nudged his way around Jason and went into the kitchen.

"I found this." Erica held up the bag. "What's going on here?"

Papa frowned, turned back toward the pantry and spoke to Jason. "She knows what it is. That's a bad sign."

Jason sighed and came out into the kitchen. "Actually, most people know what that is. If she were using, she'd have hidden the stuff, not called you in to look at it."

Erica stared at Papa, then slowly turned to Jason. There was an expression of betrayal on her face. "You guys were testing me?"

"Yes, ma'am," Papa said. "And if the expert here is right, you passed with flying colors."

"You thought I was a drug addict?" She looked from one to the other, then flung the bag onto the counter.

"And so you set this up to test me, instead of asking me outright."

Jason waded in to defend his grandfather. "Papa just had to be sure. No addict would answer a question about being on drugs honestly, right?"

She rolled her eyes and crossed her arms, holding her elbows.

"And you know Kimmie well, obviously," he stumbled on. "She's struggled with addiction for years, as I'm sure you know, and it would make a lot of sense if you'd had a problem, too. But I've watched how addicts respond to drugs, and I can tell you're clean."

She straightened, her jaw set. "Yes, I am," she said, and stalked back into the front room.

Leaving Papa to look at Jason. "Guess that wasn't such a good idea," he said. He turned and followed Erica back into the front room.

And Jason just leaned back against the counter, disgusted with himself. He should have somehow stopped that from happening. Now they'd not only hurt her but lost her trust.

A few minutes later, Erica came back into the kitchen and glared at Jason, then at Papa, who'd followed after her. "I don't appreciate that you tried to trick me. That you thought I was an addict." From all the free therapists she'd seen in the course of living with her mother, she knew she ought to say next: when you mistrust me, I feel hurt.

She *did* feel hurt. But she didn't trust them any more than they trusted her, and especially not with her feelings.

What could you expect from men, anyway?

The thing was, Jason had been so nice to her and the twins. It had seemed like they were getting to know each other, that they might become friends. And Papa Andy… He'd seemed so warm, so welcoming.

In reality, they'd been conspiring against her, plotting.

"I'm sorry. It was a bad idea and we shouldn't have done it." Jason crossed his arms and looked at the floor.

"We trust you *now*, honey," Papa Andy said.

"Hey, what's going on out there?" Ruth's merry voice broke in. "I could use a hand here!"

The men turned toward the front room.

As Erica followed, years of feeling unworthy came back to her, an emotional tsunami she always tried to tamp down when it arose. But it refused to stay in its usual closed mental container.

She'd always been known as the addict's kid. Never any pretty clothes or new toys. Regular stints of homelessness, of trying to stay clean by way of public rest room sinks. The dread of Mom getting arrested, which meant another few months in a foster home.

Always moving somewhere unfamiliar, always the new girl in school. People didn't like her, didn't trust her, didn't want to be with her.

"Ma-ma." Mikey batted her ankle and reached up his arms.

Automatically she picked him up and cuddled him close, and the sensation of a warm baby in her arms grounded her. She couldn't give in to that old, familiar sense of worthlessness.

But she also couldn't stay in an environment where she was being tricked and treated badly. That was toxic.

"Hey, Ruth," she said to the older woman, who was

sitting on the couch beside Papa, trying to encourage Teddy to pull up and cruise along it. "You said you could babysit for me. How about giving me an hour right now?"

"You're going somewhere?"

"That's right. I can pay you your usual hourly rate, whatever's fair." Her cache of money was going down at an alarming rate, and she had to deal with that. But first things first.

"Why, sure, honey. I don't have anyplace I have to be until later in the afternoon."

"And if she has to go, I'll look after the little guys." Papa's voice was soft.

Erica spun toward Jason, who still stood in the doorway between the front room and the kitchen. "Could you show me the cabin?"

"What?"

She walked over to stand in front of him, out of earshot of the elders, feeling stiff as a robot. "The cabin on this property. Where Kimmie originally told me to go. I'd like to see about fixing that up."

"You don't want to do that, Erica. It's cold. It's a mess—"

"I can go alone if you don't want to take me." She turned toward Papa. "Could you give me directions to—"

"I'll take you!" Jason interrupted.

After she'd made sure Ruth had what she needed for the twins, after Jason had insisted on outfitting her in boots, gloves and a warm hat, she followed him outside.

He looked back as if he wanted to say something, but she glared at him and he faced ahead and beckoned for her to follow.

The walking was easy when they started out toward the barn. A trail was broken like a gully, with two-foot-deep snow on either side.

The brisk air stung her eyes and nose. Sunshine glinted on the surrounding snow, and trees extended lacy branches into the bright blue sky. Low chirps and chatters sounded from a row of evergreens, and as Jason turned from the path into fresh snow, a bright red cardinal landed on a fence post beside them, chirping a *too-eee, too-eee.*

Jason moved steadily and methodically in front of her, breaking trail. Despite his doing most of the work, she stumbled and struggled her way and was soon plenty warm, panting in the chilly air.

Impossible to maintain anger in God's beautiful world. Her emotions settled into a resigned awareness: something about her, probably an attitude or set of mannerisms she didn't even know she had, made people suspicious of her. If it hadn't changed by now, it wasn't going to. And if she was going to be alone, raising the babies, she needed to find a safe, healthy place for them to grow and thrive. And she needed to be away from painful encounters like what had happened this morning. She had to take care of herself so she could take care of the twins.

Her foot caught in an icy lump of snow and she stumbled and pitched forward on one knee. She caught herself with her hands, didn't sprawl full facedown, but snow pushed up the wrists of her jacket and sent its chill through her thin jeans.

"We're almost—" Jason turned, saw that she'd fallen and made his way back to her. "What happened? Here, give me your hand."

It would be silly to refuse. She grasped his glove-clad hand and he pulled her upright easily, brushing snow from her arms and then retrieving her hat.

"You okay? Anything hurt?"

"Fine," she said, her breath coming out fast.

"You're sure?" He was looking into her eyes. Very direct. Very intense.

She turned away and nodded. "I'm fine. Snow's soft."

"We're almost there," he said.

After a few more minutes slogging through the snow, Jason gestured ahead. "There it is, in all its glory."

Erica looked to see a weathered log cabin, small, with a steep, slanting roof and a front porch topped by a snow-covered wooden awning. One of the small front windows was boarded up, and the other needed to be, its glass clearly broken.

Behind the cabin and on one side, pine trees, their branches heavy with snow, gave the area a deep quiet and privacy.

"You still want to see inside? It's pretty run-down."

"Yeah," she said, breaking off into fresh snow to check out the sides of the cabin. It *was* run-down, but with work it could be cute.

For just a moment she flashed back on years of living in crowded, dirty cities. She'd always dreamed of a country getaway, a place that was safe, with privacy and no one to bother her. A place of her own—not just an apartment but a whole little house.

"Let me go in first." Jason tested the strength of the front porch boards before unlocking the door and going in.

Not much point locking it when someone had broken the windows out, but whatever.

"Come on in. It's just us and the chipmunks."

If he thought a few critters would scare her, he was sadly mistaken. She stepped over a broken stair and into the cabin's single room.

She'd feared it would be dark and gloomy, but it was bright, with side windows larger than those in front. A ladder led up to what must be a loft bedroom. The wood-plank walls looked sturdy, and a sink and stove lined one wall. No refrigerator, but that was easily obtained, and in the meantime, a gallon of milk would keep just fine in the snow.

A concrete floor showed through linoleum torn in one corner. That would have to be repaired, but for now, a thick rug would cover the ugliness. She walked to the back of the cabin and opened a door, discovering a storage area and bathroom.

She gave Jason a brisk nod. "It'll do. What would be the steps to getting the heat going? And I assume that once we turn on the water, the plumbing is okay?"

"Erica, you can't live like this. It's primitive and it's filthy." As if to punctuate his words, a small mouse raced across the floor, and he gestured toward it and looked at her.

"I grew up with an addict. I've lived in much dirtier places, with rats *and* scorpions." She tested the ladder, found it secure and started up to peek at the loft bedroom.

"Besides which, there's no heat per se—there's a wood-burning fireplace. Do you know anything at all about keeping that going so you and the kids won't freeze to death?"

"I'm a fast learner."

"You're not going to find someone to clean it during the holidays."

"I can clean it myself," she called down to him. The loft was even dirtier, if that was possible, littered with beer cans and newspapers and something that looked like a dead bird. Ugh.

Against one wall was a stained mattress that smelled bad even in the cold. Kids or hunters—or vagrants—must have taken refuge here.

For just a moment her courage failed as she relived dozens of dirty sleeping rooms she'd stayed in as a kid. Was she going backward in her life? Was filth and desolation her destiny?

She clenched her jaw. She was going to get rid of that mattress and clean this place to a shine. The twins wouldn't grow up as she had. She'd make sure the lock was sturdy and that the window got fixed. As a kid, she hadn't had a choice, but now she did. She would do better for her boys.

She climbed down the ladder. Now that she wasn't moving, she was getting cold, and she noticed Jason stamping his feet. Their breath made steam clouds in the cabin air, which she would've thought was cool if she'd been in a better mood.

"Look, Erica, I'm sorry. I was a jerk. I should have realized you weren't one to do drugs."

"I've never used in my life," she told him. "You don't make the same mistakes your parents made, though you might make different ones."

"You could be right about that." He rubbed his hands together. "But look, I'm sorry I was deceptive. That wasn't right."

His choice of words brought her to attention. Yes,

Jason had been deceptive and it had made her angry. But his deception paled in comparison with the one she was trying to pull off, the fact that the twins were Kimmie's.

Certainly, her own deception was bigger. But she didn't know what he'd done to make Kimmie so mistrustful, only that he was rigid and judgmental, seeing everything in black-and-white. A perfectionist with a mean streak.

Not a person to raise kids.

Moreover, if Jason were sneaky and suspicious enough to attempt to trap her into revealing an addiction, he'd certainly be able to discover the truth about the twins, once his suspicions started to move in that direction.

And that couldn't happen, because he'd take the twins away. Kimmie hadn't wanted that. She'd wanted Erica to raise them.

Erica wanted that, too. They belonged to her and she loved them. In her heart, which was what mattered, she was their mother.

All the more reason to move out of Jason and Papa's house immediately.

"I can start cleaning the place tomorrow," she said, "and if you'll give me the information, I can make calls about the water and heat today. The twins and I can move in within a few days."

"You can't live here!" Jason lifted his hands, obviously exasperated. "How are you going to manage the twins when there's a ladder to get to the bedroom? Are you going to leave one up there while you carry the other down? There's no railing. It's dangerous."

"I can make it work," she said, feeling uneasy. He did have a point.

"And there's water, sure, but no washing machine or dryer." He shook his head. "It's the kind of place someone totally down-and-out would live in, not a mother and kids. In fact, no doubt we'd have some drug squatters here if Papa didn't keep such a close eye on it."

His objections were valid, but... "I'm sure we can figure out something."

"You run the risk of Children and Youth stepping in. These are bad conditions."

And you'd like nothing better. You'd probably call them on me yourself.

"Look, the property is half yours, once the will goes through probate. If it's because you're angry at me, I can stay out here and you stay in the house." He frowned. "I'd only ask that you let Papa stay in the house with you. He shouldn't be climbing the ladder."

"Of course!" She'd never kick an old man out of his home. "No, you and your grandfather need to stay at the big house. I'm the interloper. I'll move out here."

He shook his head. "No, Erica. Listen, I...I'm rotten at friends and family. Anyone will tell you. I apologize for treating you badly. It's nothing about you. It's me."

He looked forlorn and bitter all at the same time. She steeled herself against the temptation to feel sorry for him.

"I really don't think you can get the place cleaned up yourself, but if you want to try, I'll help you."

Now, *that* would be a disaster. Working closely with the man who'd tricked her, but whom she still, to her chagrin, found attractive. The man she was starting to feel sorry for, at least a little. The man who looked so good in his lumberjack flannel and boots.

"I should get back to the twins," she said. And she

needed to figure out whether living in the cabin was really viable. And most of all, she needed to figure out how to keep Jason and his grandfather at a distance—both so they didn't hurt her anymore, and so they didn't figure out the truth.

Chapter Four

By the time they got back to the main house, clouds had covered over the midday sun. And Jason had a feeling that, once they went inside, any chance of a private conversation would be avoided or lost.

The need to know about his sister's last days and why she'd bequeathed half the farm to Erica overpowered his politeness. If he was going to be a jerk, he'd really be a jerk. "We need to find a time to talk about Kimmie."

"You don't quit, do you?" She skirted him to walk ahead in the snow.

All of a sudden she stopped, looking toward the house.

Since the skies had darkened, the front room was illuminated like a theater. Papa stood there alone, holding some small object in his hand. As they watched, he put it down and picked up something else.

"What's he doing?" she asked.

"Those are my grandmother's crèches," he said, and the lump in his own throat wouldn't let him say any more.

What would it be like to have a relationship as close as his grandparents' had been?

He opened the front door, and Mistletoe barked excitedly. Between the dog and the noise Jason made taking off his boots and helping Erica with her coat, he hoped Papa had the chance to pull himself together.

But when Papa came to the doorway of the front room, he had to clear his throat and blow his nose. "The twins are upstairs napping," he said, his voice a little rough. "Ruth fed 'em some lunch and put them down, and she says they're out like lights. She had to take off."

Erica touched Papa's arm. "I'm curious about your decorations," she said. "After I check on the twins, will you show them to me?"

Maybe it was cowardly, but Jason couldn't cope with looking through the family treasures and dredging up a bunch of memories. "I'll make lunch," he said.

In the kitchen, he soon had tomato soup heating and cheese sandwiches grilling in plenty of butter. Comfort food. Even if he wasn't good at sharing feelings with his grandfather, he was a decent short-order cook.

He started to check and see what everyone wanted to drink, but stopped on the threshold of the front room.

Papa was pointing to the star atop the tree, one of Gran's prize possessions, and pulling out his bandanna to wipe his eyes.

And rather than backing away, Erica put an arm around him. "Do you have any photos of her?"

Was she crazy? Or was she trying to butter Papa up, to get something out of him the way she'd gotten something out of Kimmie?

Papa nodded, his face lighting up. "Would you like to see our family albums?"

Jason beat a hasty retreat. If Erica could get outside of herself enough to comfort an old man to whom she owed nothing, then he was impressed. But was anyone really that nice? Most likely, she had some selfish motive. Most people did.

Once he had the plates on the table, he couldn't delay any longer. Still, when he walked into the front room to see Erica and Papa sitting on the couch side by side, the gray head and the red one bent over an old photo album, he had to swallow hard to get his voice into cheerful mode. "Lunch is ready," he said with only a little hitch.

Funny, the twins didn't have red hair. They must take after their father. Erica hadn't mentioned one word about the man, and from her reaction to being asked about Kimmie, she probably wouldn't welcome Jason opening the discussion.

As they ate their lunch, Erica kept the conversation going with questions about Gran, which led to talk of Jason's and Kimmie's childhoods.

"Our daughter was a bust as a mother," Papa admitted, his spoonful of tomato soup halfway to his mouth. "She had her reasons. I'm glad we could step in."

"I heard about that, some," Erica said. "Kimmie spent a lot of time talking her mom."

She did? Jason got up, ostensibly to get some extra napkins, but really to cover his own surprise. How much had Kimmie told Erica? What else did she know? If Kimmie had aired their mother's dirty laundry, it spoke to Erica's ability to get close to people and find out their secrets.

Papa obviously didn't have the same suspicions. "I just wish…" he said, and then broke off.

"What do you wish?" Erica asked.

"I just wish it had worked out better for Kimmie." He put down his spoon and shook his head, staring off out the window.

Enough of taking Papa down their family's unhappy memory lane. It was time to learn something about Erica. "You said your mom had issues, too. Did you have grandparents to step into the gap for your mother?"

"Estranged," she said. "So Christmas can be sort of sad for me, too." She looked from Jason back to Papa. "Did you know there's a movement called Blue Christmas for people who are mourning at Christmastime?"

"What won't they think of next?" Papa waved a dismissive hand. "People are oversensitive these days."

"Or maybe more in touch with their feelings?" She softened her disagreement with a smile. "I think it's a good idea. Pretending you're having a Currier and Ives Christmas when you're not can make you even more depressed."

Papa chuckled. "Got your own opinions, do you?" He took a big bite of grilled cheese.

"Yes, and sometimes I'm even right."

As they talked on, Jason took note of the fact that Erica had neatly evaded his effort to probe into her background. He tucked that bit of knowledge away.

Against his will, though, he got caught up in Erica's description of the special church services they'd had back in Arizona for people who had a hard time dealing with the holidays. He wanted, in the worst way, to ask whether Kimmie had attended any such services. Had his sister been sad, missed the family during the holidays? Had she maintained the strong values she'd had as a younger woman, the faith they'd shared with Papa and Gran?

Guilt washed over him. Why had he let Kimmie become alienated from the rest of the family? Why hadn't he tried harder to find her and mend their differences?

He studied the woman talking with animation to Papa. No, she hadn't been Kimmie's drug friend. And yes, he was starting to care for her more and more.

But he still had questions. Okay, Erica had been lonely, had needed a surrogate sister in light of her own mother's absence. But what had Erica done for Kimmie in return that she'd gone so far as to leave her half the farm?

Later that afternoon, Erica got the twins strapped into their car seats and tried to back out of the space her little car had occupied since they'd arrived at Holly Creek Farm three days ago.

In the icy tracks, her wheels spun.

After a couple more attempts, she stopped and looked up "how to drive in snow" on her phone.

Go forward and back, get traction. She could do that. She put the car into Drive.

The wheels spun.

She clenched her jaw. She didn't even really want to attend the charitable clothing giveaway, but when she'd seen the flyer, she'd forced herself to copy the information in her planner, because the twins needed warm clothes. Now, to have this kind of obstacle getting there… She switched into Reverse and floored it.

The wheels made a loud spinning noise.

The car didn't move.

Teddy started to cry.

Why would anyone want to live in this snowy, obstinate state, when the blue skies and warm air and green palms of Arizona were just a few days' drive away?

A knock on her window made her jump. Jason. Great. She put the car into Park and lowered the window.

"Having problems?"

She clenched her jaw. "Obviously."

"Where are you headed?"

"I'm going to town," she said over Teddy's wails, "if I can get unstuck."

He squatted and studied her front tire, then stood. "Tires are almost bald," he said, "and this is a lightweight car. Why don't you let me drive you in my truck?"

"No!" The refusal was reflexive, automatic. Help usually came with strings. That, she'd learned at her mother's knee.

"I was planning to go in anyway. Give me five minutes to grab my things and pull the truck around."

"I don't need any help." Even though the evidence was blatantly to the contrary.

"My truck has a back seat. It's going to be a lot safer for the twins."

The one convincing argument. "Fine," she said, and then realized she sounded completely rude and ungrateful. "I mean, thank you. I would appreciate that."

Five minutes later, as they drove down a snowy, twisty, evergreen-lined road, she looked over at him. "Thank you for doing this. You're right. It wouldn't have been safe in my car."

Which meant she needed to get a new car, or new tires at least. Add that to the lengthening shopping list in her head.

"No problem. Where are we headed?"

"The church." Heat rose in her face, but she forced herself to continue, staring straight ahead. "They're having a clothing giveaway."

"Oh." He steered around a sharp curve and then asked, "So money's a problem right now?"

"Yeah."

"What were you doing for work, prior to coming here?"

Her stomach tightened. Not because of the probing—he'd earned that right, driving her to town—but because of what he might find out.

She hated lying, always had. But she didn't want to put the detective in Jason on high alert, and she couldn't dodge the feeling that any talk of the past might do that. "I worked as an aide in a nursing home." Which was true. "And I was taking classes at the community college."

"Studying what?" If he'd sounded skeptical, she would have cut him off, but he actually sounded interested, like he believed her.

"Human Services. It could lead to Social Work or Early Childhood Education, if I went on for a bachelor's degree." She looked at him quickly. A few acquaintances had laughed about someone of her background going to college. If Jason did...

"Makes sense. What all had you taken?"

Relieved, she shrugged. "College Writing. Intro to Psychology. I was actually in a class called Introduction to Gerontology when...when Kimmie got sick." She clenched her teeth. *Stop talking.*

"No wonder you get along well with Papa."

Good, he was going to let the past—*her* past—go. "I

like old people," she said. "Old people and kids." She opened her mouth to say that it was the people in the middle who caused most of the problems in the world, but she snapped it shut again. The less information she volunteered, the better.

"So you were out of a home and you went to stay with Kimmie?" he asked abruptly. "Did she take care of your kids while you worked?" An undertone of censure ran beneath his words.

"It wasn't like that." She crossed her arms over her chest. *Think, think.*

"What *was* it like?"

She had to give him some information, the bare bones at least, or he'd never leave her alone. "She was too sick to care for herself. I left my apartment empty to live with her and care for her." *And her babies.* Which of course, she couldn't say.

"If she was too sick to care for herself, how'd you manage the babies and the job and the schooling?"

She blew out a sigh. "My class was online, and I finished it." She was still proud of that accomplishment. "My job... I didn't have the time off, so..."

"So you lost it?"

"Yeah." She'd actually given notice and quit, but to someone like Jason, the difference wouldn't signify.

He was pulling into the church parking lot, and he didn't respond. She glanced over at him, expecting contempt, but instead he just looked thoughtful.

Inside, the church basement was crowded with people of all ages looking through tables full of clothing, toys and small gifts. Large signs explained the rules: one item from each table, as needed.

The stale smell of used clothes and unwashed people

brought back memories. A girl of ten or eleven flipped through a rack of girls' clothing, her face tense.

Erica's gut twisted with sympathy.

She'd been that girl, desperate to find used clothes that didn't look used. Once, she remembered, she'd been excited to find a beautiful shirt with lace around the neckline and sleeves. She'd worn it to school, proudly, only to be found out by the rich girl who'd donated it.

She's poor. Look, she's wearing my old shirt.

She's poor.

She's poor.

"Let me hold one of the boys so you can see what you're doing." Jason held out his arms, and when Teddy reached for him, Erica let him go, swallowing hard.

She was reduced to charity, for now, but it wasn't what she wanted for the twins. She wasn't going to make a practice of this. She *would* get a job. Right here in this area, because thanks to Kimmie's bequest, she had a rent-free place to stay. She'd find a way to manage a job and child care.

Her kids were *not* coming to events like this once they were old enough to understand what it meant.

"Aw, are they twins?" A woman about Erica's age, but much better dressed, came over and ran a long, polished fingernail down Mikey's cheek, tickling his chin. "Such cute boys! Let me see if I can get permission for you to take two things from the tables."

"Thank you." Erica swallowed and started searching through the jeans and sweaters, trying not to wrinkle her nose at the stained ones, putting aside a couple that would be wearable, even cute, with a good washing.

The woman came back. "I'm really sorry, but rules are rules. You see, if we let one person take more than one thing—" she brushed back her hair and waved an arm around "—everyone would want to, and it wouldn't be fair, because—"

"It's fine," Erica interrupted. "Thank you, anyway."

Jason coughed and she looked over to see him lift an eyebrow and point to his own chest, clearly offering to claim the additional item as his own. She just shook her head a little, picked up the little pair of elastic-waist jeans she'd found for one or the other of the twins and moved on to the next table.

"Nothing like treating other adults like kids," he muttered.

"Yeah. Annoying, isn't it?" Of course, Jason wasn't accustomed to being spoken to in a patronizing way; he had a good job and had never been reduced to accepting handouts from anyone.

"What all do you need? I'll have a look around."

"Pretty much anything warm. They're fifteen months, but we could go as high as eighteen to twenty-four months, sizewise."

"There are more boys' clothes over here." Another well-dressed woman about Erica's age approached, this one with hollows under her eyes. She gestured Erica over. "Your babies are…" She swallowed hard. "They're really sweet." Her voice got rough on the last words, and she excused herself and walked rapidly out of the hall.

There was some story there. And it was a good reminder to Erica: just because someone was pretty and dressed in designer clothes, that didn't mean her life was easy.

Most of the people working were incredibly kind, and Erica ended up with a useful little stack of clothing that would help the boys manage winter for now.

As she was trying to figure out whether she was done and could escape, there was a small commotion at a table behind her.

"Mommy! That girl has my Princess Promise game," the little girl behind the table said, pointing at a bedraggled mother and daughter.

"Oh! Oh, no, ma'am, that's my daughter's. These are the free toys." She indicated the much less shiny toys on the table.

"I'm sorry." The poor mother blushed as she handed the toy back and knelt to comfort her disappointed daughter.

"What'd she say, Chandie?" A scruffy-looking man with bloodshot eyes and the pinpoint pupils of an addict came to stand beside the woman and child. "She disrespecting you?"

"Nothing, it's fine." The young woman, Chandie, took the man's arm and steered him away, beckoning for her little girl to follow.

The little girl hurried after, looking frightened.

So there were drug problems even in the sweet little town of Holly Springs.

Erica made an internal vow. Once she got on her feet, she'd keep the twins miles away from anyplace people with those sorts of issues hung around.

She spent a few more minutes thanking the volunteers, then turned to locate Jason. She was done here. And from the look of things, he hadn't found anything for Teddy. She wanted to leave.

They came together near the door. "Do you want to stay for dinner?" he asked. "I usually do. It's a holiday-type meal and it's open to everyone."

So that was the source of the mouthwatering smells, of turkey and pie.

"If you're staying, we'll stay, too," she said, squaring her shoulders. "If the twins fuss, though, I'll probably have to take them out to the truck."

"There's child care in the church nursery. In fact, Ruth usually takes charge of it, so she'll know what to do with the twins."

"That's good, then." She reminded herself to be grateful for the church dinner, and for the kind people who had put this event together, rather than being ashamed that she had to participate.

"Here, I'll take the stuff to the truck, and then I have to run out on a quick errand. By the time you get the twins settled, it'll be about time for the dinner. Do you want to shop a little for yourself?"

"Is something wrong with my clothes?" She narrowed her eyes, daring him to say it. Kimmie had always been on her to wear things that showed her figure rather than hiding it.

He backed away, palms up. "Nope. Nothing at all. I just thought most women like to shop."

"Nice of you to call it shopping." *Get that chip off your shoulder, girl. You're poor.* She forced a smile. "I really do appreciate your help. Take as long as you need. I'll see if Ruth needs help in the nursery, and if she doesn't, I'll meet you wherever those great smells are coming from."

On the way out, she saw Sheila, the woman who'd already given her the snowsuit for the twins, beckoning her over.

"Hey, I'm going to say something, and if it makes

you mad, just tell me and I'll shut right up." She smiled at the babies. "They are so cute."

"I doubt you'll make me mad. Shoot."

"There's this green winter dress here. It's great quality and it's only been worn a couple of times." She flipped through the rack. "Look. Pretty, isn't it?"

And it was, absolutely gorgeous. A sheath dress with a lace overlay of the same shade over the shoulders and sleeves, and a row of gold grommets around the neckline.

"It's gorgeous," Erica agreed, fingering the fabric.

"I donated it, and it hurt me to do it, but—" she gestured down at herself "—these hips are never fitting into that dress again. You should take it."

"Oh, I couldn't."

"Why not?" Sheila held the dress to her. "It would fit you perfectly. And you'd rock it, with your red hair and being so tiny."

"Someone else could use it more. I never go out."

"It's not super fancy. You could wear it to a Christmas party, or a church service."

"That's true..." Temptation overcame her. She'd feel like a queen in that dress.

"It's been hanging here all evening and nobody wanted it." She tickled Mikey's chin, making him laugh. "Go on, take it. Otherwise it'll just stare at me from my closet and make me think about how much weight I've gained."

So, feeling a little foolish and a little excited, Erica let the woman wrap it up for her.

Once the twins were settled in the nursery with plenty of attention—no help needed, as Ruth had two other assistants—Erica went to the door and looked out into the parking lot. If Jason's truck were here, she'd find him, get his key and put the silly dress in the truck before going to dinner.

He was just pulling in, as it happened, so she went out to meet him. Cold wind whipped through the icy parking lot, and she was grateful for the coat she'd borrowed from the front closet back at the farmhouse.

Jason emerged from the truck, and when he saw her, he looked almost guilty.

"I got something for myself, like you suggested," she said, holding up the bag. "Can I just stick it in the truck?"

"Um, sure."

When she did, she saw that the floor of the back seat was full of bags that hadn't been there before. A red snowsuit peeked out of one, a big plastic tool set from another.

Slowly, she backed out of the truck and looked at him. "You…have friends with babies?"

"I hope you consider me a friend."

She stared at him, then at the bags, then at him again. "You did *not* just go out and buy a bunch of stuff for the twins."

"I actually did. But I kept the receipts. I got the sizes you said, but we can exchange them if anything doesn't fit or if it's not what you like."

"Why are you doing this?" Inside, emotions churned. She didn't deserve for someone like Jason to treat her well. She'd never had that. People like her didn't get treated well.

And beyond that, she was deceiving him, so she *really* didn't deserve his help.

Not to mention that taking such big gifts—charity, really—from anyone made her uncomfortable.

"You lost your job to take care of my sister, okay?" His voice was rough. "It's the least I can do."

"I didn't do that to get something." Which she could see now was exactly how it looked. Did people think she'd bribed Kimmie? *I'll care for you if you give me half the farm?*

"I can afford it," he went on. "I have a good job and a good salary." He frowned. "At least, I think I'll go back to it."

That distracted her. So he might not return to Philadelphia? Did that mean he might stay here?

"You're a good mom, you're doing your best, you love your kids." He said all those things flatly, as if they were facts, and the words buoyed her up. "We all need a hand sometimes. Kimmie did, and you gave it."

She opened her mouth to protest some more and then closed it. Looked up at the stars for guidance and didn't find any.

"Just accept someone doing something nice for you and your kids," he said, his voice persuasive now. He reached out to adjust her coat, pulling it higher on her neck against the cold wind. Then he cupped her chin in his work-roughened hand and looked into her eyes. For a breathless moment she thought he was going to kiss her.

And she thought she might let him.

But he pulled his hand away, his eyes dark and unreadable, and nodded toward the church. "Come on, we'd better get some of that good food while we can."

As they turned toward the church, she felt his hand at the small of her back, guiding her, gently caring for her.

It was appealing. Beguiling. Tempting.

And incredibly dangerous.

Because getting close to Jason—as her heart longed to do—meant betraying Kimmie's wishes for the twins.

Chapter Five

Normally, Jason loved church dinners. He'd eat massive amounts of fried chicken, marshmallow fluff salad and green beans cooked to within an inch of their lives and still save room for a couple of pieces of pie.

Today, sitting across the long table from Erica, he wasn't even hungry.

This thing with Erica was getting weird. Intense. Dangerous.

He hadn't dated anyone since Renea, and for good reason; she'd pegged him correctly as bad at relationships. Before her, he'd dated a lot, but it had all been shallow. His heart hadn't been involved in the least.

But against his will, he was connecting with Erica, feeling strangely close to her. To the point where, when he'd seen her tension at the clothing giveaway, he'd wanted to ease it.

He'd *wanted* to pull her into his arms, but he knew better. So he'd done something to help her sons, instead.

He hadn't even minded, because he liked Mikey and Teddy, which was weird because he was *not* a baby kind of guy. He'd bought them a couple of matching outfits, flannel shirts and jeans, rugged country winter clothing they could wear as they crawled around the floor of the house.

That was the thing, though: he wanted them in the house, not out at the cabin.

He could blame his desire for them to stay on Papa, but the truth was he wanted them there for himself.

Wanted Erica there for himself.

"Eyes bigger than your stomach, young man?" Mrs. Habler, an apron tied around her waist, scolded as she looked at his still-full plate. "I made that three-bean salad, you know."

"And it's delicious," Erica said, giving Jason a chance to shove some into his mouth and nod.

Mrs. Habler turned to focus on Erica. "Still staying out at Holly Creek Farm, are you? Tongues have been wagging, I'm afraid."

"Erica was a friend of Kimmie's," Jason interjected. "Having her and her boys there is making Papa happy."

"Then that's reason enough, and I'll try to quell the gossip."

"Wait a minute, Mrs. Habler." Erica put a hand on the woman's arm. "You seem like you know a lot of what's going on in town. Do you happen to know of any job openings?"

Now, *that* was interesting. Suggested that Erica would stay around, as did her desire to fix up the cabin, actually.

The thought put way too much joy into his heart.

"I might know of a couple of things." Mrs. Habler pulled out a chair and sat down beside Erica. "I just heard Cam Cameron is looking for help at the hardware store. And there's going to be an opening at Tiny

Tykes Day Care, since Taylor McPherson got put on bed rest today."

Erica's eyes widened. "I love kids. And maybe the twins…" Her cheeks flushed with obvious excitement. "Does anyone from the day care happen to be here to-night?"

"Ruth Delacroix is in the nursery, I believe. She's the owner."

"I know her!" Erica clapped her hands together. "Maybe that's what God has in mind for me. Thank you so much, Mrs. Habler!" She leaned over and gave the woman a one-armed hug.

"You're surely welcome." Mrs. Habler bustled over toward a small group of women clustered near the kitchen, clearly delighted to have put her interfering skills to work.

Erica looked to be brimming with excitement, but before they could discuss the possibility of her working at Tiny Tykes, Pastor Wayne stood to offer a message.

"Keep it short, Pastor!" one of the men cleaning off tables called, grinning.

"That's not in my skill set, George," the pastor called back to general laughter.

As he launched into a message welcoming guests and focusing on coming home to Christ if you'd been astray, Jason finished his plate of food, listening to the pastor's remarks with half an ear.

He hadn't felt the presence of God in some time, even though he dutifully attended church with Papa when he came home. He'd gotten angry at God for letting Kim-mie go downhill so badly. Which was wrong, of course.

He hadn't done things right, faithwise. It looked like Kimmie hadn't, either. It occurred to him that he didn't know whether Kimmie had been right with the Lord or not when she'd died.

As for himself—was he right with the Lord? He'd certainly strayed far away.

Appropriately enough, the pastor was sharing the story of the prodigal son. As he started to wrap it up, Ruth Delacroix came into the fellowship hall and approached Erica. For a moment Erica looked excited, but as Ruth whispered to her, she looked increasingly concerned. As soon as the pastor finished, Erica followed Ruth out of the fellowship hall.

Jason debated with himself. He shouldn't follow after Erica, should he? For one thing, as Mrs. Habler had said, tongues were already wagging. For another, Erica could handle things herself and didn't need him interfering.

But the worry on her face...

Before he half knew what he was doing, he was out of his chair and headed out the same door where Erica had gone.

When he reached the nursery, the twins looked to be fine—a relief.

But Erica didn't.

She was sitting on the floor next to Lori Samuelson, the local pediatrician and an active member of the church, while Ruth dealt with the twins and two other toddlers and listened in.

It wasn't his business, and it wasn't right to eavesdrop. The twins were fine. But as he turned to leave, he caught Erica's concerned question: "So you think it's serious?"

"They're quite delayed for fifteen months. The earlier you get help for them, the more likely they'll catch up by the time they're in school."

He forced himself to walk away, but he couldn't force away the look on Erica's face nor the worried tone of her voice.

The twins were in some kind of trouble. And for better or worse, he cared. He wanted to help.

"Can I take you to lunch as a thank-you?" Erica asked Jason the next morning as they drove away from Ruth Delacroix's big Victorian home, half of which operated as the Tiny Tykes Day Care.

She felt like she was about to burst—with anxiety, with gladness, with worry and anticipation.

She'd basically gotten the job. She could start right after the Christmas week closure, provided her paperwork turned out fine. Best of all, the twins could come. They'd be together in the infants and toddlers' room, and Erica would be alternating between that room and the preschoolers' room. It would give the twins a lot of time with her, and some time without her, too, to get more accustomed to other people and to get a different kind of stimulation.

Their life here was shaping up—except for the secret she had to keep and the worry of getting the twins the help they needed. She had an idea about how to handle the early intervention issue, but she had to talk Jason into it very carefully.

"You don't have to buy me lunch," he said as he steered the truck through the snowy streets of downtown Holly Springs.

"I want to. What's the best lunch place in town?"

He grinned over at her and her heart just about stopped. "Well, if you insist... I do love a good burger at Mandelina's."

"Let's do it." It was just a thank-you, she assured herself. Nothing more.

In the corner diner, overwhelming stimulation confronted them. The combined aroma of grease and coffee. Bright Christmas streamers, multicolored lights and three Christmas trees. "Grandma Got Run Over by a Reindeer" blaring from corner speakers.

"The best place, huh?" she murmured as the hostess took them to the only empty booth.

"You'll see."

When the menus came, Jason plucked hers out of her hand. "I know what you're going to do. You're going to order a salad. It would be a mistake."

"How'd you read my mind?" She lifted an eyebrow.

"You're a light eater most of the time. But when in Rome…"

"Don't make assumptions. I might surprise you."

"Oh, really?" He held her gaze for a second too long.

The man was way too good at flirting. He was even tutoring her, a remedial student, in the art.

A chubby, twentysomething waiter appeared, pencil and pad in hand. "And what can I offer you fine people today?"

"I'll have a burger and fries, please," she said, earning a nod of approval from Jason.

"Same for me," he said, and gave her a gentle fist bump. "Only trick is, Erica, you have to save room for pie."

"You absolutely do, because it's coconut cream today," the waiter said as he took their menus. "It's to die for. I had two pieces for breakfast, which was a mistake, but one for dessert will make you the happiest you've been in weeks."

Hmm, she wanted Jason to be happy when she floated her idea. Should she wait until after dessert to suggest it? No, better do it now while he was smiling at her.

"I have a proposal for you." She leaned forward.

He smiled and lifted an eyebrow. "I'm flattered, but we barely know each other."

Her face heated. "Stop it! I'm serious." And then she plowed into an explanation of her idea.

His face grew more disbelieving as she spoke. Not a good sign. "So you want to sell me your half of the farm, but let you live on it?"

"In exchange for my fixing up the cabin, yes. If you need me to pay a small amount of rent, I could do that."

"But why would you do that, when you already own the place?"

She blew out a breath. This was the tricky part. "I need cash." Which was true. "It's been an expensive time, moving the boys across the country."

"And losing your job," he said, frowning. "But the farm will bring you a steady income. Surely that'll be a plus for you as the boys grow up."

She nodded and swallowed. "It would be. But I need the cash now."

"Why?"

The waiter appeared with their drinks. "Don't argue, be happy," he said. "Hey, Jason, did you hear about what's happening with Chuck and Jeannine Henderson?" And he launched into a dramatic breakup story that Jason appeared to want to avoid, but couldn't cut off.

Their conversation gave Erica a minute to think. She'd anticipated that Jason wouldn't warm to the idea immediately, so she couldn't let that discourage her. She'd been pondering and praying all night, and this was the solution she'd come up with—especially now that she'd gotten a job.

Staying in the area would be good for the twins. Staying near their relatives.

But she had to get them early intervention. And she couldn't get public assistance without a lot of paperwork, including birth certificates, which she didn't have.

She knew that someday she'd have to go through the appropriate channels to get the twins their birth certificates and other paperwork. Probably, she'd need to hire a lawyer, maybe that one who'd been a friend of Kimmie's.

But for the time being, lawyers' fees were out of reach.

And the boys needed early intervention, now, and on an ongoing basis. A onetime trip to some clinic wasn't going to be enough.

So she had to get private help, which would be no questions asked. The fact that it cost money was okay— as long as Jason would buy her half of the farm.

A busboy brought out plates, and their waiter waved a hand. "Thanks, Ger. Sorry I got to talking." He put steaming plates down in front of them, and the aroma of burgers and fries wafted up.

"Here you go, Jason and…what did you say your name is?"

"I'm Erica." She held out her hand.

"Pleased to meet you. I'm Henry, but you can call me Hank. And I need to get it in gear." He turned and headed off.

The burger was enormous, so Erica sawed it in half with her butter knife.

Jason picked up his whole burger. "There are two kinds of people in the world," he said, grinning. "The ones who are dainty with a hamburger and the ones like me." He took a big bite.

Good. Let him eat up and get into a good mood. In fact, this burger could put her in a good mood, too; it was delicious.

Hank returned to their table, coffeepot in hand. "How is everything? More coffee, Erica?"

She swallowed and held out her cup. "Yes, please."

She kept quiet during the rest of their lunch, letting Jason eat and thinking about what she needed to say or do to convince him. *Be strong, girl. It's for the twins.*

Jason finished his meal and Erica ate half of hers and asked Hank to wrap up the rest. After he brought Jason a piece of pie, she launched into her proposal again. "Will you at least think about making a deal with the farm? You wouldn't have to buy it all right away. We can do payments. Figure something out."

He held up a big bite of pie. "Sure you don't want to try it?"

"No, thanks. It's just that," she pushed on, "I need some of the money pretty soon, here."

He put down his fork. "For the twins?"

She bit her lip. The fewer details he knew, the better.

"Is the reason you're wanting to sell property so that you can pay for therapists and specialists?"

She looked away, trying to figure out how much to tell him.

"Look," he said, pushing the rest of his pie away, "I'd

hate to see you sell. It's going to appreciate in value. You're thinking short-term."

"But they need help now," she protested, shredding a napkin with nervous fingers.

He put a hand over hers, stilling them. "There's a children's health insurance program for low income people. They should have good services. Pennsylvania usually does."

She pulled her hands away. "I don't want to get public insurance."

"I respect not wanting a handout, but programs for children's health are different. You've had a hard time here, and you have two little ones. That's exactly what those programs are for."

"I don't want it," she said. Let him think it was pride.

Around them, the noise of the diner went on: forks clattering, people talking, the bells jingling on the door as it opened and closed.

"Could their father help?" Jason asked.

"No."

"He should."

"He's in prison and he has no claim on them."

Jason looked startled, and for a moment, she could see him sifting through images in his mind, trying to figure her out. He'd thought she was a drug addict, but he seemed to have ruled that out now. However, having the father of her children imprisoned put her back in that same sketchy camp in his mind, she could tell.

What he didn't know, of course, was that the twins' imprisoned father was Kimmie's partner, not her own.

"I don't understand why you won't at least see a doctor and start the paperwork for CHIP. You could make a final decision later."

He was trying to be so reasonable, and it was killing her, because under normal circumstances he'd be right.

Oh, Kimmie, why'd you put me in this position? Why couldn't you have been up front with your family?

"Hey, Stephanidis." A man with a military haircut, about Jason's age and with similar muscles came over and shook Jason's hand, an encounter that ended in a slight test of strength. "How's the hard-line detective? Didn't expect to see you out of your mean streets. How's Philly going to stay safe without you?"

Jason introduced her but didn't try to draw her into the conversation, which was fine.

As the two men talked, Erica bit her lip and pondered. She'd prayed and she knew that God would be with her no matter what. And yes, Kimmie had been a flawed person, and maybe wrong about Jason, but he *would* be angry about the deception, right? Angry enough to take the twins.

And once he had them, he'd have no reason to keep her around.

A guy like Jason wouldn't *want* to keep someone like her around.

She loved the boys too much to let them go. Her desire to mother them grew every day.

As his friend left, Jason turned back to her, smiling. "Come on now, Erica. Won't you just try signing up for CHIP?"

"I'm not getting public insurance!"

"Don't you care about your kids?"

"It's because I care about them that I won't—"

"Hey, you two, I said no fighting." Hank was back with the check. "Look, I brought you kisses to make you feel all better." He put down the check with two foil-wrapped candies on top of it and spun away.

Erica reached for the check at the same time Jason did. She grabbed it, but his larger hand closed over hers. "Let me get this."

"I said I was taking you out to lunch."

"You need the money more than I do."

"I can afford a lunch!"

"Put the money into your fund to help the twins." Deftly, he got the check out of her hand, but she closed her hand on his.

His dark skin and large hand contrasted with her own small, pale one. But as far as calluses, she had as many as he did. She'd worked hard in her life, as had he.

"Let me have my dignity," she said quietly, and immediately he let the check go. Understanding and sympathy shone in his eyes.

"Thank you for lunch. I appreciate it and it was really good."

She could see that it cost him to let a woman pay, especially when Hank came over and took the money from her and lifted an eyebrow at Jason. But he didn't protest any more.

"Look," he said while they waited for change, "we need to talk more about the farm and what should be done with it. That's not a discussion to finish in an hour, over lunch."

"What do you say we talk about it while we're working on the cabin?" she suggested. Because she *had* to get out of that house.

"Possible," he said, nodding. "I have tomorrow afternoon free. Would that work for you?"

"As long as I can get Ruth to watch the twins again, yes."

"It's a date, then." His words were light. But she could tell that his suspicions about her had been raised again.

Chapter Six

Jason pulled his truck in front of his friend Chuck's house, looked over at Erica and hoped this was all going to go okay.

They'd spent the afternoon working on the cabin, and *that* had been great. She'd opened up a little bit about Kimmie and their friendship, how they'd been in and out of touch, how Kimmie had been like a sister to Erica, albeit a flawed one.

It was what he'd done *after* working on the cabin that had him sweating a little. He was going to have to tell Erica about it tonight.

Instead, he told her the easier thing. "This could be a little awkward. They're both still living here."

As they headed up the sidewalk to Chuck's house, Erica touched his arm, stopping him. Almost stopping his heart. He was getting way too sensitive to casual contact with her.

"This is a nice house. I'm not going to be able to afford anything they have." Her voice was husky. Behind her, the sunset made her loose red curls glow like fire.

"I can afford it." As she started to protest, he lifted a hand. "It's an investment in the property."

"Does that mean you're buying it from me?" She raised her eyebrows.

He rang the doorbell. "I'm considering it."

Chuck opened the door, looking like he'd aged thirty years since they'd hung out together in high school. "Hey, come on in."

"This is Erica," Jason said once they were inside and taking off their coats. "She's going to move into the cabin on the property and she's looking for some furniture."

"Great—we could use the cash." Chuck ran a hand through his already-sticking-up hair and grabbed a roll of colored stickers. "Here, just put one of these on anything you want. Only not if it already has a sticker. I'm green and Jeannine's yellow. You can be orange."

Erica's eyes widened, and Jason felt his own gut twist a little. He'd never been this close to the sad details of a marital breakup before.

"Go on, walk through. She's out somewhere and I'm packing up the basement." Chuck sounded mechanical.

"If you're sure, man." Jason clapped his friend on the shoulder.

"*She's* sure." Chuck turned abruptly and strode out of the entryway.

When Jason and Erica walked into the front room, both of them stopped at the same moment.

The mantel was half decorated with evergreen garland and red bows, and a box containing more of the same sat on the hearth. A Scotch pine, unadorned, sent waves of Christmassy scent through the cozy room.

Erica looked over at him. "I don't feel right about this."

From the back of the house, a door opened. "Hey, I'm…" called a woman's voice, trailing off into dejection. Like she'd forgotten for a moment that happy greetings to her husband weren't part of her life anymore.

There was the sound of a heavy tread climbing the basement stairs. Chuck.

Erica's brow furrowed. "What should we do? Should we leave?"

"No, he was serious about wanting to sell stuff, and he said they both knew we were coming tonight. Come on. Maybe we should start upstairs." They headed toward the staircase, and if Jason put his hand on the small of Erica's back, he was just guiding her. Right?

"Were you ever married?" she asked as they climbed the stairs.

"Nope. Just engaged."

"What happened?"

He shrugged, nodding toward one of the smaller bedrooms, guiding her toward it with a light touch. "She regained her sanity and dumped me."

"You don't sound very upset."

"I'm not. Saved me from going through *this*." He waved an arm to indicate the whole house, the breakup of a marriage.

But Erica pressed a hand to her mouth as she looked around the room. "Oh, wow."

It was a nursery, perfectly decorated but empty of the clothes and sheets and paraphernalia that indicated a baby. There were no stickers on any of the furniture.

"Do they have a baby? Or…is she pregnant?"

He shook his head, opening the little blue dresser's drawers to confirm that they were empty. "This might be nice for the twins, huh?"

"Yes, it would, but…" She trailed off. "Are they sure they want to get rid of all this?"

"They did years of infertility treatments." He explained in the same matter-of-fact way Chuck had explained it to him. "She finally got pregnant, but about six weeks ago, she lost the baby. I guess…that and all the doctor's bills…" He shrugged.

"That is so awful." Erica's eyes got shiny as she ran a finger along the railing of the brand-new crib.

"Should I put a sticker on it?" His hand hovered over the dresser.

"Yeah. I guess. If it'll help them."

He really, really wanted to wipe that sadness off her face. He even felt a strange urge to do it by kissing her, but that would be a mistake. "What are you doing tomorrow?" he asked instead, to distract her.

She considered, then shrugged. "I don't know. The twins are getting bored. I'd like to find somewhere new to take them."

Footsteps sounded on the stairs. Light. A woman's.

Jason didn't know Chuck's wife very well, but he recognized her when she looked in the door. "Hey, Jeannine, good to—"

"Just don't." Her face crumpled and she spun and hurried away from the room.

"Oh, wow, that's the woman who looked so upset at the clothing giveaway. I've got to see if I can do anything for her." Erica went after Jeannine.

So obviously, Erica had had a better instinct about this than he did, or than Chuck did, either, for that matter. *Christmas, a miscarriage… Duh.* Not the time to participate in dismantling a home.

He heard a low murmur of voices from what looked

like the master bedroom and headed downstairs to see what he could do for Chuck.

An hour later, he and Chuck were watching hockey when Jason heard the doorbell ring. It sounded like someone was singing outside. Maybe a lot of people.

Jason looked over at Chuck. The man was still staring at the TV, obviously trying to distance himself from what was happening in his life. "Want me to get that?"

"Sure." Chuck sat upright, elbows on knees, fists under his chin.

So Jason opened the door to a group of about ten carolers, adults and kids, singing one of his favorite Christmas carols: "O Little Town of Bethlehem." Behind them, in the light from a lamppost, he could see that snow had started to fall.

There was a sound on the stairs behind him, and he turned to see Jeannine descending, Erica right behind her. When she saw what was going on, Jeannine sat abruptly on a step about halfway down the stairs and started to cry. Or maybe she'd been crying all along.

Erica sat beside her and put an arm around her, murmuring quietly.

Chuck had come out to the entryway, too, and he stood listening as the carolers came to the last verse of the song: *Oh holy child of Bethlehem...cast out our sin and enter in...abide with us, our Lord Emmanuel.*

For sure, this household needed the Christ child to enter in. And Jason did, too. He was saved; he accepted Jesus as his redeemer, but he didn't always let Christ in. Too busy trying to control things himself, fix the world by himself.

He waved a thank-you to the carolers and closed the door.

Chuck turned and took a couple of steps toward the staircase where the two women still sat. Erica got up and came quietly downstairs.

"She needs you," Jason said to Chuck.

"She doesn't want anything to do with me." Chuck's expression, looking up at his crying wife, was full of frustration and yearning.

Jason put a hand on his friend's shoulder. "You've got so much here, man. You should fight for it."

And then his eyes met Erica's, and they turned as one toward the door, grabbed their coats off the banister railing and walked out of the house.

"Wow," Erica said once they were outside. "Pretty emotional."

"Very." It was natural to take her arm on the icy walkway. "I don't know if you'll get that dresser or not."

"I hope not. I hope they work things out and get the chance to be parents."

"Me, too." He held the truck door open for her and helped her to climb in. And meanwhile, he hadn't gotten the chance to talk to her about what he needed to, and this was his last chance. Once they got home, it would be craziness, Papa and Ruth and the twins. A full house and a lively one, and he liked that, but it didn't allow time for quiet discussion.

Quiet persuasion.

For that, he knew exactly where he needed to take her.

Erica was so lost in thought, worrying about Chuck and Jeannine, that she didn't notice the direction the truck was going until it stopped. In the middle of a parking lot full of cars, apparently in the middle of a field.

"Where are we... Oh, wow!" She stared down at a wonderland of colored and white lights. "What is it?"

"It's the Mistletoe Display. Will you walk through with me?"

Her breath seemed to leave her chest. Why had he brought her here?

Against her will, her heart was warming to Jason, and maybe, just maybe, he was feeling similarly toward her. Why else would he have brought her to such a romantic place?

"We don't have to. If you'd rather get home to the twins—"

"No, no. I...I'd love to."

They walked down the path to a ticket shed, and he insisted on buying her ticket. "My idea, my treat."

Definitely date-like.

They strolled through winding paths, stopping to admire the light-made scenes scattered along the way. Here was portrayed a group of children carrying gifts; there, a family building a snowman. A brass ensemble played "Angels We Have Heard on High," and no sooner had those sounds faded than a quartet of singers in old-fashioned costumes sang "God Rest Ye Merry Gentlemen." Pastor Wayne was at a wooden stand selling hot chocolate and passing out invitations to the church's Christmas Eve service. Jason stopped, assured the pastor he'd be there and bought them both cups of hot chocolate, complete with peppermint-stick stirrers.

It was lovely and romantic, especially when Jason draped his scarf around her neck to keep her warmer.

"So, you're probably wondering why I brought you here," he said, sounding nervous.

"I wasn't, but…is there a special reason?" Her heart leaped to her throat. Was he going to make some kind of declaration? They weren't dating, although the things they'd been through together had made her feel closer to him than to anyone she'd dated. Not that there had been a whole lot of boyfriends in her life.

"There's something I want to tell you. Ask you." He led her to a bench beside a snowy lane, a little off from where most people were walking. "I…I'm going to Philadelphia tomorrow."

Her heart sank a little. She had grown accustomed to having Jason around, and she'd miss him if he left. But of course, they weren't really accountable to each other. "How long will you be gone?"

"Just a couple of days, three at the outside. I have to testify in the case that put me on leave."

"Okay." He'd told her a little bit about why he was on administrative leave, something to do with a corrupt partner. "Will this fix the problem?"

"It's a start." He took her hand. "You might be upset with me for what I did, but…how would you and the twins like to come with me?"

Erica's head spun. "Come *with* you? But…why?"

Her mind spun with possibilities. Was this a romantic proposition? Did he think she was easy and that, away from Papa's watchful eye, they could have a fling? But if that were the case, why bring the twins?

"I made an appointment with a specialist," he said, looking hard at her as if to see her reaction.

"What kind?" She wasn't following.

"A pediatrician who's, like, world renowned for helping delayed babies catch up."

Her jaw about dropped as emotions warred within her, chief among them an absurd sense of disappointment. He didn't want anything romantic, and this wasn't a date. "I *told* you I wanted to do this my own way. And I can't afford a famous specialist. You know that." She stood up.

"No, no, sit down." He tugged her hand, pulling her back down to the bench. "I just thought... I was talking about my visit to my buddy who has a child with Down syndrome, and he was telling me about everything they're doing for his daughter...you know, Philly has world-class hospitals and so I thought..."

"You thought you'd go over my head and get medical treatment for my boys?"

"You don't understand. It's so hard to get an appointment with her, but she had a cancellation. So...I went ahead and did it." He paused. "It's the day after tomorrow."

She stared at him as her head spun. Partly from his high-handedness and partly from fear. If a specialist wanted to look at the twins' medical records, she didn't have them.

"I wasn't planning to do this, Erica, but when it came up, I couldn't help but think of the twins. I care about the little guys. And about you."

"No." She was shaking her head before having even formulated a response. "Just...no. I don't want to visit some strange doctor, all the way over in Philadelphia, only to hear about treatments I can't afford in a place I can't get to—"

"My friend says lots of people come and consult with

her and then do treatment in their own towns. And as for insurance…when I made the appointment, I explained that you didn't have coverage or the money to pay privately, and they sent some paperwork. The receptionist said it's not complicated at all, and that Dr. Chen works with a lot of…of low income patients. Don't you see, Erica? This way, you won't have to sell me the farm to get help for the boys. You can keep it for them."

She squeezed her eyes shut and tried to think as the hot chocolate curdled in her stomach.

He hadn't brought her here for a date. He'd brought her here to butter her up so he could find out the truth.

"No." She shook her head. "No. I'm not ready to take that step."

"You won't even do it for the twins?" His voice held a touch of censure.

He thought she was a bad mother.

She stared down at her denim-clad knees as waves of confusion and shame passed over her. She *was* a bad mother. Not fit for the wonderful gift Kimmie had given her.

Jason reached an arm around her shoulders, gave her a quick couple of pats and then pulled his arm away. "Look, I'm sorry to spring this on you, and I know you'd rather have time to think about it. You're a great mother. You want to take time and figure out what's best for your kids. You like to plan things out, and here I'm just throwing this at you."

You're a great mother. She looked over to see if he was mocking her, but his face was serious, earnest.

"For all kinds of reasons, I'd like for you to go. Mostly for the twins and the specialist, of course, but there's a Christmas party…" He trailed off.

"A Christmas party?" She couldn't keep up with the way his mind was working.

"For my department. It's at the home of my good friends, who have little kids, so you could bring the twins. We could even stay with them." He paused. "I'd really like for you to meet them."

She felt her forehead wrinkle. What was he saying?

That he wanted her to meet his friends because he was serious about her? Or that he wanted her to come to Philly for a fling?

He seemed to read her mind. "They have a huge farmhouse. You and the twins would have a big room and your own bathroom. I'd bunk down on the couch in the den."

Now she was thoroughly confused. "Do you... Why are you asking me to come? Besides just being kind about the twins?"

He dug at the snowy ground with the toe of his boot. "Look," he said, "I'm bad at this stuff. I'm bad at talking to people, working things out. I'm bad at, well, relationships, but...I'm trying to improve. Especially now that I have a reason to." He propped his elbows on his knees and rested his cheek on his hand, facing her. "I really like you, Erica."

Her heart pounded like a drum.

He was holding out a chance, however small, at everything she wanted: connection, someone to value her, a good family.

She couldn't have even a chance at that if she didn't take him up on what he'd offered, the trip to Philadelphia and the appointment with a specialist for the twins.

She looked up at the stars, sparkling in the cold air. *Should I go, Lord?*

The very question reminded her how much in the Christmas story depended on following a star, on faith.

Jason had overstepped by making the appointment, for sure. And figuring out how to manage that appointment without revealing Kimmie's secret was going to be a challenge.

Not to mention that any kind of a relationship with Jason was out of the question, as long as she was withholding the truth about the twins. How could she judge him for being a little pushy, when she herself was lying to him?

She glanced up at the stars again, took a couple of breaths and then met Jason's eyes. "Thank you for the offer and for what you're doing for the twins and me. We...we'll go."

His eyes lit and he pulled her into a spontaneous hug. A hug that went on a little longer than something friendly.

She pulled back a little and looked at him, her heart fluttering like a startled bird in a cage.

His eyes went dark with some unreadable emotion. He cupped her chin in his hand and studied her face.

"You are so beautiful," he said. And then he pressed his lips to hers.

All logic slipped away, replaced by almost-complete feeling and warmth and care. Almost complete, not fully, because something nagged at the edge of her melting consciousness: *this isn't going to work, because he doesn't know the truth about the twins.*

Chapter Seven

The small box was sitting on the table beside the door, where Papa always tossed the mail he didn't have time to sort.

Jason spotted it as he came whistling down the stairs. Something compelled him to take a closer look.

He could hear Erica talking to Papa in the kitchen. "No, no phone calls about the dog yet," Papa was saying.

"I think his foot is getting better," Erica replied, "Look, he chewed the bandage off again."

"It looks okay, but I don't think that fur is growing back. He'll always have a scar." There was the homey sound of dishes clinking and water running.

The box was addressed to him, in Renea's handwriting.

He should probably just leave it there, get on with loading up the car. They needed to head out so they could get to Brian and Carla's house and settle Erica and the twins before he hustled to meet with the lawyers.

But it would nag at him; he knew it. So he set his suitcase down and carried the little box upstairs.

In his room, with the door closed, he opened the box

up, feeling as if a viper might jump out. Renea had been furious about their breakup even though she'd instigated it, and the sight of her handwriting brought her angry feelings and words back to him. His sense of dread increased as he used a pocketknife to slit through the tape.

Inside was a small envelope and a wad of newspaper. Cowardly, he opened the wad first.

There was the engagement ring he'd bought her.

Okay, that wasn't a problem, really. He hadn't wanted it back, hadn't wanted the reminder of his failure, but he was getting past that now. Things were new and promising in his life, he reminded himself.

The thought of kissing Erica made him sit down on his bed and close his eyes, still clutching the ring and the note in his hands. She'd been hesitant but then so sweet and giving as he'd held her. And although he'd kept the kiss short and respectful, he had seen the emotion in her eyes and he knew it had been reflected in his own.

She didn't throw her kisses around and neither did he, these days. It meant something.

She was beginning to care for him, and that thought had filled him with way more happiness and joy than he'd had any right to expect.

He heard Erica trotting up the stairs, and then a minute later, something heavy bumping down. Erica must be dragging her suitcase down herself, and she shouldn't be; he should be helping her. He ripped open the note.

I've lost weight and they want to put me in the clinic again. Haven't been able to eat since we broke up. Can you get this ring resized down? Call me.

He looked at the ring, already the size of a child's ring. The sight of it brought back the short two months of his engagement.

How he'd looked up some formula of how much an engagement ring should cost based on his salary and saved up that amount. How he'd consulted with his friends—clueless guys all—about what type of ring to buy. How she'd said yes, and instead of feeling happy, his heart had gone cold with the feeling of a cage door slamming shut.

And from then on, the whole relationship had gone downhill. She'd been discontented with the ring and with how he expressed, or didn't express, his feelings for her. He'd tried to whip himself up into a proper type of enthusiasm for a groom-to-be, not helped by a few of his friends who viewed their wives as nags and marriage as a ball and chain. And others of his friends, the more serious ones, who thought he'd made the wrong choice of mate.

Most of all, there'd been the sinking realization that being involved with a man brought out Renea's severe eating disorder. Although she'd hidden it before their engagement, she hadn't been able to hide it after. Her parents had begged him to break it off with her so as not to complicate her recovery. He'd tried, but she was so fragile that it had never seemed like the right time.

When she'd gone into a rage one night and broken up with him, he'd taken it as a blessing, especially since his only feeling had been relief. And he'd held fast against Renea's multiple attempts to get back together, each one ending in accusations that he had ruined her life.

He guessed the breakup had been fortunate. But had he changed any since then?

He didn't want to ruin anyone else's life the way he'd ruined Renea's. And obviously, he knew nothing about choosing a mate; he'd gone solely for beauty with Renea, and he'd almost made a huge mistake.

Ruined his fiancée's life.

Didn't save his sister.

He stood and looked out the window. Erica and Papa were loading things into the back of the truck, talking and laughing.

It would be wrong to go forward and try to get something started with Erica. Yes, she was beautiful, but Renea had been, too.

Why on earth had he kissed Erica? More of the same poor choices?

She's different, his heart cried as he trotted down the stairs double time, intent on setting right the wrong he'd committed. *She's a good person. Stable. Not hiding things.*

Papa must have gone inside, but Erica was there beside the truck, her breath making steam in the air in front of her beautiful face, a cap on her head unable to tame her red curls. Her cheeks were pink, and when she saw him, her eyes lit up.

"Hey." He sounded abrupt and he knew it, but that was what he needed to be. Short. Abrupt. Not paying attention to how pretty she was or to the concern starting to appear in her green eyes.

"Listen," he said quickly, "I shouldn't have kissed you last night. I want to apologize."

She frowned, tilted her head. Opened her mouth to say something, and then closed it again.

"I…I didn't mean to give you the wrong idea. I'm

not… I'm not…" He trailed off, then forced himself to say it. "I'm really not up for dating or anything."

She waved her hand, her eyes shuttered. "It's fine. It was a romantic setting. Anyone could make a mistake like that." She turned to lift a bag of baby supplies into the truck. "Or… Did you still want us to come with you? Because we don't have to. Maybe it's best if we don't—"

"No, no. I want you to come. Gotta keep that appointment."

"Right, the appointment." Wrinkles appeared between her eyebrows and she frowned down at the ground. "But we could go another time. Get there another way. I don't want to impose—"

"No imposition," he said, trying to sound happy and hearty and like his heart wasn't aching. "I'd welcome the company and we're all set up."

She looked at him, confusion clouding her eyes.

"It's important for the twins. And that's what friends do for each other, right?"

She swallowed and bit her lip and looked away.

All the work he'd done to convince her to trust him, gone.

"I'm sorry," he said.

"I… Well, if you're sure you want us to come, I'll go get the twins."

"I'll help."

"No, it's okay. I'll bring them myself." And she turned and went back into the house.

Loser. He was such a loser. She'd been happy, excited about the trip, and then he'd come down with his hurtful announcement. Now she was sad. And this trip across the state was going to be extremely awkward.

I'm doing it for her. I don't want to ruin another woman's life.

Let alone the lives of a couple of sweet babies.

But the whole thing made his chest feel as heavy as if a three-hundred-pound barbell were resting on it.

Two hours later, Erica was just about to scream into the awkward silence when Jason spoke.

"You want to stop?" He indicated the road sign announcing a service plaza.

"Okay." Anything to get out of this truck. "I shouldn't let the boys sleep much longer or they'll never sleep tonight."

"Papa packed some lunch for us. Want to eat it now?"

"If that's all right with you, sure."

They were being painfully polite with each other. As if they hadn't gotten close over the past week and shared a kiss last night. A kiss she'd thought meant something.

Apparently not to Jason. Apparently he thought it was a big mistake, and that was fine. Just fine.

Say it often enough and you might even start to believe it.

She got Mikey out of his car seat, and when she turned, Jason was standing there, so she thrust the baby into his arms. Then she unlatched Teddy. The way he lifted his arms to her with a crooked smile made her heart melt. "Aren't you the happy little man?" she cooed as she pulled him out and grabbed the diaper bag.

Mikey and Teddy were her priorities. She couldn't forget that, couldn't get too sad or upset. She had to take care of herself so she could take care of them. Like they'd said the one time she'd taken a plane ride: put your own mask on before assisting others.

She'd thought that Jason might be a positive part of her life, but if he was going to be negative and hurtful, then she didn't want anything to do with him. She flipped back her hair and followed him into the service plaza, determinedly not noticing how handsome he was and how easily he carried Mikey and the picnic container.

Once they'd put their bags down, Jason handed Mikey to her and then went to grab high chairs. Before she could ask it, he found disinfecting wipes and scrubbed the chairs down.

He was pretty good with babies, for being a novice.

"Aw, they look just like their daddy," a woman said as she carried her tray to a nearby table.

Jason gave her a half smile as he got out plastic containers of food, but Erica's heart pumped a little harder. *Did* the boys look like Jason? They were his nephews, but she'd never noticed a resemblance. Sometimes you didn't see things that were right in front of your eyes.

They each fed a twin. "You're getting pretty good at that," she said as Jason used a plastic spoon to scrape some food off Mikey's mouth. Then she froze. He didn't want to pursue a relationship, so did that mean she wasn't even supposed to talk to him?

But he smiled. "I'm a quick learner. And I think he's getting neater, isn't he?"

"Let's hope so."

Teddy wasn't hungry. He yelled and squirmed to get down, but Erica didn't like the look of the floor. She glanced around, trying to figure out what to do with him.

Jason seemed to read her mind. "I'll put my coat down and he can sit on it."

"But your coat will get filthy!"

He shrugged. "It'll wash." He spread it on the floor, and after a moment's hesitation, Erica put Teddy down on it.

Mikey, neglected, started to make some noise. "Mama!" he complained.

Jason looked over at her, grinning. "Now I see what people mean about traveling with kids." He lifted Mikey out of his chair and put him beside his brother, and Erica hurried to wipe both boys' faces.

"I couldn't do this without you. I'm really grateful."

"It's my pleasure." He met her eyes for a moment and then looked away.

But she needed to get the necessary words out now, all of them, while they were speaking to each other. "Mikey's getting more frustrated that he can't move around. And Teddy's fussing more, I think because he can't communicate. They really need the help, so... thanks for setting up this appointment and making me keep it." And please, God, let it not get them all in trouble.

"You're welcome. And, Erica..." He looked away and blew out a breath. "I'm sorry I was... This morning. I hurt your feelings."

Who *was* this man? He'd kissed her like he meant it, taken it back harshly like he meant *that*, acted as if he were the twins' loving father, and now he wanted to talk feelings?

"Look, there's something in my past. A broken engagement."

She blinked and nodded. So he'd been engaged and it had ended and that had somehow caused his seesawing behavior. "Okaaaayyy..."

"I didn't handle it well. The breakup."

"You mean you were upset about it, or you didn't do it right?" It seemed crucial to know whose idea the breakup had been.

"Mostly, I didn't do it right. I'm a perfectionist, hard on people. And I'm not good at talking to a…a girl-friend, I guess. Communicating."

"You're talking now," she said before she could think better of it. More than that, he was admitting to the problem that Kimmie had accused him of: being a perfectionist, being rigid. So maybe he was changing. Maybe he wasn't the hard-core, hard-line guy Kimmie had thought he was. Look how he'd analyzed his broken engagement, how he was trying to share his feelings.

And if this, the past relationship gone bad, was his big secret…

She needed to tell him the truth about the twins. Sooner rather than later. But how did you begin to say something like that? And would it be better to do it be-fore or after the doctor's appointment?

If she told him and he got outraged at her and the twins, where would they be? She'd better wait.

"I'm talking now because I don't want you to feel hurt. I don't suspect you of sharing Kimmie's bad hab-its anymore. And… It was fantastic to kiss you, Erica. I don't want to have any expectations out of it, or for you to, but I sure liked it."

He looked up and met her eyes, and she couldn't look away. Couldn't stop herself from saying, "I liked it, too."

In fact, she very badly wanted it to happen again. But Teddy crawled off the coat onto the dirty floor, and Mikey started to cry.

"We'd better get on the road. I've got to meet the

lawyers at three, and we still have—" he checked his phone "—about two hours to Brian and Carla's place."

They rode in silence for a while, but it was friendlier, more relaxed. Jason found a radio station the twins seemed to like, and Erica even managed to doze off for a bit.

She sat up, refreshed, and looked around, and Jason glanced over at her. "Feel better?"

"A lot."

"I've been thinking," he said, "about Kimmie."

Her heart rate accelerated. "Yeah?"

"Did she talk about her family at all? About us?"

Erica considered how much to say. "She did a little."

"Was she angry at me? Did she see what I did as a betrayal?" The words seemed to burst out of him.

She blew out a breath. "It's water under the bridge."

"Yeah, but it's my bridge. I want to know."

"Why? So you can torture yourself some more, like you do with your ex-fiancée?"

He glanced over at her, looking startled. "Is that what I'm doing?"

"It seems like it. Blaming yourself for everything. Kimmie made her choices. She did what addicts do." *Like have kids and neglect them.*

"Wait a minute. You did Al-Anon, right?"

"Yeah, it was pretty much forced on me when I was a teenager. Why, does it show?"

"Uh-huh." He put on the truck's blinker. "And the other thing that shows is that you're good at being evasive."

She stared at him as sweat gathered on her neck and chest. "What's that supposed to mean?"

"I asked you about Kimmie, and all of a sudden we're

talking about me. And this isn't the first time. Is there some reason you don't like talking about Kimmie or the past?"

Tell him. Tell him now.

Instead, she sidestepped the question. "I grew up having to keep a lot of secrets. It gets to be a habit." And it was one she should break. Look how Jason was trying to do better at communicating. "Kimmie talked about happy times when you guys were kids. She really seemed to love you."

He glanced over at her as if to see whether she was telling the truth. "Really?"

"Yes. And, Jason, she had good values in a lot of ways. It was just… Addiction is hard to break. Drugs nowadays are so strong…"

"Tell me about it." He shook his head slowly. "I remember when she was in high school, those chastity rings were the thing. She got one. Go figure." He looked over at her. "I don't suppose… I mean, she used to talk to me about how she wanted to wait for marriage."

Erica froze. Kimmie hadn't waited for marriage; not only that, but she'd had twins out of wedlock. Twins who were sleeping peacefully in the back seat right now.

"Is that pretty important to you?" she asked.

"It's the ideal, and I hope…" He trailed off and looked over at her. "I'm sorry, Erica. I don't mean to judge. I haven't been perfect myself by any means."

Erica almost laughed and then restrained it. No need to give in to hysteria. Jason thought he'd offended her because of her supposed impurity, as an unmarried mom. Little did he know that she *wasn't* actually a mom. And that she'd barely dated, let alone gotten close enough to someone to conceive a child. Waiting for marriage hadn't been a challenge for her.

But there was a desperate hopefulness in Jason's eyes. She felt for him and she wanted to provide comfort, as best she could. "If you're asking whether there were a lot of men in her life, I don't think so. Times when I was around her, she was mostly on her own."

She was saved from expanding on that by the sound of a siren. She looked back, and red and blue lights flashed. Her heart raced and she felt guilty, like the police had somehow guessed she wasn't being completely honest.

Jason let out an exclamation and pulled over. "Wonder what's up. I wasn't speeding."

"Police make me nervous."

"You gotta remember I'm a cop myself. And in fact…" He was looking in his rearview mirror, and suddenly he laughed and opened the driver's-side door.

"Don't get out!" She couldn't keep the panic out of her voice. Bad things happened when you confronted cops. "Just sit still and keep your hands visible!"

"It's fine. Old friend. He's just busting my chops." He jumped out of the truck and walked back to meet the uniformed police officer, and a moment later they were thumping each other on the back and laughing.

She couldn't take her eyes off him as he talked to his friend. That strong square jaw, dark with the beginnings of a beard. The messy-cut black hair that contrasted so sharply with his blue eyes. His athletic build, the confidence of his wide-legged stance.

Was she falling in love with him?

No sooner had she thought it than she shook her head

and let her face sink onto one fist. No. Not that. She couldn't be in love.

Jason needed to hold on to a positive picture of his sister. It would help him heal.

But knowing Kimmie had had children out of wedlock would tarnish that image.

The web of lies kept getting trickier, more complex. Now, if she revealed the truth, she wouldn't just be breaking a promise to Kimmie. She wouldn't just be risking that Jason would take the twins away from her.

She'd be risking his own happiness, the image he was trying to create of a sister who'd been an addict but otherwise, had stuck to the values she was raised with.

Male laughter rang out, Jason's, and despite her racing worries, she couldn't help smiling.

When Jason was happy, she was happy. When he tried awkwardly to explain things and apologize, truly attempting to do better at communicating, her heart warmed toward him. When he unquestioningly helped with the twins, she felt safe, protected.

Yes, for sure. She was hooked. Falling, falling, fallen.

With the one person it would be a complete disaster to love.

After they'd arrived at Brian and Carla's house, escorted by his old friend Diego, Jason knew it wouldn't take long for someone to grill him. Sure enough, the moment he'd helped to carry the twins and the luggage to the guest suite, Brian was on his case, dragging him out to the garage, ostensibly to look at his new motorcycle. "Why didn't you tell us? She's a knockout."

"She's a friend. That's all."

Brian made a skeptical sound as he went to the refrigerator in the garage and pulled out a couple of sodas. "I saw the way you were looking at each other."

He shrugged. "I like her, sure. But you know better than anyone how I am with women."

"So you've made some dumb mistakes." Brian tossed him a soda. "You can't judge everyone by Renea."

He wasn't; he was adding Kimmie into the mix, and Gran if it came to that. He'd let them all down.

"How are you doing with Erica's twins?" Brian took a long swig of soda and then squatted down by his bike. "Check out these straight pipes. I never thought I'd go for them, but they're cool."

Jason snorted. "And that makes you think *you're* cool. I like the twins, if you can believe it. I even feed 'em and put 'em in their car seats."

"You?" Brian shook his head as he swung a leg over his bike and sat on it, despite the fact that, even with the garage door closed, it was freezing. "I'm itching to ride this thing, man."

"Might be time for a trip south."

"Can't. Carla's expecting again."

"This soon? You better slow yourself down, boy."

Brian grinned and spread his hands wide. "What can I say, man. I look at her, she gets pregnant."

"And then you brag about it while she does all the work." He clapped Brian on the back. "Seriously, man. Happy for you."

Brian got off the bike and gave it a regretful pat. "I'm getting over my shock that you like a woman with kids. But family's everything, and if she's willing to put up with a loser like you, you better grab her."

"Thanks, pal." But as they walked back into the house to a cacophony of babies rolling on the floor, guarded by Carla's two teen daughters, he was surprised to find himself actually considering his friend's advice. Family life was looking surprisingly good to him.

"I appreciate your girls taking care of Mikey and Teddy," Erica said to Carla as she unpacked a few things in the guest suite. "In fact, I appreciate your letting all of us stay with you. Are you sure we're not putting anyone out?"

"Absolutely sure." Carla lounged back on the bed and waved an arm toward the rest of the house. "This place is huge. And as for the girls, they're kind of fascinated by baby twins, since they're twins themselves."

"They're sweethearts." Erica pulled out the changing supplies and diapers she'd packed for the twins and stacked them on the dresser top. "Did they have delays?"

"Not like yours," Carla said. "I mean, they were a month premature, but they caught up by age one."

"You could notice the twins' delays just from those few minutes?" Erica rubbed the back of her neck. "Are they really that obvious?"

Carla nodded. "I'm glad you're getting them checked out, and Dr. Chen is the best. Well, except for her bedside manner, from what I've heard."

"She's not nice?" Erica's heart sank. "How can a pediatrician have a poor bedside manner?"

"I know, right? It's not that she's not nice, it's just... I heard she's kind of awkward. But she's a genius researcher who knows everything babies need."

Maybe she'll be too preoccupied or oblivious to notice their lack of a medical history. Erica sat down on the room's other twin bed and looked around. "This is really nice."

Carla smiled. "I'm glad to have another adult woman around. Believe me, the fifteen-year-old girls can be a challenge, and other than that, it's just me and the baby when Brian's on duty." She patted her stomach. "And another on the way, so believe me, I grab every moment of girl talk I can get."

"You're expecting? Congratulations." Erica liked the openness of the woman already. It would be nice to be so relaxed and confident in your family life. Even though Erica was blessed, *so* blessed with the twins, she didn't anticipate ever being the kind of comfortable-in-her-own-skin wife and mother that Carla was.

"Maybe we can get the girls to make us tea." Carla leaned forward and listened at the door. "Nah. It's pretty loud out there. We should hide out in here for a few more minutes."

Erica stood, stretched and strolled around the room. "I like your samplers. Embroidery like that is getting to be a lost art." She leaned closer to read them. "Are they just for decoration or from your family?"

"Mine, my parents' and my grandparents'. And all of us are still around and still married."

Wow. What would it be like to come from that kind of legacy?

"So where's your family?" Carla asked, flopping back down on the bed.

Normally, that type of question made Erica self-conscious, but with Carla, she just felt a little sad. "I never knew my grandparents or my dad. My mom had a lot of issues." Then she broke off.

"Had? So you're alone in the world?"

"Pretty much. Except for the twins."

The sound of men's voices resounded through the house, contrasting with the girl and baby sounds. Jason came to the doorway and looked in. "This looks comfortable."

"It is. And it's Erica's. You get the couch, pal." Carla grinned at Jason with the familiarity that bespoke long friendship. She stood and slipped around Jason to exit the room. "I'm going to go manage the chaos."

"I'll be right out," Erica promised.

"Hey," Jason said to Erica, "we got a reminder call from the doctor. We're supposed to arrive fifteen minutes early and bring the babies' medical history."

Erica's stomach twisted with anxiety.

Tell him.

"Listen," he said, "I've got to run to that meeting with the lawyers. You okay here?"

She nodded. "Brian and Carla are really nice."

He walked a little into the room, hooked an arm around her neck and gave her a fast, hard kiss. Then he spun and left the room, and a moment later she heard the front door slam.

She put her hands to her lips, swallowed. This morning he'd apologized for kissing her, and now he'd kissed her again. She could smell his cologne on herself, just a trace of it.

She sank down onto the bed, needing just a moment before she went out to take care of the twins. Just a moment to think about and relish that kiss.

And a moment to try to calm her worries about tomorrow's appointment, the doctor with the poor bedside manner and the fact that she didn't have any medical history at all to show her.

Tomorrow would turn out okay. It was for the twins. She'd figure out an excuse. Wouldn't she?

Chapter Eight

As soon as Jason walked back into Brian and Carla's house, he noticed the smell of Christmas cookies and heard the sound of women's laughter.

The contrast with the hard-edged, seamy lawyer meeting he'd just come from couldn't have been greater. He loosened his tie.

He wanted to come home to this world.

Still, he had to remember that he wasn't ready. Screwing this up by acting too soon would be disaster. On some level, he knew that was what had happened with Renea; he'd been tired of the tomcatting life, had met Renea, thought she was something special, and had moved too fast. He couldn't make that mistake again.

Girded against his impulses, he walked into the kitchen.

"Where's Erica?" he asked immediately. So much for not focusing on her.

"We…we kind of made her go change," Carla said, laughing.

"Hey." Jason's protective instincts took over. "Don't be hard on her. She's new to how we all joke around."

"No, no, we were nice! It's just that…she didn't know this is an ugly sweater party. How could she?"

"And her sweater really was kind of ugly…" That was Lisa, Randall's wife. She had a good heart, but no filter. "But not ugly in the way it was supposed to be."

"Stop." Carla frowned at her. "I dug up one of my ugly sweaters for her and she's changing and getting the twins ready."

"So you really like her?" Lisa asked. "How'd you guys meet?"

He didn't want to contribute to the gossip train. "Long story. I gotta go get out of this monkey suit."

And on the way, as much as he'd intended not to do it, he found himself heading upstairs and knocking on the door of the guest suite.

When she called for him to come in, he had to stop and stare.

Normally, Erica wore loose, plain clothes. But now she was dressed in a snug-fitting sweater in a bright shade of pink with white fluffy fur on it. He supposed the sweater was a little silly, but it certainly wasn't ugly. She looked stunning, sitting on the floor with the twins while they played with a stack of blocks. He couldn't help but stare.

"What's wrong? I shouldn't have let them give me this sweater, should I?" She stood up and came over to him.

He reached out and took one of her hands. "You absolutely should have. You look gorgeous."

She looked down at herself. "It's a little tight. And it's supposed to be ugly, but…"

"Hey." He touched her chin so she had to look into his eyes. "You look really pretty, and it's not too tight. I say wear it. But…" He dropped his hand from her face because he was so extremely tempted to kiss her. And he'd decided he wasn't going to do that again. "You wear whatever's comfortable."

The hallway outside the guest suite was balcony style, with a direct view into the main family room, where the party would take place. Trying not to focus on Erica, Jason stepped outside and leaned over the balcony, looking down. Christmas lights twinkled on the tree, and a real fire glowed in the fireplace. Brian and Carla stood together, arm in arm, talking quietly.

Jason wanted what Brian had with a longing so intense that his chest hurt.

Erica came to stand beside him. Her wistful expression matched the way he felt.

"I hope they know what they've got," he said.

She nodded.

"Make you sad?"

"A little." She paused, watching as Brian tugged Carla into a hug and kiss. "But we have to remember that not everyone has it like that. For so many people, it's not like the commercials."

"Yeah. True."

"And," she added, putting an arm around his waist, "it's not what Christmas is really about."

The fact that she'd voluntarily touched him made him go still, every muscle controlled. He had to treat her like a bird that had landed on his arm, with gentleness, no sudden movements.

He turned to her and smiled, determinedly keeping his elbows propped on the balcony railing rather than letting them wrap around her as he wanted to do.

"You're right," he said. "Joseph and Mary weren't living the dream when Jesus was born."

"Exactly." She smiled up at him and then looked down at the cozy room below. "They're great, Carla and Brian. I like them."

There was a sound from the bedroom behind them, and they both turned back to see the babies. "I need to get them dressed for the party. Wish they had something cuter to wear."

She'd given him the perfect cue. "Hold that thought. I'll be right back."

When he returned to the guest suite, she was back on the floor with the twins, who were now stripped down to diapers. Teddy's scooting crawl was already a little more efficient, and Mikey seemed to be stage directing, waving his arms and babbling at his brother.

"Don't be mad," he said, holding out a bag to her. "I was walking from the car to the lawyer's office, and there was a kids' clothing store... I couldn't resist. Consider it my Christmas present to them."

She took the bag, looked at him with a wrinkled forehead and then opened it. He held his breath. Too silly? Not classy enough? He was opening his mouth to offer to return them when she let out a little squeal. "Oh, these are perfect!"

The joy on her face spread warmth through his whole body. He wanted to keep giving her joy, whatever the cost.

She laid the outfits on the floor beside each other. They were one-piecers with snaps on the bottom; he'd been with the twins enough now to know that was what you needed for the diaper set.

"Should Teddy be the elf and Mikey the Santa, or the

other way around?" She studied them and then looked up at him.

He sank to his knees beside her. "I was thinking Mikey's more the Santa type. Even though he doesn't move around much, he's kind of the boss. Teddy's like the sidekick who gets things done."

She turned and put her hand on his arm, and when he looked into her eyes, they were brimming with tears. "You already get that about them?"

"Hey." He reached out, and when a single tear rolled down, he brushed a thumb along her check. "I wanted this to make you happy."

She cleared her throat and nodded, her eyes never leaving his. "It does. You have no idea how much."

The sound of laughter from downstairs broke into their silence. "Come on, let's get them dressed."

As he dressed Teddy while Erica got the Santa suit on Mikey, something softened inside him. Not only did he care for Erica, but he was coming to care for her children, as well. He wanted with all his heart for Mikey to start crawling and walking and for Teddy to learn to talk. As he looked into Teddy's wide brown eyes, he felt like Teddy understood, because he offered a sweet smile before reaching out to grab for the button on Jason's shirt.

"Hey, quit that now." He batted Teddy's hand away and finished snapping the suit, then picked him up and stood him on his feet.

Teddy couldn't support himself or balance, but he was approximating a standing position, and when Erica looked up from putting on Mikey's hat, her eyes widened. "That's how he'll look when he's walking! Oh, Jason, I want so much for them to catch up."

"I want that, too." He sat Teddy down next to Mikey. "Listen, I need to run downstairs and see if I can borrow a sweater from Brian. But there's something I want to tell you."

He hadn't known he was going to say this until it came out of his mouth. He'd been thinking about how he'd given up his quest to find answers about Kimmie, but he hadn't lost track of the fact that he had some work and growing to do before he could hope to have a relationship.

The beautiful woman and adorable babies in front of him were making him want to speed up on that goal. Maybe he could learn it best by doing it. Strong, hot joy bloomed in his chest at the possibility that he and Erica might be able to build something together.

If there was any chance of that, he had to be honest. "I haven't always been the best... You know how we were talking about Kimmie's values? Well, mine haven't always been perfect."

"Whose have?" She watched him, her face accepting. "Are you worried about something tonight?"

"It's... There are some women." He hadn't been as bad as a lot of guys, but still, he didn't want Erica getting upset or hurt. "I dated quite a bit before I got engaged, and some of those women might be here."

"Trying to get you back?" she asked lightly, but there was concern underneath her light tone.

"No. But maybe not being the most... I mean, I wasn't..." He broke off and then started again. "What I'm trying to say, I guess, is that I care for you and I want to pursue something with you, if you're willing. But there's some baggage."

Her eyebrows rose a fraction of an inch. "That's not what you said this morning."

"I was fighting against what I felt inside," he admitted.

She looked at the floor and he thought he'd doomed himself with her. Then she started fussing with Mikey's outfit, adjusting his little white fur cuffs. "I…well, I have some baggage, too." She looked up at him. "Not the same kind, but it could hurt the chances that we could…"

He gripped her hand. "Whatever is in your past, I'm going to do my best to help you get over it and move on. And I hope you'll do the same for me."

She bit her lip and nodded, but this time, she didn't meet his eyes. She was shy. He had the sense that she was almost completely inexperienced with men.

He held out a hand and helped her to her feet, feeling the fragility of her slender fingers. She was vulnerable. Innocent.

He had to get this right. He couldn't ruin another woman's life, break another woman's heart. Especially when that woman was Erica.

As Erica walked down the stairs into the crowd of lively, laughing strangers, her stomach twisted with nerves. But she wanted to do this. Wanted to be a part of Jason's world. She tightened her grip on Teddy and Mikey and walked out into the party.

Immediately, she was surrounded by women, oohing and aahing over the boys and their outfits. Everyone wanted to hold them, and Teddy and Mikey, being budding showmen, smiled and laughed and agreeably let themselves be passed from person to person.

"Those outfits," a woman named Lisa said. "Where did you get them?"

Erica hesitated, not sure whether Jason would want to admit to having given the boys such a gift.

"Seriously, was it around here?" someone else asked. "Those are adorable."

"I think the bag said Children's Cloud Creations." She looked around for Jason, but he was nowhere to be seen. "Jason bought them."

"That place is expensive!" Lisa looked speculatively at Erica.

It was?

"Are you and Jason, like, together?" Lisa pressed.

Erica bit her lip and looked down, but that was bad because it made her notice that her borrowed sweater was a little more revealing than she would have liked it to be, especially now that the shield of the twins was gone. "I...uh...I don't really know."

Carla pushed between Lisa and Erica. "Don't mind her. She means well, but she's way too nosy."

"I didn't mean... Oh. I was overstepping, wasn't I?"

Carla nodded. "Yep. And you told me I should call you on it, so I am." She turned to Erica. "We're together all the time, the spouses, because our husbands work together. Well, and Delphine joins in, too, although she's the cop in the family." She nodded toward a tall, slender African American woman who was deep in conversation with Carla's husband, Brian, while a couple of toddlers played on the floor in front of them.

Carla and Lisa's ongoing conversation gave Erica a chance to regroup. She picked up Mikey and kept an eye on Teddy, who was scooting toward a bouncy toy.

She was overwhelmed with everything that was

happening, so much so that she felt like her mind was on overload.

Worry about the doctor's appointment tomorrow bounced against excitement that Jason actually seemed to like her. Her! The one with the druggie mother and church-bin clothes, the perpetual new girl and sometime foster kid, was the choice of a handsome, successful, kind man like Jason. The way he was with the twins brought tears to her eyes.

What would happen, though, when he found out that he was related to them?

Jason came inside with another man, carrying armloads of wood, which they stashed by the fireplace. Immediately, Jason looked around the room, and when he saw her, he headed her way.

All the people here and he chose to talk to her. Of course, he was kind and was acting as a host, but still, she felt special and cherished, truly honored.

Why had Kimmie been so adamant that Jason shouldn't have the twins, shouldn't even know them? Was it to maintain her own perfect image in her brother's mind, to continue thinking of herself as the big sister role model?

If that was Kimmie's reason, it was starting to seem a little bit selfish. Jason could offer so much to the twins. It was *they* who needed a role model, and Jason would be an amazing one.

A pretty, dark-haired woman stepped into Jason's path and put a hand on his arm. Erica couldn't hear the exchange, but she could read the body language. The woman was definitely interested in Jason.

He made a couple of quiet comments and nodded toward Erica. The woman turned and looked at her, cocked her head to the side and shrugged. Then she swooshed her arm as if to gesture Jason over toward Erica. He did as she bid, laughing, and behind him, the brunette pointed and nodded as if to provide an endorsement.

That was a little embarrassing, especially considering how many people had seen. But it felt good, too. If Jason was choosing her, maybe she *did* have something to offer, not just as a friend or helper, but as a woman.

Jason approached, and Erica hoped for a little time alone with him to catch her breath. But before he could get through the crowd, another couple came up to Erica. "Hi!" the woman greeted her, a toddler on her hip. "How old are your little guys?"

Erica steeled herself for the inevitable comparisons. "Fifteen months," she said, hugging Mikey a little closer.

"Hey, that's how old our princess is, too!" The woman nodded toward the little girl she was holding, all dressed up in a red-and-pink-striped dress and tights.

With the features of a Down syndrome baby.

"She's beautiful," Erica said. "Look, Mikey, this is… what's her name?"

"Miranda. And I'm Corrine. Miranda, say hi to Mikey." The woman lowered her voice. "I think…Jason talked to Ralph, here, about Dr. Chen. We consulted with her about Miranda."

"Thank you for the reference. I appreciate it." Which was true, mostly.

Jason finally arrived at their little cluster. "I see you've met. Hey, Miranda, sweetie!" He held out his arms for the baby.

Corrine and Ralph looked at each other. "You sure you want to hold her?"

Jason laughed self-consciously. "I'm known as the worst with babies," he said to Erica. To the couple he added, "I've had a little practice lately."

"He's great with the twins," Erica said, and finally the mother released little Miranda into Jason's arms.

The dad whistled. "Man, have you changed. Are you the reason for this?" he asked Erica.

She shrugged. "I guess I am," she said shyly.

Jason put an arm around her. "She's been very patient. And I've learned that you don't feed a baby in a white shirt."

Suddenly, the door to the party opened with a bang, letting cold wind blow in from outside. Beside her, Erica heard Jason draw in a breath and then mutter something. The party noise of chattering voices died down.

A woman stalked in, shaky on extremely high heels that she didn't need—she had to be six feet tall in her socks. Carla hurried to close the door behind the new visitor.

The woman looked around, obviously searching for someone. When her eyes lit on Jason, she stopped still. "There you are," she said in a husky voice. She slid off her fur coat and Erica couldn't help but gasp. In the light, the woman was starkly gorgeous, with sharp cheekbones, enormous dark eyes and blond hair down to the middle of her back. The dress she wore was red lace and fitted her like she was a model.

"Don't suppose anyone has a drink for a lady?" the woman said.

Chapter Nine

As he stared at the woman he'd once thought he loved, Jason's gut churned with the same feelings that had nearly driven him to despair two years ago.

Renea was beautiful and intelligent, but hopelessly, endlessly mired in alcoholism interconnected with an eating disorder. After knowing her parents, he could pretty well guess her problems stemmed from her childhood.

He'd tried, he'd failed, and they'd broken up. After getting the ring package from her earlier today, he'd sent her a brief text reiterating that it was over between them.

So what was she doing here now?

"Aw, look at the babies!" She teetered over toward the small circle of women and children by the fire. It looked like she was going to fall down until someone helped her into a chair.

Erica was there to see it all. And judging from the way she glanced over at him before focusing her attention on the twins, she could tell that Renea had been important to him.

"I'm gonna get married someday!" Renea gushed

in a loud voice. "I'm going to get me one of these little buggers, too!" She reached down as if she were going to pick up Teddy.

Smoothly, Erica sank to her knees and swept the baby out of Renea's grasp. "You know, he just ate, and I'm afraid he'll spit up on your pretty dress. Is that a Christoson?"

"No!" Renea looked insulted. "It's DeBrady."

"My mistake." Erica smiled a little and cuddled Mikey.

The comparison between the two women was striking. Renea was the more classically gorgeous, for sure, and there'd been a time when that had been important to him. Plenty of men had envied him having someone like Renea on his arm.

But Erica, with her wise-beyond-her-years green eyes, her natural hair and her comfortable, kneeling position on the floor, one baby in her arms and the other attempting to crawl into her lap, looked like everything he'd ever wanted—even if he doubted whether he'd get it.

Seeing that Erica and the twins were safe and that the other women had engaged Renea in conversation, Jason took the coward's route and stepped onto the back porch. He took breaths of clear, cold air and tried to think.

Now that he was learning what love was, he knew he hadn't had it with Renea. But the question was, had he mended himself enough from the mistakes of the past that he could dare to pursue something with Erica?

You don't have a choice. You're already pursuing it.

But he could put on the brakes, stop it now before anyone got hurt.

He thought of how hurt Erica had looked when he'd told her their kiss wasn't real. *Too late.*

He looked up at the stars. Sometimes God seemed that far away, too cold and distant to help Jason with what seemed like a fairly impossible situation.

Even the thought brought back the minister's words from last Sunday's sermon: nothing is impossible with God.

He needed God's help to fix an impossible situation, to get to where he could manage to head a family like his friends did. Somewhere in the neglect from his careless parents, or maybe in his own horribly mistaken tough love for his sister, he'd gotten broken.

He hoped God could fix him. "Will You try?" he whispered to the stars. "I'm a sinner, but You took care of that. Help me do better."

There was a bang behind him and Brian came out onto the porch. "You okay?"

"Just getting a soda." Jason bent down to retrieve a can from the cooler full of ice. "Want one?"

"Sure. Um…you've got a situation in there, huh?"

"Renea?" Jason shook his head. "For real."

"She's all over Kameer." Brian laughed a little. "And she's really lit."

Jason looked past Brian into the living room. He couldn't see Renea—nor Erica, which was probably for the best—but he saw three of his friends, all guys, talking and laughing as they looked in the direction of Renea's shrill voice.

She wasn't his responsibility, but then again… "I'll be back in just a minute," he said to Brian and went out into the backyard.

A minute later, he had Renea's mother on the phone.

"No, I'm not coming to get her," the woman said. "She's made her bed and she can lie in it."

"Can I talk to Monty?"

"He's washed his hands of her, as well. And he's away on business, anyway." There was a pause. "She's a lost cause. We've given up on her for the sake of our own sanity."

When he didn't answer, the phone clicked off.

A lost cause. Jason pocketed his phone and shook his head. Despite all the tough cases he'd seen on the streets of Philadelphia, he didn't believe in those.

When he walked back inside, a couple more guys had joined the crowd watching Renea. Most of the women seemed to be in the kitchen, or in the playroom with the kids. He could hear their talk, mingled with the sound of kids playing. He hoped Erica was there with the other women, enjoying herself.

He looked over at Renea and saw that a strap of her dress had fallen down. She was leaning on the much-shorter Kameer, who looked like he didn't know what had hit him.

Jason could identify. He used to feel that way about Renea, himself. And Kameer was young, a new officer on the force.

Jason crossed the room and approached the couple. "Hey, Renea. It's time to get out of here."

"I found somebody else," she said, slurring her words. "He's a *very* nice man."

"Yes, and maybe you can get to know him better another time. Right now, it's time to go home."

"You don't get to have a say over me."

"The lady's right," Kameer said, getting a little in Jason's face. "It's her choice."

Jason stared down the younger man. "Sometimes a lady isn't in any condition to make a choice. And at that point, a gentleman steps away from the game."

"You just don't want anyone else to have me. You ruined my life, made a mess of me." Renea's words were loud in the room that had suddenly gone quiet. "Or maybe it's just that you want me back?" She teetered a couple of steps to Jason and draped herself over him.

She felt like deadweight.

"Let's get you home." He looked at Kameer. "Get her coat, would you?"

Kameer gave an indignant snort, looked again at Jason's face and headed to the front closet.

Renea leaned over and vomited into a wastebasket with an alcoholic's quick, practiced move, still clinging to Jason's arm for balance. Then she stepped away from him and opened the door.

Some of the women had come back out—it looked like their husbands had summoned them, probably because they didn't want to deal with a sick woman themselves.

Erica was among them.

He shot her a quick, apologetic glance. This sort of display was just what she wouldn't want, and between Renea hanging on him and talking trash about him, he couldn't blame Erica if she decided to back off.

All the same, he couldn't leave Renea to freeze to death alone. Even though he hadn't invited her, she was here because of him.

He grabbed her coat and shrugged into his own.

"You need some help, man?" Brian asked.

"No, I've got it. Sorry for the disruption," he called back into the party crowd. "Carry on."

"Come back after you get her home."

"Sure. I'll be back."

He looked at Erica when he said that, wanting her to know that, despite this scene, he wasn't abandoning her. But she was talking to another of the women with some intensity. He could just imagine their topic.

He headed out, caught Renea and draped her coat around her. He was trying to talk her into getting into his truck when the house door opened again.

Erica emerged and walked down toward the two of them, her hands in her jacket pockets. "Do you want me to go with you?" she asked him. "I know how..." She gave a shrug. "I know how to deal with someone who's impaired."

"Who you calling impaired?" Renea slurred, but without much energy.

"But the twins..." Jason said.

"Carla's going to put them to bed, or try to. It's fine." She frowned. "Unless you don't want me here. If you'd rather handle it alone..."

"So *you're* his new squeeze." Renea patted Erica on the head. "You've gone down in the world, Jason."

Erica looked up at the woman, at least a foot taller than she was. "Yep, I'm a pipsqueak," she said. "Want to get in the car? I'm freezing."

"I don't have anywhere to go." Renea looked at Jason. "My mom told me if I went out, I couldn't come back. Can we go to your place?"

"It's sublet," he said.

"You living with her now?"

"Nope." He took Renea's arm and urged her into the truck, with a manhandling move he knew from years on the narc squad. Not rough, but not particularly gentle, either.

He could smell Renea's trademark scent of alcohol covered by perfume and breath mints. And he was still a little stunned by Erica's matter-of-fact willingness to help.

After Renea was in, Erica climbed in after her.

"You're sure about this? It might not be pretty."

She gave him a little smile. "I know. I'm fine."

He jogged around to the driver's side and started the truck. They hadn't driven two blocks before Renea made a sound like she was going to be sick. Jason skidded to a stop and she leaned over Erica, who simply opened the passenger door and scooted Renea's upper body a little bit farther out of the truck, pulling back her hair and holding her head while she vomited into the street.

When Renea was done, Jason held out a bandanna and Erica wiped off Renea's face.

And then Renea settled down with her head in Erica's lap and went to sleep.

Jason reached out and touched Erica's face. "You're made of steel, you know that?"

She shook her head, looking down. "I'm really not. Where are you headed with her? Does she live with anyone?"

"Her mom won't take her in." Even as he said it, his gut twisted tight. He couldn't judge Renea's mom, because he'd basically done the same to his sister. Oh, he'd offered Kimmie a place to stay, but he'd set strict rules on it and refused to send her money, only an airline ticket.

She'd never come home.

"Does she have a purse?"

Jason indicated the sparkling thing he'd found with her coat.

Erica opened it and riffled through. "Let's see, there's—"

"You're going through her purse?"

She shrugged. "What else are we going to do? She kind of gave up her right to privacy when she threw up on me." She pulled a couple of cards out of Renea's small bag, and a crisp hundred-dollar bill. "The way I see it," she said, "we can either take her to this Welcome Home shelter for women, or we can check her into some safe hotel, or we can call this woman, her AA sponsor."

Jason nodded, stopping the truck at a red light. "You're good. And I'd say…" He plucked the shelter's card out of Erica's hand.

"The Welcome Home shelter. Me, too." She nodded decisively. "Because even in a safe hotel, she could get taken advantage of. And sponsors aren't supposed to take the people they sponsor into their homes."

"How do you know so much about addicts? Is it all from your mom? Or Al-Anon?" He turned the truck in the direction of the Welcome Home shelter.

She didn't answer.

He glanced over at her. "Kimmie?"

She hesitated, then nodded. "Mom, Kimmie…that's part of it. I also volunteered some after Mom died. And, well…" She shrugged and spread her hands. "I just… That's the people I grew up with. You get accustomed to finding ways to help." Before he could say more, she said, "Your turn to answer. How'd you get involved with Renea?"

As if hearing her name, Renea shifted restlessly, and

Jason slowed. But then she sighed and settled back into sleep, her face childlike.

"She got caught up in a sting, but she was never convicted. We liked each other, so after a while, I gave her a call." Like an idiot.

Erica nodded but didn't speak.

"I guess I like to help people," he said. "Or maybe I was on a power trip. That's what Kimmie always said."

"Maybe you were trying to replace Kimmie in your life," Erica suggested quietly.

He frowned. "I don't think so, but..." He pulled into the shelter's parking lot.

"It's a Christian place?" She was looking at the blinking cross on the side of the building.

"Big-time."

"That's the only thing that'll help her. You feel okay about leaving her here?"

"She'll be as safe as she can be."

"Then go ahead on in and do whatever paperwork you need to. I'll wait here with her. Better to wait and wake her up when we have a place she can crash."

He shook his head, amazed at Erica's generosity and kindness. "If you're sure."

"It's no problem."

He nodded and got out of the truck. "You know all my dirt," he said, "but you still can tolerate me?"

A strange expression crossed her face. "Of course."

He walked into the shelter quickly, smiling.

The next morning, when her quiet phone alarm went off, Erica hit Snooze and buried her head under her pillow.

They were going to see the specialist today, and she didn't know if she could face it.

She was excited, of course she was. Maybe the famous doctor would have ideas of what Mikey and Teddy needed, some particular combination of physical therapy and nutrition that could move them along toward where they should be developmentally.

Being with the other women and children last night had just confirmed how far behind they were. She needed to get them help, the sooner, the better.

But she'd be walking through the doors of the prestigious research hospital with zero paperwork on these babies and a police detective at her side. That combination could mean disaster.

Upping the ante was the fact that she truly cared about Jason. He'd been nothing but kind to his drunken ex last night. And after they'd gotten Renea into the shelter, he'd had tender words for Erica as they'd driven back to Brian and Carla's house.

She hugged her pillow, happy butterflies dancing in her stomach, thinking of the tender moments they'd shared after coming back into the quiet house and checking on the twins.

He thinks I'm an amazing woman. Who had ever said such a thing about her, unless it was someone wanting to get something out of her?

But Jason hadn't had anything on his mind except helping her find towels for a shower and a snack because she hadn't managed to eat anything at the party.

He was truly a good and kind man. And the way he looked at her gave her the insane hope that maybe, just maybe, they could have a future together.

Except you couldn't build a future on a lie.

More than ever, she wondered why Kimmie had painted Jason in such negative colors, why she'd refused to let him, or her mother or grandparents, know about Mikey and Teddy.

Had Kimmie kept the secret to cover her own sins? Though she'd put on a party face for much of the time Erica had known her, the contrast between her and the rest of her family made Erica suspect that Kimmie had carried a deep sense of shame inside herself.

Teddy stirred, then rolled over in the crib. His round eyes met hers and he smiled, and Erica's heart gave a painful little twist. How was it possible to love a tiny little being so much? To want his good more than her own?

She reached a hand in for Teddy to play with and sank to her knees beside the crib. She couldn't control what happened today, and she knew she'd probably done some things wrong. But it hadn't been for bad intent.

I put it into Your hands, Father, she whispered. *If it's Your will, let this doctor help the boys. And let me raise them or at least help to raise them.*

Praying for something to work out with Jason was just way too much to ask, so she didn't. She just remained there, focused on her Lord and Savior, trying to rest in Him, until the clock and the babies forced her to stand up and face the day.

Chapter Ten

Jason pulled the truck into the Early Development Center's parking lot and looked over at Erica. "Ready?"

"This place is huge!"

"That's the university hospital over there," he said, waving a hand toward the big block of buildings to the left. "The Center is just this part, here." But he could see why she was impressed, or maybe intimidated. The two-story brick building looked brand-new and everything, from the signage to the landscaping, spelled *tasteful* and *exclusive* and *expensive*. His big, late-model truck was probably the cheapest vehicle in the lot. "This is the kind of facility you get when you're the best in the country. Dr. Chen has published lots of books and articles and done all kinds of studies. It was a good thing we had strings to pull and that she had a cancellation."

"Yes, and I appreciate what you've done. Really." She put a hand on his arm, squeezed and let go. Despite her tension, she was still appreciative. That was Erica.

He came around to her side of the truck, where she was leaning into the back seat to get Mikey out. As had become routine for them now, she handed him to Jason and climbed in to free Teddy.

He noticed the fine sheen of sweat on her upper lip as she emerged from the back seat with Teddy, and he extended a hand to help her down. Teddy dropped a toy, and when she bent to get it, the diaper bag on her shoulder spilled out half its contents.

"Oh, man," she said, "I'm a walking disaster today."

"Slow down." He squatted to pick up a diaper, a container of wipes and a plastic key chain toy and handed them to her. "I'm sure this parking lot is cleaner than some people's tabletops."

The day was cloudy, but the temperature was above freezing and the piles of snow were starting to melt, making the streets sloppy. Here, though, the parking lot was clear and dry.

"You know," she said as they carried the boys inside, "I'm still not sure this is such a good idea. I won't be able to come back here to get them any treatment."

"Dr. Chen does consultations for people from all over," he reminded her, wondering why she still seemed resistant. "She can refer you to local practitioners and therapists."

"And I don't have any of their medical records."

He held the door for her. "Why not?"

She hesitated. "They're back in Arizona." She didn't look at him, intent on studying the wall listing of offices. "It was a spur-of-the-moment decision to move. I have some stuff in storage. Oh, there's Dr. Chen. I guess we go to office 140."

"Did something happen in Arizona that made you decide to move?" She never talked about the twins' father, except to mention that he was in prison and had no claim on the twins. But a breakup would explain why her decision to move had been sudden, and also why she was so skittish with men. At least, with him.

Although her skittishness seemed to be fading, which was very, very nice.

Still, his detective instincts were aroused, just a little, by the way she avoided answering his questions. But then Mikey dropped his pacifier and started to cry, and Teddy let out a few sympathy wails, and it didn't seem to be the moment to probe.

Inside, the waiting room was plush and quiet. Despite the small box of toys and the shelf of children's books, it didn't look much like a pediatrician's office. One other couple was waiting, and a mother had a sleeping baby in a carrier. Diplomas and awards lined the walls.

When they approached the receptionist, she greeted them cordially and smiled at the twins. "You must be Erica Lindholm. With Mikey and Teddy?"

"That's right," Erica said.

"I'll just need your insurance card."

Erica bit her lip. "We're paying privately. Do I need to prepay?" She fumbled in her purse.

"It'll be taken care of." Jason slid the woman a credit card. "I'll handle whatever needs to be paid for today, and you can send the bill to the address I'm going to write down for you, if you have a piece of paper."

The receptionist lifted an eyebrow as she handed him a notepad and pen. "Here you go."

"Jason!" Erica hissed. "What are you doing?"

He finished writing down the address, handed the woman his credit card and turned to her. "Don't worry about it. The officers in my precinct always pick a Christmas charity for children, and this year..."

"We're your Christmas charity?" she interrupted. "Are you serious?"

She walked over to a seating area near the toys and sat, putting Teddy down to crawl.

Jason finished his transaction and brought Mikey over. "I thought you might be happy. Did I do something wrong?" Even as he said it, he knew where she was coming from; independent as she was, she wouldn't necessarily be thrilled at accepting the gift.

"I don't feel right about accepting charity. I mean, I'm going to own half that farm. I won't need that kind of help, and it should go to someone who does."

"You need it now, and the guys were looking for an opportunity." He touched her hand. "Accept it in the spirit it's given. It'll help the babies."

She looked down at Mikey, then Teddy, and then she nodded. "You're right. Thank you."

"Mrs. Lindholm?" a nurse called at the door.

Erica stood, hoisted Mikey and the diaper bag, and squared her shoulders. When she didn't turn to get Teddy, Jason took it as an invitation to join the appointment. He picked up Teddy and followed her in.

"Let's weigh and measure them right here." The nurse was a broad-faced, no-nonsense-looking person in scrubs. "They're fifteen months? Were they preemies?"

"Only by three weeks."

The nurse made a notation and then passed a tape measure around Teddy's head, then measured him from heel to the top of his head. "Just a few questions before you see the doctor. Let's talk food. Breastfed, bottle fed?" She looked inquiringly at Erica.

"Ummmm…breast?"

Odd that her answer sounded like a question.

"How long?"

"Just a couple of months."

"Okay. And when did they start on solids?"

Erica opened her mouth and then closed it again.

The nurse turned from the computer to face her. "I asked about solid food. Is there a problem?"

Erica closed her eyes for just a moment. Then she opened them. "Look," she said, "there's a whole period of their lives that I don't know much about."

Jason tilted his head, wondering if he'd heard that right.

The nurse's lips flattened. "And why's that?"

Erica sat up straight and gave the nurse a level stare. "I'd rather hold the rest of my discussion for the doctor."

"But our protocol is for me to—"

"Can the doctor see me even if I don't answer all of your questions?"

"Ye-es…"

Jason felt like his world was spinning off somewhere he didn't understand. He'd never seen gentle Erica act quite like this.

Well, actually, he had. When she was defending her kids.

"Then I'd rather save the rest of the interview for the doctor herself." Erica didn't look his way.

Something was *definitely* going on here.

The nurse looked at him as if to say, can't you control your wife? But he didn't rise to the bait. If he admitted he wasn't any relation to Erica and the kids, he'd probably be sent out into the waiting room. And despite her huffy attitude, he had the feeling Erica needed support.

"Fine." The nurse stood. "Follow me." She stormed down the hall and flung open the door of an exam room. "The doctor will be in shortly." She slammed Erica's folder into the plastic holder beside the door and stomped off.

Erica went into the exam room and he followed behind, Teddy in his arms. "So what was that about, how there's a period you don't know about? Did you just not like her attitude, or..." He didn't want to contemplate the other alternative. That she didn't remember because she'd been in some way out of it, in trouble personally or with the law.

He'd known people with big blackouts in their pasts, but drugs or alcohol were usually involved.

She'd set Mikey down on the carpeted floor, and now she lifted Teddy from his arms. "Jason."

There was a funny tone to her voice. "Yeah?"

"I'd like to speak to the doctor alone."

"Of course, I can leave after—"

"No, I mean now." She lifted her chin. "I don't want you here."

The words shocked him. He'd thought they were getting closer, thought that she liked and needed him. He wanted to hear what the doctor said about Mikey and Teddy.

And why would she—

"So could you leave?"

She was standing there with her shoulders squared, facing him, but she wasn't meeting his eyes.

"You want me to leave."

"Yes, please." She glanced up then, and he saw that her eyes were a little shiny. "If you don't want to wait around for me, it's okay. I can call for a ride. A taxi or something."

"Car seats?" He shook his head, backing out of the

room. "No. I'll be outside." He turned and spun out of the room.

He walked right through the waiting room and outside. *Goodbye, softhearted nice guy. Welcome back, Detective Stephanidis.*

In the windy parking lot, he pulled out his phone and scrolled through his contacts. "Hey, Brian," he said a moment later. "Could you do a little bit of investigating for me?"

An hour later, Erica sat in the examining room with the two babies cuddled on her lap. "I realize that you might have to report me," she said to the white-coat-clad doctor in front of her, "but I hope you won't."

Dr. Chen tapped a pencil on the table. "There's such a thing as doctor-patient confidentiality, and I believe in it. On the other hand, I'm *required* to report any situation where a child is at risk."

Erica nodded, dismayed. She was making one move at a time here. She'd only thought of kicking Jason out of the pediatrician's office this morning. If he wasn't there, she'd realized, she would be able to be completely honest with the pediatrician.

And she had been. She'd spilled the entire story: what she knew of Kimmie's pregnancy, of the early months with the twins, of their father and of Kimmie's relapse.

And she'd explained all the things she *didn't* know.

Dr. Chen had listened and watched the twins on the floor. She'd asked questions, held out toys for them to grasp, listened to their babble. Her forehead wrinkled with focus, her questions for Erica pointed. Erica didn't find her awkward at all, as Carla had said; she was just very, very intense.

Finally, after about twenty minutes of observation, Dr. Chen had nodded briskly. "Teddy's just about to crawl, and that mobility will help his mind develop," she'd said. "But he'll come along faster with some physical therapy. Speech, too. Mikey…" She'd studied Mikey's feet again, bent his legs at the knees, rotated his ankles. "He may just go directly to walking. His muscle tone is pretty good."

"I'm so relieved that you think they'll be okay," Erica said. "Look, I know there are probably a million ways I could have done better with the twins. Maybe I should have stayed with Kimmie, let them be taken into foster care. I just…" She shook her head. "I've *been* in foster care, and I know how wrong it can go. I know how siblings can be separated. And Kimmie didn't want that for them. So…I did what she told me to. I brought them here."

"Do you think she was trying to get them back together with her family?"

Erica shook her head. "For whatever reason, she didn't want her brother to find out. She thought he was hostile, judgmental. And… I realize now, she was ashamed of having them out of wedlock, and she didn't want him to know. He idealized her, you see."

"Why did you bring the twins here," Dr. Chen asked, "knowing you might be reported?"

Erica shrugged, her arms still around the boys. "Once they were able to get me the appointment and I thought about it and prayed about it, I knew I had to do what was right for the twins." She met the woman's steady brown eyes. "I know you're the best, and I want the best for them. They need to get started on early intervention, like you said. If I didn't tell a specialist—tell you—everything I knew about their past, they could suffer for it."

The doctor held her gaze, then nodded. "From what I see at this moment, the twins are loved and well cared for."

Erica's breath went out in a sigh of relief.

Dr. Chen held up a hand. "However, if you decide not to get them the help they need, now that you know more about it, I would consider that to be neglect." She leaned forward. "You're going to have to come clean about all of this, you know. Their need for medical attention will be ongoing. Nothing in medicine is inexpensive." She glanced at the chart. "Even without seeing test results and writing it up, I know they'll need therapy. Speech and physical, at a minimum. That's not cheap."

Erica nodded. "I know, and I mean to go through their mother's things and contact the hospital where they were born, do a little digging. I need to… I need to let their other relatives know about them."

"Is the man who accompanied you one of those other relatives? Or is he just a boyfriend?"

"He's a relative."

"The courts might leave them with you, even once your lack of formal guardianship comes out. Unless there's another relative claiming them. Just keep doing what you're doing and after the holidays, when you can get all the testing done and I can analyze it, we'll figure out a program of treatment."

As they exited the turnpike and headed toward Holly Creek Farm, Erica breathed a sigh of relief that this hard day was almost over.

It had been an uncomfortable ride home. Jason had

rushed them back to the house after the doctor's appointment with literally not a word, his face set and angry. Then he'd headed off to testify while she got the twins ready to go home.

He hadn't spoken except for short, efficient communications since they'd gotten in the car.

He'd taken off his overcoat but was still in his dark suit, white shirt and thin tie, and he looked so handsome he took her breath away.

And she'd ruined any chance of being with him.

The moon made a path on the snowy fields and stars sparkled above. A clear, cold night. As they rounded a corner on the country road, she couldn't help drawing in a breath. "This is where I went off the road, right?"

"Yep." He didn't volunteer more.

But emotions flooded Erica. She'd been desperate then, worried about Kimmie, not knowing where she'd land with the twins, not knowing if she could manage them.

Now she was half owner of a farm and she'd started to become part of a community. Sad, because she'd lost Kimmie, but stable.

A big part of why was Jason.

They were almost home. There wasn't time for a full discussion and she recognized her own cowardliness in that. But she had to say something. "Look, Jason, I'm sorry."

He didn't speak, didn't look over. Just steered the truck.

She looked back and saw that the twins were still sound asleep. "I'm sorry about shutting you out. You've been nothing but kind to us and… I'm sorry I had to do that."

He was silent a moment more, and then he glanced over. "I'm trying to be an adult about this, but I don't understand."

"I just… There are some things about the twins' early months that are private."

"You said you didn't remember. Was that true?"

She thought. Should she just tell him now? But no, they were only a few minutes away from home and Papa would be there, and the twins would wake up…

"Is it their father? You've never really talked about him and I've respected your privacy, but did he do something to you or them? Because that can be prosecuted. He should have to pay. Let alone pay child support, but to cause a blank out of months or to cause delays…"

"No, it's not that."

He fell silent. A waiting silence.

She couldn't form the words.

"I thought we were building something together!" He hit the steering wheel and stepped down on the gas.

She cringed. "Be careful! The twins!"

Immediately, he let up on the gas. "Sorry. I'm angry and upset, but that's no way to act."

He was going to be *really* angry when he found out the truth. "I'll talk to you about it tonight," she said. "There *is* something you need to know about their background, and I… I promise, I'll tell you."

She was promising herself, too.

Jason pulled into the parking place at the rail fence in front of the farm.

The house was dark.

Jason frowned. "Wonder if Papa had something to do. He didn't mention it."

He turned off the truck, opened the door. She opened hers, too.

And looked at him. "Wouldn't the dog…"

"I have a bad feeling. Let me go in first," he said.

Protective to the core, and why should that surprise her?

He went inside, and from the way his hand moved under his suit jacket, she knew he carried a gun. But she also knew he was safe. She trusted him with that gun. She watched as he disappeared inside. He flipped on lights, and she saw him moving from room to room.

Papa must have gone somewhere. They were being overcautious. Surely that was all it was.

Still, she felt lonely and vulnerable, just her and the twins in the cold truck. She slipped out and into the back seat between their car seats. Cramped, but she wanted to be there when they woke up.

Father God, she prayed, *help me to tell Jason the truth.* And then she prayed what she hadn't dared to this morning. *And if it be Your will, let me be with him, Lord. I love him. Keep him safe.*

He wasn't coming back out. Her prayers got more fervent. *Keep him safe.*

The twins were stirring.

She loved them so much.

Jason didn't emerge. Should she go to him?

She opened the door, torn as to what to do.

Then, suddenly, she heard an explosive sound, not from the house but from somewhere off beyond the barn.

A gunshot.

Chapter Eleven

The sound of the gunshot crashed into Jason's consciousness. He ran out of the house, and Erica met him beside the truck.

Papa. If Papa were hurt…

"It came from the barn area, maybe beyond," he told her. "I'm going out. Take the twins inside and lock the doors."

"Should I call the police?"

"Call and tell them we heard a shot and Papa's missing. He could be out in the barn, and the shot could be hunters, but…"

"I'll do it. And my phone's on." She gave him a fierce, fast hug, but she didn't offer to go along. She needed to stay with the babies and he needed to move. Fast.

He saw lights in the barn and walked toward it on the path worn through the snow, now icy. When he glanced back, he saw Erica framed in the doorway of the house, waving to let him know they were safely inside.

His breath froze in his nose and his mouth. Was Papa

out here somewhere, in the cold, freezing? Why had he left Papa alone?

Of course Papa didn't want protection or babysitting, but maybe he needed it.

His phone pinged and he glanced at it. Brian from Philly. He turned it off.

When he got to the barn, the door stood open and the lights were on. "Papa? Hey, Papa."

There was no answer, and disappointment pushed in. He checked out the whole place, though. Maybe Papa had fallen or even fainted.

But the barn was empty.

Back outside, he noticed there were tracks leading away from the barn. Human and animal. Why would Papa have gone that way? Unless...it was the direction of the cabin, but why...

Another shot rang out, close this time.

He gripped his own weapon tighter and sent up a prayer. *If You let Papa be all right, I'll stay here with him. I'll take care of him.* You weren't supposed to bargain with God, Jason knew that, but he was desperate.

He moved forward. Heard a faint sound. Then barking that sounded like... Mistletoe?

He ran toward the sound, and a moment later an excited snow-covered dog leaped up at him, bounced off and turned toward the woods, looking back over his shoulder, his tongue lolling out.

"Where's Papa, Mistletoe?"

Mistletoe gave one short bark and trotted toward a small stand of bushes. Jason followed.

There was a rustle and a grunt. Then: "About time you got here."

Jason had never been so glad to hear Papa's crotchety voice in his life. He rushed forward, nearly slipping on icy ground, and sank to his knees beside his grandfather. "What happened? Did you break a bone? Where does it hurt?"

"It doesn't hurt, but I'm cold. I can't seem to get myself up."

Mistletoe romped in a circle around them, kicking up snow and barking.

"Hit an icy patch and my legs went out from under me." Papa propped himself on an elbow and grimaced. "Every time I try to stand up I fall back down. And that's not good at my age, so I figured I'd call for help this way." He patted his rifle. "Might scare out the squatters in the cabin, too."

"You came out here alone because you thought there were squatters in the cabin? You could've been killed!"

"You're not going to be in town forever. I have to be independent." Papa was breathing heavily as he got himself into a sitting position. "Except that crazy dog wouldn't leave me alone. Curled up right beside me. Kept me warm for close to an hour." He rubbed Mistletoe's head. "Didn't like me shooting off the gun, though."

Jason ran a hand over the dog. "Steak bones for you tonight, buddy." Then he braced himself and lifted Papa's not-insubstantial weight, getting a shoulder under him, almost falling himself. "We'll talk more once you're inside and warm." He clicked on Erica's name and dictated a text. "Papa's fine but cold. Turn up heat."

And then, as he and Papa made their way toward the house, he sent up a prayer to God. *Thank You. I'll keep my promise.*

* * *

Erica couldn't stop looking at Papa's dear, tired face. She fussed over him, bandaged a scrape on his hand and brought stacks of blankets downstairs. The front room was toasty, and they soon had Papa ensconced by the fire.

"Tell us what happened." Erica sat down at Papa's feet.

"All of it," Jason added.

Papa pulled up the blanket Erica had put over his legs, settled back in his chair and smiled from Erica to Jason, almost as if he were enjoying the attention. "I missed you two and those babies," he said. "Aside from Ruth Delacroix calling to check on me, I didn't speak to a soul while you were gone. Got to feeling blue, and the cure for that is work, so I went out to do some extra chores in the barn."

"Papa!" Jason sounded exasperated. "You could've let it go until I got home."

"I told you, son, I was feeling blue. So I was out there mending that broken board on the front stall, and I thought I heard noises. When I went outside, I saw a light bobbing up and down out toward the cabin."

Erica glanced at Jason, who was studying his grandfather, and wondered if they were both thinking the same thing. Had he really seen something, or was his mind wandering? Papa seemed sharper than she was, most days, but he was definitely old.

"A light like…a lantern? Headlights?" She adjusted Papa's blankets again.

"I couldn't tell. So," he said righteously, "I got my shotgun and headed down there."

Jason let his head sink into his hand. "Papa. What

were you going to do if you found a crowd of drug squatters out there?"

"Why do you think I brought the shotgun? And the dog?"

Jason shook his head. "You should have just called the police."

"I'm a farmer. Independent. We don't call the police unless we really need 'em." He looked suddenly concerned. "Did you call them when you didn't find me here?"

"Of course I did," Erica said.

Papa made a disgusted sound.

"We were worried! Anyway, I didn't tell them to come right out. I just wanted to have them on alert. I called them back as soon as Jason let me know you were okay."

Papa sat up. "I'll never live this down. They'll be busting my chops at the diner for weeks."

"Those guys!" Jason snorted. "If anything, they'll be impressed."

"Wait, so you headed toward the cabin," Erica said. "Then what happened? You didn't see anybody suspicious, did you?"

Papa gestured toward his leg. "What happened next is that my bad knee went out. I fell and I couldn't get up."

The image of Papa struggling alone in the dark and cold twisted Erica's heart. "You could have frozen to death! Papa Andy, promise me you won't go out without one of us anymore."

Papa Andy looked at her as if she'd lost her mind. "I'm not making a promise like that, young lady. I'm fine ninety-five percent of the time. It's just, that path to the cabin turned into an ice rink, what with the thawing and freezing. I couldn't get a grip on anything."

Jason shook his head and added another log to the fire.

"I didn't want to break a bone," Papa said matter-of-factly, "so I shot off my gun. Figured somebody would hear me."

"That was smart... I guess," Erica said. "Where I grew up, shooting off a gun was an invitation for someone else to open fire on you, but you country folks are different."

"It would have been smarter to call someone on your cell phone. You took a couple years off my life!" Jason actually still looked shaken.

Papa looked at the phone on the end table with obvious irritation. "That cell phone is a nuisance. Keeps going off, and by the time I find it and answer, there's no one there."

"I don't care if you don't like it." Jason glared at his grandfather. "I don't want you anywhere without a phone in your pocket from now on."

"One little mishap," Papa grumbled, "and every young person thinks they can tell you what to do. I have more knowledge in my little finger than you—"

"Would you like some more tea?" Erica said to interrupt their argument.

"Tell you what I'd like," Papa said, "is to take a look at those babies, and then get in bed. I know it's early, but lying out there in the cold took a lot out of me. I'm just going to listen to the radio and stay warm."

And that way, he wouldn't get into more of an argument with Jason. Men. When they felt emotional, they fought.

After they'd taken Papa upstairs to peek at the babies, they got him settled in his bed, propped up with pillows, TV remote in hand.

"One more thing," he said as Jason and Erica were leaving. "I want you to check the cabin."

"Papa..."

"I saw lights," he insisted. "I'd check it out myself, but I've had enough for one night."

"I don't think it's anything," Jason said. "Just moonlight or an animal."

"If that's the case," Papa said, "then why was that path worn to an icy gully instead of just snowed over?"

Erica and Jason looked at each other. "Good point," Erica said, suddenly uneasy.

Jason's phone went off for the second time that evening. He looked at the lock screen and shoved it back in his pocket. "You stay with the twins," he told Erica, "and I'll go look over the cabin."

"I'll keep an eye on the twins," Papa said, sounding irritable. "I'm good for something at least. She should go with you. Not to confront anyone, mind you, but to call for help if needed."

Erica looked at Jason. "He's right." And she wanted to help. Wanted to build a closer bond with Jason before she told him the difficult truth about the twins.

Jason turned to Papa. "I'll only consider you staying here if you have that cell phone out and on. If anything goes wrong, with you or the twins, you call me and then the police."

Mistletoe jumped onto Papa's bed, seeming to smirk at Jason and Erica.

"You're not supposed to be there, boy, but we'll let it slide tonight," Jason said, thumping the dog's side.

"You and Papa watch out for each other, okay, Mistletoe?" Erica massaged the dog's large head and then punched her own number into Papa's phone. Quickly, she enlarged the text, just as she'd used to do for the seniors where she'd worked. "See? One click. I made myself and Jason your favorites."

"You *are* my favorites," Papa said gruffly. "Thank you for getting an old man out of a tight spot."

Erica felt tears rising to her eyes. She was growing so fond of Papa, almost like he was her own grandfather.

Out in the hall, Jason turned to her. "You've done nursing work, right? Do you think he's really okay?"

"He's fine. Probably needs a little time to himself to regroup." She turned toward the twins' room. "I just want to check on them once more, and then we can go out together."

"As long as you agree to stay well back, out of any trouble we might find."

She held up her hands. "I'm not aiming to be a hero."

In the twins' room, she listened to their even breathing. Then she leaned over the crib railing and touched a kiss to each beloved forehead. "We're going to get you the help you need, little ones," she whispered. "I promise I'll take care of you."

Outside, the sky had cleared, leaving a mass of bright stars. Heaven seemed close enough to touch.

She followed Jason, and when he got to the icy section where Papa had fallen, he broke new trail so they wouldn't have to walk on the same precarious path Papa had.

The aroma of wood smoke grew stronger. "Do you smell that?" she asked. "Is it coming from the main house or the cabin?"

"I think maybe Papa was right," he said. "Look."

Sure enough, in the direction of the cabin she saw lights. Jason turned slightly and held out a hand. "Stay back."

"Okay." Her heart pounded, hard and rapid as a drumbeat.

He crept forward, his body naturally graceful, practiced in the moves of surveillance and detection. He approached the window cautiously and peeked in.

Then he stepped back, rubbed the window with the sleeve of his jacket and cupped his hands to his face as if making sure of what he saw. Why wasn't he being more careful to avoid getting caught?

Then he turned in her direction. "We need an ambulance!" he yelled. "Somebody just had a baby!"

Jason experienced the next ten minutes as a crazy blur. Erica, staggering through the deep snow toward him as she shouted into the phone. Himself, giving the dispatcher exact directions, and then pounding on the cabin door. A pale-faced young husband answering, acting protective—and then, when he realized Jason and Erica wanted to help, looking relieved.

Inside the cabin, on a sleeping bag with a blanket over her, was an exhausted-looking, smiling woman and a squalling newborn.

Jason was afraid to even approach the damp, fragile little being. He'd gotten confident with babies of the twins' sturdy size, but not this tiny thing. Erica, though, waded right in. "Is she...he...okay?" She knelt beside the blanket-covered woman, who was propped on one elbow, wrapping the baby in a towel that at least looked clean. "Here, let me help you. Oh, he's precious!"

"We didn't cut the cord yet." The man stood beside Jason, sounding shaky and worried. "I was afraid... none of this is sanitary." He waved an arm around the cabin.

"How'd you even know what to do?" Jason nodded at the mother and child. "I mean...the baby looks fine."

"Truth?" the young man said. "YouTube videos. My phone's running out of juice and it's super old, but I got enough to know how to help her, and what to do right after the baby was born."

Jason was impressed to see, now, that the area in front of the fireplace had been scrubbed clean. An old cast-iron pot sat beside the blazing fire, and a bucket of snow was nearby. "You melted snow for water."

"We found some dishes here. I didn't expect the baby to be born so soon. We don't even have a name yet." He rubbed his hand through his hair. "This is our home-town, and I thought we'd find someone to take us in, but everyone's busy at Christmas."

Erica glanced up from her position beside the mother and child. "We want to help, right, Jason? Although I think a hospital is the first place for you. All three of you."

"Absolutely." The young man sat down on a large cut log as if it were a stool. "Man, look at this. I'm shak-ing." He held out his hands to illustrate.

"You did a good job," Jason told him.

"He did," the young woman said.

"And so did you." Erica smoothed the young woman's hair back and found a backpack to tuck under her head as a pillow. "You made an amazing baby." Her voice was soft.

Jason's phone buzzed. Brian, again. When would

his friend get the message that Jason was way too busy for a chat?

"Come down here?" The woman was looking at her husband, and he immediately got down on the floor beside her, slipping an arm underneath her neck and touching the baby's hand. "I love you, babe. And I love him, too."

Erica found another sleeping bag in their stack of gear and put it over the two of them, leaving the baby free. Then she scooted back, stood and looked at Jason. "Can the ambulance even get back here?"

"It's four-wheel drive. They'll be fine."

"Then let's give them privacy." She walked over to the cabin's kitchen area and leaned against the counter, and Jason came to lean beside her.

"Is it okay that they didn't cut the cord, do you think?" Jason was still processing the fact that a kid under twenty had just helped his equally young girlfriend have a baby.

"Smart, I would guess. The paramedics will know what to do."

"Where'd you have the twins?"

"What?" She looked at him blankly.

"The twins. Did you have them at a regular hospital, or at a birthing center or something?"

She hesitated. "They were born in a regular hospital."

There was something odd, off, about the way she said it. "Does this bring back memories?"

She shook her head. "These guys seem loving and happy, even though they're basically homeless. It's so sweet."

Their disagreement of earlier that day, the fact that she'd kept him out of the doctor's office, seemed trivial in the face of what this young couple had just experienced and of the scare about Papa Andy. He put an arm around Erica's shoulders, and after a moment, she cuddled in, slipping her own arm around his waist.

It wasn't romantic, not this time. It was comfort, a desire for human closeness, and she seemed to feel it to the exact same degree that he did. As the couple lay together, bonding with their baby, so he and Erica, two people alone in the world, bonded, as well. It was a Christmas moment.

Soon enough, though, the ambulance pulled up, right to the cabin's back door, and all the tranquility was lost. The paramedics asked questions of the mother and father, did tests on the baby and loaded them all into an ambulance in a matter of minutes. Jason and Erica gave their names and numbers, and the ambulance pulled out.

And then they were gone, and it was just Erica and Jason at the cabin. They made short work of putting out the fire and locking up.

"You know," she said, "you were right about something."

"You're kidding," he joked.

She swatted his arm. "I can admit when I'm wrong. And I was wrong to think I could have lived here with the twins. It would never have worked. It's too primitive."

"You're welcome," he said. "Just ask me anytime you need advice."

"You're impossible," she said, and then yawned hugely. "We'd better get back to Papa Andy and the twins. I'm beat."

Jason felt the same, only with a bit of an edge of adrenaline still hanging on. He wanted to hold her in the worst way, but he also knew they had differences to resolve. And they were both exhausted. "Let's head back."

Halfway down the new broken path, his phone buzzed yet again. He looked at it and rolled his eyes. What did Brian want? Impatient, he clicked into the phone call. "I'm kinda busy here, and it's late. What's up?"

"I have some news," Brian said, his voice stiff, guarded. "About that matter you asked me to investigate."

Erica. Kimmie. Arizona. "Oh, man, it's been crazy here. I forgot all about that."

Erica glanced back at him, questioning. He waved her ahead. "I've got to take this," he said to her. "Go get warm. I'll be right there."

She nodded and headed toward the house. Jason walked slowly behind. "What's up?" he asked Brian.

"You're going to want to be sitting down to hear this," Brian said.

Chapter Twelve

Jason stood outside the house and listened to Brian's incomprehensible words. Surely his friend had gotten it wrong. "You didn't find this out for sure, right? It's just a theory."

"It's true." Brian's voice was flat. "Those twins are your nephews. Your sister was their mother."

"But why—" He broke off. "What could Erica…"

"Can't say. She trying to get something out of you? Money? Land?"

He thought of the will, how Kimmie had left Erica half the farm. But his head was spinning too much to understand.

While he and Brian had been talking, Erica had gone into the house. Now lights came on in the front room, and he watched as she moved around there, picking up a cup from the coffee table, adjusting an ornament, bending down to pat Mistletoe.

From where he stood, it was like watching a Christmas movie. The perfect setting, the beautiful woman. A happy home.

And it was all a lie. "Was she married?"

"What do you mean?"

His hand was sweating on the phone. "Kimmie. Was she married to the father of the twins?"

"No." There was a dim sound of papers rustling. "She didn't name a father on the birth certificates, but my contact out there did a little digging, looked up her past addresses and other public records. Apparently she was cohabitating with a man around the time they must have been conceived, but he went to prison before the babies were born."

Cohabitating with a man.

People did that all the time. Who was he to judge?

All the same, the image he'd always carried of his sister—beautiful, laughing, pure—seemed to shatter into a million jagged fragments.

"You still there?" Brian asked. "Listen, I wouldn't worry about the father having any claim on those kids."

"Yeah. Thanks, man. I'll… We'll talk."

"One more thing," Brian said. "When I spoke with Kimmie's landlord—piece of work, that guy—he said there was a box of your sister's personal effects that was sent to your grandfather's address. Should have arrived by now."

Maybe it had, and Erica had hidden it. Suddenly, he wouldn't put anything past her.

"I guess there could be a note, some kind of explanation."

He closed his eyes for just a second, then opened them again. "Yeah. Thanks, buddy." He clicked off the phone.

And then he just stood still and looked up at the starry sky. The twins were Kimmie's. His, now. He'd been getting to know them, coming to care for them, never even realizing—

The front door opened. "Jason? Everything okay?"

Erica was framed in the doorway. The soft light behind her made her skin and hair glow.

A little bit like Kimmie had always glowed in his mind.

In truth, Erica, like Kimmie, had lost her luster, if she'd ever even had it.

He strode up the front steps and brushed past her into the entryway. Sitting down on the bench, he took off his snowy boots and tossed them into the pile of shoes by the door. They made a satisfying crash.

"Shh! The twins!"

He looked at her, and it was like she was a different person from the woman he'd been getting close to. "Yeah," he said. "We should talk about the twins."

Her eyes widened. "What was the phone call about?"

"Let's take this discussion into the front room." He watched her face. "We wouldn't want to wake up Kimmie's babies."

Her hand flew to her mouth and her eyes went impossibly wide. "You know."

Until that moment, in a corner of his mind, he'd thought Brian might have gotten it wrong. Or that maybe, Erica hadn't known the babies were Kimmie's. Which didn't make any sense, but was easier to believe than that sweet, gentle Erica—the woman he'd fallen in love with—had been lying since the moment they'd met.

"Jason…"

He jerked his head sideways toward the front room. "In here."

She walked in ahead of him, shoulders slumping, and

perched on the edge of the couch. He sat in the chair that was kitty-corner. Mistletoe lifted his head from his bed in front of the fire and whined softly.

They both stared at the floor.

Finally, she spoke. "Jason, I've been wanting to tell you about the twins practically since the first day I knew you. It's just… It's been complicated."

Understanding dawned. "That's why you didn't want me in the doctor's office."

"Yes. I knew I had to tell the doctor the whole truth, and—"

"You owed more honesty to the doctor than to me?" He knew dimly that his remark wasn't fair, but he couldn't make himself stifle it.

"It was for the twins." She leaned forward, elbows on knees. "The doctor needed to know everything so she could give them the best help possible."

A log crackled and fell in the fireplace. Mistletoe stood, turned in a circle and flopped back down with a sigh.

"All this time," he said. "Knowing it, being what I thought was close, and you didn't see fit to tell me those boys are my own *nephews*?" His voice was too loud, but he couldn't seem to control it. "What does that say about you?"

"I… Jason, I'm so sorry. I wanted to tell you."

He pressed his lips together so he wouldn't say the immediate, awful things he wanted to say.

She'd lied to him. That was one thing to focus on.

The fact that the twins were his sister's, were his blood—that was too big to take in right now.

His body felt like it was going to explode. He jumped up and paced the room, picking things up and putting them down. "Why'd you do it, Erica? What are you trying to get out of me and Papa?"

"Nothing. I don't want anything from you."

"Why, because you already got everything you need from Kimmie? What was that will about? Blackmail? Did you steal the twins from her?"

"No! I—"

"Because I'll prosecute. If you in any way made my sister's last days harder, if you..." He nearly choked as all the possibilities whirled in his thoughts. "If you caused her death, taking away her kids and stressing her out—"

"No, no!" She held up a hand, looking up at him, her eyes filling with tears. "Jason, it wasn't like that at all."

"Child abduction," he recited, his voice flat because he'd said it so many times before, though never in such a personal context. "Wrongfully removing a child by persuasion, fraud, open force or violence. I don't doubt that you'll see prison time over this."

"She gave them to me." Erica's face was white. "She asked me to take them, because she couldn't care for them herself anymore, and she didn't want them to go into foster care."

"You expect me to believe that? Why would they have been put into foster care when they had a perfectly loving family back here and a mother there?"

"Because..." She stopped, shook her head, looked away.

"Can't think of an answer, can you?"

She hesitated, then met his eyes. "I don't know if you want to know the answer."

He clenched his fists. "I want to know. Not that I'll believe one thing you say."

"She was using," Erica said quietly, "and the police were coming."

Jason pounded a fist into his hand as bitterness spread through his chest. "With her babies there, she was using?" All this time he'd been trying to maintain an image of Kimmie, and it had been false. For that matter, the same was true of Erica.

He shook his head. "So she asked you to bring them to me and Papa, and instead you—"

"No." Erica shook her head. "You have to understand, it was all hectic and hurried. She thought I could live in the cabin until I got on my feet. It was all she had to offer me for…for raising her children. But, Jason, I love them like they're my own and I want what's best for them. I'm not trying to pull something over on you. I did this—I've been taking care of them since leaving Arizona and even before—because I cared for Kimmie and I've come to love her boys." Her voice choked up on the last words.

"You can do better than that. You're a great liar."

"She didn't want you to have them." She was staring at the carpet, her voice low.

He wasn't sure he'd heard her right. "What did you say?"

She looked up at him. "Kimmie didn't want you to have the twins. She asked me to raise them and not to let you know."

Jason grabbed a plastic snow globe he'd loved since childhood and threw it against the wall.

Erica flinched as it shattered, water and little plastic pieces flying everywhere. Her shoulders hunched in, like he was going to hit her.

"That can't be true. Kimmie would have trusted me

before someone like you. A liar with nothing. No connection to the family, no experience, no resources…"

She was looking at him now, her face set and serious, except that tears were running down her cheeks.

"Kimmie was smart," he continued, trying to work it out in his mind. "She knew the babies would need help—"

"They need help now," she said, standing up.

"What?"

"I heard one of them crying. Coughing. Something." She hurried toward the stairs.

He followed her. "You're faking this to get away from me. But I'm watching you. I'm not letting you take the babies again—"

"Or maybe you woke them up, throwing things like a little boy because you're mad at your sister." The words, tossed over her shoulder, cut into him.

Still, he followed her into the room she shared with them. Her nightgown hung on the bedpost, slippers at the foot of the bed. Her Bible and a little devotional book on the bedside table.

He swallowed the bile that rose in his throat and approached the crib.

The twins lay in striped Christmas pajamas, Mikey with his head toward one end of the crib, Teddy with his head toward the other. Their legs were intertwined, and as he watched, Mikey tossed back and forth, coughed and let out a fussy little cry.

They were Kimmie's babies. His nephews.

Jason's throat tightened.

Erica's breathing sounded choked and she brushed the backs of her hands over her cheeks. The flowery smell of her hair rose to his nose.

He ignored the tiny shred of sympathy and caring that pushed at him. He'd been about to fall for this liar.

He always picked the wrong person—as witness Renea and now Erica. He had a knack for it, choosing those who were already on the way to some kind of emotional ruin, and then nudging that train along to full speed.

Mikey fussed some more, kicking his legs restlessly, and Erica picked him up carefully, trying not to disturb Teddy. She jostled Mikey gently in her arms. "You've picked up a cold, haven't you?" she said in a quiet, bouncy voice. "Let's wipe your nose, huh?" She carried him over and got a tissue from a box on the dresser, wiped the baby's nose. Then she grabbed another tissue and blotted her own eyes.

Teddy thrashed in the crib as if looking for his twin and then let out a wail.

Before he could think about it, Jason had Teddy in his arms. He gently bounced him, stroking his soft hair.

This was his nephew. His blood.

The babies Kimmie had borne and hadn't told him about.

"Did she try to get in touch with me?" The question burst out of him. "Or Mom, or Gran and Papa?"

Erica shook her head. "She didn't want any of you to know."

"But the safety of her own children, their health!"

Teddy started to cry again and Jason swayed with him. Erica had found a little medicine bottle and a dropper and was filling it, blocking Mikey from rolling off the bed with her body. "Here you go, sweetie, this'll help your cold," she said, propping Mikey up and popping the syringe into his mouth.

Mikey turned his head away and spit out some of the bright red medicine. "There, but some got inside, huh?" she crooned, using another tissue to wipe Mikey's chin. "There, that'll help you feel better and sleep. Rock with Mama."

"You're not their mother."

She drew in a little gasp and her eyes flashed up to Jason's, and then she looked back down at Mikey again and rocked, back and forth.

"So when the nurse asked you if they were breast-fed…"

She shook her head, still rocking the baby. "I don't know. Kimmie said she was able to stay clean while she was pregnant and for a while after. I'd assume she at least tried."

"You weren't around her then?" His hunger for more information made him keep talking to the woman who'd betrayed his sister and lied to him.

She shook her head. "I wish I had been. I wish it so much. But that was when my mom was having so much trouble and I could barely… Anyway, I lost touch with Kimmie."

"Lost touch until when?"

"Until she called me two months ago and told me she was dying and she needed help."

He bit down the pain those words roused in him. "Why wouldn't she call us? Why would she call a young woman, a stranger with who-knows-what intentions…"

"We were friends, Jason, and I didn't judge her."

His mouth had been open to ask more questions, to vent more feelings, but her words made him stop. *Would* he have judged Kimmie, had he known what had happened in her life?

"Hey, what's going on in here?" Papa pushed through the half-open door, clad in flannel pajamas with a plaid robe tied on over them.

"I'm sorry we woke you up," Erica said.

He waved a hand. "Old folks don't sleep well. Are the babies sick?"

She glanced over at Jason. "I think they picked up a cold or something. They were at the doctor's and around other kids so much, it's inevitable."

"Why don't you tell him what else has come out tonight," Jason said to Erica.

She narrowed her eyes at him. "Is this the right time?"

"No," he said, "that would've been when you met us for the first time. But you didn't choose the right time, did you?"

She sighed. "No, I didn't."

"What's going on between you two?" Papa Andy sat down on the bed beside Erica.

"I... Papa, I'm really sorry," she said, "but there's a secret I've been keeping since I came to Pennsylvania. Jason just found out about it, and he's angry. Understandably. You'll probably be angry, too."

"Oh, now," Papa said, patting her back, "what could a sweet young woman like you do that would make an old man angry?"

She swallowed hard. "I... You know how Kimmie and I were friends, right?"

Papa nodded, tickling Mikey's foot.

"Well, one reason she and I spent a lot of time together, toward the end, was that..." She trailed off and looked at Jason.

"What she's trying to say, Papa, is that the babies aren't hers. They're Kimmie's."

Papa's mouth opened in an O. He stared from Erica to Mikey to Teddy.

Erica thrust the baby into his arms and fled from the room.

Erica ran down the steps and into the front room, gasping with sobs.

Why, oh why, hadn't she told them on her own terms rather than letting the truth be discovered? And what would happen now?

Would the twins be taken from her? Was her dream of motherhood already at an end?

"I'm sorry, Kimmie," she whispered. She picked up a photograph of Jason and Kimmie as kids with Santa. It was one of Papa's favorites, and she often saw him looking at it.

What had gone so wrong in this family that huge, painful secrets were needed?

She saw a tiny plastic Christmas tree on the floor in a little puddle of water. The nearby shards of plastic looked sharp.

She walked into the kitchen and got paper towels, feeling stiff in every part of her body, exhausted, old. She came back into the room and started cleaning up the mess.

Jason had been so furious. Of course he had. No one liked being lied to, and this was the lie to end all lies, a lie of major proportions.

She inhaled the piney scent of the Christmas tree as she searched out all the little pieces of a broken Christmas scene. For a moment she thought about saving them. Maybe the snow globe could be put back together.

She studied the bits in her hand. *No. Hopeless*.

She carried the pieces to the trash can and threw them in. Upstairs, she could hear Jason's and Papa's low voices, but no sound of crying babies. The boys had probably gone back to sleep. They were exhausted from their big day.

Loss, a huge hole in her chest, opened with such an ache that she sat down on the couch and hunched over, clutching her elbows.

She was a horrible person, not deserving of a family.

That little moment in the cabin, when Jason had put his arm around her like she was his longtime wife, when she'd cuddled into him, was the last time she'd have the opportunity to touch him.

And they'd take the babies from her—she was sure of it. Why wouldn't they? Papa and Jason were kind, loving men who could raise Mikey and Teddy to adulthood. If Kimmie had stayed in touch with her family, she would have known that, and Erica would never have even been in the picture.

Her heart felt broken into three distinct pieces. Four, actually: one for Mikey, one for Teddy, one for Papa and one for Jason.

The fun, happy moments they'd spent together played through her mind. How they'd decorated the tree, how Teddy had scooted toward it. The capable way Papa held a baby on his lap like he was born to it. The sleigh ride to church, bells jingling, the twins laughing.

There wasn't going to be any more of that for her.

Unbidden, a memory from childhood spread into her mind. She'd rushed home from school to the motel where they'd been living, excited to have a Christmas gift for her mother. A clay dish, fired in the school kiln. Now, as an adult, she knew it had been a lopsided, ugly thing. And indeed, her mother had laughed when she'd seen it, given Erica a quick pat on the head and gone back to partying with her friends.

Erica got up, walked over to the Christmas tree and looked at the little lump ornament Jason and Papa had laughed about. In a family like theirs, children's humble efforts at art were treasured and kept.

She'd always longed to be in such a family. And she'd had a brief moment there. But now that time was over.

Heavy footsteps sounded on the stairs. Jason came to the doorway and looked in at her, his expression a perfect storm of hurt and anger and mistrust.

He spun away. A moment later, the front door slammed.

It's over. She sank to her knees and pressed her hands to her mouth. *Help me, Lord.*

Chapter Thirteen

The next morning, at dawn, Jason was awakened by a rhythmic scraping sound. He looked around and blinked at the interior of his truck and the pink-and-gold glowing world outside. What was he doing here? And why was he so cold, despite the down coat stretched over him and his big boots and warm socks?

He turned on the car and cranked up the heat. Slowly, the night before came back to him. The revelation about the twins. The fighting with Erica. Storming out.

He'd driven aimlessly and then realized it wasn't so aimless; he was headed to the suburban Pittsburgh home where his family had lived during his elementary school years, after they'd moved back from Arizona. He'd sat in his truck in front of their old house, thinking about his sister, until he'd fallen asleep.

Now, as the defroster cleared the windows, he looked out to see that the Michaelson place next door was decorated with the same blue icicle lights and big blue-lit deer that the older couple had always argued about: he'd loved them, and she'd thought they were tacky.

As a kid, Jason had found the blue lights to be much

cooler than his family's plain old white lights, and he'd loved the way the blue deer had raised and lowered their heads. He remembered the year that Kimmie had taken him over to pretend-feed the deer with burned, broken-up Christmas cookies they'd made. He'd been young, first or second grade. Probably, he realized now, she'd thought of the scheme to make him feel better after their cookies had turned out inedible.

Years later, she'd covered for him, taking the blame herself, when he and his friends had dragged one of the deer over to their bonfire and accidentally burned part of its back leg. He squinted through the dim morning light. Sure enough, one of the deer had a hind leg half the length of the other three.

How had he and Kimmie gotten so far apart that she'd died alone, not even telling him she'd borne two sons? That she didn't want him, the little brother who'd idolized her, to get to know her children?

Tap-tap-tap. He lowered his driver's-side window to see a bundled-up woman, white hair peeking out from beneath a stocking cap. "You're going to freeze out here, sir. What's your business in this neighborhood?"

The voice was familiar, if a little raspier than when he'd last heard it. "Mrs. Michaelson? I'm Jason Stephanidis. I used to live next door."

The old woman cocked her head to one side and studied Jason. "You're the little kid who once decorated my front bushes with those tinsel icicles?"

Another memory Jason had forgotten about until just now. "The very same," he said, turning off the truck, climbing out and shaking her hand. "I'm sorry about that. I'd guess you were picking those things up out of your yard for weeks."

Mrs. Michaelson chuckled, leaning on her snow shovel. "That we were, but we didn't mind. We always enjoyed the kids in the neighborhood, since we didn't have any of our own."

"I see you're still putting up the blue lights," Jason said, gesturing to the Michelsons' house.

"Sure do, every year, and sometimes I leave 'em on all night. The mister has been gone these past eight years, but it doesn't seem like Christmas otherwise."

So Mr. Michaelson had passed away. And Mrs. Michaelson, although she looked spry enough, had to be well up into her eighties. She'd seemed ancient even when Jason was a kid.

"Can I help you shovel your driveway?"

"No need. I just do the walkways, and they're done. I don't drive anymore." She sighed and gestured at her thick glasses. "Vision problems. I turned in my license before they could take it away from me."

"Sensible decision." He looked around the neighborhood. "I have good memories of living here."

"You look like you could use a cup of coffee," she said "If you'd like to come in, I could fix you some breakfast, as well."

There was the tiniest undertone of eagerness in the old woman's voice. "I would appreciate that," he said, and followed Mrs. Michaelson inside.

After breakfast and promises to stay in touch, Jason drove back to the farm. He felt ashamed of having left Papa alone to deal with Erica and the twins, but when he arrived, Erica's car was gone and the house was quiet. He had a moment of panic. "Papa?"

"Up here," his grandfather called.

Papa was putting on a Christmas sweater-vest that

had to be as old as Jason was, his hair wet from a recent shower, his face freshly shaved.

"Where are Erica and the twins?"

"She took 'em to the Santa Claus breakfast at the church."

After the bomb that had exploded here last night, she'd gone to a Santa Claus breakfast? "You let her go? What if she abducts them?"

Papa waved a hand. "If she were going to abduct them, she'd have done it already. She'd never have come here at all." He leaned closer to the mirror to straighten his bow tie. "She said she'd promised to help with the breakfast, and she didn't want to let Mrs. Habler and the ladies' crew down."

"Oh." Jason stepped next door to her room. The bed was neatly made, but all her and the twins things were still there. A weight seemed to lift off his chest, even though he *thought* he wanted her to leave, to get out of their lives.

"Where are you going?" he asked his grandfather.

"Christmas Eve ham delivery," Papa explained. "Remember? The Men's Group has been doing it since I don't know when."

Jason did remember, how Papa went to a Christmas Eve luncheon with other men, out at some restaurant, and then did a surprise ham delivery to some of the poorer members of the congregation.

He didn't want to ask, but the words burst out of him. "How was Erica?"

Papa shook his head, pressing his lips together. "We didn't talk much. She was broken up, though. Red eyes. Kept apologizing." He eyed Jason. "I don't know what to think or do about this whole situation, except to make sure those babies are cared for and loved."

"What's she going to do?"

Papa picked up a comb and ran it through his hair. "I doubt if she's gotten that far in her thinking."

"I just can't understand what she did. Kimmie, either."

"Some things don't make a whole lot of logical sense." Papa put on his dress shoes and checked himself in the mirror again. "Tell you what you need to do, though. Get a shower. Get yourself cleaned up. You'll feel better."

Jason gave Papa a half smile he didn't feel inside. "Sure. Will do."

As he left Papa's bedroom, he heard a car approach and a door slam. His heart leaped. He hurried to his bedroom window to look out.

It was only Papa's ride.

Jason didn't want to see Erica, anyway.

After he'd showered and put on clean clothes, he didn't know what to do with himself. Erica and the twins hadn't come back yet, not that he was waiting for them. Once again, he got into his truck.

As he started to turn out of the farm's long driveway, a brown delivery truck appeared and stopped in front of the drive, brakes squeaking. When Jason saw that the driver was a high school acquaintance, he waved.

"Got a package for you and your grandfather," Elmer called, hopping down and carrying a two-foot square box to the truck's window. "Want me to throw it in the back of your truck, or should I take it up to the house?"

"Throw it in the back. Thanks."

"Merry Christmas!" Elmer waved and the brown truck chugged off.

Jason stopped at the hospital to check on the young couple who'd given birth in the cabin. He found them in good health, just waiting for the doctor to release them. He admired their new son and envied the loving smiles on their faces. Exhibit A that you didn't need material things to be happy.

Since it seemed they had no idea where they'd go once they left the hospital, Jason found the hospital's social worker and made an anonymous donation for a month's rent for them.

But it didn't make him feel a bit better.

Aimless, he drove around and finally ended up at the mall two towns over, thinking to pick up a little something more for Papa. He wandered until he found a bookstore and picked up a copy of Papa's favorite author's new hardcover spy novel. The thought of Papa's reaction—"I could have gotten this at the library for free"—gave Jason a minute's pleasure. Secretly, Papa would be glad he didn't have to join the long waiting list to get the book.

He looked at his watch and realized he'd killed only half an hour. Package in hand, Jason sat down on a bench.

Repetitive Christmas music played, audible over the sounds of people's voices, some irritable but most happy and excited. People crowded through the mall and into the stores, and he heard snippets of conversation.

From a man in a wheelchair, talking to the young nurse pushing him: "Figures my disability check would be late this month. But I know, I know, I should stop complaining and be grateful I can still get something for the grandkids."

From one frazzled-looking young mom to another: "Did you see the Dino Dasher is finally on sale?"

From a pretty teenage girl: "If I get Aunt Helen an extra large, she'll be insulted, but if I get her anything smaller it won't fit."

Families. None of them having perfect Christmases, but the holiday spirit shone through the complaints and the crowding.

The smell of candied nuts tickled his nose, and he looked around, spotting the source in a kiosk in the middle of the mall. His mother had always loved those nuts. He should call her.

He turned away from the crowds and covered one ear and put in the call, but there was no answer. Either she was out or maybe all the circuits were overloaded, it being Christmastime. Did wireless circuits get overloaded?

He strolled over to the kiosk and bought a paper cone of candied nuts, then wandered through the mall, nibbling them.

"There's the most handsome detective in Holly Springs." The voice behind him was merry and loud, and he turned to see Ruth, as always with a baby in her arms. "Doing some last-minute shopping, are ya?"

He held up his bag. "You, too?"

"Sure am. Do you know the Glenns from church?" She introduced him to a bedraggled-looking man who didn't smell any too good and his much younger, stressed-out-looking wife. Then she held up the baby for him to see. "And this is little Maria. We're out doing some shopping for her. Gotta make her Christmas bright!"

"Nice to meet you," he said, and watched the small

group head into a baby store. He could guess who'd be footing the bill there. Ruth was widowed, and she wasn't wealthy herself, but she had a generous heart. She must have taken it upon herself to play Santa for the Glenn family.

On his way out to his truck he spotted Chuck and Jeannine, walking arm in arm through the parking lot. He was happy they were back together, but he didn't want to intrude on their holiday.

But Chuck called out a greeting. "Jason! Come hear our good news!"

Standing in the cold parking lot, they explained that they'd decided to keep all the baby furniture because they were planning to adopt.

"I finally figured out it doesn't matter how kids come into a family," Chuck said. "I was on some kind of male ego trip, wanting my descendants to be my own blood."

"But he finally realized that was ridiculous." Jeannine squeezed her husband's arm. "What's important is how much love is there."

How much love is there. Jason wasn't feeling any excess of love, himself. He had Papa, of course, but even Papa had plans today, long-standing friends in the community. Everyone in Holly Springs, single or married, seemed to be rooted and connected. Everyone except him.

Maybe he ought to think about staying here, settling down. The pace of life, the way people cared for each other, was starting to appeal to him. Maybe, like Papa and Ruth, he could build a life here even though he was single.

He drove by the Mistletoe Display and, on impulse, turned in. Twilight was gathering, and he figured he might see a cheerful crowd. He didn't feel like being alone.

But as he drove up to the gates and parked in an almost-empty lot, the display's lights clicked off. A worker came out and hung a sign. "Sorry, buddy, we're closing down."

"No problem. Merry Christmas." Jason waited until the guy had gone back in to lock up the office and then read the sign. "Closing early so our workers can spend Christmas Eve and Day with their families."

Jason wandered along the fence, looking into the now-dark display. In the rapidly deepening twilight, he spotted the bench where he and Erica had shared their first kiss.

The emotions from that evening washed over him, and this time, he didn't even try to push them away.

He'd cared so much for Erica. He could admit it to himself now: he'd fallen in love with her.

But in the end, she'd betrayed him. Just like Kimmie had, and Renea, and even his own mother.

A nagging, honest voice inside his head said: Who's the common element here?

I know. It's me! I make bad choices!

Honesty compelled him to push further. Was it really just about choices?

Renea had been his own bad choice. But he hadn't chosen his mother or Kimmie. They'd been his family, and while his mother had definitely been the one to distance herself from her children, he'd followed up on that by judging Kimmie, pushing her away.

It was a decision he regretted, and would regret his whole life.

Erica had come into his life as a result of that decision; in all probability, she'd have never been involved with Kimmie if he had taken the proper responsibility for his sister.

Or maybe not; Kimmie had been her own person, and she might have still chosen to run away.

God works all things to good.

Even bad things, like Kimmie's death, God had worked to good by bringing him, Erica and the twins together.

Except that, last night, he'd judged Erica harshly, yelled at her, pushed her away. Just like he'd done with Kimmie.

But she lied to me! He banged back into his truck and drove too fast to the diner. That empty feeling inside him was hunger. He hadn't eaten anything since Mrs. Michaelson's breakfast and a few of those candied nuts.

He had a moment's fear that the diner would be closed, too, but it was brightly lit. When he pushed the door open, bells jingled and steamy warmth hit him, along with the homey scent of turkey and stuffing.

He'd have Christmas Eve dinner here and then go to church services. He'd done holidays alone plenty of times, back in Philly. And there were other solo diners here, too.

Hank came out to take his order, dressed in a Christmas apron atop his black slacks and shirt. "Where's your friend?" he asked.

"What friend? I have a lot of 'em." Which wasn't true, at least not here.

Hank lifted his hands like stop signs and took a step back. "Whoa, I meant the cute redhead. But I *didn't* mean to touch a nerve. What can I get for you? Coffee first?"

Just to prove he wasn't pathetic, Jason ordered the full Christmas Eve platter—turkey, stuffing, potatoes and vegetables. "Give me pie, too."

But when the food came, he could barely stuff down a quarter of it.

He sat back and waited for the check and thought about the day. Thoughts about Kimmie, and then about Erica, edged their way into his mind and wouldn't leave.

He'd gotten so rigid lately, judged people harshly. Partly it came with the police work, but he knew himself well enough to understand that he was trying to keep control.

He'd condemned Kimmie harshly when he'd learned she was using. He'd gotten all strict and judgmental, and that had pushed her away.

Would he do the same to Erica?

But how could he forgive what she'd done to him and Papa?

He gave Hank a credit card for the check, leaving an oversize tip as befitted the occasion and the fact that Hank had to work on Christmas Eve.

And then he ended up at church, even though he was an hour early for services.

It was where he probably should have been all along.

Erica carried the twins upstairs, her muscles aching, her mind and heart calling for rest. She'd stayed out all day on purpose, and it looked like her plan had worked; Jason's truck wasn't here. She wouldn't have to see him, to say goodbye.

Saying goodbye to Papa and the twins would be hard enough.

She set Mikey down on the floor and placed a basket

of colorful blocks in front of him. Then she fastened
Teddy in the bouncy swing she'd found at the thrift store
a few days ago, and right away, he began to babble and
jump. His legs were getting stronger by the day.

"Ma-ma, Ma-ma," he chortled, waving his arms.

She did a double take. *Teddy* had said a word. He'd
called her Mama.

It was the first time. She knelt in front of him, laughing and crying at the same time. "Oh, honey, I'm not
your mama. But what a big boy you are for saying it."

"You *are* his mama, or the closest thing he's got to
one." Papa Andy stood in the doorway.

She looked up at the old man who'd become so dear
to her, and her heart twisted in her chest. "I guess I am.
But that's all going to change now."

"Does it have to?"

She sat back and wrapped her arms around her up-
raised knees. "Jason's going to report me to the local
police. He said last night that I'd probably do jail time."
Which was terrifying, but even worse was the prospect
of losing the twins forever.

"What a man says when he's angry and what's true
can be two different things."

Papa hadn't heard the icy determination in Jason's
voice. "I hope you're right about the jail time, but no one
will disagree that he has more right to raise the twins.
Along with you. You're their closest relatives, whereas
I…" She was a nobody.

"Something you need to know about Jason. He's always seen things in black-and-white. I think he's growing out of that, but…"

"I don't." Erica hugged her knees tighter. "He sees

me as evil now. I'm on his bad list, and I don't think there's any chance of a change."

"Huh." Papa gestured toward Mikey. "That one might walk before he crawls. You'd best keep an eye on him."

Erica turned to see Mikey next to Mistletoe, both little hands buried in the dog's fur. He was trying to pull himself up to his feet, and it had to hurt poor Mistletoe, but the dog didn't seem to mind. In fact, he tugged to the side a little as if he were trying to help Mikey to stand.

Erica pulled in a breath, her hand going to her heart. Was it possible to die of love?

"They grow fast," Papa said, and paused. "Mind if I come in a minute?"

She gestured toward the rocking chair in the corner of the bedroom. "I'm going to start packing, but I'd love some company."

"Where are you headed?"

She shook her head. "For the moment, to town. I lined up a room at the Evergreen Hotel." She sat down on the edge of the bed, facing Papa. "I'll say goodbye as soon as I've packed. I'll leave…" She stopped, swallowed hard. "If you can handle them, I'll leave the twins here tonight."

Papa leaned forward, elbows on knees. "You're a pretty strong woman."

"How do you figure?" So she wouldn't have to focus solely on her misery, she knelt to pull her suitcase out from under the bed and opened it.

Inside were all her shorts and T-shirts. Arizona clothes. It seemed like a lifetime ago that they'd been what she put on every day she wasn't working.

Maybe she'd end up going back there, get away from

the cold. But the thought didn't give her the least iota of happiness.

Restraining a sigh, she opened her drawerful of cold-weather clothes and started refolding them and placing them, carefully, on top of the summer things. If she focused, maybe she wouldn't cry in front of Papa.

Mistletoe trotted over, toenails clicking on the wood floor, and nudged his shaggy head under her hand, whining faintly. Automatically, she tugged the dog against her leg, rubbing his back.

"It took a strong woman to care for your friend, sick with cancer. And then you drove her kids across the country, which couldn't have been easy. You got them early intervention. You've made yourself a place in a brand-new community, even though you've got barely two nickels to rub together."

"I had your help with that," she said. "Thanks to you, I've had a place to stay and food to eat." Honesty compelled her to add, "And it's thanks to Jason that I got in to see the developmental specialist. I could never have done that on my own."

Papa ignored her remarks. "It just surprises me, that's all."

"What surprises you?"

"That you'd give up so easily."

She stared at him. "Give up? What do you…"

"You love those boys, don't you?" In the midst of his wrinkled face, blue eyes shone out, bold and challenging.

"Like they were my own." As if to illustrate, Mikey held out his arms, and she scooped him up and hugged him fiercely.

"And I suspect you have some feelings for my grandson, as well."

Erica set Mikey down in the crib and went back to folding clothes, avoiding Papa's eyes. "You see too much."

"I see what's there. And I see what's there on his side, too. He's a hard one, that Jason, but you've helped him to soften up. You and the twins. That's worth something."

"Thank you, I…" She didn't know what to say, how to respond, but she stumbled to put some words together. "I hope there was something good he got from knowing me. It's been…" Her throat was too tight to go on. She took a sweater out of the suitcase and refolded it, blinking away tears.

"You also did something that hurt him. Hurt me, too, but—"

"I'm so sorry, Papa." She dropped the sweater and hurried across the room to kneel at his side. "You've been so good to me. It was unforgivable of me to deceive you."

He took her hand in his own hard, leathery one. "I'm also old enough to know that nobody's perfect and everybody makes mistakes. Yours wasn't for a bad cause." He tipped her chin up to look at him as her tears spilled over. "Seems to me our Kimmie put you in a mighty confusing dilemma. You tried to do the right thing for her and for the twins. How can we fault you for that?"

She swallowed and wiped at the tears rolling down her cheeks. "Thank you, Papa Andy. That means a lot to me."

"You mean a lot to me, sweetheart. You and these boys have helped me more than you know." He squeezed her hand. "Now, why don't you go find yourself a corner and do a little praying? I'll watch the twins."

"But I need to pack—"

"You in too big of a hurry to listen to God?" He lifted a bushy eyebrow, his sharp eyes pinning her.

"I... No. Thank you. I'd appreciate a few minutes." She grabbed her Bible from her nightstand and hurried downstairs to sit beside the Christmas tree and the nativity scene.

Half an hour later, she knew what she needed to do. Something terrifying, something unlikely to work, something against her whole shy nature.

And she needed to get started right away.

Chapter Fourteen

"I'd love to stay and talk more, but I have a sermon to preach." Pastor Wayne pounded Jason on the shoulder. "I think between you and the Lord, you can figure out what to do. You're welcome to my office, if you need a place to think."

"Thanks." Jason watched the pastor gather his Bible and leave, confident, ready for his next challenge.

That was how Jason had used to feel about his detective work, too. Now he wasn't sure of anything.

He needed to stay in Holly Springs with Papa. And he needed to take care of his sister's children.

But the big question was Erica.

Could he forgive her? Could she forgive him?

The church bells rang, announcing that services would start soon. Jason closed his eyes and slumped forward, elbows on knees, his forehead on his folded hands.

Ten minutes later, he still wasn't certain what to do, but he'd gained a measure of peace. The Lord didn't leave His sheep without a shepherd.

He stood and looked out the window into the twilight-darkened parking lot. People were starting to arrive for services.

And it hit him like a missile.

The box the postman had delivered.

Brian had mentioned that a box of Kimmie's belongings should be on its way.

Was it possible…?

He strode out of the pastor's office and into the parking lot, almost running to his truck. He grabbed the box from the back and brought it up into the cab, turning on the vehicle for warmth, clicking on the interior light.

He studied the package. An Arizona return address.

Hands shaking, he used his pocketknife to slit the tape and opened the flaps. Inside, there was a stack of envelopes held together with a rubber band and about four or five newspaper-wrapped items.

He set the letters aside and was opening the first packet when there was a knock on the window.

He lowered it.

Outside was Darien, the father from the couple who had given birth in the cabin. "Dude, mind if I get in for a minute?"

Yes. "No. Come around." He clicked open the locks and moved the box from the passenger seat to the middle.

"I got a ride here," Darien told him. "Hoping I'd see you. Thanks for setting us up with rent, man!"

Jason nodded. "Glad to do it. How're Caylene and the baby?"

"They're great. We're gonna live in a carriage house that belongs to one of my aunts. Now that we can pay rent, the relatives are being a little nicer."

"Good." Jason's eyes strayed to the box on the gear area between them.

"What's that?"

He picked up the packet he'd been opening, too curious to wait for Darien to leave. "Stuff from my sister." He cleared his throat. "She passed away recently."

"Sorry, man."

Inside the packet, metal clanked together. He got it open. "Gran's cookie cutters." He cocked his head to one side. "Wonder why she kept these."

"Must've been important to her."

"Yeah." Jason thought back. "At Christmas, as soon as us kids got there, Gran and Kimmie would always bake a bunch of cookies." He remembered it like yesterday, them laughing and talking, bringing out the final results for him and Papa to rave over and eat. Under Gran's watchful eye, the cookies had always turned out well. Good memories.

"What're these?" Darien was holding the stack of envelopes. "They all have your name on them, man." He held them out to Jason.

"I don't..." Jason shook his head. "I don't think I can deal with these right now."

Darien flipped through and whistled. "Some of these look pretty beat-up. But this top one here looks new. Maybe it's recent." He handed it to Jason.

Jason couldn't deal with it, but he couldn't resist it, either. He opened it up and read the first line:

I'm sorry I'm not what you think I am, but please don't hold it against my sons.

His throat tightened and he couldn't speak. He kept reading and learned that the reason Kimmie had relapsed into drugs was her terminal diagnosis. And that she'd strayed away from her faith, but with Erica's help, she'd read her Bible and discussed Jesus and prayed in the last days.

Erica is really a special woman. If you're reading this, give her a chance.

Words of wisdom from beyond the grave.

At first, I wanted Erica to keep the twins away from you. But now, I keep remembering the good times. I love you, Jason, and I know you love me. I hope you'll give that love to my sons.

Jason's chest hurt. He closed his eyes.

"Check this out." Darien nudged him, reached into the box and pulled out a plastic sleeve with official-looking papers inside.

Darien pointed to the top document, visible through the plastic. "That's a keepsake birth certificate," he said. "Just got one of those for our boy today. See the footprint? And then you order the official one online."

"What's the Post-it say?" Jason heard the hoarseness in his own voice.

"For Erica Lindholm." Darien held the packet closer to the dome light. "Looks like there's medical records in here, too."

So Kimmie *had* meant for Erica to have the babies.

Jason didn't trust his voice, but he pulled the one remaining packet from the box, hard and flat. With trembling hands, he opened it.

Inside was an old picture frame he recognized as one Papa had made, years back, from barn siding. The photo in the frame was of the twins. He studied it, trying to figure out what looked familiar.

It was their clothes. They were just a little out-of-date.

They were Jason's own baby clothes. He'd seen them in photographs. In fact, Teddy's outfit was the one in the Santa picture back at the house.

How had Kimmie managed to keep those clothes for all these years, for all her moves through the gutter?

A whole wave of memories came back to him then. How Kimmie had loved dolls, had collected them when she got too old to actually play with them. How she'd showed him outfits that had belonged to him as a baby, outfits she'd saved from the trash or donation bin.

She'd told him how she'd played with him like a doll when he was a baby, and though Jason had no memory of it, he suspected that a good portion of the mother love he'd gotten had come from Kimmie rather than their mother.

And she'd kept his baby clothes, put them on her own sons.

He stared up at the ceiling of the truck to keep the tears in his eyes from falling.

"What's up with the picture?"

Jason drew in a deep breath. Let it out slowly, and then repeated the process. Cleared his throat. "My sister helped raise me and I guess she kept my baby clothes. She put them on her twins for this picture."

"Wow, heavy."

It *was* heavy, but Jason felt like a huge weight was lifting off his shoulders.

Kimmie had kept these things. She'd loved him and had remembered Gran and Papa warmly. She'd wanted

Erica to have the twins, and she'd wanted Jason to give Erica a chance.

Kimmie hadn't been perfect. And that was okay.

Erica wasn't perfect. Also okay.

And that meant Jason didn't have to be perfect, either.

A strange warmth came over him. He looked out at the parking lot, where more and more people were heading into the church, to celebrate the birth of the Christ child.

He grabbed Darien's hand and pumped it. "Thanks."

"Anytime, dude. I gotta get back to Caylene and the baby. You hang in there, hear? Let me know if there's anything I can do for you."

After Darien left, Jason put the precious items back into the box and set it on the seat behind him. Then he dropped his head into his hands. *I'll do what You tell me, Lord. Not my will but Thine.* He left the truck and walked into the church foyer.

As soon as he got inside, he saw Erica. Her back was to him, and she wore a green dress that hugged her slender silhouette and showed off her clouds of red hair. She had Mikey on her hip, and Papa walked beside her, holding a squirming Teddy.

His impulse was to go to them, but he was trying to follow God, not his impulses. So he leaned against the church wall and just watched and thought.

He loved her—he knew that. His feelings for any woman in his past paled in comparison.

But love was tricky and messy and people didn't live up to his standards. More important, he himself didn't live up to his own standards. The question was, did he want to hold back and judge, or did he want to wade in?

And if he made the latter choice, was he healed enough to do it right this time?

She turned and looked over and saw him. He saw her mouth drop open a little, her posture tighten. Then she lifted her chin and held out her arms, low, palms facing him. As if she were offering him an embrace.

In front of all these people. He felt a wave of love for her that she would try.

But people surged around her, between them. Partly, of course, because the twins were so adorable. Partly because Papa was such a popular figure.

And partly because Erica was so incredibly appealing that all the males between fifteen and fifty were drawn to her like bees to a colorful flower.

Organ music rose up from the sanctuary, the signal for people to stop milling around and come in to worship. There was a general movement toward the sanctuary.

Jason had lost sight of Erica, but he was going to find her, no matter what.

Erica followed Papa into what was apparently his usual front-and-center seat in church. She probably would've chosen a seat in back, given that she had two wiggly babies to contend with, but she treasured that Papa had forgiven her, had wanted to come to church together.

When she'd seen Jason across the foyer, leaning against the wall, her heart had swelled with love for him.

Had she made a fool of herself, reaching out to him in that obvious way? He hadn't jumped into her arms, that was for sure.

On the other hand, maybe her gesture hadn't been clear enough. Maybe she should have run across the room to him and begged forgiveness. There would have been no ambiguity in that gesture, but it was totally against her nature.

People stood for the opening hymn, and she and Papa each scooped up a twin and joined their voices in "It Came Upon a Midnight Clear." The dimly lit sanctuary, smelling of fresh pine and spruce, the advent wreath at the front of the church, the greenery and red bows decorating the pews and railings—all of it brought her calm. Not joy, not yet, but calm.

It was a time of new life, new birth. She wanted so badly for that new life to be right here, raising the twins with their great-grandfather and their uncle.

And her prayers this afternoon had reminded her that she was forgiven, ultimately forgiven by God. That she had value and was worthy simply in Him, regardless of her own significant mistakes.

Feeling like she deserved love and good treatment and a chance—that would take a little more time. God had a lot of work to do in her, but she was starting on the path.

When it was time to share the peace, Papa tapped her shoulder and gestured toward a gray-haired man in a wheelchair, alone in the back of the church. "Need to go sit with Tommy. He's a Vietnam vet and this is his first time at church in years. He shouldn't be alone."

"Of course."

She cuddled the twins, one on either side of her, giving Mikey a board book to look at and Teddy a couple of colorful blocks. Surprisingly, they played quietly while the Bible passages and carols continued on.

They were so dear to her. How could she possibly say goodbye to them?

And what was in store for her afterward? A prison of loneliness? A real prison?

"Fear not, for behold, I bring you good news of great joy that will be for all the people."

Fear not. Erica repeated it to herself, over and over.

They were half an hour into the service when Teddy got restless. He slid down from the pew and tried to scoot along it, which was awesome—he'd walk soon—but he kept falling, and the effort to pull himself up again, the frustration of it, made him cry. Mikey, as was his way, babbled instructions, which got progressively louder.

Erica scooped Teddy up and put him on the seat beside her, but he wasn't having it. He cried harder.

Erica was starting to gather her things to leave when someone behind her picked Teddy up. She expected more crying, but instead he quieted down immediately.

She turned partway around.

It was Jason. "I'll hold him," he said, and his slight smile made her heart soar.

That hadn't been an "I hate you" smile.

With only Mikey to contend with, she was able to keep him entertained and even to listen and sing a little more. But she was hyperaware of the man behind her, singing in his deep bass voice, whispering to Teddy.

The lights dimmed for the candlelight part of the service, and as "Silent Night" echoed out from the choir and organ, Erica's heart filled to the brim.

Christ had been born for all of them. In this fallen world, how badly they all needed Him, and He had come.

God had seen fit to send His son to save sinners like her.

The candles were lit, person to person. She was struggling to keep hold of Mikey and sidle to the nearest person when Jason came around from his pew to hers. He lit her candle and met her eyes. "I'm sorry," he whispered.

"I'm sorry, too," she said.

And then she turned away to light her neighbor's candle and the twins babbled and everyone sang. But she was still unsure about the man next to her. What could it mean, his kindness, in contrast to the outrage he'd shown her yesterday?

Soon enough, the lights came back on. Joyous music rang out and people greeted each other, stopped to chat. Children shouted and ran with the excitement of staying up late and presents to come.

Ruth and Papa Andy approached as the crowd thinned out. Without a word, each took a twin, and they headed toward the reception in the foyer of the church.

That left Erica and Jason alone together, side by side.

His arm was draped along the back of the pew, behind her but not touching. "I've been thinking—"

"So have I, and, Jason, I'm so sorry."

He opened his mouth to speak again and she held up a hand. "Let me say this. I was wrong to pretend the twins were mine. Especially as you and I got closer. It was deceptive and that's a horrible thing to do. I was trying to do the right thing, but that's no excuse. I just... I really care for you, Jason, and I apologize for the wrong I did to you."

He looked at the floor, then met her eyes. "Thank you for that."

And then there was no sound but the organ music and a little distant chatter as people left the sanctuary.

Was that all? Erica wondered. Now that she'd apologized, were they done?

And then he took her hand and held it. "I've made a lot of mistakes in my life. One of them was saying some pretty harsh things to you, things that came out of my sadness about Kimmie and my anger at myself, more than being about you." He shook his head, looking away, then looked back at her. "I can be judgmental. A perfectionist. I've been like that all my life, but I'm trying to improve. I was hurt by what you did, but I shouldn't have said those things to you." He paused, cleared his throat. "To the woman I love."

"To the woman you…" Erica's heart pounded so quickly she couldn't catch her breath. "You *love* me?"

He nodded and smiled, touching her cheek. "Is that so hard to believe?"

She laughed a little as tears rose to her eyes. Jason wasn't angry anymore. He wasn't expecting her to be perfect.

He *loved* her.

A lifetime of feeling inadequate seemed to rise up in her like a wave, and then crash and dissipate. "Yes, it's hard to believe," she whispered. "You might have to tell me more than once."

"Then you'll…" He broke off. "We should be practical."

"Practical?" She lifted her eyebrows and clutched his hand. She'd never had an experience like this and didn't know how it was supposed to go. But *practical*?

"I want to stay in Holly Springs, at Holly Creek

Farm. Papa needs me, and I...I owe it to him to be here, like he was here for me and Kimmie."

"Of course," she said, hardly breathing.

"I can find work here. Probably police work, but there's so much to do on the farm, as well. I need to figure all that out."

She nodded. Inside, she was thinking, *He wants career counseling? Really?*

"Look, I'm making a mess of this because I don't know... How do you feel about me, Erica? Would you want to..."

She closed her eyes for a moment. *You have value. And you're strong.* "My dream would be to stay here, too, and to raise the twins with you."

There. She'd said it and it was out on the table.

"Like, coparenting?" He shook his head. "No. Erica, that's not going to be enough for me. I know it might take you a while to have the feelings, but I'd like to try to move toward a true, permanent partnership. Toward..." He swallowed. "Toward marriage."

"You want to *marry* me?"

"Kimmie knew what she was doing when she left us each half of the farm, I think," he stumbled on.

Was that true? Would Kimmie have left her part of the farm because she was *matchmaking*? Erica's head spun and her heart pounded. Jason loved her. He wanted to marry her.

"I know it's soon and we haven't known each other long, but—"

"But sometimes you just know," she interrupted, her eyes pinned on his face. "I love you, Jason. And my answer is yes. Yes, let's move toward marriage but I...I'm pretty sure that my answer is yes, forever."

He pulled her into his strong arms, and Erica knew she had found the home and the family—and the Christmas—she'd always dreamed of.

Epilogue

Twelve months later

Erica tucked the blanket tighter around Teddy and Mikey, nestled in back of the old sleigh.

"Ready everyone?" Up front, Papa made a clicking sound with his tongue, and the horses started to move.

"Ready as we'll ever be." Jason held Mistletoe by the collar and reached across the twins to squeeze Erica's shoulder.

As they approached the covered bridge, white with a simple Christmas wreath, Erica couldn't help but remember the first time she'd ridden in the sleigh, one year ago. Her life had undergone a radical change she never could have envisioned, and she was loving it.

Sunlight caught her wedding ring, making it sparkle like fire.

Papa cleared his throat. "Thought I'd stop and pick up Ruth," he said over his shoulder.

Erica looked at Jason, raising her eyebrows.

He leaned over. "Maybe Papa has some news to share, too," he whispered.

As they approached Ruth's house, Mistletoe spotted a rabbit and started barking, straining to escape Jason's strong grip.

"No, Miss-toe!" Mikey scolded.

"No, Miss-toe," Teddy echoed.

"Are you sure it's okay to bring the dog along?" Erica asked as Papa jumped spryly out of the sleigh and strode up the sidewalk to Ruth's front door, sporting its Tiny Tykes sign—a spot very familiar to Erica, since she'd spent a lot of time working there in the past year.

"Mrs. Habler wants to try him out as a camel in the pageant, and Hank promised to watch him during the service. He and his friend are running the hot chocolate and cider stand for Sleigh Bell Sunday." Jason shrugged. "Could be a disaster, but they insisted."

Ruth came out, dressed all in red, and Papa helped her into the front of the sleigh.

She twisted around to see the twins, laughing at them and pinching their rosy cheeks.

"Roof, Roof!" they said in rapturous voices, their adoration obvious.

"And don't you both look handsome in your new snowsuits," she said. "New boots, too!"

"Boots," Teddy agreed, holding a leg out.

Ruth looked over at Erica. "Honey, do you think you can sub for a few hours tomorrow? I know you want part-time, but—"

"Of course, no problem. You know I love the center." Erica gave Jason and the boys a mock-stern glare. "Just as long as these three let me study for my test tonight. You're not on duty, are you?" she asked Jason.

"No more evenings, remember? That was my condition for the promotion." Jason was enjoying small-town police work, but he was clear about making time for family. "And it's hard for me to let you study, but I'll do my best."

Erica blushed. "Leave your hat on, Teddy," she ordered as the sleigh drove on.

"No!" He looked up at her to see what she thought of his opinion.

"Told you he'd started his terrible twos," Ruth sang out from the front seat. "He's late, but you're not going to escape them."

"I know." But she relished every stage the twins went through. And now she could look forward to sharing every future stage with Jason. She snuggled down under the blanket, Teddy on her lap now, Jason at her side with Mikey on his lap, the dog at her feet. Papa and Ruth in the front seat.

Glorious stuff, for a girl who'd never had a real family.

At the church, they tied up and the twins were immediately off, shouting and running in the snow under Ruth's watchful eye. Papa started to follow them, but Jason put a hand on his grandfather's arm. "Papa," he said, "we have some news."

Papa stood still and looked from Jason to Erica. "Is it what I think it is?"

Jason nodded. "A little girl."

Papa folded them into his arms. "I was already happy, but you two young people just made me even happier."

Erica pulled back so she could look up at both of them. "I've been thinking about names," she said. "If it's okay with the two of you…I'd like to call her Kimmie."

It was just as well the church bells rang at that moment, because none of them could speak. They just stood, holding on to each other as the twins came back to grab legs and Mistletoe barked to be let out of the sleigh.

Full circle. Erica lifted her face to heaven with a prayer of gratitude and joy. And it seemed to her that her old friend Kimmie, all sins forgotten, must be smiling down at the entire family.

* * * * *

If you enjoyed this story, try these books in
the RESCUE RIVER *miniseries*
from Lee Tobin McClain!

ENGAGED TO THE SINGLE MOM
HIS SECRET CHILD
SMALL-TOWN NANNY
THE SOLDIER AND THE SINGLE MOM
THE SOLDIER'S SECRET CHILD

Available now from Love Inspired!

***

And don't miss the next
CHRISTMAS TWINS *story,*
TEXAS CHRISTMAS TWINS
by Deb Kastner,
available December 2017!

Find more great reads at www.LoveInspired.com

Dear Reader,

I've always been fascinated with twins, so research for this book has been a joy! Watching videos of how baby twins "talk" to each other, mock-shopping for Christmas outfits and peppering every twin parent I know about their memories of the early years...what could be more fun? And since my own daughter benefited from early intervention services, it made me happy to give a nod to the amazing work doctors and therapists do to help babies catch up.

I also loved figuring out Erica and Jason's story. Both of them have baggage from childhood hurts, and both are insecure about their ability to make a relationship work. But as they discover, God is there to help all of us grow closer to perfection, as we seek Him and follow His will.

My prayer is that each of you experiences love and peace this Christmas season. Please visit my website at www.leetobinmcclain.com and stay in touch. I love to hear from readers!

Warmest Christmas wishes,
Lee

COMING NEXT MONTH FROM
Love Inspired®

Available November 21, 2017

TEXAS CHRISTMAS TWINS
Christmas Twins • by Deb Kastner

All Miranda Morgan wants for Christmas is to be a good mom to the twins she's been named guardian of—but their brooding cowboy godfather, Simon West, isn't sure she's ready. Can they learn to trust in each other and become a real family for the holidays?

HER AMISH CHRISTMAS SWEETHEART
Women of Lancaster County • by Rebecca Kertz

When Peter Zook and Meg Stoltzfus are forced to work side by side to throw a surprise Christmas party, they struggle to put their long-held differences aside. Yet as they succeed in their planning, they realize they have a lot in common—and that opposites really do attract!

AMISH TRIPLETS FOR CHRISTMAS
by Carrie Lighte

Spinster schoolteacher Hannah Lantz had given up on having a husband and children—until Sawyer Plank asks her to be nanny to his triplets. Now she's falling for the handsome widower and putting a future together on her Christmas wish list.

THE RANCHER'S CHRISTMAS BRIDE
Bluebonnet Springs • by Brenda Minton

Unable to face family and friends after being left at the altar, Marissa Walker goes searching for the grandfather she's never met. But she couldn't imagine the holidays would bring a second chance at love with her grandfather's neighbor, rugged rancher next door Alex Palermo.

THE CHRISTMAS BABY
by Lisa Carter

Pregnant widow Anna Reyes returns to her seaside town for the holidays and reunites with her first love, Ryan Savage. Ryan hopes to go back to the career he once sacrificed, but as they work together with three at-risk kids, he's realizing his friendship with Anna is turning into a wish for forever.

THE DEPUTY'S HOLIDAY FAMILY
Rocky Mountain Heroes • by Mindy Obenhaus

Lacie Collier makes a trip to her hometown to give her orphaned niece the cherished Christmas traditions she had growing up. Reuniting with her childhood crush, deputy Matt Stephens, throws a wrench in Lacie's plans—and her heart—when they discover he's little Kenzie's real dad!

LICNM1117

Get 2 Free Books,
<u>Plus</u> 2 Free Gifts—
just for trying the Reader Service!

Love Inspired®

LI17R2

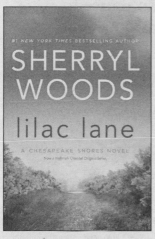

Inspirational Romance to Warm Your Heart and Soul

Join our social communities to connect with other readers who share your love!

Sign up for the Love Inspired newsletter at **www.LoveInspired.com** to be the first to find out about upcoming titles, special promotions and exclusive content.

CONNECT WITH US AT:

Harlequin.com/Community

 Facebook.com/LoveInspiredBooks

 Twitter.com/LoveInspiredBks

LISOCIAL2017

THE
TROUBLE
WITH
LEMONS

Daniel Hayes

SCHOLASTIC INC.

New York Toronto London Auckland Sydney
Mexico City New Delhi Hong Kong Buenos Aires

Copyright © 1991 by Daniel Hayes.
All rights reserved. Published by Scholastic Inc., 557 Broadway, New York, NY 10012, by arrangement with David R. Godine, Publisher, Inc.
Printed in the U.S.A.

ISBN 0-439-12415-8

SCHOLASTIC and associated logos and designs are trademarks and/or registered trademarks of Scholastic Inc.

LEXILE is a registered trademark of MetaMetrics, Inc.

1 2 3 4 5 6 7 8 9 10   23   13 12 11 10 09 08 07 06 05

LYMIE TOLD ME we'd be sorry if we went. Which I didn't listen to, seeing how Lymie was the kind of kid who thought you'd be sorry if you got out of bed in the morning. Besides, nobody ever really listened to Lymie. Not even Lymie.

But this time he was right.

I suppose it had to happen sooner or later, Lymie's being right, that is. It's the law of averages or something. And it didn't surprise me that in Lymie's muddled-up mind, his warning me proved that all the trouble that followed was *my* fault. Of course he doesn't say how it was his idea to go swimming, not mine, and if we'd stayed out of the water, nothing would have happened. At least not to us.

Sure, it was my idea for us to sneak out to the quarry that night. But only to see it. Period. I'd discovered the quarry by accident a few weeks earlier and it was wicked cool, this huge basin of gray-green water sitting right there in the middle of nowhere, surrounded by these solid rock walls like a miniature Grand Canyon or something. I couldn't believe my eyes. It was the kind of place part of you'd like to keep all to yourself, but another part of you'd like to bring all your friends to. Only since we were hardly a week into the new school year, and since school was already out for the summer when I moved to Wakefield, and since I'm kind of quiet anyway, all my friends stood for Lymie. And if it wasn't for Mom, I wouldn't've even had Lymie. She'd met Lymie's mother at the Wakefield library one day and after that we used to drive out to this farm she lived on for fresh eggs and milk and stuff. And this lady just happened to have a kid my age, and Mom just happened to invite him over all the time. I knew it was a setup because Mom is one of these lowfat, low-cholesterol people who wouldn't be caught dead eating an egg, and any milk my family used was bound to be skim.

It worked though. Lymie and I did end up being best friends. But not right off the bat. And it wasn't easy. For starters, Lymie and I are like total opposites. I'm a city kid; Lymie's a farm kid. I'm on the thin side; Lymie's on the chubby side. I'm a strict vegetarian; Lymie thinks real men eat cows and pigs and stuff. That kind of thing. But the real problem was Lymie'd always do a million things that'd drive me crazy. Like if he'd see a Porsche or something, he'd make barfing noises and go, "Piece of foreign junk," even though he knew my brother had a Porsche. And if he saw a Trans Am or something jacked up in the back so high it looked like it was getting ready to do a headstand, he'd whack me in the arm and go, "You wanna see a car? Now there's a car." Early on, about the only thing we agreed on was that at least a couple of times a day we'd have to try to punch each other's faces in.

2

Still for some reason our mothers seemed to think we'd be good for each other.

I asked Chuckie about the quarry (Chuckie's our groundskeeper), and all he told me was to stay away from the place or I'd probably end up drowning because the water was about fifty feet deep all across it. And if I didn't drown, he told me I'd get arrested for trespassing. Big help. Lymie was no better. He'd never even seen it. That really blew me away, him having lived in Wakefield his whole life. Talk about not taking an interest in your environment.

The quarry wasn't much more than a mile from my house and I'd walked there alone quite a few times. They had signs stuck up all over the place warning you to keep out unless you wanted to get prosecuted, and every once in a while somebody did. A couple of nights after I found the place, the Miller sisters were arrested there with two college guys. They were all in the water swimming away and when the cops pulled in with their spotlight and told them to get out, they did. Only according to the two deputies, they weren't wearing anything and the girls started doing like a hula dance or something right on the rocks. In the spotlight. Everybody was talking about it. Their father was some big minister who'd run for the school board because he said there were dirty books in the school library (Lymie checked and couldn't find any), and everybody said he almost busted a blood vessel. He even tried to get the cops fired for not turning off their light.

That story didn't mean much to me, not really knowing these people, except it got me thinking about checking out the quarry at night. Places are different at night, and a place that beautiful in the daytime would probably knock your socks off in the moonlight. But having been raised under streetlights, I'm no Daniel Boone, and traipsing through the wilderness at night wasn't something I was about to do. Not alone anyway.

That's where Lymie figured in. Even though he moans and complains, it's usually not so tough for me to get him to do what I want. I knew Lymie was staying over that Saturday night so I slept in that morning like I do on New Year's Eve or any other day when I know I'll want to stay up late. And as soon as Lymie got there I started building up the place, painting this cool picture in his mind. Plus, I reminded him about the Miller sisters' episode. With Lymie's mentality, something like that elevated the place to a historical landmark practically. It didn't hurt either, my telling him that our housekeeper, Mrs. Saunders, was a heavy sleeper. She wasn't really. But she was kind of heavy. And she would be sleeping.

"It's almost midnight," Lymie had said for about the hundredth time after we left my house. "I must be crazy."

"Yeah, what else is new?" I said finally, backpedaling and watching Lymie chug along, his pudgy face all scrunched up with effort. Between complaints he'd click his tongue and burp. Lymie was always snorting or belching or something, like he thought the whole purpose of his head was to make goofy noises. He's kind of a funny kid.

Passing the last streetlight on the edge of town, we took a left into the shadows and hopped a gate into this huge pasture. With the moon almost full, seeing was no problem. I followed a zigzaggy cow trail, watching my step closely to make sure I didn't step in anything

4

some cow might have left behind. I could hear Lymie muttering and snorting and clicking right at my heels. Pretty soon I slipped through a barbed wire fence on the other side. Nothing but a bunch of brush and some bushes separated us from the quarry now.

"Okay, Lymie, you gotta be quiet till we make sure nobody's there."

"Yeah, Tyler," Lymie sputtered as I tried to unsnag his shirt from the barbed wire, "like the whole stupid world is probably climbing out of bed in the middle of the night and ripping its clothes to get to this stupid place. Duh!"

Lymie always said "duh" when he thought I was saying something dumb. He said it quite a bit.

I started down the narrow path, probably an animal path or something, that led to the water's edge. The brush was alive with mysterious squeaks and twitterings and buzzes. I stood still for a second and pricked up my ears. I could make out the sound of crickets and a few tree toads maybe, but that was it. The rest was pure mystery, like we were surrounded by some kind of strange and secret world out there in the shadows. I felt kind of like Alice in Wonderland or something (if she'd been a guy).

"Lymie," I whispered. "Listen."

Lymie let out this big belch. Then I could hear him scratching himself.

"Listen to what?"

I remembered who I was talking to.

"Forget it," I told him.

"Forget what?" he said. "First you get all spastic and act like you heard something and then you say forget it."

5

"Just shut up, Lymie."

"You're the one that started talking, dirtbag."

That's the kind of exchange that might have led to us punching each other out earlier in the summer, but we hardly ever did that any more. Lymie didn't notice the same things I did. That's all there was to it. And it wouldn't matter if I beat him over the head with a two-by-four.

We tiptoed forward and before we knew it the path opened into a clearing, and we could see the water. A slight breeze blew our way, and you could tell by the sound of the leaves around us that they were getting ready to change color. They were drier and rustlier than a month ago. And the moon made one of those rippling orange ribbons that stretched from one side of the water to the other. I held my breath. It was beautiful.

I turned to check if Lymie appreciated any of this and was surprised to see he was all wide-eyed. In fact, you'd think he'd just inhaled a fly or something. I looked where he was looking. Across the water on the entrance lane, less than a hundred yards from where we stood, was the lighted red interior of a car. The light hadn't been there a few seconds ago. A guy in a dark jacket climbed into the driver's seat. Another figure sat on the passenger side. Before I could make out much else, the door slammed, plunging the car into darkness again. The engine rumbled, a big V-8 from the sound of it, and the car peeled out, splattering pebbles across the water. Tires screeched as the car skidded onto the highway. Finally the headlights came on, flashing like a strobe light through the trees as the car sped toward town.

"I wonder who that was," Lymie whispered.

"Beats me," I said. "It's kinda weird how they took off like that. Maybe they saw us. You think?"

"Yeah, Tyler, real smart. Like they're old enough to drive and they're gonna panic when they see a couple of eighth graders sneaking through the bushes. Duh!"

"They don't know we're eighth graders, cow breath."

"Oh, yeah, Ty. I forgot how big and tough you look in the dark. We're lucky they didn't have heart attacks right on the spot. We coulda got sued."

He laughed and shoved me to the side in case I might have forgotten he was stronger than me, something Lymie always had to prove. I jabbed at him but without much interest. Big deal, so he thought I was scrawny. I was a runner like my brother Christopher, and no runner in his right mind wanted to be built like Lymie. He might not be what you'd call fat, but he was a little too close to it for my taste.

I sat on the rock ledge dangling my feet over the water. Lymie did too. We were quiet for a long time, looking around and listening to make sure we had the place to ourselves. Gradually I relaxed enough so I could start soaking up the atmosphere. Lymie fidgeted.

"Hey, Lymie," I said, feeling like I had to entertain him, "I'll show you where I scratched my name on the rock wall. It's right under us."

"Boy, Ty, you really know how to show somebody a good time."

We rolled to our stomachs and peered down the side of the rock wall over the water. Lymie struck a match and immediately let out a whoop. Etched in big upside-down letters I saw:

and under that, or over it, I guess, in big scribbly letters:

SUCKS

"Oh, no," I moaned. I swear to God you could carve your name on the inside of a double-locked cast iron safe and when you opened it back up somebody'd've written something nasty about you.

"Whoever did that must know you," Lymie said, elbowing me and yucking it up for all he was worth. " 'Cause they sure got the facts right!"

"Don't be a jerk, Lyme," I told him.

"Hey, *I'm* not the jerk," he said laughing. "You're the one who got caught taking a snooze in Old Lady Waverly's class the other day, not me. My whole bus was talking about it."

I groaned, remembering for the thousandth time how it felt waking up eye to eye with Old Lady Waverly, and everyone in the class giggling and gawking at me. It was like waking into a bad dream. My first week at a new school and already I looked like a total spazola. Exactly the kind of thing Lymie would find amusing.

"You're pitiful, Lymie. You can't appreciate anything unless it's totally stupid."

"Why do you think I hang around with you?" That cracked him up all over again. "Boy, everybody said Old Lady Waverly really went hyper. It must have been great."

"Yeah, Lyme. I'm real sorry you had to miss it," I said sullenly.

Finding a rock, I began scratching out somebody's lame excuse for a joke. Lymie lit matches for me and kept up with the stupid cracks. I scratched out a large area surrounding my name so it'd be harder for anyone else to add their two cents' worth.

"So, Ty, when is Chris coming here again?" The last match flickered out and Lymie rolled to his back and stared up at the stars.

"I don't know." I chucked my rock into the bushes, hard, and turned to my side. "Not till Thanksgiving probably."

"And your mom?"

"In a few weeks maybe. Depends how her shooting schedule goes."

"Awesome," Lymie said. "I can't believe I actually know two movie stars. Me . . . Lymie Lawrence." He grabbed his head. "Then again, why not me? I'm good looking. I'm bright. I'm . . ."

"You're an idiot."

"I'd like a second opinion."

I knew he was waiting for me to say he was ugly too, but I wasn't in the mood to play along. Sometimes I wished my mother and brother did something normal for a living like delivering mail or teaching school. Something where you didn't have to constantly trek all over the planet. It was the same with my father when he was alive. Only he was a producer.

I hadn't seen my mom or Chris since last month when I was in the hospital with a concussion. I'd been sleepwalking and fell down the stairs. (The doctors said that was a first.) Christopher came all the way from our old house in Los Angeles and Mom came all the way from where she was shooting on location in Colombia. First thing Chris said when he saw me was, "I told Mom we should make you sleep on a leash, Timmy Tyler, but she said your head was unbreakable." Mom had poked him in the side and said, "Now don't you pay any attention to him, Tyler," but she knew I didn't mind the teasing.

I answer to a lot of different names. See, Mom wanted to name me Tyler after her favorite uncle, and Dad had insisted on Timothy because he didn't like the name Tyler. Or Mom's favorite uncle either. So I ended up with both names. Mom and Mrs. Saunders called me Tyler (when they weren't calling me "lamb" and "doll" and that kind of thing), and my dad called me Timothy, and Chris, being in the middle, called me Timmy Tyler. Dad and Mom had already separated before I started school, and Mom put me down as T. Tyler McAllister on all my school records. So that's what I am officially.

"Hey, Ty," Lymie said, climbing to his feet. "Cut the moping act and let's go swimming."

I sat up and thought for a second. It wasn't really warm enough, but seeing how I'd dragged Lymie there, I said okay. We were both decent swimmers.

Lymie hopped out of his clothes and took a running leap into the water three feet below. Bobbing to the surface, he yelled, "This is great!" but knowing Lymie he would've said that if his head had smacked into an iceberg. I was freezing before I was half undressed, so I whipped off the rest of my clothes and dove in before I had a chance to change my mind.

The shock of the cold water took my breath away and

made me a little spastic for a few seconds. I knew pretty soon my teeth would start chattering like crazy. That's something that happens to skinny kids. Lymie could be packed in ice for two days and not get cold.

I warned Lymie not to swim too far from the low rocks about twenty feet to the right of where we'd dove in. That was one of the few places you could climb out without a long struggle. After all, we were naked. What if girls or cops or somebody pulled up in a car? I didn't feel like putting on a show like the Miller sisters.

As usual Lymie ignored me, but I paddled toward the low rocks. When I was close enough for a quick getaway, I rolled onto my back and floated. Kind of. If I didn't kick or stroke every so often, I'd sink like a rock. That's another advantage Lymie had. He could float on his back for a week without so much as wiggling his ears.

I was really getting into the silky cool feel water has when you skinny-dip, staring at the moon, letting my mind drift. Suddenly I felt something sliding down my back.

"Watch it, Lymie, you weirdo."

"What's your problem now, hyper-spaz?"

A shiver shot up my spine which seemed to lift my hair. Lymie's voice was in front of me and quite a ways off. I lay frozen for a few seconds, afraid to move, praying that some big friendly fish was getting into rubbing my backside. Then, taking a deep breath, I flipped to my stomach. My hands pushed into a heavy, wet, woolly thing. As I instinctively thrust the thing away, something rose up out of the darkness into the moonlight. And I saw it.

11

A face, pale and bloated. And hands, slimy hands reaching for my throat.

I jabbed at it. I kicked at it. I felt the bone on bone of my elbow on its head. As I broke away something slid down my stomach and I came up hard with my knee, so hard my head went under. My feet pushed off it and I came up screaming.

"Lymie! Lymie! OH MY GOD, LYMIE!"

I might have screamed out of control for a week if I hadn't sucked up a mouthful of water. Gagging, I beat a hysterical path toward the shore until my head bashed into the rock ledge. I clawed my way over the bluff, scraping elbows and knees, and flopped belly down on the cold rock platform, choking, gasping for air. Cold water pumped painfully out my nose, and I thought I'd suffocate for sure. My head throbbed and my heart pounded against my rib cage.

Something touched my shoulder and I almost left my body.

"Tyler, you all right? Come on, can you breathe, man?" Lymie was out of breath and his voice trembled.

"Did you see . . ." I gasped, my chest heaving in fits and starts. "Did you . . ."

"Shut up!" Lymie yelled. "I saw it. Just breathe, will you!" He yanked me up and shook me like a rag doll. He probably thought I was having one of my asthma attacks.

"I almost drowned . . . It was grabbing at me!"

"Shut up, Tyler. Just breathe!" Lymie sounded like he wanted to cry, but by now I was crying enough for both of us. He tugged my arm. "Come on. We gotta get dressed and get out of here."

My teeth jackhammered away as I struggled into my

clothes. I kept peeking back at the water, half expecting something to crawl out. I felt my shirt rip as I tried to jam my wet arms through the arm holes. Lymie finished getting dressed and leaned over the ledge.

"I can see it, Ty. Under the water. Come 'ere."

Dropping my other sneaker, I crept up beside him. As much as I dreaded it, I knew I had to look. Maybe I had to see for myself that the thing was dead and powerless. I gasped when I saw it, a man, floating at an incline with arms and legs outstretched, like a freeze frame of a hopping frog.

Then I threw up, right into the water. Lymie held my belt so I wouldn't fall in. He didn't need to worry. There was no way I was going back in there.

II

E VEN MY ROOM felt cold. I was freezing to death in the comfort of my own home.

We knew we had to call somebody about the body, but we weren't sure who. Lymie said the rescue squad, but I told him that guy was way beyond being rescued. And Lymie said to forget about the village police because the quarry was out of their jurisdiction, and they wouldn't care. So it was a toss-up between the sheriff and the troopers. Lymie knew the sheriff's son and had even been to his house a few times. According to him, the sheriff was a pretty decent guy.

Neither of us wanted to make the call. Lymie claimed the sheriff might recognize his voice, so I was elected. I was still shivering something wicked even though I had thrown on dry pants and two sweatshirts, and I was wrapped in this electric blanket my father's aunt had given me because she said New York'd be cold. I had it cranked up all the way. My breathing still hadn't settled down to the point where talking was that easy. Lymie and I sat on my bed for a while staring at the phone.

"Lymie, I can't. I don't know what to say."

"It's easy, Tyler. Tell them there's a dead guy floating in the quarry. And that somebody should get him out."

"If it's so easy, why don't you do it?"

"I told you. If the sheriff recognizes my voice, I'm dead. My parents would ground me till I'm ready to retire." Lymie picked up the receiver and started dialing. "The longer you wait, the harder it'll be. And remember, NO NAMES." He stuck the phone in my face.

Taking a couple of deep, hitching breaths, I grabbed the phone, closed my eyes, and tried to rehearse what I'd say.

"Sheriff's office." The deep voice sounded tired and annoyed.

"Hello, Sheriff . . . this is . . . ooof!" Lymie had slammed his elbow into my ribs. "Is this who you'd call if you find a person who's dead?" My voice was really shaking now and I had a pretty good idea how stupid I sounded.

"Look, kid, if this is some kind of a joke . . ."

"No, you gotta believe me. This is for real!" I was almost shouting now. "We found this dead guy and we don't know who he is or anything . . ."

"All right. All right. Slow down, son. Take it easy. Where did you find him?" The guy sounded nicer now. He talked slower and softer, like he thought I might be hysterical. I almost was.

"At the quarry. We were swimming." I drew in more air. "I swam right into him."

"I see. And this would be the Wakefield Quarry?"

"Yeah, right outside of town. You better . . ."

"And where are you now? Are you all right?"

"Me? Yeah, I'm all right now. But I coulda drowned! I was . . ."

"Settle down, son. Take it easy. How many of you were there?"

"Two of us. My friend and me. Plus the dead guy."

"Listen, son, we're going to need your name and the name of your friend."

"No."

"It's important, son. We need to make sure you're all right. And we'd like to talk to you. I know how you feel. You're afraid that . . ."

Lymie snatched the receiver from my hand and slammed it down. Good thing too, because I can never hang up on anybody, let alone a sheriff.

"Tyler, don't you know they're probably tracing your call? You told them about the body. It's their problem now." Lymie looked at me sitting on the bed all scrunched up in my blanket. "You think they believed you?"

"Yeah, I sounded like too much of a jerk to be playing a joke."

"Boy, finding that body really spazzed you out, didn't it? Your hands are shaking like crazy."

I looked at him. "I don't get it, Lymie. Usually when I wrestle with a dead guy and almost drown, I'm much better than this."

"Sorry. But I've never seen you this way." He paused. "Still pretty cold, huh?"

"I think I'm going to be cold for the rest of my life." I scrunched even tighter into the blanket so only my eyes were showing.

We sat silently. We were both exhausted but neither

of us wanted to go to bed. Lymie was clicking his tongue the way he always does when he thinks.

"Ty?"

"Yeah?"

"Who do you suppose he was? I mean, I know you probably don't like to think about it that much, but was there anything about him you can remember? Like how old was he? What color hair? Something."

The bloated face flashed before me again and I felt the cold, slimy hands sliding down me for the fiftieth time. I gulped and fought back another wave of panic and nausea.

"I don't know. It was pretty dark. And I didn't exactly stick around to pose with the guy. He was pretty big, I think. Definitely not a kid."

"Yeah, well, it doesn't matter," Lymie said, putting his feet up and lying back on the pillow. "The police will figure out who he is."

We were quiet for a long time, me huddled up in a ball and Lymie stretched out across the bed.

"Lymie?"

"Yeah?"

"What do you think happened to him?"

"That's easy. He drowned." Lymie sounded half asleep.

"Yeah, but if he was an adult, why would he be swimming at the quarry? That's more like something kids do."

"Who knows. Like he could have been a bum or something, just passing through. And he decided to take a bath, maybe."

"With all his clothes on?"

"Well, maybe he was a bum who was drinking, and he fell in. How should I know?"

"Lymie, what if he was murdered?" The thought sent another chill up my spine. "And what if we saw the murderers?"

"Naw, nobody ever gets murdered in Wakefield. That's city stuff."

"But remember how that car squealed outta there with no lights? I should have told the cops about the car. It might be a lead."

"A lead?" Lymie sat up and rolled his eyes. "You don't even know there was a crime, and already you're finding leads. 'Oh, and by the way, Sheriff, if you happen to see two people drive by in a car, you'd better arrest them. I have reason to believe they murdered someone and tossed them into the quarry.' Duh!"

"Don't be a jerk, hemorrhoid. I'm not in the mood. Besides we know the car had a red interior. And it sounded like one of those big jobbers with a V-8."

"I don't know, Ty. It's almost morning and I'm pooped. Let's go to bed and not think about it any more. By tomorrow they'll have the whole thing figured out."

Lymie stripped down to his underwear and climbed under the covers. Ordinarily when Christopher wasn't home, Lymie slept in his room. He got a charge out of having a room all to himself since he has to share his room with two little brothers. I was relieved he decided to stay in my room without me having to ask. If I was going to have bad dreams and go on another sleepwalking binge, tonight would be the night.

III

THE FACE RIPPLING in the water was my own. I glided effortlessly across the shimmering surface and the face floated under me, playfully bending and twisting itself into funny house-of-mirrors shapes. I lifted my head, and the face stretched long and thin like a horse's. I touched my nose to the water and the face mashed itself out, wide as a pancake. It was so funny I raised and lowered and turned my head again and again, fascinated by the fish-eye lens distortions of my features. I touched my nose to the water once more but now my nose touched a nose and I could feel it. I heard a "whoosh" and felt a splash as my other face disappeared, like it had been sucked beneath the black waters. I stopped gliding and waited, puzzled at this new game of hide-and-seek. I felt lonely now and wanted to go home. Suddenly a new face appeared, an evil face, pale, bloated, and leering. My heart pounded and I paddled with all my strength, but a strong current held me fast. As I flailed at the water, the face smiled. Rising up from the deep was a pale, puffy body with hands outstretched as if in silent prayer. Icy fingers clutched at my sides, and I screamed louder than I've ever screamed, but no sound came out. I kicked hard into the squishy belly and it burst, a black cloud rising from its tattered white edges. The swollen eyes stared in disbelief as I struck out wildly in every direction.

Now I was dry and running down a long hallway. Boys in blue uniforms with black stripes grabbed at me. I recognized one kid, a fat kid with a high pitched whiny voice. He took my arm and led me to a room, my room. When I turned to thank him, I saw that his face had become the evil face, and I lunged past him, knocking him to the floor. His cold hands snatched at my ankles and tore at my striped pants as I raced out the door, running until my throat and chest burned. The boys lining the hallway watched as I flew by. A foot tripped me, and I sprawled hard on my hands and elbows. Flopping to my back, I saw the boys gaping down at me. They too were wearing evil faces.

A man spoke softly. I knew the voice and peeked up to see my father smiling down at me. His gentle hands lifted me to my feet. My raw elbows throbbed with pain. I tried to tell him what I'd been through, but he didn't understand. When he saw my ripped clothes, he became angry and shook me. I told him it wasn't my fault, but he squeezed harder and shook harder until I squirmed and gasped for air. I grabbed at his hands and felt nothing but bone. Then before my eyes his face melted into a skull. I pulled myself free and suddenly I was alone again, cold and trembling.

Again, a hand on my arm. This time softer, shaking more gently. I pulled away, but I was too tired. I couldn't fight it any more.

"Tyler, honey, wake up. Come on. You're all right now. It's only a dream."

I blinked a few times and squinted up at Mrs. Saunders standing by my bed. Still bleary-eyed, I regarded her suspiciously, making sure I was awake and she was real. Her smile was warm, but her eyes looked worried. I turned to see Lymie wrapped in most of the covers, still snoozing peacefully. My sweatshirts were soaking wet and my pillow felt cold and damp. I grabbed a handful of blankets off Lymie and pulled them around my neck.

"You were having those dreams again, weren't you?" She sat on the edge of my bed and smoothed back the hair that was plastered to my temples. "I thought they had stopped."

"Yeah . . . me too." My voice sounded weak and hollow.

"Is this the first night?" Mrs. Saunders's forehead wrinkled as she peered down at me over her glasses. She was a big woman, and old, but the sort of old that made her seem kind and warm and understanding.

I nodded my head and pulled the covers more tightly around my chin.

"Was it bad? You don't look too good. You want to tell me about it?"

I couldn't keep her questions straight, so I just lay there staring up. She felt my forehead. Her hand was warm and soft and dry.

"You don't feel hot." She stood up, placed her hands on her large hips, and studied me. "Is it possible that the two of you disobeyed orders and decided to stay up half the night watching that trash on 'Chiller Theater'? Now look me in the eye and tell me the truth." She still looked a little worried, but her face was gradually growing more menacing. "Come on. Tell me the truth."

"Uh, uh," I mumbled. "We didn't. We didn't even have the TV on." I could feel her gaze trying to probe my head for secrets. I was too woozy to answer any more questions, so I flipped over and dunked my face into my soggy pillow.

"Well," she said, "I've never known you to lie. But I sometimes suspect you don't always tell me everything you know." Her voice was moving away from me. "But old ladies aren't supposed to know everything boys are up to. I lived through it with your brother, and God willing, I'll live through it with you."

I could hear the shades roll up, and when I lifted my head, the morning brightness splashed over my pillow. I rolled over and sat up, and tried to rub some life back into my head. Mrs. Saunders paused at the door and studied me again.

"If you're planning on running today, honey, you best get a move on. Your brother will be calling at noon."

I do a short run four or five days a week, but Sunday's my big day. I usually get in five or six miles on Sunday morning, and then when Chris calls, I give him my times. But today I didn't feel up to it.

"I think I'll pass on running today, Mrs. Saunders."

"That's fine with me," she said. "I'm always telling your mother I don't think all that running is good for you. You're too thin as it is. Well, come on then. Drag yourself out of bed. Maybe after a nice shower, you'll have enough energy to roll Lyman out. I'll expect you both down at the table in a half hour."

After Mrs. Saunders left, I collapsed on my back and managed somehow to slam my head into my headboard.

"Ow!" I popped back up and felt my head for a lump. I looked at my clock and noticed it was almost 11:00. Seeing how Lymie and I hardly ever slept past 8:00, I was lucky I hadn't had to field more questions.

I had to almost cook myself for ten minutes under the steamy water before I was warm clear through. Then I grabbed the soap. Mom told me when I was a little kid that if you used enough soap, you could practically scrub all your troubles and worries away. I knew now that she probably told me that so I wouldn't be so grubby, the way little kids usually are, but it's funny the way a suggestion can stick with you for life. To this day you can always tell my state of mind by how sudsed up I get in the shower. Today, within a few minutes my whole body was lathered up like that guy's face in the Gillette Foamy commercial.

Then I grabbed my lemon shampoo, the same kind I've used since before I could remember. When I was a little kid Christopher used to always call me the Lemon because my hair was so yellow and it always smelled lemony from that shampoo. I used to think that was funny. But then Mom got this car that was always conking out in the middle of nowhere, making her late for work and appointments and stuff. It was in the shop as much as it was on the street. At first I didn't know why, but I'd always stick up for that car, and every time we'd pick it up from the shop I'd tell Mom it was probably all fixed now. And I didn't know why I felt so lousy when Mom got rid of it. Mom couldn't figure it out either. She sat me down and tried to explain how the car had been nothing but a lemon from day one.

She told me how she could never really depend on it because even when they'd fix one thing, something else would go. She was always worried because she never knew what it'd do next. And that, she said, was the trouble with lemons. Then it finally dawned on me. Right while I was sitting there. I was just like that car. By the time I was ten, I'd been in and out of more doctors' offices than I could count. Mom and Chris thought it was dopey, me comparing myself to some dumb car, but I couldn't help it. If you looked at things objectively, I'd been ten times as much trouble as that car. And it was probably twenty times more expensive to keep me going. Only you're not allowed to trade in a kid on a new one. Thank God.

I blasted my head with icy cold water and watched the suds swirl down the drain, trying to imagine that each sud was dragging a little trouble down with it. It didn't work. All I could think of was that body.

Throwing on a bathrobe, I went out to check on Lymie. He was still snoozing away like nothing had ever happened.

"Hey, Lymie. Get up. Come on, it's after 11:00." I grabbed his arm and started shaking him. Then I bounced up and down on the bed. One thing you'll never catch me doing is tickling feet. Mom does that and I hate it.

Lymie sat up and looked at me like I was a green alien or something. Talk about a vacant expression.

"Lymie, you awake?" I happen to know people can move around and still not be awake.

"What's your problem, Tyler?" He rubbed his head, grunted, stretched a few times, and then gave me that green alien look again. "Why don't you finish me off?"

24

"What are you talking about?" I figured maybe he'd been dreaming too.

"Tyler, you scumbag, they oughta make you sleep alone in a padded room." He was definitely awake. "For crying out loud, I should have worn a hockey goalie's uniform to bed. All night long you were rolling around growling and kicking me and jabbing me with your bony elbows. What are you training for—the Olympics or something?"

"Sorry, Lyme." I still felt lousy, but I had to laugh, seeing Lymie scowling at me and looking so crabby. "But it's not my fault you're so delicate. I hope I didn't hurt you too bad."

Lymie muttered something that had the word "kill" in it and stumbled toward the bathroom. I threw on a pair of jeans and a tee shirt. Sitting on the stool in front of the mirror, I began working a comb through my hair. I still looked kind of pale and I felt about the same way. I thought I had finally outgrown these nightmares, but last night they were back as bad as ever.

Only different this time.

When I was little, I had this recurring dream where for some stupid reason I'd always fall off the edge of the earth. I'd hear my mother scream as I fell over this cliff which I never seemed to know was there. I'd fall for the longest time, but when I landed I never got hurt. And I'd look up and see Mom and Dad and Christopher and Mrs. Saunders leaning over looking down at me from the edge of our yard or someplace. They'd always look so sad. I'd yell to them but you could tell they couldn't hear me. Or even see me. It was like I was gone, disappeared, kaput. Mom and Chris and Mrs. Saunders would start to cry, and Dad would lead them away. By then I'd be screaming and jumping around like crazy, even though I knew it wouldn't do any good. Then I'd wake up in a cold sweat, too terrified to even move. By this time, everybody in the house would have come running because I'd been screaming out loud.

I had that dream again after Dad's funeral. When it got real bad there for a while, I started staying in Chris's room with him, and that seemed to help. Chris is a light sleeper, and if I'd start in dreaming and making noise and tossing and turning, he'd wake me up, let me know everything was all right, and I'd go back to sleep. After a few nights, the bad dreams pretty much disappeared. We went through the same thing last month when I started dreaming again and added sleepwalking to my repertoire, and Chris straightened me out in no time flat. But he had his own life to live, and you couldn't expect him to hang around forever to see what stunt I was going to pull next. So when things with me were looking fairly normal, he went back to work in Los Angeles. Mom stayed longer and when she was convinced I was all right, she went to finish her film in Colombia.

Since then I'd been fine.

The doctors told Mom that all this dreaming and sleepwalking probably had something to do with my allergies. Unless people have had some experience with them, they wouldn't believe how bad allergies can be. Just ask me. I could be the poster child for allergic reactions. If there's something around and you can touch it, breathe it, or eat it, there's a decent chance I'm allergic to it. My allergic reactions have run anywhere from regular stuff like itchy eyes and runny nose all the way up to asthma attacks which have almost killed me.

And in between I've had bouts of dizziness, or hyper-activity, or migraines. You name it.

But, all in all, with my shots and stuff things had gotten quite a bit better, and to look at me you'd think I was a regular, everyday kid and not some spazola who was allergic to half the planet.

Besides, any kid that swims into a dead body in the middle of the night is entitled to a few nightmares. I only hoped they weren't back to stay.

Having finished combing my hair, I studied my face. Sometimes I think I'm really starting to look a lot like Christopher, and that makes me feel good. My eyes are dark blue like his, although mine maybe have a little more green in them. And we both have light hair, except his is more wheat-colored and mine is more yellow. My face is a little narrower, but still, lots of times I'll look in the mirror and it's like looking at an old picture of Chris.

But not then. Right then I seemed too pale and too delicate to resemble anyone with my brother's carefree confidence. I tried to look tougher, and stronger, and braver, but all I looked like was a jerky kid making faces in the mirror.

The bathroom door opened, and Lymie's reflection appeared behind me wrapped in a towel.

"You staring at yourself in the mirror again?" he said. "I mean, it's not like you had anything to look at."

IV

I COULDN'T WAIT to get to Buster's and get the scoop on the body. Buster ran this cruddy game room on the east side of town, and if there was any news, we'd hear it there.

Christopher called at noon. It about killed me not to be able to tell him what happened, but I'd promised Lymie, and paranoid as Lymie was, he stood right over me waving his fist in my face. Mrs. Saunders must have clued Chris in about my nightmare because he asked a zillion questions to find out if something was bothering me. He wondered if I felt bad that he and Mom were going to miss my thirteenth birthday next week. Actually I did, but I didn't want Chris to think I'd have nightmares over something dumb like that. I'm not that big a baby.

Then stupid Lymie got on the phone and started in with the questions about Allie St. John, Chris's co-star. You know, does she take off her clothes in the movie, and if she does, does she take them off right in front of everybody on the set. It was really stupid because if she did take them off, about fifty million people would get to see her, and Lymie was all excited thinking about the cameramen and the lighting crew getting to see her. Plus, what did he think, the camera guys were going to shoot the film wearing blindfolds or something? Chris liked Lymie all right, so he probably didn't mind, but I poked at him until he said good-bye. We had things to do.

On the way out the door Lymie grabbed another chicken leg and a roll. Mrs. Saunders always cooked tons of things like fried chicken and hamburgers and stuff when she knew Lymie'd be around, because except for my dad when he was alive, my family hardly ever ate meat. (I never did.) She said it did her heart good to watch Lymie eat.

"You got it made in the shade, Tyler. You got it made in the shade."

I skipped backward watching Lymie munch his way toward me.

"Why?" I said. "You don't get fed at your house?" I knew that wasn't what he meant, but I wasn't going to make it easy for him.

"Real funny, Ty. You know what I mean. You got a brother with lots of bucks who feels guilty about missing your birthday. And a servant. You practically got your own servant. Made in the shade!" He stopped walking and gnawed on the chicken bone. "Play your cards right and I bet you can get anything you want for your birthday. Anything."

"Cut the crap, Lymie. First of all, Chris probably already bought my present. And second, all's he said was he feels bad about missing my birthday, and you're making a big deal out of it."

"It is a big deal." Lymie lumbered up to me. "That's

guilt you're talking about. And you oughta learn to use it. You know, get the most out of it."

"You're a jerk, Lymie. You know that. A total jerk." I pushed him away from me and kept walking. "And Mrs. Saunders isn't a servant."

"Yeah, well what is she then, scumbucket? She gets paid, doesn't she? She wouldn't take care of you for nothing, would she?"

"She's more like part of the family. Like a grandmother or something. She took care of Chris when he was a kid too. And I bet she would do it for nothing."

"Well, if she's like your grandmother, why do you have to call her Mrs. Saunders? I mean if you're paying her, she oughta call you Mr. McAllister."

"Shut up, Lymie."

No sense wasting any more breath on the subject. He wouldn't get it anyway. See, my mom had this thing about money and respect, you know, how people who had more money lots of times thought they deserved more respect. She'd even point it out to me if I was watching something like "The Brady Bunch" on TV. According to her, it was a prime example of social injustice that Alice, the housekeeper, had to call the parents Mr. and Mrs. Brady, while everyone, including all the kids, got to call her by her first name. And Alice was older than both Mr. and Mrs. Brady, not to mention the kids. When I told Mom that Alice seemed happy enough, she told me that was beside the point because the guys who wrote the show could make even a slave seem happy if they wanted to. Plus, she said, most of the writers had maids, and their kids and everybody probably called them by their first names too.

I thought that was pretty silly at the time, but since

then I've seen what she meant. Especially at that snobby prep school my father sent me to. All the maids and gardeners and people like that had to call us "sir" or "Mr. McAllister" or whatever, I guess since we were paying so much to go there. But nobody told us what we had to call them or how we had to treat them, and I couldn't believe the way some of the guys acted. Guys would yell at a maid old enough to be their mother or grandmother, "Get outta here, you old goat. Can't you see I'm busy?" And the poor old lady would have to say something like, "Forgive me, sir. I'll check back later." Because she probably really needed the job and was afraid to complain.

It gave me the creeps to think that Mrs. Saunders might have gotten a job with one of those guys' families instead of ours.

I took off and jogged ahead before Lymie could come up with anything else to discuss. When I reached Main Street I waited for him, so I wouldn't have to walk into Buster's alone. Buster's wasn't the safest place in the world for a new kid. Buster's wasn't even that safe for an old kid.

When we got there, I couldn't believe it. The place was deserted. Buster was sitting on a chair in the doorway wearing his change apron and his usual scowl. He probably tipped the scales at over three hundred pounds, but no one ever let on they noticed. At least not to his face. Every pound of Buster was mean. He had a face like a pit bull. A fat one. And he'd watch the kids every second like he was hoping somebody'd scratch a pool table, or get rough with one of his machines, or cause trouble, or do anything else he wasn't in the mood for. When Buster shook his fist and roared something like,

"Hey, you with the goofy face! Outta here!" every kid in the place made sure his sneakers were packed and ready to go. Because Buster looked at all of us like he thought our faces were goofy, and any of us could have accidentally rubbed Buster the wrong way.

Even though Buster made his living off the town's kids, he acted really put out if you needed change for the games, or were crazy enough to order one of his greasy Buster Burgers. He'd growl, "Whaddaya need now, pigeon face?" and then look down at you like he was wondering whether he could get away with squishing you into the floor. And if a fight broke out, Buster wouldn't even break it up. He'd just pick up a kid in each hand and toss them both out the door onto the sidewalk and snarl, "Go ahead and kill each other, but not around my games."

But it was just as well. With the kind of kids that hung around Buster's, they'd have probably torn the place apart years ago if Buster had treated them halfway decent.

We looked at Buster, and Buster glared at us. Even his chewed-up cigar looked angry.

"Whaddaya want?"

"Hey, Buster, where is everybody?" Lymie asked.

"Do I look like the town historian?" Buster answered. He never could give you a simple answer.

"We thought you might know," I said, squeezing closer to Lymie.

"Yeah, what if I do?" He gave us that "Can I get away with squishing you into the floor" look. Lymie and I stood there waiting. Like fools.

"It so happens I do know," Buster continued. "I figure right now every stupid, nosy, rubberneck in town is out at the quarry watching 'em fish for some bone-head who decided to take his last swim." He chuckled. "Knowing the cops around here, they probably won't find nothing till they drain the place and bring in blood-hounds."

Buster stood up, and Lymie and I backed up.

"Get lost. I'm closing."

"Are you going to the quarry?" I asked. I heard Lymie swallow. Buster looked down at me like I was a mosquito pumping blood out of his arm. I swallowed.

"What's it to ya?"

"Can we ride out with you?"

I couldn't believe my own ears. Here I was having nightmares because of this body, and all of a sudden I get this big urge to go back to where it is. But I couldn't help it. I had to see this thing through to the end. And I didn't even want to waste time walking.

Buster yanked his angry, chewed-up cigar out of his angry yellow teeth and studied me.

"Five bucks. One way. And you keep your traps shut."

I heard Lymie groan.

"Okay, good," I told him. "Deal." I stuck out my hand and really thought Buster might spit on it. I yanked it back.

"That's apiece, baby face. Up front."

I had seven bucks and Lymie only had two. He groaned again but he gave it to me.

"We'll have to owe you one," I said.

Buster snatched the money from my hand.

"I'll trust ya. I never knew anybody that owed me money more than a week."

Buster smiled. Lymie and I didn't.

33

V

BUSTER OWNED A faded old gray Cadillac with fins pointing out the back that looked like rocket engines. It even sounded like a rocket when Buster tromped on the gas and roared onto Main Street. The guy drove like a total maniac. Sitting between Buster and Lymie, I sank into a few layers of Buster each time we screeched into a hard right turn and got elbowed by Lymie on the lefts. Buster blew thick clouds of cigar smoke that quickly filled up the car. I wondered how he'd take it if I threw up all over his front seat, and I tried to get the thought out of my mind. Thinking about throwing up isn't that far away from actually throwing up.

Dozens of cars lined the road on both sides of the quarry entrance. The people strolling down the lane looked like they could have been going to the county fair. At least until Buster veered in, blasting his horn and swearing out the window. A volunteer fireman in an orange vest planted his feet in front of us and thrust out his arm. Until Buster hit the gas, that is. Then his feet got unplanted pretty quick.

A fire truck, two state trooper cars, a sheriff car, and

a rescue van were parked by the water, all with lights flashing every which-way. A large crowd milled about. The new arrivals craned their necks to see, and the ones who'd been there a while shook their heads and spoke in hushed tones like people do at a wake.

We scrunched up behind Buster as he plowed through the crowd to the water's edge. Way out in the middle a state trooper sat in a blue and yellow trooper rowboat peering over the side into the gray water. Every so often two divers in black suits would surface and direct him to move the boat this way or that. The body must have sunk, and it would probably be tough to spot it in the dark water.

A few yards from where we stood, a large, shapeless woman sobbed quietly and two men tried to comfort her. She kept repeating, "I know it's him. He's never stayed out all night. Oh, God, I know it's him."

The men looked awkward and helpless, and every once in a while they'd say something like, "Now, Claire, we don't even know for sure anyone is in there."

But it didn't do any good. She seemed to know, as surely as Lymie and I knew, that a body *was* in there, and it was pitiful to watch her stunned misery. The men might as well have shut up. There was no way anybody could make her feel any better.

I turned away and fixed my eyes on the water, and closed them pretty fast when I remembered what might come floating up. Suddenly I wanted to get out, to be as far away from the poor woman and the body as possible, but I was walled in by people. I wished I could go do something, play basketball, run, anything that would take my mind off this woman, and the body, and all the misery and suffering that come from tragedies like this one. I drew in a deep breath and tried to stop thinking, but it was too late. My mind was already back to last summer. The worst summer I'd ever had.

Dad had been furious that I'd screwed up so bad at prep school, less than three months there and they didn't even want me back. I told him I wouldn't have gone back anyway, and that sent him through the roof again. My allergies were going crazy, and I was practically a basket case. By early August I'd had three or four asthma attacks within a month, as well as a bunch of other symptoms that came and went, like dizziness, and nosebleeds that wouldn't stop, anxiety, nightmares, you name it. I'd spent half my summer in one doctor's office or another as they all tried to find out what was going wrong. Mom blamed Dad for having insisted I be sent away to military school. And Dad said I had pretty serious problems before I ever even heard of Grant Academy. They fought whenever they saw each other, which was usually only on weekends when Dad stopped by to see me or take me someplace. I was terrified that one time he'd decide not to come back, that I just wasn't worth it.

When things seemed to be about as bad as they could get, Chris woke me one morning saying he needed a vacation, so why didn't we take off for a few days. He had the keys to a friend's cabin on Lake Granby, in Colorado. I couldn't believe it. Chris never took time off in the middle of a picture, and I knew it was me who he figured needed a vacation, but I didn't wait to be asked twice. We left before breakfast, flew to Denver, rented a car, and were floating on the lake by evening. It happened so fast, it didn't even seem real. It was like living in a dream.

If it's possible for a person to be happier than I was those three days on the lake, I'd be surprised. Prep school, and doctors, and allergies, and arguments seemed to belong to another world, one I could only vaguely remember. Our cabin was surrounded by a dense, cool forest which crept up to the brightest, bluest lake you could ever imagine, a place right out of a postcard. Every day Chris and I would go out in a boat for hours and fish and swim and talk. The water was so clear sometimes it felt like we were floating on air. In the late afternoon we'd hike up the side of the mountain or around the lakeshore and see deer and rabbits, and birds I didn't even recognize. When evening came, I'd bustle around collecting firewood, and we'd cook outside as the sun disappeared behind the trees. Then we'd sit around the campfire talking for hours. I told Chris all about prep school, and it was like talking about the scary part of a fairy tale, where you knew no matter how bad things got, everything would turn out happily ever after. And I told him how one of these days I'd make Dad proud of me even if he wasn't now. Then I'd fall asleep outside staring up at the stars, bright sparkly ones, not your dingy L.A. kind. I'd wake early in the morning, snug and warm in my sleeping bag, to a world that was kind and clean and where nothing bad could get in.

Each morning we'd drive to this little store and call Mom, and I'd tell her about the place and tell her she was crazy not to fly there right away. Then Chris would send me inside to pick up whatever supplies I thought we'd need for the day. And at eleven years old, I felt smart to know they wanted to talk about me, how did I feel, was I happy, that kind of thing. It was a world created for me, all mine, and five senses weren't enough to take it all in.

I even got thinking that Mom and Dad would get together again. My allergies would disappear, and Dad would never dream of sending me away to a boarding school again. We'd all be one big, happy family. I thought all this and believed it.

Until the fourth morning.

It was Tuesday, a beautiful Tuesday, with the bright morning sun peaking through the trees and a cool breeze blowing across the open porch of the store. This time Mom stopped me when I started in. She told me the news that only I hadn't known. Four days earlier, a private jet carrying Dad to New York had gone down somewhere north of Flagstaff. The searchers combing the area had finally found the wreckage. There were no survivors. Dad, his business manager, and the pilot were all dead. I felt like I'd been slammed hard against the wall, hard enough to knock the wind out of me. But I didn't cry. I couldn't. Something inside me had stopped. And that's the part that would have cried.

I don't remember much of the trip back to Los Angeles. I had been yanked out of my dream world so fast that my mind was reeling with a kind of mental whiplash. Chris talked to me a lot but I didn't know what he said. And I didn't say a word. There was nothing to say.

At the airport Mom took my arm and led me to the car. She spoke softly into my ear, and Mrs. Saunders patted my knee as Chris drove home. A while later we turned onto the Santa Monica Freeway. I remember that I had trouble sounding out the letters on the huge green sign. And even when I did recognize the words, I didn't see any point to them.

Or to anything else.

I coughed once . . . twice . . . and I felt an awful tightness gripping me from behind my ribs. It was like someone huge was sitting on my chest. I sat bolt upright, and listened, as if I were outside myself, to the slow, wheezy breathing. My pulse quickened as every muscle in my chest, my whole body, struggled to draw in air. I felt like a distant observer, watching some stupid kid whose shocked eyes bulged, and whose hands grabbed for air that couldn't be grabbed. Somebody pushed my head forward over my knees, and I heard a voice shout, "He's turning blue!" It sounded like Mom, but it was coming from far away. I heard coughing that became more violent, and I felt pity for this frightened body which didn't even have the sense to breathe.

Bright lights buzzed over me, and strangers in white held my head over my knees. Words floated by me like cartoon captions. I felt I could have grabbed them if I sat up. Certain words came by more than once, and they took on colorful, three-dimensional shapes. "ASTHMA . . . NURSE . . . ADRENALIN." The words didn't mean anything to me. They were just shapes and colors.

I tried to raise my head and couldn't. Something cold was put on my arm. A sharp stabbing pain over the cold spot made me jump. I struggled to get loose, trying to remember where I was and why I was being handled by so many people. I couldn't. A light tremor grew from inside my heart into shaking that I could watch in my arms and legs. I heard crying and was surprised to realize it was my own. I cried harder and harder and

39

someone said it was all right. Even though I was crying much harder than Dad would have ever allowed.

Once I pulled out the stops, that was it. I was crying like crazy and I couldn't stop. I cried until I hardly even knew what I was crying about. And I didn't care if Chris saw me or anyone else. And that was strange for me. Even when I was little I never gave in like that. It was almost like I was crying for all the other times that I'd held it in. And even though I was more miserable that night than I'd ever been, there was something good about letting go. Like an awful weight had been lifted from my chest.

As I listened to this woman sobbing pitifully, I knew how helpless everybody must have felt being with me that night. There was nothing anybody could do for her. It was something she'd have to go through on her own.

Suddenly I was startled by a change in the crowd. It had grown quieter, more attentive. Opening my eyes, I saw one of the divers disappear under the water. The trooper in the boat was hunched over the edge peering down, but more intently than before. The spectators slowly and silently crowded the rocky rim, and I sat down, afraid I'd be squeezed into the water.

"Looks like they got him." Lymie's whisper startled me. I'd nearly forgotten he was next to me.

The divers and the trooper were awkwardly hoisting something from the water. As the boat tipped up, we could see the body of the drowned man. My stomach lurched and I looked away. When I looked back, the boat had straightened up and most of the body was hidden on the bottom. Both divers had scrambled into the boat after it.

The sobbing woman was silent now, not even breathing, with a hand across her heart and leftover tears in her eyes. She started bouncing slightly and wrapped her hands around her jaw like some game show contestant waiting to see if her answer was right for the grand prize. I hoped like crazy she'd be wrong, and the body would be someone who didn't belong to anybody. The woman turned away from the boat, walked a few paces from the water, wrung her head, and returned. She did this two or three times, until the boat reached the edge a few feet below us. The two men around her held her arms as she leaned dangerously over the water. All she needed was a peek, and this awful wail rose from her throat. She would have toppled into that boat for sure if the guys hadn't yanked her back. She screamed and kicked at them as they dragged her away. A few more hands fumbled to help control her, but most of the crowd backed off looking stricken and helpless.

"Tyler, it's BooBoo Anderson!" Lymie's eyes were wide and his jaw had dropped.

Almost against my will, my head turned to watch the body being lifted toward the waiting stretcher. I almost gagged but I kept looking. It was bloated some and kind of pale, but not as bloated or pale as I remembered it. Big, fat Buster, perched on his hands and knees, gently lifted the body onto the stretcher and his face almost looked tender and sad. When the body landed, water gurgled out the mouth past the blue lips and splashed down the chin. My stomach reeled but my eyes kept watching. As the stretcher was lifted, he gurgled some more water up. Finally a rescue squad guy came running up with a white sheet and covered him up.

Buster cleared a path for the men carrying the body, and they headed for the van. The air seemed hollow, and whenever anybody coughed or anything, you could almost hear an echo off the rocky ledges. Staring wide-eyed at the body, I had nearly forgotten about the sobbing woman, but suddenly she broke free of the men and charged the stretcher. She snatched the sheet up and screamed, "Bobby, Mommy's here now! Listen to me, Bobby! Mommy will take care of you."

She shook the body like she thought she could wake it up. She had this distant kind of scary look, as if she were possessed by demons or something. When her son didn't move, she flung herself at the stretcher and nearly toppled him off it. Buster gently but firmly lifted her up, and led her through the crowd past where we could see.

Lymie and I stayed sitting on the edge of the rock wall, neither of us caring to see any more. I was thinking about BooBoo and about how I'd never even heard his real name before or even wondered what it was. I never thought about him as having a mother or anything like that. BooBoo, or Bobby as his mother called him, worked at the school. I'm not sure if he was a janitor or only a janitor's helper, but I'd seen him a lot working around school my first week. He must have been around twenty or so, and I think he was a little retarded. He got his nickname because when he talked, he sounded like BooBoo, Yogi Bear's sidekick. If a water pipe or something would break, he'd say to his boss in this sad, nasally voice, "Gee, Mr. Bremmer, what'll we do now?" That cracked everybody up when he did that. Especially the kids who weren't much smarter than BooBoo to begin with.

But he was a nice guy. On the second day of school, after I'd been thrown out of Old Lady Waverly's class for sleeping while I was supposed to be filling out a stupid worksheet, he saw me sitting on a chair outside Mr. Blumberg's office. I was feeling pretty low. BooBoo pulled up another chair and asked me who I was. When I told him who I was and what I'd done, he really seemed to feel bad. I told him how everybody'd laughed at me, and he said, "That's all right. They laugh at me too. Just don't forget, they've done dumb stuff too."

I even ended up telling him how it was easier for me to fall asleep around a crowd of people, like in a classroom, than it was for me to fall asleep alone in my room at night. And I never told people that kind of stuff. He wanted to know all about California and I told him. He said he wanted to go there someday. Before he left, he told me that Old Lady Waverly used to put him to sleep too, and that didn't mean I was bad.

That really got to me, BooBoo caring enough to worry about whether I thought I was bad.

My stomach sank thinking about him drowning.

Buster growled from behind for us to get into his car, and he'd drop us off in town. When we looked suspicious, he told us there was no charge. We could hardly believe it. And not only that, but he drove us right to my house. As we were climbing out of his car, he mumbled, "That BooBoo. He spent a lot of money at my place."

That's what he said. But I looked at him. And I don't think he cared at all about the money.

VI

"AW, CRAP!"
I almost barfed all over my assignment pad.
I looked again, and I still didn't believe it. Over the
weekend I was supposed to have collected twenty rocks
for Old Lady Waverly and be able to tell what each one
was by looking at it, feeling it, and scratching it on
things. What a way to end a perfectly lousy weekend.
As if I didn't have enough on my mind.

"What's the matter, dear?" Mrs. Saunders yelled
from downstairs.

"Nothing. Just my stupid, idiotic, lamebrained science homework!"

"Well, don't be long. It's getting late."

It was getting late all right. I had finally finished all
my other work, and I could barely keep my eyes open.
I almost climbed into bed without even being told. Then
when I flipped my pad open to double check, I saw the
science assignment. I couldn't believe it. And Old Lady
Waverly would be in all her glory if I showed up empty-
handed.

I stumbled downstairs and out the door in a kind of
sleepy version of panic. It was too dark and I didn't

have the ambition to search the whole yard, so I ended up grabbing a bunch of rocks from the flower beds. I thought I'd struck the jackpot. I lugged them upstairs in a paper bag and dumped them on the floor.

"Aw, crap!" I stared in disbelief at the bright red, white, and blue stones the old owners had left behind. "Why me?"

"What's the matter now, dear?"

"My stupid, moronic science rocks! They're painted like Fruit Loops."

I found a file and started scraping them down, but it didn't do any good. All of them were the same kind of crushed stone. And there wasn't one listing for crushed stone in the whole stupid science book.

I was trying to decide whether to slit my wrists or go outside for another bunch of rocks when Mrs. Saunders came in and told me I had to go to bed.

"Come on, Tyler. Your work will keep. Right now you need your rest." She smiled when she saw my stupid red, white, and blue rocks and put them back in the bag.

"It's easy for you, Mrs. Saunders. You don't have to face Old Lady Waverly tomorrow with those goofy looking things." Even though I was pouting, I was really glad to get to bed. I told myself I'd get up early and find some more rocks.

I didn't. I should have known. Monday morning is the pits. That's one thing you can always count on. When Mrs. Saunders woke me up, I was so groggy I felt like I'd been drugged. It took all my concentration just to get out of bed and take a shower. I did make it to school on time, barely, and that was only because Chuckie happened to be painting the front porch when

I came stumbling out of the house ten minutes late, dropping my books all over the driveway, and he gave me a ride. I weaved my way through groups of loud, laughing kids who didn't have enough brains to be miserable, and sped up the stairs to my locker.

Mary Grace Madigan was calmly organizing her locker and sorting out all the books she'd need for the morning. Exactly what I needed to see. It's kids like her who make kids like me look worse than we really are. Mary Grace sat behind me in nearly all my classes because her name was after mine on the teachers' alphabetical lists. For some reason the Mc in McAllister is alphabetized under Mac. That's also why her locker was next to mine.

I scooted up beside her and tried three or four different ways of dialing 40-20-8, as half the messy stack of books and papers I'd scooped up from the driveway started slipping out from under my arm and tumbled around my feet. The lock finally released and I pulled the handle up and out. The bottom of the locker door gaped open an inch or so, but the top was jammed. I jiggled the handle up again and yanked harder until the door flew open and banged me in the nose. The remaining books dropped from under my arm, and a few others toppled out of my locker and piled up with the others around my feet. I groaned. Nice way to start a new week! I crouched down and began stuffing layers of junk on top of the other layers of junk already at the bottom of my locker.

"You're funny. You know that?" Mary Grace, having finished making her locker look like something out of *Better Homes and Gardens*, was standing above me looking down at my jumbled mess of books and papers.

"You probably love it when people fall down the stairs, too," I said.

"Depends who it is," she said, laughing. "Look, you want some help? I'm good at this. Really."

She didn't wait for an answer. She brushed past me and began pulling everything from my locker, including the large textbooks and permanently twisted notebooks wedged on the bottom, and began stacking them neatly up on the shelf. Before I knew it, my books were perfectly arranged in a beautifully tapered pile, titles facing out, and the books I needed for the morning were waiting in a neat pile at my feet.

"How could you possibly do that to a locker in less than a week?" She shook her head in disbelief.

"I don't know. It's a gift, I guess."

She laughed. "Do you clean your own room at home? I can't imagine."

"Kind of. Well . . . sort of," I said and then I laughed too. "Not really."

If Mrs. Saunders didn't help me keep my room straightened up, our house might have been condemned by now. I'm the only one in my family who's a total slob. If I didn't look a little like Chris, everybody probably would have thought I was adopted or something. It drove Mom and Dad crazy. It was the one thing about me they agreed on. Dad, being a former military man, couldn't stand any kind of clutter. And Mom said it was deplorable that I thought since I was a boy I didn't have to pick up after myself. I told her that wasn't fair. I know if I'd been a girl, I still would have been a slob. It's just . . . I don't know . . . I always seem to have other stuff on my mind.

One time Mom told Mrs. Saunders not to go near my

room. Mom always warned me about Mrs. Saunders's heart not being so great, and maybe she figured cleaning a room like mine could really hurt her. Plus she probably wanted to see how rotten I'd let it get. After a few days she marched me up there with a vacuum cleaner, a laundry basket, and a Hefty garbage bag, and told me not to set foot outside the door until my room looked the way a room should look. That meant the way she thought a room should look. Christopher tossed in a baseball bat and told me to use it if I saw any suspicious movements under all the crud. And he said not to worry, that he'd sneak food to me every day. Ha, ha. Later that afternoon, Mrs. Saunders came sneaking in and gave me a hand. It was to be "our little secret." She said, "Don't you worry, Tyler. I used to have to tidy up after your father and your brother too, and they didn't even know it. A man just can't clean the way a woman can."

She was careful not to talk like that in front of Mom. Mom was always trying to liberate Mrs. Saunders. When Mom would start in on her "this is the twentieth century" lecture, Mrs. Saunders would always wink at me. I think she knew Mom wouldn't have much luck at reforming either of us.

I looked down at Mary Grace's pile of stuff.

"Hey, Mary Grace. Where's your science rocks?"

"Home. They're not due till next week, remember."

"Oh, yeah, right." Something inside me did a cartwheel.

Mary Grace hurried off to homeroom almost before I could thank her. I watched her for a moment, thinking. Mary Grace was one of the prettiest, most popular girls in the eighth grade. I wondered if she kind of liked me, or if she thought I was some kind of pathetic pig. I couldn't tell.

I slipped through my homeroom door right as the bell went off and joined the other kids in mumbling the "Pledge of Allegiance." Then after a few warm-up clicks and rapping noises, Mr. Blumberg's voice came over the P.A. system with the morning announcements. The first thing he did was ask for a moment of silence in memory of Robert Anderson, who he said would be sorely missed around school and around town. I hadn't even formed a good picture of BooBoo yet when Mr. Blumberg raced on with the rest of the announcements. No crying over spilt milk for that guy.

Everybody was talking about BooBoo all day, but nobody knew that much. At lunch, Jeff Hunter, whose father was county sheriff, told us that some scared little kid had called a deputy in the middle of the night to report finding the body. The cops were hoping that little kid, or the other kid that was with him, would come forward so they could get more information out of them. As it stood they didn't have much to go on. They could tell that BooBoo had suffered a knock on the back of his head, but that could have happened if he fell in. They were hoping the coroner's report would turn up something.

A scared little kid. I was glad Lymie hadn't let me give names. And Lymie was glad we wouldn't get caught.

"Really, Ty, it was good you sounded like such a little jerk. They'll never guess in a million years that the body was found by a couple of eighth graders."

"Thanks, Lyme," I said. "Anything to help."

After seventh period, Mary Grace helped me pack the

49

books I'd need to bring home, figuring in which work I'd be able to get done in study hall the next day. She had eliminated most of the guesswork from school. She knew which teachers graded on neatness and punctuality, which ones admired original thought, and which ones wanted nothing but their own words flung back at them on exams. I couldn't believe it.

"You're in the top group, Tyler, and you need to know these shortcuts. But don't worry. Since you're new here, I can fill you in."

But it didn't matter that I was new. Not really. Schools were always kind of mysterious to me. Most teachers I'd had seemed to like me all right, even though most said I worked below my potential. But success or failure was hit or miss with me, like walking through a mine field and hoping you didn't get blown up. But for kids like Mary Grace, it was like they had studied the mine field and drawn maps so they never accidentally stepped on anything that would go bang. It wouldn't hurt being more like that. And it sure would have made Dad happy.

We walked down the front steps of the school toward the street.

"Wasn't it awful about BooBoo Anderson?" Mary Grace said. "He was the sweetest guy."

Everybody claimed to feel bad about BooBoo but with Mary Grace it was different. She didn't sound excited, like it was some fun kind of mystery or something.

"Yeah," I said. "That was pretty bad."

"I can't help thinking about those poor little kids who found him. Imagine little kids running around on their own in the middle of the night. Some parents, huh?"

50

We had almost reached Main Street. I watched the way the breeze and the sunlight played through her sandy hair.

"Maybe they weren't so little," I said. "That old deputy probably thinks anybody under thirty is a little kid. Plus, they probably sneaked out. And maybe they couldn't tell their names because they had the kind of parents who'd really be upset if they knew their kids were outside fiddling around at night."

"Maybe," she said. "But I bet those kids are having some kind of nightmares after that experience."

I knew one of them was.

I left Mary Grace in front of her house and kept walking home. I almost wished I had told her.

VII

I N THE FEW months since I'd come to Wakefield, I hadn't gotten to know Chuckie very well. I'd see him every day as he worked around the yard or fixed up the house, which Mom wanted restored to its original condition, but Chuckie didn't talk much. He'd answer me if I asked him a question, barely, and he'd say hi if I said hi, but that was about it. I figured maybe he didn't like kids too much. Or maybe he thought I was some kind of spoiled rich brat.

I did know that Chuckie had just gotten out of the marines or something, and that he held black belts in both judo and karate. I also knew from Lymie that he had quite a reputation around town; nobody messed with Chuckie Deegan. Even though he was six feet tall and real muscular, he moved with the smoothness and grace of a cat. Like he could walk through the woods without crackling the leaves.

I'm not sure what his official job description was, but I figured that in addition to keeping up the place, Mom had asked him to keep an eye on Mrs. Saunders and me. I knew that even with all his references, Mom wouldn't have hired him unless he agreed to live in the guest cottage at the edge of our property. Being in the movies made Mom kind of a public figure. Which she didn't mind so much for herself; she said that went with her career. Besides, she knew how to handle people and crowds and everything. But I was quite a bit quieter, more shy, and even though we moved here because Mom thought small town life would be good for me, I think she worried that outside L.A., where celebrities are a dime a dozen, people might bother me all the time. They didn't. Sometimes I'd see kids gawking at me. And a couple of times some girls came up to me, all giggly and trying to hide behind each other, wanting to know if I was Linda LaMar's son (LaMar is Mom's maiden name), but mostly everybody left me alone. Since Chris's first big movie wouldn't be out till around Christmas, and since my last name is different from my Mom's, maybe a lot of people just didn't make the connection. Who knows?

Anyway, since Mom knew she'd have to be away from time to time, it didn't surprise me that she'd hire some tough guy like Chuckie to be around and keep an eye on things. And I didn't figure there was much more to know about Chuckie. He was the tough, silent type, and that was that. Only on Tuesday, I found out that wasn't that. Because sometimes a person will do something for you, some little kindness or whatever, and it's one of those things you know you'll never forget for the rest of your life, no matter what. And that's how I came to consider Chuckie part of my family, the same as we all considered Mrs. Saunders part of the family.

By Tuesday I still hadn't recovered completely from the whole BooBoo thing, and I was kind of counting on a normal day with no hassles. After school Mrs. Saunders was driving me to Albany for my weekly allergy shot, and then we'd go out to dinner and maybe see a movie or something. I was kind of looking forward to it this week. I needed to get away from Wakefield for a few hours. I'd already made it through three periods, and I was hoping to lay back and coast through the rest of the day, no sweat.

Then disaster struck. Disaster has lots of faces, but this time it appeared in the form of Beaver Bruckman. Beaver was one of those kids who'd probably been in the eighth grade since the school was built. And since the junior high wing was like his permanent home, he probably figured he had seniority rights over the smaller, scrawnier kids who were merely passing through. Half the kids who experienced a growth spurt in last year's eighth grade class thought it was because Beaver had picked them up so many times by the head.

The only class Beaver was good at was gym. In fact, in gym he was the undisputed king. But you had to watch out for him. By fourth period gym class every day, Beaver had stubble on his chin, and the friction of exercising with stubble might have made him irritable or something. In touch football, Beaver's touch was more like a full body slam. Kids were so scared of him, he could block by giving a dirty look. And if you were lucky enough to make it through the game in one piece, you still had to make it through the shower. Beaver was the kind of kid who got his jollies by reaching over and turning your faucet to scalding, and he'd actually get mad if you didn't stay under it and burn. Then came towel snapping. Beaver would always dampen the towels to improve their action, and he could make them crack like a whip. One guess what his favorite target was. Beaver was one guy you *had* to turn your back on. And he was persistent too. Last Friday he snapped at me so much, I felt like I'd been blow dried.

Each day after getting into our gym clothes, we'd dash out to the gym floor for attendance and the word or two of daily instruction which made up the phys. ed. curriculum. Today's lesson, which Mr. Johnson delivered in a voice that must have started down around his ankles was, "Laps," and then he chucked a football at the kid closest to him. I knew from last week that the "laps" part meant we had to go outside and run four laps, and the football meant we'd pick up sides for a touch football game. The first kid to finish would get to be a captain and Mr. Johnson would pick the other captain. So far it'd always been Beaver who finished first. And Mr. Johnson would always pick this other humongous kid, Ralph Martin, to be the other captain.

"Lymie, buddy," I said as we trotted out to the track, "Today I'm gonna get to be a captain."

I took off ahead at an easy pace and smiled when I heard Lymie yelling for me to stop. I'd plodded along with him every other day, but today, for some reason, I really wanted to be captain. I don't know . . . maybe I needed to feel like I had some control over my life. Anyway, I was used to running five miles with Chris, and when Chris was away, I worked on increasing my speed because I knew he always had to run slower than he'd like to so he wouldn't leave me behind. I wanted to be as fast as him by the next time he came home. Not only that, but running was also making my lungs stronger and would probably cut down on the chances of my having another serious asthma attack.

I hadn't run since Saturday morning. I really hadn't

been sleeping all that great since swimming into poor BooBoo's body that night and I was waking up later than usual. And since Mrs. Saunders thought rest was more important than running, she never got me up for school until it was too late for me to go out and run. And I'm a morning runner. By Tuesday I felt fine and light like you do after you've laid off for a few days. Four laps was a piece of cake. It was only a mile. I knew I'd win easy, and I could be captain of my own team.

I wished Christopher could have been there to see me. I finished half a lap ahead of everybody else. Mr. Johnson told me he'd like to see me on the track team next year and that I should keep practicing and stay off the booze and cigarettes. I laughed. I couldn't picture myself sitting around with a six pack of beer and a pack of Winstons.

Mr. Johnson picked some other smaller kid to be the other captain, probably so the teams would be fair. I picked Ralph Martin first so we'd have at least one big guy. Then I picked Lymie. I didn't pick Beaver even though he was probably the best player because I figured he'd try to run the team. Lymie wasn't too thrilled about the whole thing. I heard him mumble, "You'll be sorry." But that's the way Lymie is. How was I supposed to know that Lymie would be right for the second time in less than a week? What are the chances of that happening, like a thousand to one?

The first time I went out for a pass, Beaver was right there covering me, and rather than going for the ball like he was supposed to, he slammed me hard into the ground. I hit so hard I got dirt in my mouth. I called pass interference, but Beaver said he never touched me.

56

I looked over at Mr. Johnson, but he seemed to be daydreaming. Probably thinking about lesson plans for his next class, I thought angrily. Beaver called it an incomplete pass, and nobody argued it.

On the next play, Beaver sideswiped me before the ball was even close, jabbing his elbow into my ribs for all he was worth. I called pass interference again, and Beaver swore again he never touched me. Now I was mad. My whole body tensed up with rage, and I wouldn't have backed down for ten Beavers. I didn't care. I mean what could he do, anyway? Brushing past him, I grabbed the ball and moved it to where he had slammed me. When I straightened up, Beaver's face appeared in front of my face. It was almost deadpan, except for the clenched teeth and the hate in his eyes.

"You callin' me a liar, rich boy?"

"You slammed me," I said, backing up a step. "Let's just play the game, all right?"

"Tell me I'm a liar!" He pushed hard into my chest and I fell back another two steps. My whole body shook with fear and anger.

"Tell me I'm a liar, rich boy. Come on." Another push, harder this time, and I nearly landed on my butt. I stood facing Beaver's cruel eyes.

"Are you chicken, rich boy?" I could smell Beaver's hot, sour breath. "Whaddaya sleepin'? Wake up, boy."

He cuffed me a good one on the side of the head, hard enough to knock me sideways a good couple of feet. Before I knew it, all the anger and fear and pain I'd ever felt burst through my arm with an almost electrical jolt. My fist caught the hard jaw before the mouth had formed its next taunt. I heard teeth grind under my knuckles. I knew I was dead meat now, and knowing that electrified my entire body, my arms windmilling punches, and my legs driving me forward into Beaver. I could feel myself being hit back, but I felt no real pain. It was like my heart was pumping novocaine instead of blood. Then large powerful hands yanked me in a semicircle, and a large body wrapped around me and held me in a tight grip.

"That's enough! Stop it now!" The voice in my ear was Mr. Johnson's, and the arms holding me down were Mr. Johnson's. Now they jerked me to my feet.

"McAllister, go in and get yourself cleaned up. And Bruckman, sit on the bench. Somebody should have hit you years ago."

Beaver's nose was dripping blood which trickled over the corners of his mouth and swollen lips like a bloody Fu Manchu. His eyes smoldered with hatred. He took one last seething look at me before retreating to the bench.

My tee shirt was bloody, but with whose blood I didn't know. I could taste blood around the corners of my own mouth. When I touched my face, it felt wet, and my hand turned magically red. I probably staggered a little because Mr. Johnson grabbed my arm. He tipped my head back, jiggled my nose, and looked into my mouth. Then he patted me on the back and told me again to get cleaned up.

Now that Beaver was out of range, a few kids mumbled, "Good for you, Tyler. He had it coming."

My head pounded something fierce and I felt lousy, but something inside me felt good about not letting myself be pushed around. I spit and a few specks of blood landed on the new white sneakers Mom had bought me for school. I knew this wasn't over. Not by a long shot. Beaver didn't strike me as the forgive and forget type.

Mom always told me I had a temper like Dad's, and she didn't mean that as a compliment. Mom claimed she never hit anybody in her whole life, and I believed her. I could remember the long, loud fights she and Dad would have if he hit me. The worst time was after Dad got the letter saying I wouldn't be allowed back to Grant Academy in the fall because I'd been in too many fights and wasn't adjusting, according to them. Mom had to climb right in between us that time. Dad had me by the neck and was all set to belt me when Mom wedged herself between us and pushed on him so hard it pinned my head against the wall. That was as close as I ever saw my mother to getting hysterical.

She screamed, "Only an idiot would hit a child to teach him to stop fighting!" Then she told him if he ever touched me again, she'd get a court order to prevent him from seeing me.

Dad had shouted, "You're to blame for all his problems, not me! I could straighten him out in a week if you'd let me."

It would have been ten times easier to have gotten belted. I was pretty mad at Mom because now I was sure Dad was gone for good. I was wrong. He picked me up the next Sunday at the usual time. But he never mentioned Grant Academy again. And I never had a chance to explain my side of things. Never.

Chris took after Mom. He had more patience than anyone I knew, and I had never known him to fight. Even when I blew up at him for some stupid reason, he wouldn't get angry. I'd be swinging and kicking like some kind of crazy person, and he'd just move in on me and pin me down. And he'd say something like, "Listen to me, Timmy Tyler, in a second I'm going to let you go. And if you still want to hit me, you can. But I'd rather you tell me what you're really upset about." I couldn't get into hitting him then. And it was funny, after we talked, I usually discovered it wasn't even him I was really mad at.

I wished Chris were around now. I tried to think how he would have handled Beaver, but I couldn't figure it out. Chris wasn't the kind of guy to back down from what he knew was right. But still, I couldn't picture him carrying on like I did. I really didn't know what he'd've done. As I got dressed I wondered if I'd ever reach the age where I wasn't always so confused about things. I doubted it.

The rest of the day I was treated pretty good by everybody. Kids I didn't even know came up and told me they wished they had been the one to smack Beaver around. It felt good to know kids were pointing me out saying, "Yeah, that's the kid that belted Beaver in gym class." My lips were cut inside from where they had been mashed into my teeth, and my nose was feeling a little sensitive, but I felt pretty decent.

Until lunch when I saw Lymie. Mr. Doom and Gloom.

"So how are you planning to get home, Ty?"

"I'm gonna walk, same as usual."

"Yeah, that's real bright, Ty. Like Beaver isn't going to mash your face into the sidewalk as soon as you step outside the school."

"You're always such an optimist, Lyme." I tried to act like his words didn't bother me that much. "Besides, he'd really look stupid beating on me. He's twice my size."

"Duh, real good, Ty. Like Beaver's gonna stop and think like a regular person. I'm telling you, Tyler, you're living on borrowed time. Beaver wants one thing. Revenge. He's not gonna sleep until he beats the crap out of you."

"Yeah, so?" I said, because I didn't know what else to say.

"So Beaver isn't the type to lose sleep. He'll be waiting for you after school." Lymie was talking real slow like he thought I was a foreigner or something.

"Yeah, so?" I said again.

"How can you stand there saying 'Yeah, so' like that?" Lymie threw up his arms in disgust. "Look, come home on my bus, and have Mrs. Saunders pick you up at my place."

"Naw, if he's gonna do something to me, I'd rather not have to wait around all week for it. Besides, I don't think he will." If I was trying to convince myself, it wasn't working.

"Suit yourself. But I've gotten kind of used to seeing your goofy face the way it is. And after Beaver gets done with you, I won't recognize it." He shook his head, tapped my shoulder, and left for class. Shoulder-tapping was pretty affectionate for Lymie. He must have been pretty worried.

As much as I hated to think about it, Lymie was right. The fact that I was so much smaller than Beaver probably made him all the madder, having to wear those cuts and bruises from somebody he could have killed if a teacher hadn't stopped him. I could still see Beaver's heartless eyes glaring at me from his bloody face, and

I got chills thinking about meeting that face and those eyes where there weren't any teachers or anybody around.

I spent the afternoon trying to think up a plan. Begging for mercy was tempting, but that was out. Even if I could bear the humiliation, Beaver would never buy it. He'd probably wait till I got done, and then slam his fist down my throat. And avoiding him was out. I couldn't avoid him forever unless I moved back to Los Angeles, and he might even come for me there, if someone told him where it was. And reasoning with him was out. Lymie was right about that. I might as well try to reason with a killer grizzly bear.

Every time a teacher called on me, Mary Grace jabbed me between the shoulder blades to snap me out of it. After our last class as we walked to our lockers, she asked me if I felt all right.

"You're really out of it, Tyler. How hard did you get hit?"

"Not very," I said. "I'm all right."

"I can't believe you fought that guy. You must be crazy."

"Gee, thanks, Mom."

"I'm serious. What if that gorilla is waiting for you after school?"

"I don't care," I said. "It's a free country."

"Macho isn't cool anymore, Tyler. Grow up. He's twice your size."

"Look," I told her. "I'm sorry. But what am I supposed to do? I've been thinking about it all afternoon. Believe me, I don't like getting beat up. But what do you want me to do, buy a gun?"

"Why don't you wait and go home with me after my history club meeting? Beaver'll be gone by then."

"No, I'll be all right." I didn't want to tell her about my allergy shot. I already felt like enough of a wimp.

"Well, at least you're a runner. You outran him once today and if he tries to grab you, you'll just have to do it again. After a while he's bound to cool down."

"I have a feeling the sun cools down faster than Beaver."

We finished putting our books in our lockers and taking out the ones we needed for the evening. Mary Grace automatically switched a couple on me as we talked. Then she looked me right in the eye.

"Promise me you'll be careful, Tyler. Can you at least do that?"

"I will. I'll be careful. Really."

She gave me a long, hard look, probably trying to remember me as I was. Then she turned and left for her meeting. I was alone. Surrounded by kids, but still alone.

As I left school, I could feel kids watching me, but I didn't feel good about it like I had earlier. I walked staring straight ahead, not looking at anyone. I know it's stupid, but I felt like I should be given a last meal or a last cigarette, even though I was too scared to eat, and I don't smoke. When I reached the corner of Main Street and headed down it toward Academy Park, I was sweating something fierce. And when I saw the crowd of kids milling around the fountain, a drop of icy sweat rolled down the inside of my arm. My legs felt rubbery, but I tried to look nonchalant, like a normal kid walking home after a normal day at school.

As I got closer, I saw that many of the kids were

older than me, high school kids. They watched me approach and some of them poked each other. All conversation stopped and they stood there, edgy and excited. What better way to end a day than by watching some scared kid get mauled. One of them yelled, "Get ready, Beaver. He looks real tough." He laughed and a few other kids joined in. The kid that spoke was Mark Blumberg, the principal's son. I'd seen him lots of times at Buster's. He and his goofy friend Jack used to hang around with BooBoo, but I couldn't figure out why. Mark was a lousy wise guy. The type of guy who got his kicks by watching people squirm. He was a junior and you'd think he would have gotten over that by now. He was smart, and mean, and I think I hated him worse than Beaver. At least Beaver was dumb.

Beaver pushed his way to the front of the group and stepped into my path. He pulled his shirt slowly over his head and handed it to Mark. He flexed his muscles and looked down at me with a smile that wasn't a smile at all. His shoulders were thick and well developed, but his stomach looked soft and paunchy like a beer drinker's. I stared at the dark hair which crept up to his navel. I thought foolishly that it wasn't fair for someone to beat me up who had hair around his navel. I stood frozen, waiting for something to happen.

"We got something to finish, don't we, rich boy?" He jerked his hand up and I flinched. A few kids laughed.

My mouth was dry and tasted like tin. I knew my voice would shake if I tried to speak, so I kept quiet, hoping Beaver wouldn't drag it out too long.

A sudden shift of Beaver's weight, and a punch flew at my head. I ducked and delivered a hard one with all

64

of me behind it into the soft, hairy belly button. As I straightened up I heard almost before I felt a sickening thud on the top of my head. The force of it drove me backward into waiting arms which trampolined me back into the action. My hair was grabbed and my head was yanked back. A crushing forearm knocked through my upper body, and my head flopped forward until my jaw slammed my chest. The world sounded like it was under water. The side of my face was being hammered and I stumbled backward, no longer understanding what was happening to me. A knee slammed up under my ribs lifting me off my feet, and I felt something warm, almost hot, spreading over the insides of my icy cold legs. My bones seemed to rattle as my rear thumped the sidewalk. I lurched forward instinctively, jamming my head between my knees, and locking my fingers behind my ears. And I hid motionless over the sidewalk like a rabbit under the shadow of an eagle. Footsteps pounded past me. Almost from another world. I was distantly aware of one sharp kick in my side, and then all was silent.

I didn't move. For what seemed like a long time.

"Can you get up?"

I knew the gruff voice.

"Come on, Tyler. Get up and let me have a look at you."

Hands tried to rock my head back, and I locked my hands and knees all the tighter around it.

"Go away. Leave me alone, Chuckie. Please." I was crying now, and pleading.

"I'm bringing you home," he said. "I'm not leaving without you." As he spoke, he was firmly prying my knees down, tearing down the walls of my hideout.

"Chuckie, will you just get out of here!" I cried. "I pissed my pants. Why can't you leave me alone?" I was really sobbing now and my face burned with shame.

Chuckie pulled me to my feet and held my head from turning away as he examined my face and mouth. I could taste his fingers feeling around my teeth. Then he felt around my nose and wiped his snotty, bloody hand on his own tee shirt.

"Get in the car." When I didn't move, he pulled me, opened the door, and pushed me in. "Don't worry about the seat. You're not that wet."

He got in the other side, and I collapsed forward with my shame into my old retreat. I wished I'd never have to face Chuckie again in my whole life.

"Looks like you took quite a beating."

I didn't answer.

"But you did all right this morning, huh?"

That almost made me look up. I wondered how he knew about that.

"I ran into Mr. Johnson in the diner at noon," he said, stepping on the gas. "You're a gutsy kid. Not too sensible, maybe, but gutsy. I'll say that for you."

I felt the car pull into my long driveway. Drops of water from the sprinklers spattered the hood and windshield. Chuckie stopped the car, and I peeked up out the windshield. Mrs. Saunders and two old neighbor ladies were sitting on the porch, watching us and talking. I looked down at the dark splotches of dampness on my light blue corduroys. I lowered my head to my knees again and prayed I'd disappear.

"Come on." Chuckie got out. I heard my door swing open, but I didn't budge.

"Come on, hothead! You ought to know better than

to be fighting.'' Chuckie was talking loud, and he hardly ever talked loud. He wrenched me from the car. In my misery I tried weakly to shake loose from his grip, to keep from having to walk past those ladies with wet pants.

"A kid that's a hothead needs to be cooled down. Then maybe he can think straight." Picking me up by the neck and the seat of my pants, Chuckie hoisted me over the nearest sprinkler. Cold water stung my face, and I struggled clumsily to kick and punch my way free. Chuckie laughed and kept waving me over the sprinkler. I wanted to kill him.

"Chuckie, have you lost your mind? Put him down!" Mrs. Saunders yelled from the porch.

Chuckie yanked up on my neck, and swung me to my feet. He couldn't let go of me completely because I was still kicking and punching like a wild man. Mrs. Saunders came tearing down the porch steps but froze in her tracks when she got a look at me.

"Tyler, what in the world . . .''

I stopped struggling and looked from her bewildered face to down at myself. I could only imagine what my face looked like, but my shirt and pants were streaked with blood, and more thin watery blood still dribbled from my nose and chin down my front. I was soaked from head to toe.

"Tyler, you poor . . . What in . . . Chuckie, how could . . .'' Mrs. Saunders didn't know whether to examine me or hug me, so she did a little of both. Plus she tried to pry me away from Chuckie.

"He needed to be cooled down, that's all. He's all right now." Chuckie looked at me and winked. And I suddenly realized with a burst of joy that my pants were no longer any wetter than the rest of me. Chuckie smiled and pulled my arm. "Come on, tough guy. Let's get you inside and cleaned up."

Mrs. Saunders yanked me back, and looked at Chuckie the way you'd look at a mad dog.

"It's all right, Mrs. Saunders," I said, smiling. "It worked. I feel a lot better now."

As Chuckie led me up the porch steps, he stopped for a second and nodded politely to the ladies.

"Good afternoon, ladies. Lovely day."

Their jaws flopped down and their eyes widened at the sight of me. Chuckie pushed me into the house before they could say anything.

And that was how I came to adopt Chuckie Deegan into my family.

VIII

IT TOOK ABOUT fifteen minutes of holding my head back before my nose stopped bleeding. By then my whole face felt stiff, and I talked through clenched teeth because it hurt to move my jaw. My teeth felt like they'd all been jarred loose, and my bruised ribs hurt if I breathed too hard. And I noticed I was a little light-headed whenever I sat up. But it felt good to be in clean, dry clothes, and it was a relief to know that some terrible ordeal was behind me, kind of like the way I used to feel when I was little and walking out of the dentist's office.

Chuckie had shooed Mrs. Saunders out of my room after watching five minutes of her yelling and shaking her finger at me, and then hugging me and thanking God I was all right, over and over. He told her to call the doctor's office and tell them I'd be a little late for my appointment. He even said he'd drive me, which Mrs. Saunders wasn't crazy about at first, but she finally said all right. Driving through cities made her nervous, and she knew we wouldn't get home till after dark.

"Chuckie?" My voice sounded funny sneaking out from behind my teeth.

"What do you need now, Ace?"

I sat up and watched him rocking back in the chair he'd pulled up next to my bed.

"Thanks, Chuckie . . . I really mean it." It sounded stupid, but I didn't know how else to start. And I really did mean it.

"What for? I brought you home. Big deal."

"You know what I mean. When you found me, I was sitting on the sidewalk crying like a baby. I wanted to . . . I don't know . . . melt into the sidewalk or something. And you . . . you know . . . you chased everybody away and brought me home. If any of those kids had ever known I wet my pants, I swear I never would have gone back to that school. Ever. And then when we got home, you got yelled at for holding me over the sprinkler, just so I wouldn't be humiliated in front of Mrs. Saunders's friends."

"You can thank Mrs. Saunders for my showing up when I did. She sent me to get you. And as for the sprinkler deal, that was a last minute thought. You looked like you could use a good rinse." He pushed my head back again and pried the pillow under my shoulders. "Keep that head back until we're sure the bleeding has stopped. If you had a dipstick in your head, we'd probably find you were already down a quart."

"I couldn't help it," I said to the ceiling. "About my pants, I mean. He slammed me so hard I didn't even know where I was. It's not like I was being a baby or something. I usually don't even cry."

"No big deal. Don't worry about it."

"Chuckie?"

70

"Yeah?"

"Tell me about something stupid you did." I was up on my elbows now.

"What are you talking about? Who said I did anything stupid?"

"Whenever I feel really bad about something embarrassing or idiotic I've done, Chris always tells me a story about something embarrassing or idiotic he did. Then I don't feel so bad."

"Come on, Tyler, get out of here. He's your brother. He's supposed to do stuff like that." He pushed my head back.

"Yeah, but he's not here," I said. "Come on. It'll be fun."

"The next time somebody asks me to tell something stupid I did, I'll be able to tell them about being in this conversation."

"So will you do it?"

"Well, you could at least give me a minute to think," Chuckie said. "Would that be asking too much? I can't come up with something right on the spur of the moment."

"That's all right," I said. "Take your time. But remember, it has to be something so bad that even after years have gone by, you still think back and cringe because you're still so ashamed." My head popped up to study Chuckie's face.

"All right. Let me see . . . okay, I've got it. This one's bad." He pushed my head back and giggled. I'd never heard Chuckie giggle before. "This is just between us, right?"

"Yeah, and if I tell, you can tell how I pissed my pants." Now I was giggling. I tried to stop because it made my face and my ribs hurt.

71

"All right. Good enough. Now listen." Chuckie leaned forward and talked low, like we were sitting around a campfire or something. "You know how when you're in high school and taking driver ed., you have to watch these films about safety on the road? Well, I guess you wouldn't know about that yet. But anyway, in order to make you a more careful driver, they always show you these films about high school kids drinking, and driving too fast on their way to a prom or someplace."

"I know," I said.

"What do you mean, you know?"

"Chris took driver ed. and he told me."

"That's wonderful. Now shut up and listen."

"Sorry."

"Now where was I? Oh, yeah. At the beginning of the movie, you meet all the kids and see them making plans for the big day, you know, the prom or whatever. And you meet their parents and families, and you're supposed to think how these kids and their parents are like you and your parents and everybody."

"Did you?" My head popped up.

"Did I what?"

"Did you think how the kids were like you and your parents and everybody?"

"How do I know? Yeah, I guess I did. But that's beside the point. Now will you shut up and listen?"

"Sorry. But I thought that might be important."

"It's not, so shut up and listen. If something is important, I'll tell you." He pushed my head back, harder this time.

"Sorry," I said. "Go ahead."

Chuckie looked at me a minute to make sure I was done.

"Okay, so you're supposed to identify with these kids. But the thing is, you always know they're going to get into this awful, gruesome accident on the way to the prom, or wherever it is they're going."

I knew all that from Christopher, but I thought I'd better keep quiet.

"And so on the day we all know we're going to see one of these films, all the boys start bugging the girls, telling them how bloody and grisly the film's going to be, you know, to get them going. And the girls scream and carry on about how they won't be able to look, or how they'll have to leave. You follow me so far?"

"Yeah, I bet this is gonna be good."

"Sure, good for you. I'm the jerk in this story."

"Well, come on. Shut up and tell it."

"All right, keep your shirt on. So we get there, into the driver ed. room, and all the boys, myself included, are acting cool and telling the girls to make sure they get good seats so they won't miss any of the blood and gore. And the teacher tells everybody to shut up because he's been hearing the same stuff all day, and he turns the projector on. We watch about twenty minutes and get to know everybody in the film, and then we start poking the girls because we know the good part's coming. The kids are all in a convertible whizzing down the highway, drinking beer and having the time of their lives. Only they don't see this tractor trailer truck stopped right in front of them with the lights flashing, so they hit it, dead on. By now the girls in the class are going hysterical, but this is only the beginning. Now they start mixing in footage of a real accident just like the one they set you up for. And you see real kids, some of them are dead, and mangled, and twisted into funny

73

shapes on the highway, and some of them are alive and screaming for help. Then they show the parents, the actor parents, of one of the dead kids and they're saying how they hope their kid is having a good time. The camera goes back to the scene of the accident, the real accident, and shows close-ups of this mangled dead kid. And that's as far as I got.''

"You ralphed?''

"I what?''

"Ralphed. You know, upchucked, barfed.''

"Whose story is this, Ace? Yeah, I did. All over my desk. It was right after lunch, and believe me, it was a gusher. And what made it worse was that the girl I was sitting behind and poking earlier in the film had this beautiful, long blonde hair trailing over my desk. What a mess! All I can remember is girls screaming, especially that one girl with the blonde hair. And I took off.''

"Yeeooow! Whoooa, that must have been awful!''

"Yeah, I'll never forget it. I wanted to disappear from the face of the earth. And it's like you said. I still cringe when I think about that.''

"I threw up when I was watching *The Exorcist*,'' I said. "Chris had a whole bunch of his friends over and we were all sitting around our living room munching out, when the girl that was possessed threw up this green goop and it sprayed right out into the priest's face. And I threw up all over the couch. Mom was really mad at Chris for letting me watch that movie. I was only eight or nine then. Plus, the couch was brand new.''

"Now look what you've done,'' Chuckie said. "I spend all that time telling you a humiliating story so you'll feel better, and then you go and try to match it. Now you're one up on me.'' He laughed.

74

"That's my problem. I'm not even thirteen, and I've already experienced more humiliation than most adults. Probably every humiliating experience you can mention, I can match."

We were both laughing like total fools now. My face felt like it would crack, and my ribs were in agony.

"Go ahead, Chuckie. Try again," I said. "CHUCKIE DEEGAN, THIS IS YOUR HUMILIATING LIFE!" I tried to sound like that TV announcer on "This is Your Life." We were in stitches, and boy did I hurt.

Finally Chuckie said we'd better get going or I'd never make my appointment. He promised to tell me more grimy, mortifying details about his life on the way to the doctor's. We hurried down the stairs and out onto the porch. I still felt light-headed and rubbery-kneed from the beating, and when I saw the two old neighbor ladies sitting there staring at me with that same amazed look they were wearing an hour before, I burst out laughing all over again, and I couldn't have stopped if you put a gun to my head. I can only imagine how ridiculous I must have looked with a swollen nose and a bruised and cut-up face, clutching my sides with the pain of trying to stifle myself. And to top it off, when I laugh real hard, I make a shrill, squeaky kind of noise that Chris says sounds like a nail being pulled out of a board.

Chuckie wasn't any better. He grabbed my arm and dragged me down the steps and tossed me into the car. But as I watched him through the windshield heading for his side of the car, the whole thing struck him as funny again, and he doubled over in front of the hood and disappeared until his door popped open and he crawled in behind the wheel. We took off before Mrs.

Saunders had a chance to change her mind. I have to admit, we probably didn't look that sane.

It's hard to believe that anybody who was as miserable as I was that afternoon could have had as good a time as I did that evening. Chuckie and I shared some more cringe material, and we were still laughing when we got to Albany. I figured nobody could have more shame buried in their systems than we did. Except maybe Christopher. He had some pretty bad stories too.

As it turned out, the doctor wouldn't even give me my shot. One look at me and he said to forget it. With the kind of shape I was in, he was afraid the shot would send me into allergic shock or something. After he checked me all over, he gave me some kind of oral medication to take until I came back the next week.

"Oh, and by the way," he said smiling, "No driving. These pills might make you drowsy. And, hey, next time pick on somebody your own size."

For dinner I dragged Chuckie into this little health-food restaurant on Washington Avenue, even though he was afraid he'd have to end up eating tofu and sprouts. Chuckie handed me a *Times Union* he'd grabbed and told me to find something good to do. I love movies more than anybody I know and was heading for that section when I spotted an ad for this championship wrestling show at the RPI Fieldhouse in Troy. I'd seen a lot of wrestling on TV, but I'd never been to a live show before. Chuckie wasn't too keen on the idea (I think he was afraid somebody'd see him there), but he'd made the offer so he was stuck. We called Mrs. Saunders so she wouldn't worry about us.

We were lucky to get tickets. Even though it was a weeknight, the place was packed. The show was pretty much what you'd expect, a lot of fake kicks and punches, and a lot of fake interviews and arguments, and guys chasing each other with chairs and tables, and the bad guys whipping sharp things out of their trunks that everybody in the crowd could see, but the ref couldn't. But I have to admit it was pretty entertaining. I even saw Chuckie laughing a few times.

One thing that always gets me about professional wrestling is the crowd. You notice it on TV, but when you're right there with them, it's incredible. You have to wonder where they dig up some of these people. I swear they really thought this was real life. And I'm not talking about the little kids. I'm talking about full grown adults and old ladies and stuff. I made the mistake one time of cheering for the bad guy and booing for the good guy, just to be funny, and this old lady turned around and started swearing at me, and a bunch of other people started shaking their fists at me. Chuckie poked me and told me to shut up, but I was about ready to shut up on my own anyway. I couldn't believe it.

And it's like the promoters of the show knew what kind of junk the crowd would go crazy for, and they really fed it to them. Like there were these two bad guys who were on the same tag team. One of them was supposed to be some kind of sheik in this big turban, and the other was this humongous bald-headed guy who was supposed to be a Russian, or a Mongolian or something, although Chuckie said he'd give me ten to one neither of them had ever been out of this country. The guy who was supposedly the Russian or whatever made a big deal out of standing up there in the ring and trying to sing his national anthem while the sheik was running around the ring and yelling at everybody to stand up.

That made the crowd go really nuts. I mean totally bonkers. There were crazies all around us wrapping themselves up in American flags, screaming their lungs out, and shaking their fists. They weren't kidding either. Groups from all over the fieldhouse started singing "The Star-Spangled Banner" for all they were worth. People were almost knocking themselves out trying to drown out this guy's singing on the P.A. system. I couldn't believe it. Half this crowd would have probably been willing to drop bombs on Russian cities or someplace over that stupid song. And the funny thing was the stupid guy singing it was probably from Detroit or someplace.

To add fuel to the fire, the guys they were supposed to be fighting were supposed to stand for The American Way or something. They looked real clean cut, and you could tell at a glance they were the type of guys who respected women and spent their free time visiting crippled kids in the hospital. Another thing you could tell at a glance was that these guys hated loudmouthed sheiks in turbans, not to mention foreigners singing their national anthem in our country, worse than the crowd, if that was possible. The crowd could hardly stand it when they chased the Russian and the sheik away from the mike and started singing "My Country 'Tis of Thee." If I'd ever booed during that song, I'd have been dead meat.

Later, in the car, I asked Chuckie why he thought the crowd fell for the whole routine.

"I don't know, Ace. But I bet if I did, I'd know why there were wars, and terrorism, and cruelty, the whole works. Maybe it's like . . . I don't know . . . People like to feel that they're one of the good guys, and the easiest way to do that is to create bad guys and hate them and fight them. That probably doesn't make much sense to you, does it?''

"Yeah, it does," I said. "That's kind of like the reason why Mom can't stand most politicians. She says instead of trying to make the country better they just keep making speeches about how great we already are. Like we're better than everybody else."

"Hey, people eat that stuff up, Ace. It makes them feel like winners."

Chuckie pulled the car onto the interstate. I was quiet for a minute, thinking.

"Chuckie?"

"Yeah."

"You know how I went to this prep school for a few months?"

"What about it?"

"When I first got there, I roomed with this real fat kid. The poor guy. He had acne real bad, he was lousy at sports, he didn't have any personality . . . I don't know . . . He didn't have anything going for him at all. He wasn't even smart. And it seemed like the whole school ganged up on that guy. They did awful stuff to him."

Chuckie nodded but didn't say anything. He kept his eyes on the road.

"Chuckie?"

"Yeah, Ace?"

"Would you have stuck up for him?"

He waited a while before answering.

"I don't know. That's a tough one. It'd be easy to say yes, but if you're actually there . . ."

"I bet you would have."

That was the last either of us said for a while. The

79

subject was getting kind of depressing, and I was getting too sleepy to do much more thinking anyway. I slumped back in my seat and let my mind go blank, concentrating on feeling the vibrations from the road. Just as I was about three-quarters drifted off, a strange thought hit me from nowhere, like they do sometimes. I popped up with a start.

"Hey, Chuckie. Didn't you say that Mrs. Saunders sent you to bring me home from school? '

"Yeah, Ace. Why?"

"I always walk home alone," I said. "How did she know I was going to get beat up?"

"She didn't."

"Then why'd you have to come get me?" I shielded my eyes from the glare of oncoming traffic.

"I wasn't going to tell you this, but I suppose you'll hear about it soon enough anyway."

"What? Come on, Chuckie. You can tell me."

"It's about BooBoo Anderson. The coroner says he didn't drown out at the quarry. The water in his lungs was chlorinated. You know, like water in a pool. Somebody dumped him in the quarry after he was dead. And what he died from was a broken neck. He'd been struck in the head so hard that his neck snapped. Nobody knows much yet, but those gossipy ladies got Mrs. Saunders all shook up by talking about murder and everything, and she was afraid to have you walking home alone."

This was news. And to think Lymie and I may have been at the quarry right when the murderers were there!

Suddenly I was wide awake again.

IX

IT WAS ALMOST 11:00 before I got to school on Wednesday. I never even heard my alarm. Because we got home so late, Mrs. Saunders came in and flicked it off without waking me. She told me afterward that she really thought I needed my sleep, especially since Chuckie had told her the pills I was taking might make me extra tired.

Before I could go to any classes, I had to bring my note to the nurse's office and get an admittance slip. The nurse was busy arguing with some kid who claimed he had a headache and wanted to go home. He told her there was something about math class that always gave him a headache, and that somebody ought to check that classroom for chemical contamination. The nurse looked like she'd heard it all before.

"Back to class, Harvey. If you die at your desk over a long division problem, I'll take complete responsibility."

Harvey groaned and turned toward the door. When he saw me standing there, he said, "I hope you're not planning on leaving."

The nurse took my note, read it, and looked up at me.

"Got home late from a wrestling show?" she said. "From the looks of it, you must have been sitting a little too close to the ring."

I laughed, remembering my cuts and bruises.

"I got in a fight with a kid after school yesterday."

"A fight, huh," she said through her teeth, the way I was talking. "I hope you lost."

When I looked confused, she said, "If you didn't lose, I'd hate to treat the guy who did."

I laughed again. She was pretty funny.

"I didn't see much of the other kid," I said. "But I think he's all right."

This time she laughed. Then she asked me a few questions to make sure nobody at home was beating me or anything. I told her Mrs. Saunders was too old to hit me even if she wanted to, and that Chuckie was the one who had saved me from getting beat up worse than I did. She seemed convinced and wrote me an admittance slip.

"You know, Tyler," she said as I was leaving, "being tired is not exactly a legal excuse, but I have to admit it's more honest than a lot of the excuses I'm expected to swallow. See that it doesn't happen again."

The bell rang just as I stepped into the hall. And Mary Grace was at her locker when I got there.

"Tyler, thank God. You're in one piece," she said. "I was going crazy! Yesterday I called your house to see if you made it home all right, and a lady there told me you were still at the doctor's. Well, that was bad enough, but this morning when you didn't show up, I really got scared. Some of the kids said you'd been practically beaten into the sidewalk.'' As Mary Grace spoke, she was at it again, digging out the books I'd need for the rest of the day.

I explained about my allergy shots in Albany.

''Only the doctor wouldn't give me the shot anyway because he said I was too wracked up.''

''He's got that right. You're a mess.''

''I'm fine,'' I told her. ''Today I just overslept.''

''Well, one good thing came out of this,'' Mary Grace said. ''I don't think Beaver will bother you anymore. When you didn't show up this morning, Beaver was afraid you were crippled or in a coma or something.''

''I'm surprised he cared.''

''He didn't, except that he thought the police might be coming for him. And I told him I hoped they did. I almost spit in his face.''

It was funny picturing someone like Mary Grace standing up to a thug like Beaver. And I couldn't picture her spitting on even a sidewalk.

My next class turned out to be lunch. Mary Grace was on B lunch so she headed for home ec. Since Mrs. Saunders had made me eat breakfast, I wasn't hungry, but I went to the cafeteria and tried to do some of the homework I was supposed to do the night before. I had barely opened up my social studies book when an overloaded tray slid toward me, splashing milk all over my book, and Lymie plopped down in front of me.

''He lives! T. Tyler McAllister has survived the deadliest ordeal known to man, an encounter with a mad Beaver!'' He paused a second to gawk at my face. ''And he only looks a little funnier than he used to.''

83

Lymie was shoveling lunch into his face almost before his rear end hit the seat.

"Lymie, you clod. Look what you did to my book!"

"Couldn't be helped," Lymie said. "I thought I was seeing a ghost." He continued shoveling as I grabbed a couple of napkins off his tray and dried off my pages as much as I could.

"I warned you, Tyler. You never listen to me, but I told you what would happen."

"Yeah, well, if I had listened to you, I'd still be looking over my shoulder every time I took a step. At least now it's over."

"But if you listened to me, you'd be able to open your mouth a little when you talked." He imitated the way I was talking through my teeth.

"Maybe we should get Beaver to smack *you* so you'll learn to keep your mouth closed when you eat."

"Funny, Ty, you're a regular barrel of laughs, you are," Lymie said. "Hey, did you hear the news? You know, about BooBoo. It might've been murder like you said." He crammed half a roll into his mouth. A little thing like murder wasn't enough to keep Lymie from stuffing his face.

"I heard," I said, closing my book. "What do you think, Lymie? What do you make of it?"

"Who knows? BooBoo's mother told the cops that the last she saw BooBoo, he was headed down the street to Mark Blumberg's house. He used to hang around there a lot. But Mark said he never got there."

"Somehow I can't picture Mark Blumberg being nice to somebody like BooBoo. That kid's sick." I remembered how excited he got at the prospect of me getting beat up.

"Yeah, he's a sick puppy, that's for sure," Lymie said. "But who ever said he was nice to BooBoo? He and that geek Jack Robbins used to drag BooBoo around with them, but it wasn't because they were such good guys. They'd always boss him around and laugh at him if he did anything dumb. And the rotten thing was, BooBoo really thought they were his friends."

"That stinks. Why didn't anybody tell BooBoo?"

"Would you want to be the one to tell somebody that his best friends didn't even like him?"

"I see what you mean." I shook my head. Mark was an even bigger jerk than I thought. "So, Lymie, if BooBoo didn't show up at Mark's house, where'd he go?"

"According to Mark and Jack, they were both sitting on Mark's front porch about the time BooBoo was supposed to have left his house. And they noticed these two grubby looking hitchhikers walking up the street toward BooBoo's house. Only they didn't think anything of it at the time until afterward when the police questioned them, and they found out BooBoo was supposed to have showed up."

"So the police think the hitchhikers murdered BooBoo?"

"No, Tyler, you goofball, they think my grandmother did it. Duh. That's why they're running around questioning everybody trying to get more information on these guys."

"Boy, Lymie," I said, "this is really spooky. Any of us could have met them on the street that day." I tried to think what I'd do if two guys tried to grab me.

"You're telling me! A lot of kids saw them."

Lymie was right. For the rest of the afternoon everybody was talking about those two hitchhikers, and it seemed like almost everybody had seen them. If they were all telling the truth, which I doubt, those poor guys must have hitchhiked up and down every street in the village, and then headed out and crisscrossed most of the surrounding countryside. Some of the kids said the guys looked like hippies (they still used that term in Wakefield), and some said they were two seedy-looking old guys. Not only that, but it seemed like every time they were spotted, their hair color changed and they were wearing different clothes.

By seventh period I had lost interest in all the stories. Those pills the doctor gave me were really catching up to me, and probably like Chuckie said, I didn't have as much blood left in me as I was supposed to have. I felt like one of those guys in the movies who's had some kind of knockout powder put in his drink. I thought about going home, but the nurse had already made it clear that tiredness wasn't a good enough excuse for getting out of school, and I wasn't up for sneaking out. Besides, there was only one period left. I figured it shouldn't be too hard to get through one period.

Old Lady Waverly passed out one of her famous worksheets on the three basic kinds of rocks, which we were supposed to have read about in Chapter 3 the night before. Luckily it was open book because I hadn't read it, and rocks aren't really my thing anyway. But I'm a fast reader, and I used the index to find the page numbers, and then skimmed paragraphs looking for key words. The work was easy, but pretty boring, and being as tired as I was, it was pretty hard for me to keep my eyes open. I had told Mary Grace about the pills before class, so whenever my head started to droop down, she jabbed me in the back with her pen.

Old Lady Waverly sat up at her desk giving everybody the evil eye, and every so often she'd go up and down the aisles on patrol or something, making sure kids were being quiet and neat, in that order. Any kind of noise tended to bring out the worst in her. She must have had ears like a dog. And sometimes she'd stop and wad up a kid's paper saying, "Is this what you call neat?" Last week Jason Rounds got thrown out for saying, "Not anymore."

It didn't take much to rub Old Lady Waverly the wrong way.

I worked on, silently, and as neat as I could manage, jotting down information on igneous rocks, and volcanoes, and sedimentary . . . riverbeds . . . metamorphic . . . The fluorescent lights overhead buzzed monotonously. I felt another jab and straightened up.

"Mary Grace!" The whole class snapped to attention. Old Lady Waverly paused and took a few steps toward us. "Perhaps you should have brought a cattle prod to school. Then maybe you'd have to wake our friend less frequently. But today, since you don't seem to have the proper equipment, why don't you move to the front of the room."

Mary Grace grabbed her stuff and moved to an empty seat in the front. I went back to work. Old Lady Waverly's smiling face didn't fool anybody. Everybody knew she didn't have a real sense of humor. When she joked around, that only meant she was like a half a millimeter away from flying totally off the handle.

As I stared at the book, I could feel her eyes beading into my skull. It seemed like forever before I heard the slow footsteps which meant she had resumed her rounds. At least then I could relax and breathe again. Whew. I don't know why she didn't like me. Was sleeping that terrible a crime? At least it was quiet. I didn't snore or anything. It probably wasn't only me. She probably didn't like anybody. Even a goody–two shoes like Mary Grace. Rocks. They were about the only thing she liked. Somebody like Old Lady Waverly probably had them stuck all around her house. Like pet rocks or something. She probably even talked to them. It wouldn't surprise me. But I bet she hated rock music. Because that was normal. I couldn't wait to get home. I'd go up to my room, find a good album, put on my headphones, and melt into my bed. Just melt away . . . not a worry in the world . . . that'd be nice . . . real nice . . .

X

"IT IS MOST unfortunate, Mr. McAllister, that you persist on using Mrs. Waverly's class as your personal napping center. You may have surmised that Mrs. Waverly does not take kindly to the notion of her room being used as a rest stop on the freeway of public education." Mr. Blumberg leaned forward in his chair, planted his elbows firmly on his desk, and peered over his glasses at me. He looked as tired as I was, but that didn't seem to be helping me any.

A yawn was struggling to come up out of me. I fought it back by clenching my jaw while the rest of my face worked at keeping my eyes propped open. My lungs sucked in air loudly through my teeth with a couple of hitching gasps, and my eyes watered, blurring Mr. Blumberg's attempt at a smile. I blinked hard to wipe my vision clear and nodded my head although I wasn't really sure what he said. A chill had crept into my bones. Air always seems colder and damper when you wake up too fast. And Mr. Blumberg sure didn't warm the room up any.

"I notice from the attendance sheet that you arrived late this morning," Mr. Blumberg continued, holding up the paper. His other hand waved the little paper that I recognized as my note. It was a regular show and tell. "I took the liberty of checking your excuse and found that the reason for your tardiness was that you attended a professional wrestling show." He said professional wrestling slowly, in a voice dripping with scorn, like I must be some kind of lowlife to go to something like that. He even held the note away from his face between his thumb and his forefinger like it was probably swimming with germs.

"We didn't get home till after midnight," I said, because Mr. Blumberg didn't say anything more. "Mrs. Saunders thought I needed more sleep." I knew how lame that sounded. I was hoping he'd yell at me quick and tell me to get lost. No such luck.

"Mr. McAllister, forgive me for questioning the priorities of your household, but certainly you must understand that one of the purposes of a school is to foster a sense of responsibility in its students. In all its students. You do understand that, don't you?" He filed the attendance sheet and dropped my note.

"Yeah . . . yes."

"Perhaps. But I sometimes find that students who come from—how shall I put it—families with more modern notions, as it were, sometimes suffer from a kind of benign neglect. I find this especially true among the more affluent. They develop little awareness of consequences." Mr. Blumberg folded his hands, leaned back in his chair, and regarded me thoughtfully, giving me time for his words to sink in. Which didn't do a bit of good, seeing how I had no idea what he was talking about.

"I didn't mean to fall asleep on Mrs. Waverly, Mr.

Blumberg," I said, because I can't stand silence when I'm in trouble. "I told her I was sorry."

"Let's simply say that showing up late for school with an unacceptable excuse, and falling asleep on Mrs. Waverly, as you so colorfully put it, seems to say something about your general attitude toward our educational establishment. I trust you didn't fall asleep at the . . . show." He spit out "show" like it was a dirty word, and he looked at me like I was a lowlife again.

"I wasn't tired then." Sometimes I hate listening to myself.

"Of course," he said, and he closed his eyes, pulled off his glasses, and rubbed the bridge of his nose. He looked like he might be fighting off a wicked headache. "I also understand you were fighting in gym class yesterday." He put the glasses back on. "Mr. Johnson didn't see fit to file a report, but I generally find out things that happen in my school."

His school. I thought of his son, Mark, who was probably not only a sicko, but a tattletale too. I didn't say anything.

"From the looks of you, it must have been quite a fight."

"Most of these I didn't get till after school," I said, feeling my cuts and bruises. "Why don't you ask your son? He was there."

I think I sounded nastier than I meant to. You could see Mr. Blumberg stiffen up.

"That my son had the misfortune to happen upon a senseless fight is hardly pertinent. What is pertinent is that you seem to have a history of fighting. It is true, is it not, that you were expelled from a previous school for fighting?"

"Not really expelled," I said, squirming in my seat. "They just said that I probably shouldn't come back."

"You have quite a knack for euphemisms, my young friend." Mr. Blumberg's voice was meaner now. It was stupid of me to have brought up his son. "Tell me, Mr. McAllister, are you planning to carry on this pugilistic tradition here at Wakefield?"

"No." I hung my head. And I didn't even know what "pugilistic tradition" meant.

"I would like," Mr. Blumberg continued, "to have this . . . er . . . Mrs. Saunders, I believe her name is, come in to have a talk with me. I'm assuming that your mother is, shall we say, preoccupied with work and not available."

"She's in Colombia."

"Yes, I seem to have heard that." He shook his head, picked up the phone, and began to dial my number. He rapped a pencil impatiently on his desk, waiting, but no one answered. He hung up the phone and looked at me like he was puzzled. I was relieved. Maybe he'd only send me home with a nasty note this time.

"Tell me, Mr. McAllister. Are you left unsupervised much of the time?" He stared at me thoughtfully.

"Not really," I said. "I'm supervised almost all the time. Mrs. Saunders is probably out getting groceries or something."

Mr. Blumberg kept on staring at me, not saying anything.

"And even if she does have to leave," I said, "she tells Chuckie—he's our groundskeeper—to look after me."

Mr. Blumberg straightened up, and his face became less rigid. He looked like a TV detective who had stumbled onto an important clue. I knew what he was thinking.

"Your mother is out of the country. Your housekeeper is obviously out of the house. And I'm to understand that your groundskeeper will, as you put it, look after you." He paused and studied me a moment before continuing. I could almost detect a trace of kindness and concern in his face. "Tell me, son, how do you feel about this? Don't you ever wish your mother could be at home with you?"

"Yeah, I guess," I said. "But Mrs. Saunders is like family. Besides, my mom will be home the first chance she gets. It's not that bad. Really." I hated the idea of him thinking I was some kind of abandoned child, tossed from person to person with no one really taking care of me. It wasn't like that at all.

"Mr. McAllister, I'd like you to wait in the internal suspension room next to my office until I'm able to contact your maid. I don't like the idea of sending a child home to an empty house. And since your mother has chosen . . . well, let's just say we'll wait until I've made contact."

Mr. Blumberg led me down the narrow hallway that connected the main office to the guidance office, his hand on my shoulder the whole way. I think the guy really felt sorry for me. He guided me into a small room filled with two rows of desks, the kind they have in libraries that wrap around you with big sides so you can't see the kid next to you without leaning back.

"Choose a desk, Mr. McAllister, and make yourself at home. This will be a good chance for you to start on your homework, wouldn't you say? Do you need anything from your locker?"

"No, I've got stuff to work on. Thanks," I said, holding up my books.

"Very well then. I'll let you know when I've contacted your maid."

Mr. Blumberg left and I was alone in that creepy, quiet room. I headed for the farthest desk in the back corner, hidden from the door and nice and private, but with a good window view. Turning my chair to the window, I put my feet up on the sill and rocked back and forth, thinking. Thinking about how I always get myself into trouble without even trying. I was hardly into my second week of school and already Mrs. Saunders was being dragged in to have to listen to Mr. Blumberg tell her what he thought my problem was. Which made me mad at first, seeing how he'd raised a kid like Mark. But the thing was, it wasn't just Mr. Blumberg. I couldn't very well blame him for all my problems. He didn't give me allergies . . . or asthma attacks . . . or sleeping attacks. And he didn't get me kicked out of my last school. That was all stuff that happened without any help from him. Maybe I was a born loser, some kind of unfixable lemon doomed to screw up, no matter what. Besides running, school was the only thing I was halfway decent in, but lately I couldn't even do that right. Maybe I was born under a bad star or something. Maybe I was nothing more than a skinny version of Ralph Waller.

Waller was the kid I was assigned to room with when I first got to Grant Academy. He was this huge mass of blubber and the kids all called him "Waller the Whale" and "Waller the Whopper" and stuff. I didn't call him anything. I was too depressed. Dad had put me on a bus right after Easter vacation when he'd finally convinced Mom to give boarding school a shot. He said it would toughen me up and be the best thing in the world for me. When I got there, I didn't cry, but I had this sick feeling in the pit of my stomach, and I didn't feel much like talking to anybody. It felt like that dream I used to have had come true, the one where I fell off the edge of the world and was stranded completely alone. That didn't bother Waller any. He didn't seem to want to talk anyway.

At breakfast the first morning, some of the guys told me I'd better ask for a transfer unless I wanted to be stuck with Waller the rest of the year. The thing was, Waller was sitting right there listening, and they didn't even seem to care. I didn't know what to say. I ended up telling them Waller was all right, and I didn't mind staying with him, figuring maybe I could get a transfer later without making him feel so bad. The guys looked at me like I was crazy.

Maybe nobody ever stuck up for Waller before. I don't know. All I know is Waller became my shadow after that. He walked with me to class, he ate lunch with me, then dinner, and then he followed me back to the dorm, only stopping first at the candy machine to fill his pockets. Exactly what he needed.

I was miserable. As if I didn't already feel bad enough, being so homesick I could barely keep from bursting into tears, and I had to put up with the loneliness of being with Waller. The guys all hooted and jeered whenever he walked by them, and he'd slink away after me. He never even said anything back to them.

On the second night some guys came barging into our room about an hour after dinner. Six of them, all a few years older than me, and dressed perfectly in their blue uniforms with black stripes and spotless shiny black shoes. They ignored me at my desk and zeroed in on Waller. I recognized the one who seemed to be in charge as the kid who carried the flag in the flag-raising ceremony that morning. He cuffed Waller a few times before he spoke, his voice hissing with hatred. "How's it going, Fat Boy?" Another slap. "Did you miss us, Waller, buddy?" Another slap. Harder each time. A few other boys moved in and jabbed him in the side.

Waller turned away, whimpering and huddling over his desk. I started to get up, but what I saw next stopped me in my tracks. I couldn't believe my eyes. Waller's shaky hands began to open his candy, shielding it with his body and peeking sideways the way a hungry dog does when it finds food and doesn't want to share. It was horrible . . . revolting to watch. He started stuffing candy into his face. And at that moment I learned something. I learned that I hated Waller almost as much as the other guys did. I hated him for all the misery he stood for. And I hated the other boys for the cruelty they stood for. And I hated my room. And I hated the whole stupid lousy school for dragging me away from home. I hated my allergies. I hated how lonely I was, how helpless. I hated so much that tears started streaming down my face, and I slumped back into my chair.

The kid from the flag-raising ceremony struck Waller hard on the side of the head, and he rolled heavily from his chair to the floor like a plastic bag filled with guts. He was whining and still clutching his candy. The other kids kicked him as he writhed like a fat worm, curling up around his candy.

The seething, hissing threats that followed the jabs

96

and kicks, and Waller's whimpering cries rose in my head until my head seemed to expand with them like a balloon. I clutched my ears to stop the noise, but it didn't stop. It got louder. I got up and yelled at them to cut it out, and they laughed and kicked Waller some more. I screamed at them to get out, and one of them knocked me down. My arms grabbed a chair and started whaling kids with it. I heard smashing sounds and screaming, my own maybe. Arms and bodies crushed me into my bed, and punched me, and crammed a pillow in my face. The next thing I knew, the housemaster was dragging me downstairs. He'd had to practically pry the chair out of my hands.

I might as well have left that night, because that was the beginning of the end of my stay at Grant Academy. Two long months and I don't know how many fights later, I came home for the summer. I'd lost ten pounds, and I was ten times more miserable than before I left home. That was the summer I was so sick. That was the summer my father died.

Chris told me afterward that I should be proud that I stuck up for Waller. But the truth is, I didn't. I knew I didn't.

I jumped when the dismissal bell went off. Pretty soon the happy sounds of kids heading for freedom came in through my window. I watched sadly as kids laughed and poked one another, hopping on buses and zooming down the aisles to get the best seats. The town kids filed down the sidewalk in little groups heading for Main Street. I wanted to join them more than anything.

The door behind me clicked and I sat up, expecting to hear Mr. Blumberg saying I could go home too. But the door banged closed and for a moment I thought I was alone again. Then I heard a voice right behind my wrap-around desk.

"Well, what do you think?" I knew that voice.

"I don't like it. I told you I didn't like it from the start." That voice didn't quite ring a bell.

"Relax. We answered their questions, didn't we? It's over, so forget it."

"We throw BooBoo into the quarry, and you tell me to forget it!"

"Shut up about that!"

"And what about the hitchhikers? The cops asked too many questions."

I held my breath as my ears strained to hear their hoarse whispers.

"Good for them. They asked the questions and we answered them." He laughed, the same nasty, sneery laugh I heard the day before when he told Beaver I looked tough. "And Jack, the thing that really cracks me up is that *we* didn't even see any hitchhikers, but everybody else did!"

"I'm glad you're happy," Jack said. "Me, I haven't slept right since before this whole mess."

The door clicked open again. I must have been about purple now from holding my breath. I prayed they were leaving.

"What are you boys doing here?" Mr. Blumberg's stern, no-nonsense voice.

"Waiting for you, Dad. You were on the phone. I need your car keys. We have to pick up some stuff at Jack's house. How about it?"

"I suppose so," Mr. Blumberg said. "I'll get them for you in a minute. But see that you go straight there and straight back . . . Now where did that boy go? Mr.

McAllister, are you in here?'' His voice moved in on my hideout behind the row of desks. I was still frozen up against the back of my chair. ''Ah, there you are. I was afraid you'd fallen asleep again. You're free to go now. I'll meet with you and Mrs. Saunders tomorrow at two. And, might I suggest that you go to bed early tonight?''

He gave me one of those grim, principal looks, but his face seemed to soften when he saw how spooked I was. He put his hand on my shoulder and walked me out the door. Glancing back down the narrow hallway, I saw Mark Blumberg and Jack Robbins staring at me, looking like they'd just seen a ghost.

Which is what I was afraid I'd end up being if they got their hands on me.

XI

I'VE NEVER BEEN a very decisive kid. At least that's what Chris always tells me. He used to get a kick out of me when we'd be in New York or someplace and we had to cross a busy street. I'd stand there swiveling my head back and forth, waiting for just the right moment to make my move. I'd always make a couple of false starts and then hop back up on the curb. Chris would look at me and shake his head. Then he'd clamp his hand around my arm, and exactly at the right moment, he'd give a yank and off we'd go, zipping through an opening in traffic. No hesitation. No false starts. No sweat. We're different like that.

And if a kid has trouble deciding when to cross a street, you can just imagine how he'd react knowing he was the only one to know about some kind of murder cover-up. And to make matters worse, I knew they knew I knew.

I hurried down the sidewalk toward Main Street, too scared to even look behind me. I wondered what Mark and Jack would do to me. They might even kill me. Stranger things have happened. But waiting and not knowing was what scared me the most. If they didn't do something soon, I might die of fear.

A big black car pulled up next to me and the door popped open.

"Hey, McAllister, get in!"

Jack's voice shook and his face looked pinched. He jumped out of the passenger side not three feet from me, and I could see the car's red interior. I bolted before I even knew it. Running is the one thing my body understands and does well. I had zipped down a driveway and cleared a fence before my brain even caught on. A man yelled at me from his backyard, and his voice trailed off in the distance. I should have stopped. He was big and mean-looking with a face like a bulldog. Angry maybe, like people get at kids, but not a killer. I should have stopped. He could have protected me.

I poured on more steam and pumped hard, in case Jack was right on my heels. I was gasping for breath. You can only sprint for so long. When I made it to the cemetery behind our property, I glanced behind me and saw that I was alone. I wasn't all out sprinting now, but I was still moving at a pretty good clip. I stayed clear of the lanes, figuring I could outrun Mark and Jack if I had to, but not their car. My foot snagged a low marker hidden in the grass, and I sprawled to my hands and knees, but scrambled back to my feet without losing any time. It wasn't till then that I noticed I was still clutching the bookbag Mrs. Saunders had dug out of my closet for me. It was just as well. If somebody grabbed me, I could always whale him a good one with it. But I prayed it wouldn't come to that.

Leaving the cemetery at a slow jog, I cut through a narrow pine woods. I could see my house now, but instead of feeling relief, it gave me the creeps. Mark and Jack would count on my coming home, and might be waiting for me. I threw my bookbag over our black iron fence and kept my eyes peeled as I rolled over it. The sharp points jabbed into my legs and I felt my pants rip.

Dashing across the open lawn, I made it to Chuckie's cottage. I beat on the door so hard, it's a wonder the glass didn't pop out. I waited, hearing only the sound of my own wheezing, and then beat on it some more. No one answered. How would I protect myself and Mrs. Saunders if Chuckie wasn't around?

I ran past the main house, chucked my bookbag on the porch steps, and headed for the garage. Both doors were locked. I paced back and forth in front of the garage like expectant fathers always do in the movies. Thinking. Or more like trying to think. It isn't easy coming up with something when you're looking over your shoulder and jumping at every little sound. After a minute, I darted back to the house.

As I fumbled for my keys, I glanced over my shoulder down the long driveway. What I saw made my eyes almost pop out of their sockets. The big, black car was rolling to a stop in front of our entrance archway. When the door opened and Jack jumped out, my heart nearly stopped. Jamming the key in the latch, I flung myself at the door, slammed it shut, and double locked it. Me, who always got yelled at for never remembering to lock anything. I even flipped the switch to the burglar alarm which Mom had had installed, the one Chris and I teased her about because we never figured crime was too big in a place like Wakefield. I was grateful for it now. If anyone tried to open a door or a first floor window, a loud siren would go off in the house and down at the police station. Mrs. Saunders never left it on in the daytime because I was always setting it off by accident.

Dropping my bookbag, I darted into the den because it had a big bay window jutting out from the house that would give me a wider range of vision as to what was going on in the front yard. I sneaked the curtains back and peeked out, holding my breath and hoping I didn't come face to face with Mark's blistering, beady eyes. The big car was still out front, but the door was closed and Mark and Jack were both inside. From the way their heads bobbed around and the way Jack kept jerking his thumb toward the house, it looked like they were having a pretty lively discussion. Finally, Jack slumped down in the seat with his head in his hands, and the car rolled slowly down the street and out of sight.

I wondered what they might have decided. And what I should do. I remembered how Mom used to tell me how Mrs. Saunders had kind of a bad heart and that I should help her out whenever I could and lift heavy things for her and stuff like that. So I couldn't very well run up to an old lady with a bad heart and tell her there were two murderers stalking the place.

The door to the den snapped open, and I nearly jumped out the window and left my skin behind the way a snake does.

"Tyler, I thought I heard you come in."

"Whew! Mrs. Saunders," I said. "You scared me."

"You're as white as a ghost. Are you sure you feel all right?" She came over and started feeling my head like she always does.

"I'm all right," I said, trying to smile and look healthy.

"Why, you're all overheated." She stepped back and studied me. "And what in the world happened to those pants?"

103

"I kinda jogged home. And I ripped these climbing our fence."

"Tyler, is that bully after you again?"

"Naw, I think he learned his lesson." I laughed weakly. "You heard about me falling asleep?"

"Yes, I heard." Mrs. Saunders sighed and smoothed my hair back.

"Are you mad?"

"No, I'm not *mad*," she said, giving me a hug. "I know you're trying to do your best. That's all we ask."

"I'm trying," I told her, "I really am. But things . . . happen to me. I don't know. I mean, it's not like I decided to go to science class and fall asleep or something."

"I know, dear. Don't worry. I'm sure those pills you're taking didn't help any. We'll straighten it all out with Mr. Blumberg tomorrow."

"I think he thinks there's something wrong with me," I said. "He brought up about Grant Academy and said how I had a history of fighting."

"Well, there's not, and you don't," Mrs. Saunders said, suddenly bristling. "And you needn't take things people say too seriously. You're too sensitive sometimes for your own good."

"I think he thinks I'm a psychopath or something."

"A psychopath! Don't be ridiculous. You're a thoughtful, well-mannered boy. I only wish you could have heard Chuckie talking about you today. Chuckie, who doesn't usually say two words. He went on and on. It sounded like you two really hit it off after all these weeks."

"Where is Chuckie?" I asked, casually, I hoped. "I looked for him outside."

"Don't you remember, honey? Today was the day

for him to drive to New York and pick up some new things your mother ordered for the house. He won't be back until tomorrow afternoon.''

"Oh, no!" I moaned before I even realized it. "Not today of all days."

"He'll be back before you know it." She paused and gave me the eye, the one adults give you when they think you're hiding something. "Was there something you needed him for, dear?"

"Naw, I guess not," I said. "There was something I wanted to tell him is all."

"Well, you can tell him tomorrow, and I know he'll be glad to listen. Come on. I'll get you a snack. And don't forget it's time for your medication. Remember, three times a day until your shot next week." She shooed me toward the kitchen.

"I'm not really hungry, thanks. And I'm starting to think those pills are more trouble than they're worth."

"Not if they keep you from having an asthma attack," she said. "Relax, dear. We'll deal with Mr. Blumberg tomorrow. Don't be so . . . what's the word you kids use . . . so uptight."

I didn't know anybody my age who said uptight, but I didn't say anything. I tried to look pleasant as I swallowed my pills, which wasn't easy considering my brain was whirling with thoughts of murder—both BooBoo's and the possibility of my own. I kept picturing myself as a chalk outline on the carpet. Mrs. Saunders was studying me pretty close, and she looked a little worried herself. She took another temperature check on my forehead, and then started feeling around my neck for signs of disease.

"You don't have a fever, but you seem so jumpy.

Have you been eating sweets?'' She stepped back and regarded me thoughtfully.

"No, Mrs. Saunders, I didn't eat anything since you fed me. I'm all right. I feel great." I was lying. I felt all shivery and weak-kneed.

"Why don't you run up to your room and get your homework done? Then tonight you can watch a little TV and get to bed early for a change. I don't like the way you look lately." She kissed me on the forehead.

Upstairs I paced around my room, back and forth about fifty thousand times, trying to decide what to do. I thought about calling the police, but why should they believe me? Not that many people around town knew me, and I didn't have any proof of anything. Also, being in trouble with the principal and reporting that his son was a murderer wouldn't look so good. Plus, if I did that, Mr. Blumberg would be sure to drag out my school records for everybody and his brother to see, so they'd think I was some kind of dirtbag who shouldn't be believed anyway. So much for calling the police.

Then I thought about calling Chris because he's always good in an emergency. I called and got the answering machine, which was Chris's voice saying he'd be out until tomorrow and to leave a short message. What I had to.say I couldn't say to a machine.

And it wouldn't be any use to call Lymie. He'd be out doing chores. I could ride my bike to his place, but I didn't dare. I'd be a sitting duck pedaling along the side of the road. Besides, Lymie was only a kid like me anyway. How much protection could he be?

Like I said, I'm not a very decisive kid.

I moped around my room for an hour or so, unable to keep my mind on my homework. What did homework matter when I might not be around long enough to turn it in? I slumped back on my bed in misery. Why me? Why always me? I couldn't understand it. It seemed sometimes that my whole life, and especially the last few years, had been so jinxed that hardly anything went right for me. I was allergic to what seemed like half the things on the face of the earth. I had been thrown out of a school, and then only after nearly dying of loneliness. I didn't have a father, and when I did, he couldn't seem to figure me out anyway. And when Mom bought a new house, mainly for me, to give me a chance to start a new life, the bad luck followed me across the country. Sneaking out at night and going swimming, a thing that millions of kids must have done, for me turns into a disaster. Who but me would be jinxed enough to swim into a dead body? And even if they were, what would be the chances of them overhearing the body's murderers talking about it? The whole thing even sounded ridiculous. It didn't seem fair.

I wished I could be one of those people who had their lives organized and who always seemed to know exactly where they were going. No fear. No sweat. No stupid blunders. Mom was like that. In addition to her acting and reading scripts and planning film projects, she managed to do all kinds of public service things like benefits for clean air and water and rain forests and stuff. And even with all the trouble I'd been for her, she was always able to bounce back and stay on top of everything. And Chris. He was making a big name for himself and never seemed to be afraid or lonely or confused. And Chuckie. He had this quiet confident way of facing life and taking things in stride. I couldn't picture him lying around his room shaking in his boots the way I was. Even Mary Grace, a kid who was my own age, had all the ins and outs of school down pat and was always prepared for whatever might happen.

Not me. I was a lemon if ever there was one. A textbook case, clear and simple. If Mom had bought me at a store instead of giving birth to me, she could have exchanged me for a kid who worked better.

"Excuse me, sir. I have a complaint. I bought my last son here, and he's been a perfect joy. But this one is a different story. Nothing but problems. You should be ashamed of yourselves for selling such a lemon to a good customer."

"Please accept my humblest apologies, Ms. LaMar. Of course, I can see at a glance that this child is defective. You must understand that no matter how careful we are, these things do happen. Please, choose any child in the store, compliments of the house. Maybe you'd like a nice musical prodigy? Or maybe our Olympic model? That's been a big seller this year."

"To tell you the truth, at this point I'll settle for one who can breathe on his own and stay out of trouble for more than a day at a time."

Of course, I was being unfair. Mom would never do that. She'd keep worrying herself sick about me and sinking more money into doctor bills and hospital bills and new houses so I'd have a better environment and all that. And every time she got me back on my feet, I'd use those feet to rush into my next disaster. But Mom was loyal. And she really did love me. But let's face it. How long can you love a lemon?

XII

THE PHONE NEXT to my bed rang and I jumped. I looked at my clock. It was nearly 5:00. My history book lay open on my chest. Why would I go to bed with my history book and with all my clothes still on? And why wasn't it dark? The phone stopped ringing and I lay there trying to remember.

"Tyler, honey, it's for you!" Mrs. Saunders, yelling from downstairs.

I rolled toward the phone, and my history book fell to the floor with a thud. I rubbed my head and stared at the phone, not too sure what to do with it. Wait. It wasn't five in the morning. I must have fallen asleep after school. And with a sickening wave I remembered Mark and Jack and all the trouble I was in.

"Hullow."

"Tyler, is that you? I can barely hear you." The cheerful voice sounded familiar, but I couldn't remember who it belonged to.

"Yeah . . . ziz . . . Tyler," I mumbled. I don't wake up fast.

"Tyler, you sound like you're dying. I waited for . . ."

"Whoziss?"

"Tyler, are you all right? This is Mary Grace. I waited for you after school, but you didn't show up."

"Oh, yeah. I didn't . . . I just woke up." Even in my stupor it was good to hear her happy voice.

"I didn't mean to bother you, but I wanted to know if you got in much trouble."

"Uh, well . . . give me a second." I sat up and tried to rub some life into my head.

"You know you sleep more than my nephew does, and he's only two."

"Thanks, Mary Grace," I said. "You're gonna give me a hard time about that too? I told you about the pills. I can't help it."

"Tyler, I'm sorry. I was only teasing. I called because I was worried about you."

"It's not your fault. I'm just being sensitive. That's another of my many problems." I knew I sounded like a jerk, but that's what I felt like.

"Boy, what's with you today?" Mary Grace said. "Did you get in that much trouble? I mean, sleeping in school isn't that serious, is it? Actually it's probably the only sensible thing to do in one of Old Lady Waverly's classes. Let's face it, if her worksheets get any duller, they'll have to start serving coffee in her room."

I smiled. Almost.

"No, I'm not in that much trouble. Mrs. Saunders and I have to meet with Mr. Blumberg tomorrow. It shouldn't be too big a deal."

"Okay, good. So what's bothering you?"

I waited for a minute, thinking.

"Mary Grace, if I told you something, something really important, would you promise never to breathe a word of it to anybody? Ever?"

"Tyler, you're scaring me. Are you in some kind of real trouble?"

"Promise?"

"All right, all right. I promise. Should I be sitting down or something?"

"I can't tell you on the phone. I've gotta tell you in person. It's a long story. Can I come over tonight?"

"Yeah, of course you can. Look, why don't you come over right now and have dinner with us?"

"I can't. It's got to be dark. It'd be too risky in the daylight."

"Tyler!" She almost shouted. "Don't do this to me. You're really scaring me! Look, why don't I send my father over right now to pick you up?"

"No, that's all right. I'll see you sometime after eight. Don't worry. I'm just a dramatic kid. It runs in the family. Get it?" I forced a tiny chuckle.

"I hope you're right," she told me.

At dinner I told Mrs. Saunders that I had to go over to Mary Grace's and get help on math. I'm a lousy liar, and if she'd really looked me in the eye, she would have known something was fishy. She didn't notice my guilty face, but she still wasn't crazy about the idea of my leaving, what with the whole BooBoo thing unsolved, and me needing extra sleep because of the pills. Plus, she was still worried about my seeming so jumpy.

"Tyler, you turned on the alarm, didn't you?"

"I happened to think of it."

"You never thought of it before."

"Maybe I'm getting more responsible."

She was studying me close-up, but that line cracked her up. She finally said I could go but only after she cranked my head around till we were eye to eye and told me if I wasn't home by 9:30 and in bed by 10:00, I'd have some real worries.

I waited till it was pretty dark before I dared leave the house. I'd been running around upstairs since dinner, peeking out the windows, making sure I didn't see anything suspicious around the yard. The coast seemed clear. I told Mrs. Saunders to turn the alarm back on after I left, and that got her going again, and she almost locked me up for the night. I told her I wouldn't talk to strangers and I could outrun almost anybody on foot, and she gave in again. By this time, I was having second thoughts about leaving myself.

It was a breezy night and darker than I thought it would be. I crept around behind the house, looking around and listening. I couldn't really hear much because there was quite a breeze whizzing past my ears, and until my eyes adjusted, I couldn't see anything either. I didn't look forward to walking through the dark woods or the cemetery alone, but if Jack and Mark were looking for me, it would probably be right on the streets.

I headed toward the iron fence, steering clear of any trees or bushes big enough for anybody to hide behind. I stopped at the fence and looked around to make sure I wasn't being followed. The back of the house was dark and its roofline and sides were outlined by the glow of streetlights. I shuddered. It would have been easy for someone to have seen me leaving the house and be sneaking up on me right now. It was stupid of me to wait until dark. In the daytime at least you could see danger coming. Even the air felt creepy at night.

I climbed the fence without ripping my pants this time and started through the pine woods. It was too dark to run. I could make out the outlines of the big trees, but I was afraid of poking my eye out on one of the little jagged branches that hung down around my head. The pine needles cushioned my footsteps, and I seemed to glide slowly over the ground. Sometimes when I turned around to check behind me, a twig would rub against the back of my neck and my skin would crawl and my hair would feel like it was trying to climb off the top of my head. I knew that if someone had been lurking at the edge of the woods watching me leave the house, I'd be walking right into a trap. Maybe I should have taken the street. At least then I'd be able to take off like a shot and scream my lungs out if I had to. If I got mangled in the woods, no one would hear a thing. It might even be days before anyone found me.

I moved faster, holding my arms out to protect my eyes, but it still took forever to get to the end of that little woods. The cemetery was easier to manage once I found the lane, but a cemetery is a creepy place to be alone in at night, especially when your skin is already all creepy and goosebumpy. I jogged down the lane slowly, being careful not to twist my ankle on a rock or a stick. My pace picked up as I saw the silhouetted shapes of the houses on Main Street.

I hopped the picket fence into the bulldog-face guy's backyard. A real dog barked and the backyard light snapped on. I dropped flat on my face in a shadow on the dewy grass and prayed the guy wouldn't let the dog out. It didn't sound like the type of dog that wanted to play. I also prayed that snakes didn't come out at night since I hate snakes even in the daytime. Peeking up, I saw the bulldog guy's face at the back door looking right at me but not seeing me. Growling at his dog to shut up, he flicked off the light and his hulklike shape moved off through the blue glow of a TV set in the next room. I bolted down his driveway like a rocket, turned onto Main Street, and poured on the steam for all I was worth. Mary Grace's house was only a little more than a quarter mile away, but after coming this far, I didn't want to take any chances.

I was pretty well winded by the time I scrambled up the steps of Mary Grace's front porch. I hit the glowing orange button once and turned to check the street. I didn't see anybody, but when the porch light snapped on, I felt like I was in the spotlight at Carnegie Hall. I whirled around and scrunched up against the door. When the door opened I almost jumped over the top of the lady inside. Mrs. Madigan, I figured. She looked down at me kind of surprised, and then yelled up to Mary Grace that her "little friend" was here. Smiling, she led me into the living room where Mr. Madigan sat reading the paper.

"You poor dear," she said, still looking at me kind of funny, "you look like you ran the whole way."

Mr. Madigan stood up to shake my hand. He was a big guy, graying at the temples, and he had one of those grips where you could almost feel your bones cracking. He was about to offer me a seat when Mary Grace yelled for me to come upstairs.

"Nice to meet you," I gasped and headed for the staircase. It was a relief not to have to sit in a small, quiet living room making wheezing noises in front of somebody's parents I didn't even know yet.

Mary Grace met me at the top of the stairs, dragged me into her room, and slammed the door like I was a slave on the underground railroad or something.

"Door!" we heard Mr. Madigan yell from downstairs, and Mary Grace ran back and opened the door. That's all I needed, to get beat up by some girl's father.

"Tyler," Mary Grace started in, "I'm going crazy! Tell me what's the matter!" She looked down at my clothes. "Why do you have wet grass all over the front of you? And why are you all out of breath?"

"I'm lucky . . . that's all I got . . . lying around . . . in some guy's yard . . . that owns a big dog," I said, still gasping for air.

"Sit down," she told me. "Relax. I'll get you a glass of water. If you keel over and die, I'll never get the story."

It was difficult for me to get started. I didn't know where to begin. So I started with Lymie and me sneaking out of the house last Saturday and went on from there. Mary Grace stopped me a few times to ask about this or that, but no matter what I said she didn't act like I was crazy or the victim of an overactive imagination or something. And she really listened to everything I said. Before I knew it, I had told her not only about BooBoo and Mark and Jack, but also about Christopher and Mom, and Mrs. Saunders, and Chuckie, and Grant Academy. I even told her how Dad would be mad if he were around and heard me spilling my guts because he thought boys were supposed to keep things inside and work them out privately, and never in front of females. And I told him how Mom always defended me against Dad, telling him all the time that he was left over from the Dark Ages and that guys didn't have to be like that any more and to get off my back. I'd never said anything out loud about Mom and Dad's fights before, I guess because deep down inside me, I felt responsible for them not getting along and finally getting a divorce. I couldn't tell Mom this because I knew how much it would upset her, and I realized after telling the whole story to Mary Grace that I had been afraid to say anything to Chris because I was worried that somewhere deep down inside, he thought I was to blame too, although he'd never say it.

I must have gone on for at least an hour. When I realized how self-centered I'd been, dominating the whole conversation with my problems, I was kind of embarrassed and started to apologize all over the place.

"Hey, don't apologize," Mary Grace said. "Do you realize that in one evening I've gotten to know you, really, more than I've gotten to know any of the other kids I've gone through school with for eight years? It's amazing. I mean, think about it. How many times do you get a chance to really talk to somebody, you know, without all the little games and cover-ups and everything? You're crazy if you think I'm going to let you apologize for that."

"But I didn't give you a chance to say hardly anything."

"Tonight you had things to say. Maybe next time I'll have things I want to say, and I'll know I've got you."

I couldn't believe Mary Grace was my age, or Lymie's. And I didn't have to worry about her rushing to school the next day and nearly breaking her neck to blab all the personal stuff I'd told her to her friends. I knew I didn't.

"Right now, Tyler, let's get back to Mark and Jack. I think you're wrong about them."

"Mary Grace, I'm telling you. I heard them. I wasn't dreaming. They killed BooBoo."

Mary Grace shook her head.

"Think about what you really heard. Nobody actually said anything about murder. I've known Mark Blumberg all my life. His father's good friends with my father. And I know Mark can be mean, and he can be selfish, and he can be stupid, but I can't see him as a murderer. He and Jack are covering up something, but probably not murder."

That made sense. A little anyway.

"But why did they try to get me into their car, and why did they go to my house? They didn't exactly look like they wanted to take me out for ice cream."

"That's the way Mark is, and probably Jack's the same way. He intimidates people to get what he wants. And believe me, Mark's used to getting what he wants. And now he wants something from you. If you got into that car, Mark would have threatened you, probably, and maybe even hit you, but I doubt it. He wants you quiet, but he also saw you take a pretty bad beating without backing down. And you said yourself how Jack looked scared. I bet neither of them knew what they wanted to do with you. Maybe they only wanted to talk to you to see if they could find some angle to get through to you. But I think you're safe. Mark will never make citizen of the year, but I'd bet anything he's not a killer. And I don't think Jack does anything without Mark's stamp of approval."

I felt a little better hearing that. After all, Mary Grace knew Mark a lot better than I did.

The phone rang downstairs and Mrs. Madigan yelled up to me. I looked at the clock. It was almost ten. Mrs. Madigan told me that Mrs. Saunders was going crazy worrying because I should have been home by now. Mr. Madigan said he'd drive me.

Mrs. Saunders was waiting for me on the front porch. She didn't look pleased. I scooted up the steps and into the house. I didn't even look over my shoulder for Mark and Jack.

XIII

"You TOLD! I don't believe it. We had a deal, and the first pretty face that comes along you blab your guts out to. I don't believe it!"

Lymie grunted and puffed his way around the track. Beaver never needed to worry about Lymie winning his way to captain. I jogged backwards trying to explain, but Lymie wouldn't even look at me. His head was down, his eyes following the white line. I couldn't blame him really. I *had* promised to keep my mouth shut.

"Lymie, can't you get it through your thick head? I thought they might kill me or something. You're afraid you might get grounded for a week. I thought I was gonna be put in the ground. Forever! Besides, Mary Grace promised she wouldn't say anything."

"Oh, sure, like a girl can be counted on to keep her mouth shut. You're a guy and you couldn't even keep quiet."

"Good thinking, Lyme. Real modern."

"I don't want to be modern, Tyler. I want to stay out of trouble, and I thought I could count on you. I was wrong."

"Come on, Lyme. PLEASE?" I begged. I hate it when people are disappointed in me. I really hate it. "Come on, Lyme. You can at least look at me, can't you? PLEASE?"

Lymie continued to puff around the track without even raising his head. I was going crazy. Here was my best friend and he couldn't even stand to look at me. He thought I was some kind of traitor or something. I had to make him listen. I had to do something. Almost before *I* knew it, let alone Lymie, I stopped, jammed my foot in front of Lymie's, yanked his arm and rolled to the side. As he pitched forward and toppled to the ground, I rolled on top of him, pinning his shoulders down with my knees.

"Tyler, you butthead, get off of me! I'll kill you! I really will!" Lymie flopped around the ground like a madman in the middle of some kind of fit. He almost flung me off a couple of times. I don't weigh all that much and Lymie was pretty strong.

"Lymie, don't make me get rough," I told him as I jammed my knees hard as I could into his shoulders. " 'Cause I'll belt you if I have to. Mrs. Saunders is about ready to kill me after last night, and I can't stand it if you're mad at me too. What do you want me to say? I'm sorry. I was scared. I didn't know what to do. Is that a crime?" So much had happened to me so fast over the last few days I was afraid I was going to start crying all over the place.

Suddenly Lymie stopped struggling beneath me, and I felt him begin to shake. With laughter. The stupid fool was laughing at me. The laughter grew until he was choking and teary-eyed, and it was making me madder by the minute. I didn't see anything funny going on. I leaned up and ground all the weight I had into his shoulders.

"What's so funny, jerkface?" I yelled.

"You . . . you are . . ." He was so out of breath from running and laughing he could barely get the words out. "You . . . you crack me up . . . 'Don't make me get rough.' When you get serious . . . you're the funniest kid I know. Eeeoooowwww! Get your bony knees off me. They're liable to cut me." This sent him into another round of convulsions. "You look so goofy when you try to be serious . . . You crack me up . . . Eeeoooowwww . . . I'll kill you . . ."

I had to laugh, too, after a while because Lymie looked pretty goofy himself, but I didn't miss the opportunity to get a couple more knee jabs in, seeing how Lymie was nearly paralyzed.

"You boys want to be alone?" Mr. Johnson's rough voice startled us, and we both hopped to our feet and started jogging again without waiting to see if he had anything else to say. When we got out of Mr. Johnson's range, I turned to Lymie, and when his eyes met mine, he cracked up all over again.

"Lymie, don't be such a jerk. You think because you're stronger than me that's all there is. I could dazzle you with my speed." I cuffed him lightly on the side of the head a few times to demonstrate, and backpedaled out beyond his reach. "Attack and retreat. That's how I can get you. No sweat at all."

"You better hope you can run forever, Tyler," Lymie panted, "because when I get my hands on you, you know I can mash you into a bloody pulp. No sweat at all."

"Good for you, Lymie. The whole universe is proud

of you. I'm trying to talk serious here and first you act like a big baby, and now you're a tough guy.''

''Oh, I like the way you explain things, Ty. I don't call it being a baby when you're mad at somebody for breaking a promise. And I wasn't being a tough guy. I was stating facts.''

''Fine, Lymie. Great. You're tough. But what I want to know is what should we do?''

''We? Did I hear you say 'we'? Those guys weren't chasing me around in a car, Tyler. I don't know where you get this 'we' stuff.''

I wasn't in the mood for listening to Lymie's whole song and dance routine. Not today.

''Cut the crap, Lymie. You're supposed to be my friend. Besides, you know as much as I do now.''

''Yeah, thanks to you. Come to think of it, it's thanks to you we found the body in the first place. I'm telling you, you're an accident waiting to happen.''

''Tell me about it,'' I said. We had finished our laps and were walking to the football field.

''Look, Tyler, I know you're upset and worried and everything, but there's nothing we can do. Let's just see what happens. If you go squealing to the cops or somebody without any evidence, you'll end up looking like a total fool. Mark and Jack will deny everything and that'll be that.''

''How about you though? Won't you back me up?''

''Back you up with what? What do I know?''

''You were at the quarry when we found the body. And you saw two people in a car with a red interior, same as Blumberg's.''

''Hold the phone, butt-for-brains, you want to get me grounded for that lousy information? We've been

122

through this before. There must be millions of cars with red interiors."

He saw how disappointed I was.

"Really, Ty, I don't see that our saying anything will make any difference."

We walked quietly for a while, thinking.

"Well, I feel funny about not saying anything. It doesn't seem right."

"All's I'm asking you to do is to can it for a while. At least for now." He stopped and looked at me. "Just don't do anything stupid. For your sake as well as mine. Just keep your cool and we'll see what happens. You don't want to get all beat up again, do you? Huh, buddy, do you hear me?" He rapped his knuckles on the side of my head.

"I hear you," I said. I heard him, but it didn't go down easy. I couldn't help feeling we owed BooBoo something, but maybe Lymie was right. It wouldn't hurt to wait a few days.

Most of the kids had finished their laps by the time we joined the group, and they were already picking up teams. Beaver was captain again, along with Ralph, so things were pretty much back to normal.

"Hey, McAllister," Beaver yelled, "you're on my team. We can use your speed."

My heart sank, wondering what Beaver had in store for me this time. As if I didn't have enough on my mind. I trudged over to join the team, watching Beaver suspiciously to see if there was a catch. He seemed friendly enough, at least as friendly as someone like Beaver ever got. He stepped in front of me as I approached.

"Hey, McAllister." He paused, shuffling his feet and

groping for the right words. "I was glad to see you in school yesterday. You know, that you weren't really hurt or nothing. I gotta admit, you got guts. You're pretty stupid, maybe, but you do got guts."

"Thanks," I said, trying not to sound sarcastic. I knew a lot of Beaver's change of heart was because he was so happy that he didn't get arrested or sued or something. But I also knew how hard it must have been for him to say what he said, especially in front of everybody. This didn't make him Mother Teresa or anything, but I did appreciate it.

"Hey, Beav?"

He turned and looked a little uncomfortable, like he was afraid I was going to wise off to him and start the whole thing over again.

"What?"

"Can we have Lymie on our team too?"

Beaver gave me a funny look. You could tell he wasn't used to taking requests, and it threw him off for a second.

"All right," he said. "He can be center. I'll be quarterback. And you'll be going out for passes." He turned to where Lymie was. "You," he told him, "over here."

Lymie came trotting over and stood next to me. After Beaver finished picking the rest of his team, he turned and glared down at the two of us.

"We better win," he said. And then with one finger on my chest and one finger on Lymie's chest, he pushed us out of his way.

Lymie and I looked at each other and kind of smiled to show how we weren't all that scared. But I swear to God, neither of us ever played harder in our lives.

124

XIV

Mrs. Saunders stared straight ahead. She hadn't seen me come around the corner past the secretaries in the main office. I stopped for a second and watched her sitting there alone outside the principal's door. She looked tired and troubled, clutching her purse nervously, as if she'd done something wrong instead of me. If she'd known I was there, she would have perked up right away. The few times I'd seen Mrs. Saunders looking that worried were when she didn't know I was around. I felt pretty terrible about her getting dragged into the whole mess. She was old, probably sixty-five or so, not to mention her heart condition. She deserved better than to be sweating it out in front of some principal's office wondering how she'd be able to defend some dumb kid who had a habit of snoozing his way through science.

I started toward her again, deliberately squeaking my sneakers on the linoleum so she'd know I was there. She looked over and smiled, motioning me to sit in the empty chair next to her. All trace of worry had vanished from her face, and I wondered where it had gone.

"Are you still mad?" Selfish question. I should have asked her how she was.

"Mad is what dogs get, Tyler. You want to know if I'm still angry."

"Are you?"

"No, dear, I'm not angry. I just have to remind myself from time to time that you're a typical twelve-year-old boy, and your head is tied up with typical twelve-year-old boy things."

"Almost thirteen," I said glumly, "and I'm not sure all the things I do are so typical. I'm really sorry you got dragged into this."

"Don't you worry about me," she said, patting my knee. "I've been around long enough to be able to take care of myself. You're probably too young to remember, but I had to see a few teachers and principals for Christopher too."

"No kidding. I don't remember Chris ever getting into trouble." It was kind of nice to think that I wasn't the only one that messed up.

"Your brother was a good boy, same as you, but he wasn't perfect either, not by a long shot. He got into his share of fights like boys will, and believe me, he could be filled with the devil when he wanted to be." She thought for a minute. "Come to think of it, science wasn't his strongest area either. I remember one time he and a friend sneaked into the science room right before their earth science lab practical. Those two rascals went through all the rocks they were supposed to know how to identify, and figured they'd do better on the test if they threw all the ones they didn't know out the window. And believe me, they didn't know many of them." She nodded her head and smiled as she remembered. "He was a year older than you are now, Tyler, and in the ninth grade, as I recall it. The two of

126

them might have gotten away with their funny business, except it was lunchtime and the entire faculty, including their science teacher, heard those rocks pinging off the sidewalk right outside the faculty room.'' She stopped and laughed, and I smiled, trying to picture the whole thing. ''There's not much you do, Tyler, that doesn't ring a bell with me about something Christopher did. But I'll say this for the two of you, and this is the God's honest truth, I've never known either of you to be anything but good when it came to the big things, the things that really matter.''

''Wow, that's a pretty neat story. Chris never told me that.''

''I suppose he figured you could come up with enough devilry without him supplying you with ideas. And I probably shouldn't be telling you this either, except . . .'' She paused and studied me a minute. ''Sometimes I think you take things too seriously, as if you think you're the only boy in the world who isn't perfect.''

''I'm not trying to be perfect, Mrs. Saunders. I just want to be normal. You know, like everybody else.''

''Oh, Tyler, can't you see there's a million ways to be normal? Christopher was normal in his way, and you're normal in yours. And you're both special. All I'm trying to say in my own clumsy way is that you should never think of yourself as a bother or a burden to any of us. You bring a lot of joy to us, Tyler, just the way you are. Your mother knows it, and your brother, and, as tough as your father was on you, I hope you realize you were something special to him too.''

I wanted to jump right up and hug her on the spot, but I didn't. It was amazing sometimes how she could tell what I was thinking and say the things I needed to hear. Mom and Chris were like that, too. I guess I was more like Dad in that respect. We both had trouble with saying the right thing at the right time.

The door opened and Mr. Blumberg stood there, shoulders back, hands on his vest, looking as if anything he might say would be the most important thing in the world. I remembered Lymie saying how I was funniest when I was the most serious. Now I knew what he meant. Mr. Blumberg did look pretty funny standing there all smug and important, especially considering he was going to be yelling at me for snoozing in class.

"Mrs. Saunders, I presume . . . and Tyler, please step into my office and have a seat."

He made this big sweeping gesture with his hand, and we jumped up and did like he said. He followed us in and sat behind his desk, regarding us thoughtfully and giving us time to soak up the importance of the occasion. Neither of us spoke. We just gawked back at him, so he cleared his throat and started in.

"I'm glad to have the opportunity to meet with both of you. I thought maybe if we had a chance to . . . to interact, we might be able to iron out what I perceive to be some difficulties."

He wanted to discuss my problems. Which we knew before he said anything.

"This interaction may prove valuable in preventing us from having to face more grave predicaments somewhere down the line." He waved his hand toward the window, like he thought maybe this predicament would take place in the parking lot.

Mrs. Saunders sat up straight in her chair and met him eye to eye.

"Mr. Blumberg, I don't know what grave predicaments you foresee for this boy, but I can assure you he's a good boy and a good student. And while I can certainly understand your concern about his falling asleep in class . . ."

"Twice, Mrs. Saunders. Twice." He held up two fingers to help out.

"Yes, twice. I can understand your concern about his falling asleep in class twice. And I do appreciate that in your line of work you've very likely heard every excuse in the book for every behavior imaginable. But I think you should know this. You see, in the past few years Tyler has had a number of allergic reactions. In fact, a few of his asthma attacks have been quite severe. To control these reactions, he sometimes needs strong medications, and these medications *can* cause drowsiness. And that is why sometimes, especially late in the afternoon, he's not at his best. His doctors are hopeful that he'll outgrow many of these allergies, and he'll no longer require medication. But he's a good boy, Mr. Blumberg. He really is. And I'm certain you'll find, medication or no medication, Tyler will turn out to be the kind of student Wakefield can be proud of." Mrs. Saunders spoke firmly and without hesitation. She had really done her homework. Perry Mason couldn't have defended me better.

"Mrs. Saunders, please understand," Mr. Blumberg said as nice as anybody could, "we wish the boy the best of luck with any medical problem he may be encountering. But, and forgive me for being blunt, I don't think all of Tyler's problems in school are by nature medical ones. We are, Mrs. Saunders, in the seventh day of school, and the boy has fallen asleep in class twice, he's been late once, without a legitimate excuse,

I might add, and he's been involved in two fights, one in school and one after school.''

Mr. Blumberg sat back in his chair and studied Mrs. Saunders's reaction. I felt like I was watching a tennis match and it was Mrs. Saunders's serve.

"I'm afraid I'll have to take responsibility for his being late, Mr. Blumberg. And as for his fighting, well, I suppose I know as well as anyone that he can be a handful, a real handful . . . just like a lot of boys his age. But I think you'll find that given the chance, Tyler will settle into the routine soon enough.''

"I don't think I need to remind you, Mrs. Saunders, that this is not the first school in which Tyler has experienced difficulties.'' He waved my permanent record folder and I squirmed in my seat. My head swiveled back to Mrs. Saunders. She still looked pretty strong.

"Mr. Blumberg, I think if you examine the whole record, you'll find that most of Tyler's school years have been flawless. His grades are fairly good, and most of his teachers have made a point of telling us he was a pleasure to have in class. He did have one bad semester, it's true, at a boarding school where he didn't belong in the first place. That was our mistake. A child belongs at home with the people who love him. But that's all in the past, and I don't think we'll see that kind of problem here.'' She met him head-to-head without flinching, even when she said "our mistake.'' Mrs. Saunders had been against that school from the start, but it wasn't like her to lay the blame on others.

"Mrs. Saunders,'' Mr. Blumberg said, nodding his head and looking as pleased as anything. "You bring up an excellent point. A child certainly does belong at home. But in addition to that, and forgive me for my

130

candor, I also feel very strongly that a child needs a full-time family.''

Mrs. Saunders stiffened at that and looked ready to jump down his throat. Mr. Blumberg smiled and held up his hand so he could continue.

''I'm simply trying to say that parenting is a full-time job. I know. I have a son myself. And it seems to me that a mother . . .'' He paused and seemed to grope with his hands for words. ''I'm sorry, but I must confess that I have difficulty with this modern notion of entrusting one's children to the care of others.''

I turned to see Mrs. Saunders's knuckles whiten as she gripped her purse. For a moment I thought she might clobber Mr. Blumberg with it.

''Mr. Blumberg, I'm afraid you don't quite understand our situation. You . . .''

''I may understand more than you realize. Correct me if I'm wrong. The boy's mother is out of the country. He is left to the care of a housekeeper, and . . .'' He threw his hands up in disbelief. ''And if no one else is available, he is watched by the groundskeeper. Now that's hardly the stability a child needs, wouldn't you agree, Mrs. Saunders?''

Suddenly I felt bewildered by the exchange. Mrs. Saunders had tears in her eyes, and it was plain to see that her hands were now shaking.

''That is terribly unfair, Mr. Blumberg. I am available as much as any real . . .''

Mr. Blumberg held up his hand again, smiling sadly now. He knew he was in control.

''Mrs. Saunders, I didn't mean for you to take personal offense. I'm certain you're doing an admirable job caring for the boy. I only have trouble with . . . how can I say it . . . the situation.''

''The situation!'' Mrs. Saunders had been about ready to burst into tears, but the way he said ''situation'' really rubbed her the wrong way. ''You don't even begin to understand the situation.'' She was getting hot now, and patting my knee at the same time to show me that everything was all right. My jaw dropped down and my eyes popped wide. I could feel blood pulsing through the cuts and bruises on my face, and on top of that, I was starting to feel a little sick to my stomach like I do when I get tense.

''The situation is, Mrs. Saunders, that we see a child who needs, if anything, special care, being left behind by a woman who has obviously prioritized her career over her son!'' He lost his smile, and for a second you could see something like anger or impatience flicker across his face.

Mrs. Saunders gasped. I felt like I'd been hit. My mouth was dry, and my tongue tried to stick to my teeth when I spoke.

''That's not true!'' I yelled, tears starting. The blood seemed to drain from my head. I couldn't believe what I was hearing. He didn't even know my mother.

''Tyler, I'm sorry,'' said Mr. Blumberg, recovering quickly and smiling again. ''I shouldn't have said that in front of you.''

I glared at him, still shaking with anger. He didn't say he shouldn't have said it, only that he shouldn't have said it in front of me.

He turned to Mrs. Saunders.

''Perhaps we should have the boy wait outside.''

''No!'' I said before Mrs. Saunders had a chance to answer.

132

"Perhaps, honey, it would be best. I'll only be a minute." She spoke softly, but the way she looked at Mr. Blumberg, I knew she was bracing herself up for a real no-holds-barred battle.

"I'm not leaving," I said sullenly. That was the first time in my whole life that I could ever remember openly disobeying Mrs. Saunders. But it wouldn't be right to make her fight it out alone. It was my problem. Besides, there was no telling what kinds of things he might say if I wasn't there.

"I'll be all right," I said, still glaring at Mr. Blumberg, still smoldering inside.

"Perhaps," Mr. Blumberg continued calmly, "I'm wording this poorly. I didn't mean to be critical of the boy's mother. In fact, my own wife, who's as fine a woman as there is, would be working today if I had given her the choice." He paused and shook his head, giving us time to appreciate the difficulty of his decision. "But I remained firm on this one issue, and I believe it has paid off. My wife has her clubs and committees to keep her busy, and I believe, I really do, that this is why my son's permanent record folder doesn't . . . uh, shall we say, contain any surprises." He held up my folder as a kind of contrast.

"You really think your son is perfect, don't you?" Knowing what I knew about Mark made it impossible for me to keep quiet. Mrs. Saunders tried to shush me.

"I think his record speaks for itself." Again, the little flicker of anger across his face.

"Maybe the record should show that your son threw BooBoo Anderson in the quarry." My voice was quiet and cold. I felt like I was listening to someone else speak. I heard Mrs. Saunders gasp, and I was afraid she might have her heart attack right then and there.

"Tyler!" Mrs. Saunders looked at me like I was a ghost. "This isn't doing any good!" Then turning. "Mr. Blumberg, this child's mother loves him as dearly as any mother could, and you've absolutely no right to imply otherwise. Look what you've done to him. He . . ."

"No, it's true," I yelled, knowing I had already gone past the point of no return. "You gotta pool, right? Yeah, you must have 'cause BooBoo was in your pool when he died. That's why he had chlorine in him!" I pointed an accusing finger. "They moved him . . . He was in your car!"

"Tyler, please!"

"It's true, Mrs. Saunders. I know it sounds crazy . . . they're hiding it . . . I saw it . . . I heard them . . ."

"Tyler!"

"Remember how he had chlorine in him! From their pool!"

"My dear boy," Mr. Blumberg said, remaining cool through all the yelling, smiling sadly like he was on to my childish game, but still had all the patience and understanding in the world. "This outburst merely substantiates my point. And not that I feel the need to respond to your wild accusation but for your own information, Bobby Anderson couldn't have drowned in my pool. On the night of that unfortunate incident I was home, in my own backyard, and next to the pool." He eyed me smugly, with a trace of pity that I would stoop so low.

"You'd lie to protect him, wouldn't you? You'd lie in a minute!"

"I'd much rather discuss your problems, which is

why we're here. But if you choose to further embarrass yourself, feel free to go out right now—I'll even give you a pass—to share this outlandish story with any teacher whom you feel you can trust." He reached into his desk and pulled out a book of blue passes. "You see, on Saturday, almost all the teachers were in my backyard from early evening on. And a few of the hardier members of our staff were still there until after the drowning was reported. It was the night of our annual faculty party."

"Then it happened in his friend Jack's pool!" That had to be it.

"I'm afraid Jack's family doesn't have a pool."

I turned to Mrs. Saunders. She was studying me sadly as if it was useless for her to say anything more until my tantrum had run its course. And from her too, I saw pity.

"I don't lie, Mrs. Saunders," I said, jumping up, tears streaming down my face. "I don't lie . . . you know that . . . and I'm not crazy . . . I heard them . . . That's why I had to go out last night . . ." I stopped, suddenly remembering that I had told her I left because I needed help in math. She stood with tears in her eyes and smoothed my hair back. She knew I was lying and felt sorry for me.

I couldn't look at her. And I couldn't look at Blumberg gloating from behind his big desk. I kicked at my chair like some kind of baby and darted into the hallway. Two secretaries stopped what they were doing at the office counter, their eyes fixed on me in wonder. I flew past them and kept running until I was a long way from school, and all those prying eyes. I didn't want to see anybody ever again.

135

XV

I WISHED I had worn a jacket to school. Or at least a sweater. The sun was low and didn't have much heat left in it, and a steady breeze whipped across the water, chilling my bones with its dampness. I hadn't noticed it getting colder when I was walking, but I couldn't keep that up forever. I was about walked out. I had hiked to Lymie's place way out in the country the hard way, through the woods, across fields and meadows, climbing old rock fences and rusty barbed wire. It had taken me hours to get there. As it turned out, I'd even walked a few miles too far because I was quite a ways from the road and had lost track of where I was.

I had hidden like a convict in a tree overlooking Lymie's farm, far enough away so the dog wouldn't start yapping, hoping to see Lymie come out of the house or the barn alone. I spotted him once carrying a bale of hay out for the calves (I remembered how Lymie always cracked on me when I called them baby cows) in the pen next to the barn. I was about to hop down and sneak up on him when his father came out with another bale. I watched, sad and alone, as they fed the calves and got involved in some big conversation on their way to the house. Lymie's two little brothers came flying around the corner and zoomed into the house ahead of them. Dinner time. I could picture them all sitting around the big old table passing all kinds of food around. I was so hungry by this time I was tempted to run down and join them. But I knew that after I ate, Lymie's father would drive me home and I'd have to face the music.

Besides, I didn't really want to see anybody anyway. Not even Lymie. Come to think of it, after Lymie found out I'd blabbed the whole idiotic story about BooBoo a second time, I didn't suppose he'd want to see me either.

So I tramped back to the one place I knew of to hide out. A place where I could be alone and think.

The rock ledge I was dangling my legs over suddenly began to feel icy cold through my pants, and I stood up. I fired some flat shale rocks across the gray water and watched them skip and hop before losing momentum and sinking to the bottom. The last rock skipped five times before snagging the water and sinking in the exact spot that I'd swum into BooBoo. It seemed impossible that could have been just five days ago.

My stomach gnawed at me and my joints felt stiff and damp. I wanted more than anything to go home to my warm house, but I couldn't make myself do it. Maybe tomorrow. I couldn't face Mrs. Saunders tonight. My face still flushed when I thought about what I had said, and how I had slammed my way out of the office like a three-year-old having a tantrum. Maybe by tomorrow it wouldn't seem so bad. But I doubted that. This seemed like the type of rotten feeling that would linger for years.

I grabbed a sharp rock and began clearing a little cave

in the nearby brush that I could crawl into and get at least a little shelter. It wouldn't do much to keep out the cold, but at least working at it warmed me up some. After I'd hollowed out a narrow hole barely wide enough for me to squeeze into, I lay on my stomach and started sliding my legs in.

I lurched back and yelped. My nose was smack dab over a big pair of brown work shoes. I craned my head back and followed the work shoes up past a pair of jeans until I saw Chuckie's face staring down at me. His face was blank and he didn't say anything right away. I lowered my head back down between the shoes, waiting. I don't know what I was waiting for, but I knew better than to make a break for it. Chuckie was quick and athletic, and he'd snatch me back before I took two steps.

Something soft fell over my head blocking out the light.

"Put it on." It was one of my sweaters. I sat up and pulled it over my head. As soon as I was done, something else fell on me. My black denim jacket.

"Now put that on." Something in Chuckie's voice seemed to say I'd better do as I was told. Besides, I was still pretty cold. I buttoned my jacket and sat huddled up in a ball, trying to save what little body heat I had inside. Chuckie crouched down beside me, but he didn't say anything.

"How'd you find me?" I still wouldn't look at him.

"I went out to see your friend Lymie. He said you might be here."

"You heard what I did today?"

"I heard."

I waited to see if he had anything more to say. He didn't.

"So I guess you think I'm a liar along with everybody else."

"Did I say that?"

"You don't need to. I know what it looks like."

"Things don't always look like the way they are."

I peeked up. Chuckie was chewing on a blade of grass, not looking at me.

"Mrs. Saunders thinks I lied. I could tell."

"She didn't say that."

"She wouldn't. But I told her two different stories about why I went out last night. She knows one of them is a lie."

Chuckie stood up and grabbed me by the jacket.

"Let's go."

"I don't want to," I said sullenly.

"I want you to." He pulled me to my feet and waited while I brushed myself off. "So you're telling off principals now?"

"Blumberg's a big jerk. He thinks I'm no good because nobody cares about me." I walked to the rock ledge and stared across the water.

"Blumberg's not as bad as he seems. He's got his own problems."

"Yeah, like me," I said. "But he doesn't need to worry about that anymore. I'm not going back to that school."

"You're kind of conceited, aren't you?"

"No." That was about the only thing I wasn't.

"It seems to me you think everybody's problems revolve around you. I call that conceited."

"Yeah, and who made you a psychiatrist?"

"If I were a psychiatrist, I'd be charging you. I'm telling you this for free."

"Yeah, well, maybe you don't know as much as you think you do."

Chuckie pulled up alongside me, looking around like a tourist taking in the sights.

"I used to come here when I was a kid and wanted to be alone."

"Good try, Chuckie. Trying to make me feel like you were just like me. But I'm not buying it." I sat on the cold rocks. Chuckie did too.

"You know, it's funny," he said. "You tell me how Blumberg's a jerk, and yet you believe everything he says. But I can't get you to believe a word I say."

"Who said I believed him? I hate him."

Chuckie chewed on some more grass and thought for a minute.

"You might hate him. I don't know. You hated what he said, that's for sure. And I think it's because part of you really believes he was telling the truth."

"That's a load of bull. I can tell you that right now." I hate it when people think they know everything. Especially when they don't.

"Have it your way. You fly off the handle when some guy implies that your mother doesn't care about you, that she has to pay people to take care of you. And then you run off and hide because you don't think people care enough about you to trust you. What's it look like to you?"

"I took off because I made a fool of myself. Nobody likes to look like a total jerk."

"Oh, I see," Chuckie said quietly. "You're the jerk. I thought you said Blumberg was."

140

"If you're trying to make me look stupid, don't bother. You don't need to."

"Let me see if I understand this. You're stupid . . . and you're a liar . . . and you're a jerk. Whew! No wonder you thought Blumberg was telling the truth! But even if you were all those things, who ever told you a kid has to be perfect for people to care about him?"

"Perfect!" I yelled. "Everybody keeps saying that. You really think I want to be perfect? I'm a walking disaster area. Mom could retire on the money she's spent on my doctors. And you don't even know what happened at Grant Academy. You think the only stupid thing I ever did was piss my pants. Or tell off a principal. You don't know anything! You think you're so smart! You don't even know that I'm the one . . ." By now I was crying like crazy. Me, the kid that used to hardly ever cry at all.

Chuckie put a hand on my shoulder and spoke softly.

"I don't know that you're the one what?"

I drew in a heavy breath and turned away.

"I'm the one that drove my father out of the house! And even when he came back on Sundays, Mom and him still fought about me. You don't know anything!" I pulled away from Chuckie's hand and stood up. If I could have jumped into the gray water and disappeared, I would have.

Chuckie's grip, like cold iron, pulled my arm.

"Come on. We're going home."

I pulled against him but only feebly. I didn't have the strength or the will to put up much of a fight. I stumbled along miserably, like a guy on a chain gang. After a while Chuckie let go of my arm. I still trudged beside him, not even trying to get away.

"You know, Tyler, I know more about you than you might think."

"Yeah, like what?" I was being a mean, spoiled brat, but I didn't care.

He walked on for a minute without speaking.

"You remember when your mother bought your place right after finishing her last film?"

"No, my memory's bad, too."

Chuckie ignored the sarcasm.

"It was last spring, a few months before you moved here. Your mother hired me to start getting the place fixed up. I was out of the service, I needed a job, and that seemed like as good a job as any. Your mother stayed on for a week so she could show me what she wanted done. But she did more than that. She pitched right in and worked alongside me for the whole week. That impressed me, knowing that she could afford to have everybody else do her work for her, and yet seeing her in old clothes, hammering and scraping and painting."

"That's the way she is." I still sounded sulky, but I'm always a sucker for a story. I wondered what he was leading up to.

"Anyway, I really started to admire her. We talked a lot, and it wasn't long before I realized that she was really some kind of lady—smart, lively, interesting. She was good to have around. About the only thing I found wrong with her was the way she went on about you and your brother—you know the way parents do about their kids and it drives everybody crazy. I'd try to change the subject, but when she got wound up, there was no stopping her."

"Well, what did she say?" I stopped and looked up at him. He had me now. I'm such a sucker.

"I learned more about you and your brother in that

142

week than I ever wanted to know. Especially about you, probably because Chris was already grown up and on his own, and you were the one who was going to be living here. Actually most of it was kind of sickening, you know, how smart you were, how sweet and loving you were, how cute your little nose was . . ." He poked his finger at the tip of my nose and laughed.

"Cut it out, Chuckie."

"Anyway, she got to telling me how she was worried that she and your father had made life so difficult for you. She said she really needed to make it up to you. All I could picture was this spoiled rich kid whose mother would be willing to give him the sun and the moon if he asked. I didn't like you and I hadn't even met you yet."

"Why did she think that she and Dad made life difficult for me? I'm the one who made things tough for them."

Chuckie looked back at the red sun which was dropping down fast and gave me a little push to get me moving again.

"Can't you walk and talk at the same time, Ace? She said how a little while before you were born, things had already gotten pretty bad between her and your father. In fact, your father moved out and took an apartment downtown. Your mother told me they had been married too young, and as they both got older and learned more about who they each were, trouble started that just wouldn't go away. They couldn't agree on anything. Your father thought your mother should give up her career, for one thing, to take care of your brother. But it wasn't only that. No matter what the subject was, if one of them thought one way, the other thought the opposite. But when they found out you were on the way, they decided to get back together and try one more time to make a go of it.''

"How come Mom told *you* all that stuff?" I asked him. "She never said anything to me."

"I don't know. But it was all leading up to you. She wanted me to know all about you. Maybe so I'd understand you better. I don't know. And your mother probably figured you were too young to know about that kind of trouble. Even your brother didn't know any of this at the time. He was only eight or nine then, and he thought your father had been away on a job."

"So what'd she say about me?" I stopped and looked at him again.

"I'm getting to that, Ace." He gave me another little shove to get me going. "So they got back together and you were born, with your cute little nose, which personally I don't find all that irresistibly cute, and you were one big happy family again. At least that's what your mother wanted you and Chris to think. Actually your parents still couldn't agree on anything. And when you started having asthma attacks, and breaking out in hives, and all the other stuff you did, your parents thought it was psychosomatic, you know, all in your head. And both of them blamed the other for screwing you up. That's what your mother felt the worst about, looking back on it. You had become an excuse for them to fight. You were in the middle of a tug-of-war you didn't even know about. It finally got so bad they couldn't stay together, and they split up for good."

We were on the street now, less than a block from my house. I stopped again.

"I used to hear them fighting about me all the time.

144

I thought that if I was a better kid . . . you know . . . if I was less trouble . . ."

"Ace, your parents couldn't even agree on your name, and they were fighting about that before you were even born. So how could it have possibly been something you did?" He walked on past me. "There was one thing they agreed on."

"What?" I said and caught up to him.

"As much as they fought, they did love you very much. Your father too."

It seemed funny hearing a tough guy like Chuckie using the word "love."

"Mom always told me how much Dad thought of me, but I figured she only said it to make me feel better."

"Well, she told it to me too, and that's the God's honest truth. And I don't think she was trying to make me feel better." He stopped next to the archway at the end of our driveway. "So don't get smart thinking you're hiding some deep, dark secret from me."

It was hard to believe. All these years I thought I was a major disappointment in my father's life, and that disappointment was the main thing that came between him and Mom. I guess people tried to set me straight before, but I never completely believed them. It turned out Chuckie knew more about me than I knew about myself.

"Chuckie, can we go to your place? I'm still not ready to face Mrs. Saunders after what I did today."

"Yeah, why not," Chuckie said, turning toward his cottage. "But I'll never understand how you're able to squeeze so much guilt into such a little body."

"I'm not that little," I said, following him. And I couldn't believe it. I felt better than I had in a long time.

XVI

CHUCKIE MADE ME take a hot shower to get warmed up while he made something for us to eat. I knew he'd call Mrs. Saunders right away, but I didn't mind. I couldn't face her yet, but I didn't want her worrying herself sick over me either.

Chuckie was a lousy cook. He managed to burn the canned spaghetti to the bottom of the pan while the top of it was still cold. And then he scooped out some ice cream right into our dirty spaghetti dishes. It was just as well. I wasn't supposed to eat too much stuff like that anyway because sugar makes me hyper. Chuckie was funny to watch, like some clumsy mother hen, spilling things all over and yelling at me that I didn't eat enough. He cleared the dishes, dumped them into the already overflowing sink, and then sat looking at me.

"So what are you going to do now?" he asked me.

"About what?"

"You said you knew something about what happened to BooBoo. So what are you going to do about it?"

"Are you kidding me, Chuckie?" I said, irritated that he would bring that up when I was finally feeling good again. "There's nothing I can do. Nobody will believe me now.'' I sat for a minute, thinking. ''I don't understand it. I must be going crazy or something. I sat right there and heard those guys talking about BooBoo. And since the police said he had chlorine in him, and his mother said he was going to Mark's place, I was sure that whatever happened happened at Blumberg's pool. But now . . . I don't know . . . I'm really confused.''

''But you and Lymie did see a car that could have been Blumberg's at the rock quarry the night you found the body.''

I looked up, surprised. Chuckie smiled when he saw the bug-eyed look on my face.

''Lymie told me all about it,'' he said. ''I thought his mother was going to kill him. And I'm not sure Mrs. Saunders isn't going to kill you when she finds out.''

''Wow, Lymie told you that even though he knew he'd get in trouble.'' I was beaming all over the place. Now at least Chuckie wouldn't think I was completely off my rocker.

''Let me see,'' Chuckie said, sitting back and rubbing his chin. ''Blumberg said he was at his poolside with a group of teachers all night, right?''

''Yeah, that's what I don't get. They were there from early evening till way past midnight.''

''That's strange. I remember seeing Blumberg's car in front of the school that night. I didn't think anything of it at the time. I figured Blumberg was catching up on some office work.''

I popped up in my seat.

''So, Chuckie, Blumberg must be lying!''

''Not likely,'' Chuckie said. ''He wouldn't be dumb enough to lie about that many witnesses having seen him.''

"Then what?" I said, studying his face to see if he had anything.

"Think about it a minute, Ace. Blumberg is home and most of his teachers are with him. BooBoo is heading for his house, but supposedly never gets there. BooBoo dies in a pool, but it couldn't have been Blumberg's. And Blumberg's car is at the school."

"The pool in the school!" I shouted. "That's where they went. The school keys are probably right on Blumberg's key chain. That's gotta be where they went!"

"Maybe. It wouldn't surprise me a bit. But we don't have any proof."

"So what should we do? What do you think?"

"Well, we can't do anything about it tonight. And you've already had a busy enough day. You look kind of bleary-eyed. I say we'd better get you home to bed."

"Chuckie?"

"What?"

"Can I stay here tonight? I know I've already been a lot of trouble and I'm sorry, but, I don't know, I'm still not ready to go home."

Chuckie looked at me a minute before saying anything.

"I guess that would be all right. I only have a twin bed. You take it and I'll sleep on the couch."

"No, I've already been enough trouble. I'll grab some blankets and make a bed on the floor of your room." I was old enough not to be afraid to sleep in a room alone, but with all the thoughts racing through my head, I didn't want to take any chances with nightmares. I hoped Chuckie wouldn't figure that out.

"Suit yourself," Chuckie said, like it was no big

deal. "There are plenty of blankets in the hall closet. You take care of that, and I'll call Mrs. Saunders."

I headed for the blankets and stopped, thinking.

"Chuckie, can you, I don't know, can you tell Mrs. Saunders that I'm really sorry about this afternoon? I still can't believe I did that."

"Still giving yourself a hard time, huh, pal? Don't worry about it. I'll tell her. But you know, it gets pretty tiresome hearing you apologize for yourself. It's starting to get on my nerves."

"Sorry," I said and then laughed when I realized what I'd done.

"I expected you to say that," Chuckie said, "so why am I so surprised?" He looked at me like I had two heads, then shook his head and threw up his arms. He was still mumbling something I couldn't quite make out as he left. I started grabbing all the blankets I could get my hands on. One thing about me, I can never get too warm.

Chuckie's bedroom looked a little like mine would have looked if Mrs. Saunders didn't help me keep it cleaned up. I cleared off a spot right next to the bed and folded a couple blankets in half, laying them out on the carpeting. I threw the rest on top. Then I hopped out of my clothes, burrowed into my homemade bed, and closed my eyes. It had been a full day and I was pretty beat. I could hear Chuckie in the other room on the phone, but I couldn't tell what he was saying. I wished I could come up with a brilliant plan to snag Mark and Jack before I went to sleep, but my mind was too fuzzy to think straight.

A moment later a pillow whacked me over the head.

"I thought you might want this. Don't apologize again. It's an extra one."

149

Chuckie snapped off the light and turned to leave the room.

"Chuckie?"

"What do you need now, Ace?"

"Remember when you were talking about Blumberg?" I propped myself up on my elbows. "What did you mean when you said he had problems of his own?"

"It's a long story, Ace, but I'll see if I can keep it short." He sat on the edge of his bed. "You see, Blumberg's wife used to be an actress in New York, a pretty good one from what I've heard. When they first moved upstate, his wife was in an off-Broadway play, and she was away most of the time. Rumor had it that when Mark arrived, Blumberg forbid her to work until he was grown up. Well, she went along with him, but people who know them say she's never been the same. She goes through the motions of being his wife, but it's like she's never really forgiven him. Like he took something that wasn't his to take."

"Wow," I said, thinking. "Maybe that's why Mark turned out so mean. You know, growing up with all that resentment around him."

"I wouldn't be surprised."

"I bet everybody'd have been better off in the end if she went ahead and did what she wanted like my mom did."

"That wouldn't surprise me either. But anyway, the point is that when your mother moved here with you, and the whole town was buzzing about having a famous actress around, well, it was tough on both of them. People say she won't even look at him anymore."

"And that's why Blumberg wanted to prove to everybody that I turned out so lousy, I bet. Maybe so everybody would think he was right.''

''Maybe. Or maybe he just wanted to believe it himself. I don't know. But it's harder to hate a guy when you see that he's got problems like everybody else.''

''I don't hate him any more,'' I said. I felt kind of sorry for him. And her, too.

''Yeah, I know,'' Chuckie said, standing up and walking to the lighted doorway. ''Now get some sleep.''

''Chuckie?''

He stopped, silhouetted in the doorway.

''I almost made it that time. What now, Ace?''

''Remember how you said you didn't like me even before you met me? Did you . . . you know . . . have you changed your mind about me at all?''

''I'm crazy about you, Ace. I don't know how I managed to live all these years without you. There is one thing though.'' He paused for a second. ''Try not to piss all over my floor.''

I felt my cheeks get hot. I could see Chuckie's outline in the doorway, his head cocked sideways. I knew he was wearing a big stupid smile and waiting to see if I'd go hyper or throw something at him.

''Sure, Chuckie, as long as you promise not to throw up all over me.''

At that he burst out laughing. I did, too.

''You're learning. It's a deal. Now no more dumb questions. We'll talk tomorrow.''

I had to admit I felt like a pretty lucky kid. In a new town I hadn't even wanted to come to, I already had three of the best friends anybody could want: Lymie, Mary Grace, and Chuckie.

Not bad for a lemon.

XVII

CHUCKIE WOKE ME early the next morning. I half remember snuggling my head into my pillow and mumbling for him to leave me alone. Chuckie grabbed the blankets I was sleeping on and gave them a good yank, spinning me across the floor like a tipped-over top.

"What are you, crazy?"

"Maybe a little. But I'm sane enough to see that you get to school." He was snatching up the blankets quicker than I could wrap myself back into them.

"You are crazy!" I said, gawking up at him like he was some kind of madman. "I can't go to school today."

"You look healthy enough to me."

"For all I know I'm expelled or something. Come on, Chuckie, be serious. You know I can't go back there."

"You can't?" Chuckie gasped, wrapping his hands around his jaws and pretending to be surprised. "Oh, my goodness gracious, I forgot. Quick, we've got to find a cave to hide you in. At least till Blumberg dies of old age. Or maybe after twenty years the President will pardon you, and you can once again be with us who believe in you, a free man at last." Chuckie jerked me to my feet and clasped me in his arms. "Just remember, we'll think of you every day."

"That's really funny, Chuckie," I said, shaking myself loose. "But I'm not going."

"Oh, yes," he said. "You're going all right. Now quit wasting time. You get ready for school and I'll cook breakfast." He shoved some fresh school clothes in my gut and shoved me toward the bathroom. He must have gone over to my house earlier to get them. I got the feeling from the look on his face that even if I dropped dead, he'd still drag me to school. And on time.

Maybe it wouldn't be so bad. Maybe nobody'd even heard what I did yesterday. After all, it wouldn't be too smart for Blumberg to broadcast the whole thing. Even if he did figure Mark had an airtight alibi, there were enough people around who would be only too glad to believe Mark would be involved in something rotten. And deep down inside, Blumberg probably knew this. It might not be so awful. Unless I got in trouble I probably wouldn't even see Blumberg all day.

Besides, I didn't have any choice.

At breakfast I asked Chuckie if he had come up with any ideas. He shook his head.

"Nothing specific. But I know that if you have no evidence and no witnesses, you'll have to hope one of the guys confesses. There's no other way."

"Fat chance of that," I mumbled disappointedly.

"Don't be too sure. Haven't you ever read *Macbeth*?"

"No, I read *Romeo and Juliet*, but I don't think that applies here."

"You surprise me, Ace. I thought you were an expert on guilt."

"Only my own," I said.

"Yeah, well we're working on that, aren't we? Let's see. How about the 'The Telltale Heart' by Edgar Allan Poe? You must have read that."

"Yeah, I read that," I told him. I even liked it. It was about this crazy guy who killed an old man just because he didn't like the way he looked. Only he didn't know what to do with the body, so he chopped it up in little pieces which he buried under the floorboards. I figured that's how he'd get caught, when it started to smell, but it never got a chance to. When the police come to question him, he starts hearing the old guy's heart beating under the floorboards, even though the guy is dead and all chopped up. Of course the police don't hear a thing. They're still as friendly as can be. But finally the heartbeat gets so loud to the crazy guy that he jumps up and confesses the whole thing. I couldn't believe it.

"That's a good story, Chuckie, but what do you want me to do, follow Mark and Jack around making heartbeat noises?"

Chuckie ignored the wisecrack and leaned forward, thinking.

"Listen, Ace, if somebody has a guilty conscience about something, it's like that guilt is crying out inside them all the time. Except they're the only ones who can hear it. But if it's loud enough inside them, they start thinking other people can hear it too. Or see it in their faces. And if the guilt gets bad enough, they just might confess to save themselves the mental agony."

"I think Mark's conscience is on permanent hold. He probably wouldn't confess even if we had pictures."

"Maybe. But what about the other guy? All it takes is for one of them to break."

"Yeah, that's right," I said, getting excited again. "Jack was really bugged about the whole thing. He was all worried that the police didn't believe them, and he even said he hadn't been able to sleep right since that night."

"Well, that's a good sign. And that was even before he knew anybody was on to him."

"So we should probably do something to make him talk, huh? What do you think, Chuckie?"

"Slow it down, Ace. Don't go rushing into anything. It might be that he's shaken enough right now so he's ready to confess on his own. If not, then we'll try to think of something. But I don't want to see you going off half-cocked and getting into more trouble. Take your time and see what happens."

That's a thing that always happens to people when they get older. They always figure everything can keep. Me, I couldn't wait to try something.

"I'll see if Mary Grace and Lymie have any ideas."

"You do that, Ace. And let me know if you come up with anything." Then he grabbed me by the shirt and pulled my face up to his. "But listen and listen good," he said. "Don't do anything stupid. If Jack and Mark have something to hide and they're scared, I don't trust them."

"All right, all right. Don't get all bent out of shape. I can take care of myself."

"Right," he said, letting me go and handing me my bookbag. But he didn't look too convinced.

XVIII

MARK AND JACK leaned against the wall, cool and tough, their thumbs hitched into their jeans pockets, watching everybody go by. I thought about making a U-turn and almost did. Then Jack spotted me and elbowed Mark. They both straightened up and glared at me without blinking.

I did something then that surprised even me. I walked right toward them and smiled. Not a big flashy smile like a car salesman would give you, just a little "isn't it good to be alive" smile. I stared at them, still smiling, as I walked past. Mark clenched his teeth and mumbled something to Jack. Jack still looked mean, but his eyes were on his shoes now. When I got a ways down the hall, I shot another happy face their way. For a second, I thought Mark would come after me, but he didn't. And Jack looked downright sickly.

Chuckie was right.

I hurried to study hall. Lymie, Mary Grace, and I all had library passes, and I couldn't wait to sign out. Both of them had been after me since before homeroom to tell them what the big deal was, but I wouldn't say a word, only that they should meet me in the library third period.

The library was pretty empty when the three of us arrived. We plopped our passes on the librarian's desk. She kind of gave us the evil eye, probably because we walked in together. I told her I was looking for *Macbeth* because I needed to grab *something*, and she wrinkled up her face and pointed to the card catalog. Things like that always kill me. It was a small library and she probably knew where every book in the place was by heart, but all she could do was point at the card catalog. Lymie headed for the magazine rack and grabbed a *Hot Rodder* magazine, and Mary Grace browsed through fiction.

We met at a table in the back corner like we had agreed on and tried to look busy. If we seemed to be in the mood for conversation, we'd be split up right away. We waited a few minutes for the librarian to stop gawking at us and get back to her own work. Pretty soon another suspicious-looking group arrived, and she started eyeing them.

I leaned forward and pretended to be sharing a passage from *Macbeth* with Lymie. Lymie looked funny peeking out from behind his *Hot Rodder* magazine, pretending to be interested in *Macbeth*. Mary Grace kept her eyes in her own book.

"I told Blumberg about Mark and Jack," I mumbled, pointing to a Lady Macbeth speech.

"I don't believe it!" Lymie said. "Is there anybody you haven't told?"

I glared at him and he fixed his eyes back on the speech.

"Let him tell the story." Mary Grace's voice floated out from a mouth that didn't move.

"I couldn't help it, Lymie. Blumberg got nasty about my mother, and I got all hyper. It was pretty bad. I yelled at him and everything. He thinks I'm a mental case now for sure."

"Wow," Lymie said quietly, as if he were in the presence of greatness. "No wonder you ran away!"

"Tyler, you ran away?"

"Yeah, he did. Chuckie, this guy who works for him, came around looking for him. I tell you, I wouldn't want that guy mad at me."

"Tyler, why did you run away?" Mary Grace asked.

"You should see the arms on that guy," Lymie said.

I rolled my eyes. "Does anybody want to hear what I have to say? I thought that's why we were here."

"All right, all right. Shut up and tell us!" Lymie's voice carried across the library. The way the librarian flinched, you'd think something had hit her in the head. We buried our faces in our books and magazines, not saying anything for quite a while. Finally she started shelving books.

"Now listen," I said through my teeth. "Don't say anything. Just listen." I felt like a ventriloquist whose dummy had been stolen.

I probably looked pretty foolish, but I did manage to get the whole story out without us being split up. I had to kick Lymie in the shins a few times to shut him up, and he did threaten to kill me once, but at least I got it out. The whole time Mary Grace's eyes were glued to her book, and a couple of times I could've sworn she was reading it.

"Well anyway, that's what Chuckie said." I took a deep breath and looked at both of them.

Lymie shook his head. I should have known he'd

never come up with a plan because he never thinks anything will work. And Mary Grace looked like she wanted to finish her book. What a pair!

"Is the book really that good?" I said. "I mean it's only BooBoo's murder we're talking about here."

"I think Chuckie is right." Her voice floated out of her mouth again. "Jack is the one to work on. Even when Mark was a little kid, he'd never admit anything even if ten people saw him do it. But Jack, he's another story. He's scared already."

"You've got an idea?" I should have apologized for making that sarcastic remark about her book, but before I could, she had already launched herself into the details of her plan. And a beautiful plan it was—a cat and mouse plan where we got to be the cats. Even Lymie looked thrilled, and that's saying something.

"Do either of you have any plain white paper?" Mary Grace asked.

I had a bunch left over from my stupid science project which I was falling further behind on every day. I was glad to find a good use for it since I still hadn't collected any decent rocks, and I'd rather hand in nothing than those painted crushed stones.

Lymie and I watched, amazed, as Mary Grace took out a red magic marker and started drawing up a sign in her perfect block letter printing. I tingled with excitement as she finished the first one.

"Okay, Tyler, put this one up on the gym bulletin board outside Mr. Johnson's office. Try not to be seen." She started in on the next one. "And Lymie, you put this one in the main foyer, and I'll put one up on the cafeteria bulletin board."

"Mary Grace," I said, hoping I didn't sound too

much like Lymie always did, "how do we keep the teachers or Blumberg from seeing these signs and yanking them down?"

"That shouldn't be a problem. For one thing, I don't think Mr. Johnson ever looks at his own bulletin board. If the janitors didn't keep the graffiti off it, the gym probably would've been raided by the police by now. As for the other two, by the time a teacher or somebody finds them, who knows how many kids will have seen them already."

"It'll work, Tyler," Lymie said gruffly. "Don't be such a worrywart."

I bit my lip and let that one slide.

After Mary Grace finished the last sign, we all sat restless and fidgety waiting for the bell. When it rang I flew for the door like a shot and got yelled at for not signing out my book. I raced back to the desk.

"Sorry, I forgot."

"I'll bet you did," she said, giving me the evil eye again. Like I came to school just to steal her book.

I snatched the book off her desk almost before she lifted her stamp and zoomed toward the gym. A steady stream of kids filed into the boys' locker room. I hung around the bulletin board pretending to read announcements until the coast was clear. Then I grabbed a spare tack out of the football schedule and stuck up our phony sign.

I stepped back for a second to admire it.

DUE TO THE SUCCESS OF LAST SATURDAY'S
SMALL PARTY AT THE SCHOOL POOL
ANOTHER PARTY WILL BE HELD THIS SAT.
AT 8:00 P.M.

SIGN UP LIMITED TO FIRST ONE HUNDRED
SO DON'T WAIT
SEE JACK ROBBINS TO SIGN UP
BEFORE 3:00 TODAY

Beautiful.

XIX

I'M NOT MUCH in the patience department. A whole
period passed and nobody even mentioned the pool
party. I was going crazy. Maybe Mrs. Saunders was
right. She always said people don't read any more. Mary
Grace told me to relax.

At lunchtime the sign in the cafeteria started to draw
some attention. A bunch of kids clustered around the
bulletin board chattering away and pointing, and that's
all it took. Nothing draws a crowd like a crowd. Pretty
soon big kids were pushing their way through, and little
kids were craning their necks to see what the excitement
was. Mary Grace poked me and told me to act natural
and quit staring. I tried, but every few minutes my head
would swivel back to the action like a compass needle.
Not that it mattered much. A lot of other kids were
staring too.

On the way out I passed by the announcement and
sneaked a peek. A strand of spaghetti was hanging from
it and there was some chocolate milk or something
splattered on it, and somebody had written EAT ME on
the bottom, but it was still pretty readable considering.

Posters and cafeterias both bring out the animal in kids. Put the two together and you're asking for trouble.

Before social studies class everybody was talking about signing up for the party. A few kids had already tried and said Jack had been pretty nasty to them. Nobody thought that was too strange. Eighth graders are used to being shafted by older kids. Everybody figured Jack wanted to save room for all his high school buddies. A few of the activist types said it was unfair and they started up a petition saying that if the junior high kids weren't allowed to sign up, we should be able to have a party on our own. At the last minute they changed the junior high part to eighth graders because they didn't want to hang around with little seventh grade kids.

I even signed it. What the heck.

After fifth period I ran across Jack in the hall. He was swamped by kids trying to make sure they got signed up. As he pushed his way through the crowd, kids kept jumping in front of him trying to stop him. His face was bright red, and he looked like he was about ready to cry. I stood there and watched for a minute before going to class. I could hardly believe it, but I was starting to feel sorry for him. And guilty about what we were doing. Chuckie was right. I really had to work on that.

Turning to go to class, I drove my nose into some big kid's chest. When I looked up, I found myself staring at Mark Blumberg. He didn't say a word, but his jaw was clenched and his eyes were meaner than I'd ever seen them. I swallowed hard and stood frozen in my tracks until he shoved me out of his way with his forearm, hard enough so my books went flying. I hoped

Mary Grace was right about him. But he sure did look like he could be a killer.

During sixth period, Jack was called to the office over the P.A. Mary Grace poked me in the back. Ten minutes later I was called to the office. I sat for a minute feeling the blood drain from my head. Mary Grace jabbed me.

"Remember," she whispered, "you didn't write those announcements."

As I walked out of the room she smiled and gave me the thumbs up. I tried to smile back. My heart was beating something fierce.

They were waiting for me in the office. Mr. Blumberg motioned impatiently for me to take a seat. Jack was already in a chair, and he looked pretty shaken. He didn't look mean now, just plain scared.

"Mr. McAllister," Mr. Blumberg began, "it seems that hardly a day goes by that I don't find it necessary to have a little chat with you. I have a few questions I'd like to ask, and if you would be so kind, I'd appreciate some honest answers."

I nodded.

"Mr. McAllister, have you seen the announcements concerning tomorrow's supposed pool party?" He held up two of Mary Grace's signs and waved them in front of me. One of them still said EAT ME. Probably the one in the gym was still up.

I nodded again.

"Mr. Robbins seems to think, and I suspect with good reason, that you are responsible for these. I'd like to hear what you have to say about this." He leaned forward and studied my face.

I gulped. Then I shrugged.

164

"Did you write these?" Mr. Blumberg snapped, his voice jumping up a few notches. "I'd like a simple yes or no."

"No." I looked down.

"You swear you're not responsible for these? Look at me, please."

I looked.

"I'm not. I swear." As long as he asked the question that way, I was safe.

Mr. Blumberg looked tired. He rubbed his eyes, shook his head, and threw up his hands.

"Mr. Robbins, could you give us, perhaps, at least an inkling as to why you think Mr. McAllister wrote these?" He sat back and waited. So did I.

"I don't know, but I know he did it. He hates me. He probably figured he could get me in trouble." He gave me a sullen look.

Jack sounded so scared I was starting to feel sorry for him all over again. And that's saying something, because I was pretty busy being scared myself.

"Perhaps you could explain, Mr. Robbins, why you feel Mr. McAllister hates you so much he is bent on revenge?"

"I don't know," Jack said, squirming in his seat. "He just does."

Mr. Blumberg closed his eyes and pinched the bridge of his nose. When he opened them, they were fixed on me.

"Do you hate Mr. Robbins?"

"No, not really."

"Then, Mr. McAllister, let me rephrase the question. Do you like him?"

I looked at Jack and Jack looked at me.

"I don't know. I don't really know him that well."

Mr. Blumberg closed his eyes again and took in a couple of deep breaths. I was afraid he might be getting ready to have some kind of attack. When he finally spoke, I could barely hear him.

"Both of you may return to class until I decide what to do about this."

I was surprised he didn't tell us not to leave town. I dashed out the door and hustled back to class so that I wouldn't have to face Jack alone in the hall. No sooner had I slid into my seat than Mr. Blumberg's voice sounded over the P.A. announcing there would be no pool party.

One of the kids with the petition looked up and said, "I wonder if this means we can't have ours either?"

XX

I HEARD THE lawn mower buzzing around the backyard. Tossing my bookbag onto the porch, I ran out
to find Chuckie, anxious to fill him in on what we'd
done to Jack. Chuckie turned off the little John Deere
tractor and listened as I rambled excitedly through all
the details. He didn't say a word.

"Well?" I said. "I bet that'll make him confess.
You think?"

"I don't know, Ace. I thought we were going to hold
off for a while."

"Hold off for what, Chuckie? We had a good plan.
Why should we wait?" Chuckie wasn't the type to get
all excited and hop around like a kid, but I had expected
more enthusiasm than this.

"You have to be careful about pushing people too
hard into corners. You could get hurt."

"Aw, come on, Chuckie. You don't really think those
guys are dangerous, do you?" I thought about how I'd
smiled and stared them down earlier.

"Anybody can be dangerous if they're pushed hard
enough. So don't get too impatient."

"Yeah, right," I said, not even trying to hide how

annoyed I was. I figured he was probably mad that he didn't think up his own plan.

He put his hand on my shoulder and shook his head slowly.

"Ace, I'm not putting the plan down. All I'm saying is be careful. I don't want to see you get beat up again."

"I can take care of myself," I said sullenly. "Don't worry about it."

"Yeah, you're right. I'm sorry," he said, punching my arm. And then, "Oh, by the way, Ace, are your other pants dry yet?"

He blocked my swing before it connected with his jaw and wrestled me to the ground before I had a chance to swing again. And all the while he was laughing like some kind of a nut. I squirmed and kicked and swore, but Chuckie was about ten times stronger than me, and I ended up with nothing for my trouble but a mouthful of grass.

"Sorry to get you riled, Ace," Chuckie said, after his laughing fit had passed, "but I've never known anybody who could completely take care of himself, let alone a twelve-year-old with a bad temper."

"I'll kill you, Chuckie!" I spit out some grass.

"I'm waiting, Ace," Chuckie said. "Make your move."

I flailed around a little more and then let myself go limp under his weight. It was no use.

"Why do you have to keep bringing up about me pissing my pants when you know it bothers me? Is that how you get your kicks?" I spit out some more grass.

"When it stops bothering you, then I won't have any reason to bring it up, will I?"

"You're probably going to tell everybody. That is, if you haven't already."

"I told you I wouldn't. I don't go back on my word." He stood up. I rolled over and looked up at him.

"Yeah, you told me. But sometimes . . ."

"Sometimes what, Ace?"

"I don't know. Sometimes I think you deliberately try to get me mad."

"Oh, I do," Chuckie said smiling. "Definitely I do."

"Why?" I said, sitting up.

"Because you're too sensitive for your own good, Ace. That makes you a hothead, a reactor."

"A reactor?" I understood the hothead part.

"Yeah, a reactor is somebody who reacts to everybody around him. They do something and he reacts—bing! He's letting other people call the shots. They control whether he's happy, sad, mad, or whatever. And if you're a hothead on top of that, then you're really at their mercy."

I thought about that for a minute.

"You mean like how I blew up at Blumberg?"

"Yeah, that's one example. If you know what your mother is like, it shouldn't matter what anybody else thinks. It has nothing to do with you. Or like now, when I cracked on you for pissing your pants. I was ready to block your punch before you even decided to swing. You were letting me control you."

"But Chuckie, if you never reacted to anybody, then you'd be like a zombie or something, you know, stumbling around in your own little world. Then people could do whatever they wanted to you."

"All I'm saying, Ace, is that you should stay in control and call the shots yourself. You should decide what you want to do, what's best to do. Don't go flying off the handle without thinking."

That made sense. I remembered how when I smiled at Mark and Jack that morning, I felt like I was in control, forcing them to react to me, like Chuckie said. That felt good for a change.

"Work on it, Ace. That's all. You're not going to change overnight, but keep trying."

"I will, Chuckie," I told him. "Yeah, I will."

Chuckie sat down next to me, and we stayed quiet for a while, staring out across the yard.

"Chuckie?"

"Yeah, Ace?"

"You think Mrs. Saunders will let me go to Buster's tonight?"

He laughed.

"Don't even ask. You don't have a chance. You better let things cool down for a few days before making plans to resume your social life."

"Is she mad?"

"No, she's not mad. But I have a feeling she'll want to keep her eye on you for a while."

"She's afraid I'll screw up again?"

"No, she worries, that's all. She takes care of you. She's got a right to worry." He hopped to his feet.

"Chuckie?"

"Why do I get the feeling we're playing Twenty Questions?"

"Maybe you could ask her. You know, about me going to Buster's. Maybe you could even bring me there. Then she couldn't say no."

"Forget it, Ace. Stay home and out of trouble for a

change. Besides, I have to go to Albany to pick up something tonight."

"Didn't you ever hear of UPS?"

"No," Chuckie said, like it was news to him. "Did you ever hear of lawn mowing?" He picked me up by the elbows and set me on the tractor seat. "Finish up, will you, and I'll get my other work done."

"No problem, Chuckie. This kid was made to mow."

"Yeah, I bet. Just make sure you don't drive through the side of the house or something." He started to walk away. "Hey, Ace?"

"What?" I said, reaching down for the key.

"See that the seat stays dry, huh?"

That cracked him up. He was still laughing as he disappeared around the corner. I had to laugh too when I thought about it.

I finished the lawn without doing anything stupid like wracking up or chopping anything that shouldn't have been chopped, things I'd been known to do in the past.

And I was still laughing whenever I thought about Chuckie and his stupid wet pants jokes. And I started thinking, maybe there's still hope for me.

XXI

I KNOW MRS. Saunders doesn't mean any harm, but when you're going on thirteen, a little hugging and kissing goes a long way. The way she carried on you'd think I'd been away for twenty years. My mom's the same way. When they're both around, they're on me like fly paper.

And I was glad Chuckie wasn't around to hear all the apologizing I did. The whole scene would have made him throw up worse than he did in the driver ed. room that time. But it felt good to have things back to normal between me and Mrs. Saunders, to know she'd still be there for me no matter what stupid stunt I might pull next. Good thing, too—I was already planning what she might consider my next stupid move.

I had to get out of the house and go to Buster's to see if our plan had driven Jack to confess yet. If he'd done it, somebody at Buster's would know about it. Chuckie had already told me not to even bother asking for permission, so I wasn't going to. I told Mrs. Saunders that I was pretty beat and I was going to bed early. I knew that would make her happy, knowing how she feels about sleep. I even got undressed and climbed into bed so I wouldn't feel like such a liar. But by 8:30 I was out the window and shimmying down one of the porch columns. Chuckie had already left by then, so it was no sweat about getting caught. And it's only about ten times faster to escape when you're not dragging Lymie behind you.

Buster's was already alive with its usual grubby Friday night crowd when I arrived. There was a greasy thickness of cigarette smoke and fumes from the grill that made voices and the electronic bleeps and bloops of the video games seem to hang suspended in midair. Kids milled around in bunches, talking loudly, eyeing what little action there was restlessly, impatiently, waiting, like they were expecting something more. The weekend everybody had lived all week for had arrived, and no one seemed to know what to do with it.

I slipped silently through the crowd looking for Lymie. He said he'd try to get a ride to town if he could talk his mother out of grounding him for sneaking out with me to the quarry. Which was somewhere between highly unlikely and never in a million years. So it didn't surprise me that I couldn't find him. And I knew I wouldn't see Mary Grace. Kids like her didn't go to Buster's. I stuck a token into the only game that wasn't being played and started bombing terrorists and saving hostages with this helicopter. Except the game was set up too close to one of the pool tables, and high school kids kept shoving me out of their way or jabbing their cue sticks into my ribs, and I ended up annihilating about fifty hostages. Lymie didn't know it, but he wasn't missing much. Mary Grace probably did know it, and that's why she wasn't there.

I gave up on the game before it was finished and

snaked my way around trying to find a corner with some space I could call my own. I made it to the back, half under my own power and half under the power of the big kids I bumped up against.

I saw Jack standing alone behind the last pool table. He looked sickly and miserable. He spotted me, and I froze in my tracks. Next thing I knew he was headed my way, and I tried to scoot out through the crowd. Before I'd gone two steps, I bashed into this fat kid who looked like he wanted to body slam me or something. As I backed out of his range, somebody grabbed my arm.

"We have to talk." It was Jack. He didn't say it mean. His voice was dull and tired. But he didn't let go of my arm.

"Okay, so talk."

"Not here. Outside." He jerked his thumb toward the rear exit.

"Where's Mark?" I asked suspiciously. I didn't like the idea of ending up alone in a back alley with Mark and Jack. Not after what we'd done.

"On a date," he said bitterly. "As if nothing ever happened."

I didn't move.

"I won't hurt you, if that's what you're afraid of. I want to talk is all."

I watched his sullen, weary face a second before moving toward the door. The alley was dark and surprisingly silent as the door closed behind us. I stood motionless, waiting for my eyes to adjust and listening to make sure there were no extra footsteps. Pretty soon I could see Buster's big old Cadillac a few yards in front of me, but otherwise the alley seemed deserted.

"So what do you want with me?" My voice sounded weak and hollow, like when I have the flu or something.

"Sit down."

He climbed up on Buster's hood and sat with his back on the windshield. I did the same, hoping Buster wouldn't come out and catch us there. Neither of us said anything for a while, lying back, staring up past the rooftops at the stars. I buttoned my denim jacket against the cool breeze. It was really starting to feel like fall now and the air smelled clean and damp compared to the stuffy atmosphere of Buster's.

"You know what happened." It was more of a statement than a question.

"I know some. Other people do, too." I didn't want to be out there alone with Jack with him thinking I was the only one who knew anything.

"It was an accident. You know that, don't you?"

"People don't usually work so hard to cover up accidents."

"We were scared. It all happened so fast. Mark . . . we were both afraid of what his father would do if he found out about it. We took his keys . . . we even stole some of his beer, and got into the school without his permission."

"Mark doesn't seem too worried."

Jack stiffened.

"Sometimes I hate him. I don't sleep for a week, and he pretends like nothing happened, that the whole thing will just go away."

We were quiet a minute.

"You'll have to tell."

"I know. I guess I've known all week. I don't know

how I'll do it. My parents will . . . I don't know. I don't know what'll happen to me. To either of us.''

Jack started to blubber, and I didn't know what to say. It was strange. A big guy like that crying next to me.

"You were trespassing. And it was an accident." I said it like it was no big deal, but I knew it was.

"It was more than an accident. We should have known better."

"How did it happen?"

Jack didn't say anything right away. He snuffed loudly.

"We were drinking. Drinking a lot, all three of us. Mark and I were doing flips off the diving board, and BooBoo wanted to try. We shouldn't have let him. He never was any good at things like that, even if he hadn't been drinking. But we . . ."

Jack leaned forward and buried his face in his hands, sobbing uncontrollably. I sat by feeling totally helpless.

"But we thought it was funny," he continued through the tears, "the way he was so clumsy jerking around in the air . . . and then belly-flopping. And he was like a little kid running back to the diving board, yelling for us to watch the next one."

"So what happened?"

"The last time he got on the diving board, still all excited, Mark and I sneaked into the locker room. We had all his clothes, and we hid behind the door with them. We wanted to scare him, you know, make him think we left him there all alone with no clothes."

Jack had stopped crying now, and his voice had become wooden and cold.

"We waited there, expecting him to come tearing through the door. But he never did. It was so quiet out there, we wondered what he was doing. After a while we went out to see what he was up to, and . . .''

He drew a deep breath and slumped back against the windshield.

"At first we didn't see anything and we laughed, thinking he was running around the school naked looking for us. Then we saw him. He was face down, lying there near the bottom of the pool.''

"Didn't you try to save him?'' I was sorry I said that.

"Of course we tried to save him!'' Jack said angrily. "You think we wanted him to die? We dragged him out and tried to make him breathe . . . but it was too late. Way too late. I don't know . . . he must have hit his head on the board or something. He was dead.''

"Didn't you want to call an ambulance?''

"I don't know. It's different when you're there. We were so scared I hardly remember what we did. Mark said we had to get him out of the school. Somehow we got him dressed, and Mark pulled the car up to the side door. I keep thinking about how we carried him out. It was awful. He was filled with water. It kept splashing out of his mouth.''

Jack sat up and started sobbing again. I really felt sorry for him. I kept trying to picture myself in his place.

"And so you put him in the trunk and brought him to the quarry so everybody'd think he drowned on his own,'' I said, guessing the rest.

"Mark said it didn't matter what we did to him since he was dead anyway, and there was nothing anybody could do for him. Mark said we had to worry about ourselves now.''

I put my hand on his shoulder.

"It must have been tough keeping that inside all week."

"It was a nightmare. It still is, and one that you don't wake up from." He rolled off the car and slammed his fist into Buster's fender. "And the thing that really gets me is how Mark goes on as if nothing happened, like it doesn't matter about BooBoo as long as we don't get caught. He made up that hitchhiker story so the police would have something to waste their time on."

"Maybe it bothers him," I said, jumping down beside him. "Maybe he just doesn't show it."

"I don't know. Remember how he was all excited when Beaver was going to beat up on you? BooBoo wasn't dead three days, and he couldn't wait to see some kid get smacked around. That doesn't sound like somebody who's too upset."

I remembered how happy Mark looked when he announced to Beaver that I was coming down the street. And he didn't even have anything against me then. Jack wasn't like Mark at all.

"Everybody messes up," I said, jumping in front of him. "But people will stand by you. You'd be surprised, really. And I ought to know. Messing up is a kind of hobby of mine."

"Thanks," he said, "but I'm not talking about hitting a baseball through a window or something. I wish I was."

"Neither am I. And I wish I was."

He laughed and then he stopped suddenly, like he all of a sudden remembered how bad things were.

"I suppose I might as well get this over with."

"Do you want me to go with you? I will."

"No, you're an all right kid, and I appreciate it. But this is something I have to take care of on my own." He tapped my arm and continued his grim march down the street. "I'll see you around."

"See you around."

I watched sadly as Jack shuffled toward the police station, his head down, hands jammed into his pockets.

"Good luck," I yelled.

That wasn't quite what I wanted to say, but what can you say to a guy at a time like that?

I turned back toward Buster's and stopped. I didn't want to go back in.

XXII

THE STREETLIGHT BUZZED overhead, vibrating through the air and charging it with a kind of restless energy. Things were quiet inside now. Through the big window across the street I could see the cop at the desk picking up the phone every once in a while, talking, then going back to his paper work. I couldn't tell if he was filling out official reports or doing a crossword puzzle or something like that. Jack had disappeared into the back room with a couple of cops quite a while ago. How long ago I couldn't tell. I had drifted off a few times into a fitful, delirious sleep with awful thoughts and scary pictures bouncing around my brain. I would wake with a jump and not remember right away where I was. And each time I woke up I was shaking more and freezing worse than the time before. By now I was nearly numb with cold.

What was I doing there? Did I blame myself for this? That'd be stupid. I didn't cause the accident. And Jack said himself he would have confessed sooner or later. So what was holding me to that bench on the edge of the lonely darkness of the park? Why couldn't I go home?

I won. So why wasn't I celebrating?

Car doors slammed and I sat up straight. Two state troopers marched briskly into the station, pausing briefly at the desk before disappearing into the room with Jack and the two village cops.

An old car pulled up behind the trooper car, and a man and a woman climbed out. I didn't recognize them.

"Don't tell me how to act!" the man snarled. "I think I know how to take care of my own son!"

"I'm only saying that you should listen, John. Listen to him before you fly off the handle."

She chased him up the sidewalk, tugging at his arm. He shook her hand off and plowed on ahead.

"I might have a few things to say myself. Did you ever think of that?"

Poor Jack.

The door closed behind them. The man waved his arms angrily at the desk cop, who hurried him into the back room with everybody else. The woman hung back for a few seconds, probably to apologize. The desk cop raised his hands and smiled.

I lay down on the bench and curled up, trying to save as much heat as I could. I was shaking something fierce. What was I waiting for? I didn't know. I couldn't think. I closed my eyes for the longest time. Sometimes I saw BooBoo floating up out of the dark water. Sometimes I saw Jack in a roomful of angry cops, and his mother was trying to keep his father from hitting him. Either way I'd wake suddenly with a sickening feeling in the pit of my stomach.

But I still stayed.

A hand was on my shoulder. A hand in my dream.

"Is this your new address?"

I opened my eyes and the hand stayed. But I had to have been dreaming the voice. That voice.

"You know, you do have a nice home, Tyler. When did you take up sleeping on park benches?"

I rolled my head back and saw my mother, looking like some golden-haired glowing angel under the streetlight. I couldn't be awake. It didn't make sense.

I sat up, rubbed my eyes, and looked again, squinting. Mom was still there. She took off her long coat and wrapped it around me. Then she sat down and kissed my forehead, smoothing my hair back.

"Are you awake yet, honey?"

I stared at her, dazed. Then I touched her shoulder. She felt real enough, but it seemed like I was looking at her from some fuzzy dreamworld.

"I think so," I said, puzzled. "I don't know."

"Come on, Space Cadet," she said, gently shaking me. "Snap out of it."

Chris always called me Space Cadet when I woke up.

"What . . . What are you doing here?" I scrunched up inside her coat and stared at her. It still didn't make much sense.

"Oh, excuse me. Is this bench by invitation only?" She smiled. "I could ask you the same thing. Chuckie and I have been all over town looking for you."

"I'm sorry," I said weakly. That was the one thing I could always remember to say, no matter what.

"You know, I heard a rumor that there's a cute guy around here who's about to become a teenager. I was afraid there'd be a party and I'd miss it. Know anything about that?"

"I forgot. I . . . I guess I've been busy."

"So I heard," Mom said, wrapping the coat collar

182

tighter around my neck. "Are you going to tell me why you're out here freezing on a park bench when you're supposed to be home in bed?"

"It's a long story."

"Chuckie told me most of it. You're some kind of kid, you know that?"

"I don't know. I guess I'm different if that's what you mean."

"Different in a good way," she said, and put her arm around me. "Tell me, honey, did something happen tonight?"

"Jack turned himself in. He told me the whole story, and he turned himself in over there." I pointed. "It looks pretty bad for him."

"He's inside now?"

I nodded, tears starting down my face. I couldn't stop them.

"Do you want to tell me about it?"

I nodded again and started telling her everything. I still couldn't stop crying. It was like after my father died, when I let myself go and cried for everything that ever went wrong in the world.

"It'll be all right," Mom said, wrapping her arms tighter around me and squeezing.

"You didn't see how scared he looked. And you didn't see his father."

"It'll be tough for him for a while, but believe me it'll be all right."

"Will he have to go to jail?"

"No, honey, he won't have to go to jail. It was an accident. Just a terrible accident."

"Mom," I said, sniffling and wiping away the last tears on my sleeve, "it was like . . . I don't know . . .

It was like a game or something. And I wanted to win . . . you know . . . to prove I was right. And I did . . . but . . ."

"But you found out that life isn't just good guys fighting bad guys?"

I looked at her. And suddenly I realized I'd been almost as dumb as those fans at that professional wrestling show, wanting to see people as either good guys or bad guys. And thinking how the good guys' job was to make sure the bad guys got everything they deserved. It'd been easier to think that, easier and less confusing . . . Only it wasn't that simple. Jack was no bad guy. And I knew Mark had his own problems. His whole family did.

"Everything's so complicated," I said. "Sometimes I don't know how to look at things."

"I know," Mom said. "And your problem is that you're smart enough and sensitive enough to realize that." She stood up. "Why don't we get you home now? There's nothing we can do here."

I stood up. My legs felt like rubber, but I was awake now, and just knowing Mom was there made things quite a bit better. I saw the desk cop looking our way, and I took the coat off.

"Leave it on, honey. You'll catch pneumonia."

"Come on, Mom. Be serious. It's a lady's coat. I'm not walking home in that."

"Oh, I get it," she said, nodding her head. "It's better to freeze to death than to be seen in your old mother's coat."

"I won't freeze," I said. "And your age has nothing to do with it. Please, don't make me wear it." I handed it to her like it was a stink bomb.

"All right," she said, "but let's hurry. Your hands are like ice."

As soon as we hit the sidewalk, a big black car pulled up and parked beside us. Mr. Blumberg got out first on the other side, and then Mark got out right next to us. He glared down at me. All I could think of was that I was glad I wasn't wearing Mom's coat.

"I hope you're happy now," Mark snarled, brushing past me.

"No," I said in a low voice, "I'm not."

Mr. Blumberg hesitated, looking over the car, first at me, then at my mother. He came around the side of the car.

"I'm sorry," he said. "I'm really sorry."

"That's all right," Mom said gently. "He's upset."

"No, what I mean is, I'm sorry about everything. Everything." He turned and hurried after his son.

Mom looked at me, puzzled. I knew nobody had told her what Mr. Blumberg had said about her.

"It's a long story," I said.

"Well, you can tell me later," she said, tugging my arm down the sidewalk. "I have a hunch your other birthday guest may have already arrived, and he'll be wondering where we are."

"Christopher? Is he coming home, too?" I stopped walking and looked at her.

"Could be. You never know." She smiled when she saw the look on my face.

"Wow," I said, thinking how great it would be to have everybody together again. "Excellent! Let's go."

Now I was towing Mom down the street.

"Oh, my God! It's after midnight," she said. "You

know what that means? My little baby is thirteen. I can't believe it. My little baby.''

I groaned.

"Oh, Mom, don't start in on that baby stuff. Especially not in front of Chris and Chuckie.''

"Then I'd better start getting it out of my system right now. I'd hate to embarrass you.''

She wrapped her arms around me, right on the street where everybody could see, and started squeezing me and planting kisses all over my face.

"Mom!'' I whined. "Cut it out. Somebody'll see us.''

She laughed.

"I want everybody to see us. I want the whole world to know that my son is thirteen, and I love him more than ever!''

"Mom, please, don't make a . . .''

"I LOVE MY SON, EVERYBODY! I LOVE MY SON!''

"Oh, God, no Mom.'' I noticed some lights snapping on in the houses around us. "Mom, come on. People . . .''

She pinched my cheeks.

"Pee-wul . . .''

"Oh, you are too cute. You really are. And I'm glad to see you're getting some color back in your cheeks.''

She laughed as I tried to cover my face. I hoped no one would recognize us. Talk about humiliation.

"Mom, I changed my mind. You can kiss me at home if you still need to.''

"Okay, but I'm first. Promise me that. I know for a fact Mrs. Saunders will try to crowd in ahead of me.''

I groaned again. Mom laughed and took off running.

"Come on, Tyler! You're getting slow."

Oh, great, I thought. She used my name. But I had to laugh, watching her tear down the street, whooping it up like a kid. After all, she was forty years old. I took off after her, feeling pretty good myself.

Who knows? Thirteen might turn out to be a good year for lemons.